A LITTLE, ALOUD WITH LOVE

THE READER is a national charity dedicated to bringing about a reading revolution by making it possible for people of all ages, backgrounds and abilities to enjoy and engage with literature on a deep and personal level. Their Shared Reading groups, in which books and poems are always read aloud, reach across all ages, demographics and settings from nurseries and schools to care homes, via hospitals, mental health settings and prisons. The organisation started on Merseyside but has since expanded across the UK and beyond. ANGELA MACMILLAN has worked at The Reader since its inception and has run several Shared Reading groups.

Also Available

A Little, Aloud

A Little, Aloud for Children

A Little, Aloud with Love

Prose and poetry for reading aloud to someone you love

♥

Edited by Angela Macmillan

Chatto & Windus

LONDON

1 3 5 7 9 10 8 6 4 2

Chatto & Windus, an imprint of Vintage,
20 Vauxhall Bridge Road,
London SW1V 2SA

Chatto & Windus is part of the Penguin Random House group of companies whose
addresses can be found at global.penguinrandomhouse.com

Copyright © The Reader 2016
Introduction copyright © The Reader 2016

The publisher is donating all royalties in full from this book to The Reader

First published by Chatto and Windus in 2016

www.vintage-books.co.uk

A CIP catalogue record for this book is available from the British Library

ISBN 9781784740078

Typeset in India by Thomson Digital Pvt Ltd, Noida, Delhi

Printed and bound by Clays Ltd, St Lves plc

Penguin Random House is committed to a sustainable future for our business, our readers
and our planet. This book is made from Forest Stewardship Council® certified paper.

Contents

♥

Introduction

♥

O, my Luve's like a red, red rose,
That's newly sprung in June:
O, my Luve's like the melodie
That's sweetly play'd in tune.

As fair art thou, my bonie lass,
So deep in luve am I;
And I will luve thee still, my dear,
Till a' the seas gang dry.

Till a' the seas gang dry, my dear,
And the rocks melt wi' the sun;
And I will luve thee still, my dear,
While the sands o' life shall run.

And fare thee weel, my only Luve!
And fare thee weel, a while!
And I will come again, my Luve,
Tho' 'twere ten thousand mile!

Last week I sat with my reading group in a nursing home, each of us with a copy in very large print of Robert Burns's glorious love poem 'A Red, Red Rose'. As the group facilitator, I was the only member under eighty-five. I read it aloud and the silence that followed was alive with memories. At length someone said, 'Till all the seas gang dry, my dear.' And someone else said, 'And I will come again, my Love.' Someone sighed and then the woman next to me patted and stroked the paper. No one thought it inappropriate to be reading love poems in advanced age. An old man with hardly any voice remembered the poem as a song and spontaneously sang a verse, and somebody then recalled the pleasure of hearing the Scottish tenor Kenneth McKellar singing it live. It was suggested that we all read the poem aloud: nine rather shaky voices speaking the words of love in unison into the quiet afternoon. At the end, every heart was full.

Shared reading is at the heart of what we do at The Reader, a national charity that aims to bring about a Reading Revolution by making it possible for thousands of people of all ages and backgrounds to come together in weekly read-aloud book groups held up and down the country in libraries, community centres, prisons, drug rehabilitation centres, mental-health facilities, hospitals, workplaces, schools, foster homes, and in our new international centre for reading in Liverpool. In a welcoming environment, literature is brought to life. Thoughts and experiences are exchanged, feelings expressed, relationships forged, often with hugely beneficial effects on health and wellbeing. The poems and books that are important to us at The Reader as tools of our trade are the ones that make connections at a deeply personal level. Everyone in the nursing home could make such a connection with Burns's great poem, and thus we came together in shared experience both of the poem and in something understood between us.

This is the third anthology in the series, *A Little, Aloud*. The first comprised a general selection of poems and stories that had been read and well received in our reading groups. In the second, *A Little, Aloud for Children*, I wanted to make a selection of great stories and poems for children of all ages. Just because children can read for themselves does not mean they have to stop listening to stories read by someone else. Michael Morpurgo said in the Foreword: 'Reading out loud conjures a precious space and a time that is spent exclusively together.' His potent words bring me to *A Little, Aloud with Love*: a selection of poems and prose, ranging across centuries and cultures, not just for lovers (though there is plenty here to satisfy the most romantic lover) but for everyone who loves or has loved someone in an enduring relationship, in their family or in friendship. This book offers meaningful reading for that precious time and space together.

Who exactly do we have in mind? Well, for a start there is someone like me reading to and with my partner at any time of the day. Or my daughter and her husband, two years married with a baby who has just started sleeping through the night, thus giving them back their evenings. A friend whose husband was seriously ill and spent most of last year in hospital or in a wheelchair. A couple who find there is nothing on TV that evening, or a couple taking their first holiday for sixteen years without the children and who share the book on the beach. The newlyweds who read together on Sunday mornings with breakfast in bed. Best friends reading by the fire on winter afternoons. Me again, to an old man in a care home who tells me he has always been a romantic. The woman who reads with her daughter in loving memory of her husband. Or the child who reads to his mother on Mother's Day.

The literature we need the most at The Reader, as in life, is the literature that tells us what it's like to be alive, and loving includes so much of human experience: passion, joy, tenderness, intimacy, jealousy, heartbreak and loss. Loving is always complex and we often struggle to understand what it is we are feeling, but in the literary language of a book or poem we might find the sudden release of personal meaning:

> It will often happen, perhaps from the nature of things, that it is impossible to master and express an idea in a short space of time. As to individuals, sometimes they find they cannot do so at all; at length, perhaps, they recognize, in some writer they meet, with the very account of their own thoughts, which they desiderate; and then they say, that 'here is what they have felt all along, and wanted to say, but could not,' or 'what they have ever maintained, only better expressed.'
>
> John Henry Newman, University Sermon 15

A novel or poem can give shape or form to experience that we recognise as our own: here is what I have felt all along, but never quite knew until it was given words in this book or that poem. Or, here is what I have always thought and felt but thought I was alone in such feeling and thinking. Reading aloud empowers people to share these insights and feelings. Reading aloud about love with someone you love can be intimate, revealing and binding.

A Little, Aloud with Love includes literature that honours human love – the joy *and* the pain. I find it puzzling that many contemporary love stories seem in fact to be anti-love stories. By that I mean stories that merely scorn and debase or offer no holding-ground for human value. I do not want to suggest every story should have a happy ending, or be unreal, but in this selection you will find old and new literature that acknowledges, respects, and, yes, sometimes even exalts all that love means to the body, the soul, the life, the entire human being, without artful cynicism, or fatalistic pessimism. For as Thornton Wilder says at the end of *The Bridge of San Luis Rey*: 'There is a land of the living and a land of the dead and the bridge is love, the only survival, the only meaning.'

Angela Macmillan, The Reader

How to use this book

♥

There isn't a right way or a wrong way. Dip into it, start at the beginning, start at the end; of course it is up to you but I want to offer the thoughts behind the making of the anthology. The first thought was to collect together great poems and stories about this extraordinary, unfathomable thing called love in order to offer people the opportunity to read aloud to each other. The literature, diverse in form and content, ranges from the Bible to Haruki Murakami, from John Donne to Wendy Cope.

The book is divided into reading sessions: a short story or extract from a novel is presented with a poem. Hopefully one piece will resonate with the other and enhance the experience of reading and thinking about both. And these two go under a heading which is a line taken from the poem. For example, under the heading 'The Right Human Face' the prose piece is from *Adam Bede*. Written more than 150 years ago, it tells of a man who, after a deal of trouble, finally recognises his love for a woman who has long loved him in silence. This is paired with Edwin Muir's soaring poem 'The Confirmation' written a century later:

Yes, yours, my love, is the right human face.
I in my mind had waited for this long,
Seeing the false and searching for the true,

Then found you as a traveller finds a place
Of welcome suddenly amid the wrong
Valleys and rocks and twisting roads.

Occasionally you will come across two poems paired together. 'Lochinvar' and 'Lord Ullin's Daughter' are famous old ballads that some of the older generation will have learned at school, while U. A. Fanthorpe's fine poem 'Atlas' is placed beside 'A Marriage' by the American poet Michael Blumenthal, for both are about maintaining and holding up the 'rickety structures' of a relationship.

There are reading notes at the end of each section which are nothing to do with study guides or reading-group guides. They briefly recount conversations, observations, questions and connections from our existing reading groups or in shared reading one-to-one. They might describe what a group of young mothers in a run-down inner-city area made of feisty Bathsheba Everdene in Thomas Hardy's *Far from the Madding Crowd*, or what a group who meet in a drop-in centre thought about the chances of love at first sight after reading the Murakami story. These are all personal responses to reading literature about love outside the classroom or the university and are included as ways to prompt discussion.

When it came to arranging the sections, I realised that they mostly defied the usual love poetry/story categorisation, so many of them being about more than one thing: marriage *and* loneliness; intimacy *and* infidelity. I decided not to use further headings and placed them instead in implicit order of the age of the youngest character in each story. Thus we begin with a story by Carson McCullers about a twelve-year-old boy listening to a man trying to explain love, and end with Guy de Maupassant's story of the power of the love between a very elderly couple. There are of course cross-currents and tacit contrasts between the sections, but above all I hope the anthology reflects a lifespan of loving relationships.

None of the stories takes more than half an hour to read aloud. I have given very approximate reading times, but they will of course depend on how fast or slow you read and how often you stop in the course of the story to talk about what is going on and how you feel about it. These pauses for reflection are what shared reading is all about.

The stories lend themselves to being read aloud but if, at first, you feel a bit self-conscious, remember that you are not putting on a performance but simply bringing words on a page to life. It's the same with poetry, which is always enriched by being spoken aloud. Concentrate on what you are reading rather than thinking about yourself and allow the words to come into life.

At the end of the book there are a few suggestions for further reading.

The Heart Cannot Forget

♥

A TREE, A ROCK, A CLOUD
Carson McCullers

(approximate reading time 20 minutes)

It was raining that morning, and still very dark. When the boy reached the streetcar café he had almost finished his route and he went in for a cup of coffee. The place was an all-night café owned by a bitter and stingy man called Leo. After the raw, empty street the café seemed friendly and bright: along the counter there were a couple of soldiers, three spinners from the cotton-mill, and in a corner a man who sat hunched over with his nose and half his face down in a beer mug. The boy wore a helmet such as aviators wear. When he went into the café he unbuckled the chin-strap and raised the right flap up over his pink little ear; often as he drank his coffee someone would speak to him in a friendly way. But this morning Leo did not look into his face and none of the men were talking. He paid and was leaving the café when a voice called out to him:

'Son! Hey Son!'

He turned back and the man in the corner was crooking his finger and nodding to him. He had brought his face out of the beer mug and he seemed suddenly very happy. The man was long and pale, with a big nose and faded orange hair.

'Hey, Son!'

The boy went towards him. He was an undersized boy of about twelve, with one shoulder drawn higher than the other because of the weight of the paper-sack. His face was shallow, freckled, and his eyes were round child eyes.

'Yeah, Mister?'

The man laid one hand on the paper-boy's shoulders, then grasped the boy's chin and turned his face slowly from one side to the other. The boy shrank back uneasily.

'Say! What's the big idea?'

The boy's voice was shrill; inside the café it was suddenly very quiet.

The man said slowly: 'I love you.'

All along the counter the men laughed. The boy, who had scowled and sidled away, did not know what to do. He looked over the counter at Leo, and Leo watched him with a weary, brittle jeer. The boy tried to laugh also. But the man was serious and sad.

'I did not mean to tease you, Son,' he said. 'Sit down and have a beer with me. There is something I have to explain.'

Cautiously, out of the corner of his eye, the paper-boy questioned the men along the counter to see what he should do. But they had gone back to their beer or their breakfast and did not notice him. Leo put a cup of coffee on the counter and a little jug of cream.

'He is a minor,' Leo said.

The paper-boy slid himself up on to the stool. His ear beneath the upturned flap of the helmet was very small and red. The man was nodding at him soberly. 'It is important,' he said. Then he reached in his hip pocket and brought out something which he held up in the palm of his hand for the boy to see.

'Look very carefully,' he said.

The boy stared, but there was nothing to look at very carefully. The man held in his big, grimy palm a photograph. It was the face of a woman, but blurred, so that only the hat and the dress she was wearing stood out clearly.

'See?' the man asked.

The boy nodded and the man placed another picture in his palm. The woman was standing on a beach in a bathing suit. The suit made her stomach very big, and that was the main thing you noticed.

'Got a good look?' He leaned over closer and finally asked: 'You ever seen her before?'

The boy sat motionless, staring slantways at the man. 'Not so I know of.'

'Very well.' The man blew on the photographs and put them back into his pocket. 'That was my wife.'

'Dead?' the boy asked.

Slowly the man shook his head. He pursed his lips as though about to whistle and answered in a long-drawn way: 'Nuuu –' he said. 'I will explain.'

The beer on the counter before the man was in a large brown mug. He did not pick it up to drink. Instead he bent down and, putting his face over the rim, he rested there for a moment. Then with both hands he tilted the mug and sipped.

'Some night you'll go to sleep with your big nose in a mug and drown,' said Leo. 'Prominent transient drowns in beer. That would be a cute death.'

The paper-boy tried to signal to Leo. While the man was not looking he screwed up his face and worked his mouth to question soundlessly: 'Drunk?' But Leo only raised his eyebrows and turned away to put some pink strips of bacon on the grill. The man pushed the mug away from him, straightened himself, and folded his loose crooked hands on the counter. His face was sad as he looked at the paper-boy. He did not blink but from time to time the lids closed down with delicate gravity over his pale green eyes. It was nearing dawn and the boy shifted the weight of the paper-sack.

'I am talking about love,' the man said. 'With me it is a science.'

The boy half slid down from the stool. But the man raised his forefinger, and there was something about him that held the boy and would not let him go away.

'Twelve years ago I married the woman in the photograph. She was my wife for one year, nine months, three days, and two nights. I loved her. Yes . . .' He tightened his blurred, rambling voice and said again: 'I loved her. I thought also that she loved me. I was a railroad engineer. She had all home comforts and luxuries. It never crept into my brain that she was not satisfied. But do you know what happened?'

'Mgneeow!' said Leo.

The man did not take his eyes from the boy's face. 'She left me. I came in one night and the house was empty and she was gone. She left me.'

'With a fellow?' the boy asked.

Gently the man placed his palm down on the counter. 'Why naturally, Son. A woman does not run off like that alone.'

The café was quiet, the soft rain black and endless in the street outside. Leo pressed down the frying bacon with the prongs of his long fork. 'So you have been chasing the floozie for eleven years. You frazzled old rascal!'

For the first time the man glanced at Leo. 'Please don't be vulgar. Besides, I was not speaking to you.' He turned back to the boy and said in a trusting and secretive undertone: 'Let's not pay any attention to him. OK?'

The paper-boy nodded doubtfully.

'It was like this,' the man continued. 'I am a person who feels many things. All my life one thing after another has impressed me. Moonlight. The leg of a pretty girl. One thing after another. But the point is that when I had enjoyed anything there was a peculiar sensation as though it was laying loose in me. Nothing seemed to finish itself up or fit in with the other things. Women? I had my portion of them. The same. Afterwards laying around loose in me. I was a man who had never loved.'

Very slowly he closed his eyelids, and the gesture was like a curtain drawn at the end of a scene in a play. When he spoke again his voice was excited and the words came fast – the lobes of his large, loose ears seemed to tremble.

'Then I met this woman. I was fifty-one years old and she always said she was thirty. I met her at a filling station and we were married within three days. And do you know what it was like? I just can't tell you. All I had ever felt was gathered together around this woman. Nothing lay around loose in me any more but was finished up by her.'

The man stopped suddenly and stroked his long nose. His voice sank down to a steady and reproachful undertone: 'I'm not explaining this right. What happened was this. There were these beautiful feelings and loose little pleasures inside me. And this woman was something like an assembly line for my soul. I run these little pieces of myself through her and I come out complete. Now do you follow me?'

'What was her name?' the boy asked.

'Oh,' he said. 'I called her Dodo. But that is immaterial.'

'Did you try to make her come back?'

The man did not seem to hear. 'Under the circumstances you can imagine how I felt when she left me.'

Leo took the bacon from the grill and folded two strips of it between a bun. He had a grey face, with slitted eyes, and a pinched nose saddled by faint blue shadows. One of the mill workers signalled for more coffee and Leo poured it. He did not give refills on coffee free. The spinner ate breakfast there every morning, but the better Leo knew his customers the stingier he treated them. He nibbled his own bun as though he grudged it to himself.

'And you never got hold of her again?'

The boy did not know what to think of the man, and his child's face was uncertain with mingled curiosity and doubt. He was new on the paper route; it was still strange to him to be out in the town in the black, queer early morning.

'Yes,' the man said. 'I took a number of steps to get her back. I went around trying to locate her. I went to Tulsa, where she had folks. And to Mobile. I went to every town she had ever mentioned to me, and I hunted down every man she had formerly been connected with. Tulsa, Atlanta, Chicago, Cheehaw, Memphis . . . For the better part of two years I chased around the country trying to lay hold of her.'

'But the pair of them had vanished from the face of the earth!' said Leo.

'Don't listen to him,' the man said confidentially. 'And also just forget those two years. They are not important. What matters is that around the third year a curious thing began to happen to me.'

'What?' the boy asked.

The man leaned down and tilted his mug to take a sip of beer. But as he hovered over the mug his nostrils fluttered slightly; he sniffed the staleness of the beer and did not drink. 'Love is a curious thing to begin with. At first I thought only of getting her back. It was a kind of mania. But then as time went on I tried to remember her. But do you know what happened?'

'No,' the boy said.

'When I laid myself down on a bed and tried to think about her my mind became a blank. I couldn't see her. I would take out her pictures and look. No good. Nothing doing. A blank. Can you imagine it?'

'Say, Mac!' Leo called down the counter. 'Can you imagine this bozo's mind a blank!'

Slowly, as though fanning away flies, the man waved his hand. His green eyes were concentrated and fixed on the shallow little face of the paper-boy.

'But a sudden piece of glass on a sidewalk. Or a nickel tune in a music box. A shadow on a wall at night. And I would remember. It might happen in a street and I would cry or bang my head against a lamp-post. You follow me?'

'A piece of glass . . .' the boy said.

'Anything. I would walk around and I had no power of how and when to remember her. You think you can put up a kind of shield. But remembering don't come to a man face forward – it corners around sideways. I was at the mercy of everything I saw and heard. Suddenly instead of me combing the countryside to find her she began to chase me around in my very soul. *She* chasing *me*, mind you! And in my soul.'

The boy asked finally: 'What part of the country were you in then?'

'Ooh,' the man groaned. 'I was sick mortal. It was like smallpox. I confess, Son, that I boozed. I fornicated. I committed any sin that suddenly appealed to me. I am loath to confess it, but I will do so. When I recall that period it is all curdled in my mind, it was so terrible.'

The man leaned his head down and tapped his forehead on the counter. For a few seconds he stayed bowed over in this position, the back of his stringy neck covered with orange furze, his hands with their long warped fingers held palm to palm in an attitude of prayer. Then the man straightened himself; he was smiling and suddenly his face was bright and tremulous and old.

'It was in the fifth year that it happened,' he said. 'And with it I started my science.'

Leo's mouth jerked with a pale, quick grin. 'Well none of we boys are getting any younger,' he said. Then with sudden anger he balled up a dish-cloth he was holding and threw it down hard on the floor. 'You draggle-tailed old Romeo!'

'What happened?' the boy asked.

The old man's voice was high and clear: 'Peace,' he answered.

'Huh?'

'It is hard to explain scientifically, Son,' he said. 'I guess the logical explanation is that she and I had fleed around from each other for so long that finally we just got tangled up together and lay down and quit. Peace. A queer and beautiful blankness. It was spring in Portland and the rain came every afternoon. All evening I just stayed there on my bed in the dark. And that is how the science come to me.'

The windows in the streetcar were pale blue with light. The two soldiers paid for their beers and opened the door – one of the soldiers combed his hair and wiped off his muddy puttees before they went outside. The three mill workers bent silently over their breakfasts. Leo's clock was ticking on the wall.

'It is this. And listen carefully. I meditated on love and reasoned it out. I realized what is wrong with us. Men fall in love for the first time. And what do they fall in love with?'

The boy's soft mouth was partly open and he did not answer.

'A woman,' the old man said. 'Without science, with nothing to go by, they undertake the most dangerous and sacred experience on God's earth. They fall in love with a woman. Is that correct, Son?'

'Yeah,' the boy said faintly.

'They start at the wrong end of love. They begin at the climax. Can you wonder it is so miserable? Do you know how men should love?'

The old man reached over and grasped the boy by the collar of his leather jacket. He gave him a gentle little shake and his green eyes gazed down unblinking and grave.

'Son, do you know how love should be begun?'

The boy sat small and listening and still. Slowly he shook his head. The old man leaned closer and whispered:

'A tree. A rock. A cloud.'

It was still raining outside in the street: a mild, grey, endless rain. The mill whistle blew for the six o'clock shift and the three spinners paid and went away. There was no one in the café but Leo, the old man, and the little paper-boy.

'The weather was like this in Portland,' he said. 'At the time my science was begun. I meditated and I started very cautious. I would pick up something from the street and take it home with me. I bought a goldfish and I concentrated on the goldfish and I loved it. I graduated from one thing to another. Day by day I was getting this technique. On the road from Portland to San Diego –'

'Aw shut up!' screamed Leo suddenly. 'Shut up! Shut up!'

The old man still held the collar of the boy's jacket; he was trembling and his face was earnest and bright and wild. 'For six years now I have gone around by myself and built up my science. And now I am a master, Son. I can love anything. No longer do I have to think about it ever. I see a street full of people and a beautiful light comes in me. I watch a bird in the sky. Or I meet a traveller on the road. Everything, Son.

And anybody. All stranger and all love! Do you realize what a science like mine can mean?'

The boy held himself stiffly, his hands curled tight around the counter edge. Finally he asked: 'Did you ever really find that lady?'

'What? What say, Son?'

'I mean,' the boy asked timidly. 'Have you fallen in love with a woman again?'

The old man loosened his grasp on the boy's collar. He had turned away and for the first time his green eyes had a vague and scattered look. He lifted the mug from the counter, drank down the yellow beer. His head was shaking slowly from side to side. Then finally he answered: 'No, Son. You see that is the last step in my science. I go cautious. And I am not quite ready yet.'

'Well!' said Leo. 'Well, well, well!'

The old man stood in the open doorway. 'Remember,' he said. Framed there in the grey damp light of the early morning he looked shrunken and seedy and frail. But his smile was bright. 'Remember I love you,' he said with a last nod. And the door closed quietly behind him.

The boy did not speak for a long time. He pulled down the bangs on his forehead and slid his grimy little forefinger around the rim of his empty cup. Then without looking at Leo he finally asked:

'Was he drunk?'

'No,' said Leo shortly.

The boy raised his clear voice higher. 'Then was he a dope fiend?'

'No.'

The boy looked up at Leo, and his flat little face was desperate, his voice urgent and shrill. 'Was he crazy? Do you think he was a lunatic?' The paper-boy's voice dropped suddenly with doubt. 'Leo? Or not?'

But Leo would not answer him. Leo had run a night café for fourteen years, and held himself to be a critic of craziness. There were the town characters and also the transients who roamed in from the night. He knew the manias of all of them. But he did not want to satisfy the questions of the waiting child. He tightened his pale face and was silent.

So the boy pulled down the right flap of his helmet and as he turned to leave he made the only comment that seemed safe to him, the only remark that could not be laughed down and despised:

'He sure has done a lot of travelling.'

WHAT THE HEART CANNOT FORGET
Joyce Sutphen

Everything remembers something. The rock, its fiery bed,
cooling and fissuring into cracked pieces, the rub
of watery fingers along its edge.

The cloud remembers being elephant, camel, giraffe,
remembers being a veil over the face of the sun,
gathering itself together for the fall.

The turtle remembers the sea, sliding over and under
its belly, remembers legs like wings, escaping down
the sand under the beaks of savage birds.

The tree remembers the story of each ring, the years
of drought, the floods, the way things came
walking slowly towards it long ago.

And the skin remembers its scars, and the bone aches
where it was broken. The feet remember the dance,
and the arms remember lifting up the child.

The heart remembers everything it loved and gave away,
everything it lost and found again, and everyone
it loved, the heart cannot forget.

READING NOTES

Speaking of the poem, Nancy said she thought it was nonsense that a cloud would remember being an elephant, but as soon as she read the line 'the arms remember lifting up the child', she knew exactly what that meant. 'And', she added, 'there is still a space on my hip that remembers the feel of a small child perching there.' Ken said he remembered seeing a documentary about baby turtles hatching from their eggs on a beach and racing down to the sea before the terrible seagulls got them. '"Savage" is the right word for those birds,' he added.

The group spent a long time puzzling over the story and there seemed to be a lot of unanswered questions: what did the man mean when he said that love is a science; was he right in thinking that we fall in love backwards; could he be in earnest when he tells the boy he loves him or was he just crazy; and the biggest of all, what *is* love? However, the man's explanation of what falling in love did for him, 'I run these little pieces of myself through her and I come out complete', was absolutely understood. 'For me,' said Celia, 'having lost the love of his life, the man seems to have lost himself. His so-called science is just his way of carrying on. You can't love trees and rocks.' Not everyone agreed.

Love So Sudden and So Sweet

ROMEO AND JULIET
William Shakespeare

(approximate reading time 12 minutes)

In Verona, the Capulet and Montague families have long been enemies. One night Romeo, a Montague, disguises himself and gatecrashes a Capulet ball. There he meets Juliet, the daughter of the house and they fall instantly in love. Later that evening, Romeo breaks into the Capulet garden.

ACT II. SCENE II. Capulet's orchard.

ROMEO
But soft, what light through yonder window breaks?
It is the east, and Juliet is the sun.
Arise fair sun and kill the envious moon,
Who is already sick and pale with grief
That thou her maid art far more fair than she.
Be not her maid, since she is envious.

Her vestal livery is but sick and green,
And none but fools do wear it; cast it off.

JULIET appears at the window

It is my lady, O it is my love.
O that she knew she were.
She speaks, yet she says nothing. What of that?
Her eye discourses, I will answer it.
I am too bold, 'tis not to me she speaks.
Two of the fairest stars in all the heaven
Having some business, do entreat her eyes
To twinkle in their spheres till they return.
What if her eyes were there, they in her head?
The brightness of her cheek would shame those stars,
As daylight doth a lamp; her eyes in heaven
Would through the airy region stream so bright
That birds would sing, and think it were not night.
See how she leans her cheek upon her hand.
O that I were a glove upon that hand,
That I might touch that cheek.

JULIET
                        Ay me!

ROMEO
                              She speaks.
O speak again, bright angel, for thou art

As glorious to this night, being o'er my head,
As is a winged messenger of heaven
Unto the white-upturned, wond'ring eyes
Of mortals that fall back to gaze on him,
When he bestrides the lazy-pacing clouds,
And sails upon the bosom of the air.

JULIET

O Romeo, Romeo, wherefore art thou Romeo?
Deny thy father, and refuse thy name.
Or if thou wilt not, be but sworn my love,
And I'll no longer be a Capulet.

ROMEO

[*Aside*] Shall I hear more, or shall I speak at this?

JULIET

'Tis but thy name that is my enemy.
Thou art thyself, though not a Montague.
What's Montague? It is nor hand nor foot,
Nor arm nor face, nor any other part
Belonging to a man. O be some other name.
What's in a name? That which we call a rose
By any other word would smell as sweet.
So Romeo would, were he not Romeo called,
Retain that dear perfection which he owes
Without that title. Romeo doff thy name,
And for that name which is no part of thee
Take all myself.

ROMEO

                             I take thee at thy word.
Call me but 'love', and I'll be new baptized;
Henceforth I never will be Romeo.

JULIET

What man art thou, that thus bescreen'd in night
So stumblest on my counsel?

ROMEO

                                    By a name
I know not how to tell thee who I am.
My name, dear saint, is hateful to myself.
Because it is an enemy to thee.
Had I it written, I would tear the word.

JULIET

My ears have not yet drunk a hundred words
Of that tongue's utterance, yet I know the sound.
Art thou not Romeo, and a Montague?

ROMEO

Neither, fair maid, if either thee dislike.

JULIET

How cam'st thou hither, tell me, and wherefore?
The orchard walls are high, and hard to climb,
And the place death, considering who thou art,
If any of my kinsmen find thee here.

ROMEO

With love's light wings did I o'erperch these walls,

For stony limits cannot hold love out,

And what love can do, that dares love attempt.

Therefore thy kinsmen are no stop to me.

JULIET

If they do see thee, they will murder thee.

ROMEO

Alack there lies more peril in thine eye

Than twenty of their swords; look thou but sweet,

And I am proof against their enmity.

JULIET

I would not for the world they saw thee here.

ROMEO

I have night's cloak to hide me from their eyes;

And but thou love me, let them find me here.

My life were better ended by their hate,

Than death prorogued, wanting of thy love.

JULIET

By whose direction found'st thou out this place?

ROMEO

By love that first did prompt me to inquire;

He lent me counsel, and I lent him eyes.

I am no pilot; yet wert thou as far
As that vast shore washed with the farthest sea,
I would adventure for such merchandise.

JULIET

Thou knowest the mask of night is on my face,
Else would a maiden blush bepaint my cheek,
For that which thou hast heard me speak tonight.
Fain would I dwell on form, fain, fain deny
What I have spoke; but farewell compliment.
Dost thou love me? I know thou wilt say 'Ay',
And I will take thy word. Yet if thou swearest,
Thou mayst prove false; at lovers' perjuries
Then say Jove laughs. O gentle Romeo,
If thou dost love, pronounce it faithfully.
Or if thou thinkest I am too quickly won,
I'll frown and be perverse, and say thee nay,
So thou wilt woo; but else not for the world.
In truth fair Montague I am too fond,
And therefore thou mayst think my haviour light.
But trust me gentleman, I'll prove more true
Than those that have more cunning to be strange.
I should have been more strange, I must confess,
But that thou overheard'st, ere I was ware,
My true-love passion. Therefore pardon me,
And not impute this yielding to light love,
Which the dark night hath so discovered.

ROMEO

Lady, by yonder blessed moon I vow
That tips with silver all these fruit-tree tops—

JULIET

O swear not by the moon, th' inconstant moon,
That monthly changes in her circled orb,
Lest that thy love prove likewise variable.

ROMEO

What shall I swear by?

JULIET

                                    Do not swear at all;
Or if thou wilt, swear by thy gracious self,
Which is the god of my idolatry,
And I'll believe thee.

ROMEO

                                    If my heart's dear love—

JULIET

Well do not swear. Although I joy in thee,
I have no joy of this contract tonight.
It is too rash, too unadvised, too sudden;
Too like the lightning, which doth cease to be
Ere one can say, 'It lightens'. Sweet, good night.
This bud of love by summer's ripening breath
May prove a beauteous flower when next we meet.

Good night, good night. As sweet repose and rest
Come to thy heart, as that within my breast.

ROMEO

O wilt thou leave me so unsatisfied?

JULIET

What satisfaction canst thou have tonight?

ROMEO

Th' exchange of thy love's faithful vow for mine.

JULIET

I gave thee mine before thou didst request it;
And yet I would it were to give again.

ROMEO

Wouldst thou withdraw it? For what purpose, love?

JULIET

But to be frank and give it thee again.
And yet I wish but for the thing I have.
My bounty is as boundless as the sea,
My love as deep; the more I give to thee,
The more I have, for both are infinite.
I hear some noise within; dear love, adieu.

                              [*Nurse calls within*]

Anon good Nurse! Sweet Montague, be true.
Stay but a little, I will come again.

                                        [*Exit*]

ROMEO

O blessed, blessed night! I am afeard,
Being in night, all this is but a dream,
Too flattering-sweet to be substantial.

Enter JULIET again

JULIET

Three words, dear Romeo, and good night indeed.
If that thy bent of love be honourable,
Thy purpose marriage, send me word tomorrow,
By one that I'll procure to come to thee,
Where and what time thou wilt perform the rite;
And all my fortunes at thy foot I'll lay
And follow thee my lord throughout the world.

NURSE

[*Within*] Madam!

JULIET

I come, anon—But if thou meanest not well,
I do beseech thee—

NURSE

　　　　　　　　[*Within*] Madam!

JULIET

　　　　　　　　By and by, I come—

To cease thy strife, and leave me to my grief.
Tomorrow will I send.

ROMEO

So thrive my soul—

JULIET

A thousand times good night.

[*Exit*]

ROMEO

A thousand times the worse, to want thy light.
Love goes toward love as schoolboys from their books,
But love from love, toward school with heavy looks.

Enter JULIET again

JULIET

Hist, Romeo, hist! O for a falconer's voice,
To lure this tassel-gentle back again.
Bondage is hoarse, and may not speak aloud,
Else would I tear the cave where Echo lies,
And make her airy tongue more hoarse than mine
With repetition of my 'Romeo'.

ROMEO

It is my soul that calls upon my name.
How silver-sweet sound lovers' tongues by night,
Like softest music to attending ears.

JULIET

Romeo!

ROMEO

    My nyas?

JULIET

              What o'clock tomorrow
Shall I send to thee?

ROMEO

            By the hour of nine.

JULIET

I will not fail: 'tis twenty years till then.
I have forgot why I did call thee back.

ROMEO

Let me stand here till thou remember it.

JULIET

I shall forget, to have thee still stand there,
Remembering how I love thy company.

ROMEO

And I'll still stay, to have thee still forget,
Forgetting any other home but this.

JULIET

'Tis almost morning; I would have thee gone,

And yet no farther than a wanton's bird,

Who lets it hop a little from her hand,

Like a poor prisoner in his twisted gyves,

And with a silken thread plucks it back again,

So loving-jealous of his liberty.

ROMEO

I would I were thy bird.

JULIET

                    Sweet, so would I.

Yet I should kill thee with much cherishing.

Good night, good night. Parting is such sweet sorrow,

That I shall say 'Good night' till it be morrow.

                                        [*Exit*]

ROMEO

Sleep dwell upon thine eyes, peace in thy breast.

Would I were sleep and peace, so sweet to rest.

Hence will I to my ghostly father's cell,

His help to crave, and my dear hap to tell.

                                        [*Exit*]

FIRST LOVE
John Clare

I ne'er was struck before that hour
    With love so sudden and so sweet,
Her face it bloomed like a sweet flower
    And stole my heart away complete.
My face turned pale as deadly pale,
    My legs refused to walk away,
And when she looked, what could I ail?
    My life and all seemed turned to clay.

And then my blood rushed to my face
    And took my eyesight quite away,
The trees and bushes round the place
    Seemed midnight at noonday.
I could not see a single thing,
    Words from my eyes did start—
They spoke as chords do from the string,
    And blood burnt round my heart.

Are flowers the winter's choice?
    Is love's bed always snow?
She seemed to hear my silent voice,
    Not love's appeals to know.
I never saw so sweet a face
    As that I stood before.
My heart has left its dwelling-place
    And can return no more.

READING NOTES

Reading Shakespeare in our reading groups has proved to be hugely enjoyable. Taking parts, reading slowly, stopping at tricky, or interesting, or moving bits and talking about it all together, gradually gets rid of any nervousness at 'reading Shakespeare'. People often want to repeat sentences or speeches, to let the language sink in. There is often talk of the extreme youth of this pair, and people share memories of first love both here and in the reading of John Clare's tender poem. People usually remember their first love: 'Her name was Ruth and I was mad about her for about two years and never plucked up the courage to even speak to her,' said a man in a nursing-home reading group.

Two Poems: So Daring in Love

LOCHINVAR
Sir Walter Scott

O, young Lochinvar is come out of the west,
Through all the wide Border, his steed was the best;
And save his good broadsword he weapons had none,
He rode all unarm'd, and he rode all alone.
    So faithful in love and so dauntless in war,
    There never was knight like the young Lochinvar.

He staid not for brake, and he stopp'd not for stone,
He swam the Eske river where ford there was none;
But ere he alighted at Netherby gate,
The bride had consented; the gallant came late:
    For a laggard in love and a dastard in war,
    Was to wed the fair Ellen of brave Lochinvar.

So boldly he enter'd the Netherby Hall,
Among bride's-men and kinsmen and brothers and all:
Then spoke the bride's father, his hand on his sword,

(For the poor craven bridegroom said never a word):
    'O come ye in peace here, or come ye in war,
    Or to dance at our bridal, young Lord Lochinvar?'

'I long woo'd your daughter, my suit you denied;
Love swells like the Solway, but ebbs like its tide –
And now I am come, with this lost love of mine,
To lead but one measure, drink one cup of wine.
    There are maidens in Scotland more lovely by far,
    That would gladly be bride to the young Lochinvar.'

The bride kiss'd the goblet: the knight took it up,
He quaff'd off the wine, and he threw down the cup.
She look'd down to blush and she look'd up to sigh,
With a smile on her lips, and a tear in her eye.
    He took her soft hand, ere her mother could bar,
    'Now tread we a measure!' said young Lochinvar.

So stately his form, and so lovely her face,
That never a hall such a galliard did grace;
While her mother did fret, and her father did fume,
And the bridegroom stood dangling his bonnet and plume;
    And the bride-maidens whisper'd, ''Twere better by far,
    To have matched our fair cousin with young Lochinvar.'

One touch to her hand, and one word in her ear,
When they reach'd the hall-door, and the charger stood near;
So light to the croupe the fair lady he swung,

So light to the saddle before her he sprung!
    'She is won! We are gone, over bank, bush, and scaur;
    They'll have fleet steeds that follow,' quoth young
        Lochinvar.

There was mounting 'mong Graemes of the Netherby clan;
Forsters, Fenwicks and Musgraves, they rode and they ran:
There was racing and chasing, on Cannobie Lee,
But the lost bride of Netherby ne'er did they see.
    So daring in love, and so dauntless in war,
    Have ye e'er heard of gallant like young Lochinvar?

LORD ULLIN'S DAUGHTER
Thomas Campbell

A chieftain to the Highlands bound
Cries, 'Boatman, do not tarry!
And I'll give thee a silver pound
To row us o'er the ferry!'

'Now who be ye, would cross Lochgyle,
This dark and stormy water?'
'O I'm the chief of Ulva's isle,
And this, Lord Ullin's daughter.

'And fast before her father's men
Three days we've fled together,
For should he find us in the glen,
My blood would stain the heather.

'His horsemen hard behind us ride –
Should they our steps discover,
Then who will cheer my bonny bride
When they have slain her lover?'

Out spoke the hardy Highland wight,
'I'll go, my chief; I'm ready:
It is not for your silver bright,
But for your winsome lady: –

'And by my word! the bonny bird
In danger shall not tarry;

So though the waves are raging white,
I'll row you o'er the ferry.'

By this the storm grew loud apace,
The water-wraith was shrieking;
And in the scowl of heaven each face
Grew dark as they were speaking.

But still as wilder blew the wind
And as the night grew drearer,
Adown the glen rode armèd men,
Their trampling sounded nearer.

'O haste thee, haste!' the lady cries,
'Though tempests round us gather;
I'll meet the raging of the skies,
But not an angry father.'

The boat has left a stormy land,
A stormy sea before her, –
When, O! too strong for human hand
The tempest gather'd o'er her.

And still they row'd amidst the roar
Of waters fast prevailing:
Lord Ullin reach'd that fatal shore, –
His wrath was changed to wailing.

For, sore dismay'd, through storm and shade
His child he did discover: –

One lovely hand she stretch'd for aid,
And one was round her lover.

'Come back! come back!' he cried in grief
'Across this stormy water:
And I'll forgive your Highland chief,
My daughter! - O my daughter!'

'Twas vain: the loud waves lash'd the shore,
Return or aid preventing:
The water wild went o'er his child,
And he was left lamenting.

READING NOTES

An old lady in a reading group remembered learning 'Lochinvar' at school. 'Mrs Roper used to ask us to come to the front and recite a verse each. I fell in love with "Lochinvar", all those years ago.' They wondered about Lochinvar, who he was and what he had been doing in the west. Someone thought there was a loch on Scotland with the same name and there followed some memories of Scottish holidays. Gordon said the wedding sounded like something straight out of a modern soap opera.

A younger reading group was divided on 'Lord Ullin's Daughter'. Some found it too old-fashioned while others enjoyed the romance and thought it would make a great film, as there had to be quite a back-story. Laura read out the last three verses again, saying, 'Even if it is old-fashioned, it still makes me cry.' Everyone liked the rhyme and rhythm.

You Must Be He I Was Seeking, or She I Was Seeking

♥

ON SEEING THE 100% PERFECT GIRL ONE BEAUTIFUL APRIL MORNING
Haruki Murakami

(approximate reading time 11 minutes)

One beautiful April morning, on a narrow side street in Tokyo's fashionable Harajuku neighborhood, I walk past the 100% perfect girl.

Tell you the truth, she's not that good-looking. She doesn't stand out in any way. Her clothes are nothing special. The back of her hair is still bent out of shape from sleep. She isn't young, either – must be near thirty, not even close to a 'girl', properly speaking. But still, I know from fifty yards away: She's the 100% perfect girl for me. The moment I see her, there's a rumbling in my chest, and my mouth is as dry as a desert.

Maybe you have your own particular favorite type of girl – one with slim ankles, say, or big eyes, or graceful fingers, or you're drawn for no good reason to girls who take their time with every meal. I have my own preferences, of course.

Sometimes in a restaurant I'll catch myself staring at the girl at the next table to mine because I like the shape of her nose.

But no one can insist that his 100% perfect girl correspond to some preconceived type. Much as I like noses, I can't recall the shape of hers – or even if she had one. All I can remember for sure is that she was no great beauty. It's weird.

'Yesterday on the street I passed the 100% girl,' I tell someone.

'Yeah?' he says. 'Good-looking?'

'Not really.'

'Your favorite type, then?'

'I don't know. I can't seem to remember anything about her – the shape of her eyes or the size of her breasts.'

'Strange.'

'Yeah. Strange.'

'So anyhow,' he says, already bored, 'what did you do? Talk to her? Follow her?'

'Nah. Just passed her on the street.'

She's walking east to west, and I west to east. It's a really nice April morning.

Wish I could talk to her. Half an hour would be plenty: just ask her about herself, tell her about myself, and – what I'd really like to do – explain to her the complexities of fate that have led to our passing each other on a side street in Harajuku on a beautiful April morning in 1981. This was something sure to be crammed full of warm secrets, like an antique clock built when peace filled the world.

After talking, we'd have lunch somewhere, maybe see a Woody Allen movie, stop by a hotel bar for cocktails. With any kind of luck, we might end up in bed.

Potentiality knocks on the door of my heart.

Now the distance between us has narrowed to fifteen yards.

How can I approach her? What should I say?

'Good morning, miss. Do you think you could spare half an hour for a little conversation?'

Ridiculous. I'd sound like an insurance salesman.

'Pardon me, but would you happen to know if there is an all-night cleaners in the neighborhood?'

No, this is just as ridiculous. I'm not carrying any laundry, for one thing. Who's going to buy a line like that?

Maybe the simple truth would do. 'Good morning. You are the 100% perfect girl for me.'

No, she wouldn't believe it. Or even if she did, she might not want to talk to me. Sorry, she could say, I might be the 100% perfect girl for you, but you're not the 100% perfect boy for me. It could happen. And if I found myself in that situation, I'd probably go to pieces. I'd never recover from the shock. I'm thirty-two, and that's what growing older is all about.

We pass in front of a flower shop. A small, warm air mass touches my skin. The asphalt is damp, and I catch the scent of roses. I can't bring myself to speak to her. She wears a white sweater, and in her right hand she holds a crisp white envelope lacking only a stamp. So: She's written somebody a letter, maybe spent the whole night writing, to judge from the sleepy look in her eyes. The envelope could contain every secret she's ever had.

I take a few more strides and turn: She's lost in the crowd.

Now, of course, I know exactly what I should have said to her. It would have been a long speech, though, far too long for me to have delivered it properly. The ideas I come up with are never very practical.

Oh, well. It would have started 'Once upon a time' and ended 'A sad story, don't you think?'

Once upon a time, there lived a boy and a girl. The boy was eighteen and the girl sixteen. He was not unusually handsome, and she was not especially beautiful. They were just an ordinary lonely boy and an ordinary lonely girl, like all the others. But they believed with their whole hearts that somewhere in the world there lived the 100% perfect boy and the 100% perfect girl for them. Yes, they believed in a miracle. And that miracle actually happened.

One day the two came upon each other on the corner of a street.

'This is amazing,' he said. 'I've been looking for you all my life. You may not believe this, but you're the 100% perfect girl for me.'

'And you,' she said to him, 'are the 100% perfect boy for me, exactly as I'd pictured you in every detail. It's like a dream.'

They sat on a park bench, held hands, and told each other their stories hour after hour. They were not lonely anymore. They had found and been found by their 100% perfect other. What a wonderful thing it is to find and be found by your 100% perfect other. It's a miracle, a cosmic miracle.

As they sat and talked, however, a tiny, tiny sliver of doubt took root in their hearts: Was it really all right for one's dreams to come true so easily?

And so, when there came a momentary lull in their conversation, the boy said to the girl, 'Let's test ourselves – just once. If we really are each other's 100% perfect lovers, then sometime, somewhere, we will meet again without fail. And when that happens, and we know that we are the 100% perfect ones, we'll marry then and there. What do you think?'

'Yes,' she said, 'that is exactly what we should do.'

And so they parted, she to the east, and he to the west.

The test they had agreed upon, however, was utterly unnecessary. They should never have undertaken it, because they really and truly were each other's 100% perfect lovers, and it was a miracle that they had ever met. But it was impossible for them to know this, young as they were. The cold, indifferent waves of fate proceeded to toss them unmercifully.

One winter, both the boy and the girl came down with the season's terrible influenza, and after drifting for weeks between life and death they lost all memory of their earlier years. When they awoke, their heads were as empty as the young D. H. Lawrence's piggy bank.

They were two bright, determined young people, however, and through their unremitting efforts they were able to acquire once again the knowledge and feeling that qualified them to return as full-fledged members of society. Heaven be praised, they became truly upstanding citizens who knew how to transfer from one subway line to another, who were fully capable of sending a special-delivery letter at the post office. Indeed, they even experienced love again, sometimes as much as 75% or even 85% love.

Time passed with shocking swiftness, and soon the boy was thirty-two, the girl thirty.

One beautiful April morning, in search of a cup of coffee to start the day, the boy was walking from west to east, while the girl, intending to send a special-delivery letter, was walking from east to west, but along the same narrow street in the Harajuku neighborhood of Tokyo. They passed each other in the very center of the street. The faintest gleam of their lost memories glimmered for the briefest moment in their hearts. Each felt a rumbling in their chest. And they knew:

She is the 100% perfect girl for me.

He is the 100% perfect boy for me.

But the glow of their memories was far too weak, and their thoughts no longer had the clarity of fourteen years earlier. Without a word, they passed each other, disappearing into the crowd. Forever.

A sad story, don't you think?

Yes. That's it, that is what I should have said to her.

TO A STRANGER
Walt Whitman

Passing stranger! you do not know
How longingly I look upon you,
You must be he I was seeking,
Or she I was seeking,
(It comes to me as of a dream)

I have somewhere surely
Lived a life of joy with you,
All is recall'd as we flit by each other,
Fluid, affectionate, chaste, matured.

You grew up with me,
Were a boy with me or a girl with me,
I ate with you and slept with you, your body has become
Not yours only nor left my body mine only.

You give me the pleasure of your eyes,
Face, flesh, as we pass,
You take of my beard, breast, hands,
In return,

I am not to speak to you, I am to think of you
When I sit alone or wake at night alone,
I am to wait, I do not doubt I am to meet you again,
I am to see to it that I do not lose you.

READING NOTES

How often have we walked past someone who might have been a soulmate had we only stopped and recognised each other? Is the poet talking of a particular individual stranger or does the stranger represent any other person? Why is he not to speak? These were some of the questions asked and discussed in an afternoon reading group.

They say it is possible to fall in love at first sight, but it would surely take bucketfuls of courage or, as the story suggests, a miracle, to walk up to someone in a train or a café and say, 'Excuse me but I have fallen in love with you – you are perfect for me.' Someone wondered if it would be better simply to pass by because *seeing* the 100 per cent perfect man or woman is one thing, speaking to them could change everything. Maybe the memory with all attendant possibilities would be more precious, and anyway, is there such a thing as 100 per cent perfect? The discussion led to thoughts on why we fall in love. The girl in the story is 'not that good-looking' and yet he recognises her perfection. Annie loved the line in the poem 'You must be he I was seeking'. 'I don't go around consciously looking for Mr Right,' she said, 'but I think, deep down, I am waiting for him. The story seems unreal, like a fairy story, and yet it makes me feel *really* sad.'

She Who Came to Woo

♥

NICHOLAS NICKLEBY

(EXTRACT FROM CHAPTER 9)

Charles Dickens

(approximate reading time 6 minutes)

After his family falls on hard times, Nicholas Nickleby takes up the post of school teacher at Dotheboys Hall in Yorkshire. The school is presided over by the deeply unpleasant Wackford Squeers, and the boys are half-starved and generally mistreated. Squeers's daughter, Fanny, who takes after her father both physically and in character, has been visiting friends. On her return she is informed of the arrival of a handsome young member of staff and is now anxious to know more.

Miss Fanny Squeers questioned the hungry servant, minutely, regarding the outward appearance and demeanour of Nicholas; to which queries the girl returned such enthusiastic replies, coupled with so many laudatory remarks touching his beautiful dark eyes, and his sweet smile, and his straight legs – upon which last-named articles she laid particular stress; the general run of legs at Dotheboys Hall being crooked – that

Miss Squeers was not long in arriving at the conclusion that the new usher must be a very remarkable person, or, as she herself significantly phrased it, 'something quite out of the common.' And so Miss Squeers made up her mind that she would take a personal observation of Nicholas the very next day.

In pursuance of this design, the young lady watched the opportunity of her mother being engaged, and her father absent, and went accidentally into the school-room to get a pen mended: where, seeing nobody but Nicholas presiding over the boys, she blushed very deeply, and exhibited great confusion.

'I beg your pardon,' faltered Miss Squeers; 'I thought my father was – or might be – dear me, how very awkward!'

'Mr Squeers is out,' said Nicholas, by no means overcome by the apparition, unexpected though it was.

'Do you know will he be long, sir?' asked Miss Squeers, with bashful hesitation.

'He said about an hour,' replied Nicholas – politely of course but without any indication of being stricken to the heart by Miss Squeers's charms.

'I never knew anything happen so cross,' exclaimed the young lady. 'Thank you! I am very sorry I intruded, I am sure. If I hadn't thought my father was here, I wouldn't upon any account have – it is very provoking – must look so very strange,' murmured Miss Squeers, blushing once more, and glancing, from the pen in her hand, to Nicholas at his desk, and back again.

'If that is all you want,' said Nicholas, pointing to the pen, and smiling, in spite of himself, at the affected embarrassment of the schoolmaster's daughter, 'perhaps I can supply his place.'

Miss Squeers glanced at the door, as if dubious of the propriety of advancing any nearer to an utter stranger; then round the school-room, as though in some measure reassured by the presence of forty boys; and finally sidled up to Nicholas and delivered the pen into his hand, with a most winning mixture of reserve and condescension.

'Shall it be a hard or a soft nib?' inquired Nicholas, smiling to prevent himself from laughing outright.

'He *has* a beautiful smile,' thought Miss Squeers.

'Which did you say?' asked Nicholas.

'Dear me, I was thinking of something else for the moment, I declare,' replied Miss Squeers – 'Oh! as soft as possible, if you please.' With which words, Miss Squeers sighed. It might be, to give Nicholas to understand that her heart was soft, and that the pen was wanted to match.

Upon these instructions Nicholas made the pen; when he gave it to Miss Squeers, Miss Squeers dropped it; and when he stooped to pick it up, Miss Squeers stooped also, and they knocked their heads together; whereat five-and-twenty little boys laughed aloud: being positively for the first and only time that half year.

'Very awkward of me,' said Nicholas, opening the door for the young lady's retreat.

'Not at all, sir,' replied Miss Squeers; 'it was my fault. It was all my foolish – a – a – good morning!'

'Good bye,' said Nicholas. 'The next I make for you, I hope will be made less clumsily. Take care! You are biting the nib off now.'

'Really,' said Miss Squeers; 'so embarrassing that I scarcely know what I – very sorry to give you so much trouble.'

'Not the least trouble in the world,' replied Nicholas, closing the school-room door.

'I never saw such legs in the whole course of my life!' said Miss Squeers, as she walked away.

In fact, Miss Squeers was in love with Nicholas Nickleby.

A LEAP-YEAR EPISODE
Eugene Field

Can I forget that winter night
　　In eighteen eighty-four,
When Nellie, charming little sprite,
　　Came tapping at the door?
'Good evening, miss,' I blushing said,
　　For in my heart I knew—
And, knowing, hung my pretty head—
　　That Nellie came to woo.

She clasped my big, red hand, and fell
　　Adown upon her knees,
And cried: 'You know I love you well,
　　So be my husband, please!'
And then she swore she'd ever be
　　A tender wife and true—
Ah, what delight it was to me
　　That Nellie came to woo!

She'd lace my shoes and darn my hose
　　And mend my shirts, she said;
And grease my comely Roman nose
　　Each night on going to bed;
She'd build the fires and fetch the coal,
　　And split the kindling, too—
Love's perjuries o'erwhelmed her soul
　　When Nellie came to woo.

And as I, blushing, gave no check
    To her advances rash,
She twined her arms about my neck,
    And toyed with my moustache;
And then she pleaded for a kiss,
    While I—what could I do
But coyly yield me to that bliss
    When Nellie came to woo?

I am engaged, and proudly wear
    A gorgeous diamond ring,
And I shall wed my lover fair
    Some time in gentle spring.
I face my doom without a sigh—
    And so, forsooth, would you,
If you but loved as fond as I
    The Nellie who came to woo.

READING NOTES

'Wishful thinking,' said a member of an afternoon reading group in a community hall. 'Nellie sounds desperate if she is settling for darning the socks of this man with his big red hands and nose, and how come he gets the diamond ring and not her?' The conversation moved from men with moustaches to the sharing of the chores in marriage.

The group took on the enjoyable task of reading the whole of Nicholas Nickleby, aloud, in weekly sessions. It took them just over a year. When they came to this chapter, no one thought Fanny Squeers would have much luck when she went to woo. The group enjoyed reflecting on the old-fashioned word 'woo' and old stories of their courting days, and although no one had actually written with a quill pen, many recalled the perils of the 'dip' pen and the inkwell.

My Love Is Come to Me

♥

SENSE AND SENSIBILITY

(EXTRACT FROM CHAPTERS 47 AND 48)

Jane Austen

(approximate reading time 15 minutes)

Following the death of their father, Elinor and Marianne Dashwood are living in the country with their mother and younger sister Margaret. Elinor has long been in love with Edward Ferrars despite knowing that he is secretly, though most unwillingly, engaged to the artful, dishonest Lucy Steele. Colonel Brandon is a friend of the family.

Margaret returned, and the family were again all restored to each other, again quietly settled at the cottage, and if not pursuing their usual studies with quite so much vigour as when they first came to Barton, at least planning a vigorous prosecution of them in future.

Elinor grew impatient for some tidings of Edward. She had heard nothing of him since her leaving London, nothing new of his plans, nothing certain even of his present abode. Some letters had passed between her and her brother, in consequence of Marianne's illness; and in the first of John's, there had been this sentence: – 'We know nothing of our unfortunate Edward, and can make no inquiries on so prohibited a subject, but conclude him to be still at Oxford;' which was all the intelligence of Edward afforded her by the correspondence, for his name was not even mentioned in any of the succeeding letters. She was not doomed, however, to be long in ignorance of his measures.

Their man-servant had been sent one morning to Exeter on business; and when, as he waited at table, he had satisfied the inquiries of his mistress as to the event of his errand, this was his voluntary communication –

'I suppose you know, ma'am, that Mr Ferrars is married.'

Marianne gave a violent start, fixed her eyes upon Elinor, saw her turning pale, and fell back in her chair in hysterics. Mrs Dashwood, whose eyes, as she answered the servant's inquiry, had intuitively taken the same direction, was shocked to perceive by Elinor's countenance how much she really suffered, and in a moment afterwards, alike distressed by Marianne's situation, knew not on which child to bestow her principal attention.

The servant, who saw only that Miss Marianne was taken ill, had sense enough to call one of the maids, who, with Mrs Dashwood's assistance, supported her into the other room. By that time, Marianne was rather better, and her mother leaving her to the care of Margaret and the maid, returned to Elinor, who, though still much disordered, had so far recovered the use of her reason and voice as to be just beginning an inquiry of Thomas, as to the source of his intelligence. Mrs Dashwood immediately took all that trouble on herself; and Elinor had the benefit of the information without the exertion of seeking it.

'Who told you that Mr Ferrars was married, Thomas?'

'I see Mr Ferrars myself, ma'am, this morning in Exeter, and his lady too, Miss Steele as was. They was stopping in a chaise at the door of the New London Inn, as I went there with a message from Sally at the Park to her brother, who is one of the post-boys. I happened to look up as I went by the chaise, and so I see directly it was the youngest Miss Steele; so I took off my hat, and she knew me and called to me, and inquired after you, ma'am, and the young ladies, especially Miss Marianne, and bid me I should give her compliments and Mr Ferrars's, their best compliments and service, and how sorry they was they had not time to come on and see you, but they was in a great hurry to go forwards, for they was going further down for a little while, but however, when they come back, they'd make sure to come and see you.'

'But did she tell you she was married, Thomas?'

'Yes, ma'am. She smiled, and said how she had changed her name since she was in these parts. She was always a very affable and free-spoken young lady, and very civil behaved. So, I made free to wish her joy.'

'Was Mr Ferrars in the carriage with her?'

'Yes, ma'am, I just see him leaning back in it, but he did not look up; – he never was a gentleman much for talking.'

Elinor's heart could easily account for his not putting himself forward; and Mrs Dashwood probably found the same explanation.

'Was there no one else in the carriage?'

'No, ma'am, only they two.'

'Do you know where they came from?'

'They come straight from town, as Miss Lucy – Mrs Ferrars told me.'

'And are they going farther westward?'

'Yes, ma'am – but not to bide long. They will soon be back again, and then they'd be sure and call here.'

Mrs Dashwood now looked at her daughter; but Elinor knew better than to expect them. She recognised the whole of Lucy in the message, and was very confident that Edward would never come near them. She observed in a low voice, to her mother, that they were probably going down to Mr Pratt's, near Plymouth.

Thomas's intelligence seemed over. Elinor looked as if she wished to hear more.

'Did you see them off, before you came away?'

'No, ma'am – the horses were just coming out, but I could not bide any longer; I was afraid of being late.'

'Did Mrs Ferrars look well?'

'Yes, ma'am, she said how she was very well; and to my mind she was always a very handsome young lady – and she seemed vastly contented.'

Mrs Dashwood could think of no other question; and Thomas and the table-cloth, now alike needless, were soon afterwards dismissed. Marianne had already sent to say that she should eat nothing more. Mrs Dashwood's and Elinor's appetites were equally lost, and Margaret might think herself very well off that, with so much uneasiness as both her sisters had lately experienced, so much reason as they had often had to be careless of their meals, she had never been obliged to go without her dinner before.

Chapter 48

Elinor now found the difference between the expectation of an unpleasant event, however certain the mind may be told to consider it, and certainty itself. She now found, that in spite of herself, she had always admitted a hope, while Edward remained single, that something would occur to prevent his marrying Lucy; that some resolution of his own, some mediation of friends, or some more eligible opportunity of establishment for the lady, would arise to assist the happiness of all. But he was now married; and she condemned her heart for the lurking flattery which so much heightened the pain of the intelligence.

That he should be married soon, before (as she imagined) he could be in orders, and consequently before he could be in possession of the living, surprised her a little at first; but she soon saw how likely it was that Lucy, in her self-provident care, in her haste to secure him, should overlook every thing but the risk of delay. They were married, married in town, and now hastening down to her uncle's. What had Edward felt on being within four miles from Barton, on seeing her mother's servant, on hearing Lucy's message!

They would soon, she supposed, be settled at Delaford: – Delaford, – that place in which so much conspired to give her an interest; which she wished to be acquainted with, and yet desired to avoid. She saw them in an instant in their parsonage-house: saw in Lucy the active, contriving manager; uniting at once a desire of smart appearance with the utmost frugality, and ashamed to be suspected of half her economical practices; – pursuing her own interest in every thought; courting the favour of Colonel Brandon, of Mrs Jennings, and of every wealthy friend. In Edward – she knew not what she saw, nor what she wished to see, – happy or unhappy, – nothing pleased her: she turned away her head from every sketch of him.

Elinor flattered herself that some one of their connections in London would write to them to announce the event, and give farther particulars; – but day after day passed off, and brought no letter, no tidings. Though uncertain that any one were to blame, she found fault with every absent friend. They were all thoughtless or indolent.

'When do you write to Colonel Brandon, ma'am?' was an inquiry which sprung from the impatience of her mind to have something going on.

'I wrote to him, my love, last week, and rather expect to see than to hear from him again. I earnestly pressed his coming to us, and should not be surprised to see him walk in today, or tomorrow, or any day.'

This was gaining something, something to look forward to. Colonel Brandon must have some information to give.

Scarcely had she so determined it, when the figure of a man on horseback drew her eyes to the window. He stopped at their gate. It was a gentleman, it was Colonel Brandon himself. Now she could hear more, and she trembled in expectation of it. But – it was *not* Colonel Brandon – neither his air – nor his height. Were it possible, she must say it must be Edward. She looked again. He had just dismounted; – she could not be mistaken, – it *was* Edward. She moved away and sat down. 'He comes from Mr Pratt's purposely to see us. I *will* be calm; I *will* be mistress of myself.'

In a moment she perceived that the others were likewise aware of the mistake. She saw her mother and Marianne change colour; saw them look at herself, and whisper a few sentences to each other. She would have given the world to be able to speak – and to make them understand that she hoped no coolness, no slight, would appear in their behaviour to him; – but she had no utterance, and was obliged to leave all to their own discretion.

Not a syllable passed aloud. They all waited in silence for the appearance of their visitor. His footsteps were heard along the gravel path; in a moment he was in the passage, and in another he was before them.

His countenance, as he entered the room, was not too happy, even for Elinor. His complexion was white with agitation; and he looked as if fearful of his reception, and conscious that he merited no kind one. Mrs Dashwood, however, conforming, as she trusted, to the wishes of that daughter, by whom she then meant in the warmth of her heart to be guided in every thing, met with a look of forced complacency, gave him her hand, and wished him joy.

He coloured, and stammered out an unintelligible reply. Elinor's lips had moved with her mother's, and, when the moment of action was over, she wished that she had shaken hands with him too. But it was then too late, and with a countenance meaning to be open, she sat down again and talked of the weather.

Marianne had retreated as much as possible out of sight, to conceal her distress; and Margaret, understanding some part, but not the whole of the case, thought it incumbent on her to be dignified, and therefore took a seat as far from him as she could, and maintained a strict silence.

When Elinor had ceased to rejoice in the dryness of the season, a very awful pause took place. It was put an end to by Mrs Dashwood, who felt obliged to hope that he had left Mrs Ferrars very well. In a hurried manner, he replied in the affirmative.

Another pause.

Elinor resolving to exert herself, though fearing the sound of her own voice, now said,

'Is Mrs Ferrars at Longstaple?'

'At Longstaple!' he replied, with an air of surprise. – 'No; my mother is in town.'

'I meant,' said Elinor, taking up some work from the table, 'to inquire for Mrs *Edward* Ferrars.'

She dared not look up; – but her mother and Marianne both turned their eyes on him. He coloured, seemed perplexed, looked doubtingly, and, after some hesitation, said, –

'Perhaps you mean – my brother – you mean Mrs – Mrs *Robert* Ferrars.'

'Mrs Robert Ferrars!' – was repeated by Marianne and her mother in an accent of the utmost amazement; – and though Elinor could not speak, even HER eyes were fixed on him with the same impatient wonder. He rose from his seat, and walked to the window, apparently from not knowing what to do; took up a pair of scissors that lay there; and, while spoiling both them and their sheath by cutting the latter to pieces as he spoke, said, in a hurried voice,

'Perhaps you do not know – you may not have heard that my brother is lately married to – to the youngest – to Miss Lucy Steele.'

His words were echoed with unspeakable astonishment by all but Elinor, who sat with her head leaning over her work, in a state of such agitation as made her hardly know where she was.

'Yes,' said he; 'they were married last week, and are now at Dawlish.'

Elinor could sit it no longer. She almost ran out of the room, and as soon as the door was closed, burst into tears of joy, which at first she thought would never cease. Edward, who had till then looked any where, rather than at her, saw her hurry away, and perhaps saw – or even heard, her emotion; for immediately afterwards he fell into a reverie, which no remarks, no inquiries, no affectionate address of Mrs Dashwood could penetrate, and at last, without saying a word, left the room, and walked out towards the village – leaving the others in the greatest astonishment and perplexity on a change in his situation so wonderful and so sudden; – a perplexity which they had no means of lessening but by their own conjectures.

A BIRTHDAY
Christina Rossetti

My heart is like a singing bird
    Whose nest is in a watered shoot;
My heart is like an apple-tree
    Whose boughs are bent with thick-set fruit;
My heart is like a rainbow shell
    That paddles in a halcyon sea;
My heart is gladder than all these,
    Because my love is come to me.

Raise me a dais of silk and down;
    Hang it with vair[1] and purple dyes;
Carve it in doves and pomegranates,
    And peacocks with a hundred eyes;
Work it in gold and silver grapes,
    In leaves and silver fleurs-de-lys;
Because the birthday of my life
    Is come, my love is come to me.

[1] fur obtained from a variety of red squirrel, used in the thirteenth and fourteenth centuries as a trimming or lining for garments.

READING NOTES

After reading the poem one group tried thinking of more modern ways of describing how the heart might feel to be reunited with the one you love, or how you could make a splendid decoration to celebrate. Someone said the poem made her think of military wives and what it must be like counting down the days until their husbands came home.

For most of a community group, the extract from *Sense and Sensibility* was their first encounter with Jane Austen, and the difference between eighteenth-century and modern-day behaviour soon became a talking point. Marianne's hysterics were remarked upon, as was Edward's inability to simply break his secret engagement to Lucy. Someone wondered why Edward left without saying anything, and the group talked about what they might have done in the circumstances. Ken said he disliked all the crying and added that there was too much crying on TV reality shows.

How Should I Avoid to Be Her Slave

WAR AND PEACE

(EXTRACT FROM BOOK 6, CHAPTERS 22 AND 23)

Leo Tolstoy

(approximate reading time 24 minutes)

Prince Andrew Bolkonski, a disillusioned landowner, soldier and widower, has recently met the very young, enchanting Natasha Rostova on the occasion of her first ball.

Other characters in the scene:

Countess Ilya Rostova – Natasha's mother

Sonya – cousin to Natasha

Pierre Bezukhov – a friend to Prince Andrew and unhappily married to Countess Helene Bezukhov

Prince Nicholas Bolkonski – father to Prince Andrew

Chapter 22

Next day, having been invited by the count, Prince Andrew dined with the Rostovs and spent the rest of the day there.

Everyone in the house realized for whose sake Prince Andrew came, and without concealing it he tried to be with Natasha all day. Not only in the soul of the frightened yet happy and enraptured Natasha, but in the whole house, there was a feeling of awe at something important that was bound to happen. The countess looked with sad and sternly serious eyes at Prince Andrew when he talked to Natasha and timidly started some artificial conversation about trifles as soon as he looked her way. Sonya was afraid to leave Natasha and afraid of being in the way when she was with them. Natasha grew pale, in a panic of expectation, when she remained alone with him for a moment. Prince Andrew surprised her by his timidity. She felt that he wanted to say something to her but could not bring himself to do so.

In the evening, when Prince Andrew had left, the countess went up to Natasha and whispered: 'Well, what?'

'Mamma! For heaven's sake don't ask me anything now! One can't talk about that,' said Natasha.

But all the same that night Natasha, now agitated and now frightened, lay a long time in her mother's bed gazing straight before her. She told her how he had complimented her, how he told her he was going abroad and asked her where they were going to spend the summer, and then how he had asked her about Boris.

'But such a . . . such a . . . never happened to me before!' she said. 'Only I feel afraid in his presence. I am always afraid when I'm with him. What does that mean? Does it mean that it's the real thing? Yes? Mamma, are you asleep?'

'No, my love; I am frightened myself,' answered her mother. 'Now go!'

'All the same I shan't sleep. What silliness, to sleep! Mummy! Mummy! such a thing never happened to me before,' she said, surprised and alarmed at the feeling she was aware of in herself. 'And could we ever have thought! . . .'

It seemed to Natasha that even at the time she first saw Prince Andrew at Otradnoe she had fallen in love with him. It was as if she feared this strange, unexpected happiness of meeting again the very man she had then chosen (she was firmly convinced she had done so) and of finding him, as it seemed, not indifferent to her.

'And it had to happen that he should come specially to Petersburg while we are here. And it had to happen that we should meet at that ball. It is fate. Clearly it is fate that everything led up to this! Already then, directly I saw him I felt something peculiar.'

'What else did he say to you? What are those verses? Read them . . .' said her mother, thoughtfully, referring to some verses Prince Andrew had written in Natasha's album.

'Mamma, one need not be ashamed of his being a widower?'

'Don't, Natasha! Pray to God. "Marriages are made in heaven",' said her mother.

'Darling Mummy, how I love you! How happy I am!' cried Natasha, shedding tears of joy and excitement and embracing her mother.

At that very time Prince Andrew was sitting with Pierre and telling him of his love for Natasha and his firm resolve to make her his wife.

That day Countess Helene had a reception at her house. The French ambassador was there, and a foreign prince of the blood who had of late become a frequent visitor of hers, and many brilliant ladies and gentlemen. Pierre, who had come downstairs, walked through the rooms and struck everyone by his preoccupied, absent-minded, and morose air.

Since the ball he had felt the approach of a fit of nervous depression and had made desperate efforts to combat it. Since the intimacy of his wife with the royal prince, Pierre had unexpectedly been made a gentleman of the bedchamber, and from that time he had begun to feel oppressed and ashamed in court society, and dark thoughts of the vanity of all things human came to him oftener than before. At the same time the feeling he had noticed between his protégée Natasha and Prince Andrew accentuated his gloom by the contrast between his own position and his friend's. He tried equally to avoid thinking about his wife, and about Natasha and Prince Andrew; and again everything seemed to him insignificant in comparison with eternity; again the question: for what? presented itself; and he forced himself to work day and night at masonic labors, hoping to drive away the evil spirit that threatened him. Toward midnight, after he had left the countess' apartments, he was sitting upstairs in a shabby dressing gown, copying out the original transaction of the Scottish lodge of Freemasons at a table in his low room cloudy with tobacco smoke, when someone came in. It was Prince Andrew.

'Ah, it's you!' said Pierre with a preoccupied, dissatisfied air. 'And I, you see, am hard at it.' He pointed to his manuscript book with that air of escaping from the ills of life with which unhappy people look at their work.

Prince Andrew, with a beaming, ecstatic expression of renewed life on his face, paused in front of Pierre and, not noticing his sad look, smiled at him with the egotism of joy.

'Well, dear heart,' said he, 'I wanted to tell you about it yesterday and I have come to do so today. I never experienced anything like it before. I am in love, my friend!'

Suddenly Pierre heaved a deep sigh and dumped his heavy person down on the sofa beside Prince Andrew.

'With Natasha Rostova, yes?' said he.

'Yes, yes! Who else should it be? I should never have believed it, but the feeling is stronger than I. Yesterday I tormented myself and suffered, but I would not exchange even that torment for anything in the world, I have not lived till now. At last I live, but I can't live without her! But can she love me? . . . I am too old for her . . . Why don't you speak?'

'I? I? What did I tell you?' said Pierre suddenly, rising and beginning to pace up and down the room. 'I always thought it . . . That girl is such a treasure . . . she is a rare girl . . . My dear friend, I entreat you, don't philosophize, don't doubt, marry, marry, marry . . . And I am sure there will not be a happier man than you.'

'But what of her?'

'She loves you.'

'Don't talk rubbish . . .' said Prince Andrew, smiling and looking into Pierre's eyes.

'She does, I know,' Pierre cried fiercely.

'But do listen,' returned Prince Andrew, holding him by the arm. 'Do you know the condition I am in? I must talk about it to someone.'

'Well, go on, go on. I am very glad,' said Pierre, and his face really changed, his brow became smooth, and he listened gladly to Prince Andrew. Prince Andrew seemed, and really was, quite a different, quite a new man. Where was his spleen, his contempt for life, his disillusionment? Pierre was the only person to whom he made up his mind to speak openly; and to him he told all that was in his soul. Now he boldly and lightly made plans for an extended future, said he could not sacrifice his own happiness to his father's caprice, and spoke of how he would either make his father consent to this marriage and love her, or would do without his consent; then he marvelled at the feeling that had mastered him as at something strange, apart from and independent of himself.

'I should not have believed anyone who told me that I was capable of such love,' said Prince Andrew. 'It is not at all the same feeling that I knew in the past. The whole world is now for me divided into two halves: one half is she, and there all is joy, hope, light: the other half is everything where she is not, and there is all gloom and darkness . . .'

'Darkness and gloom,' reiterated Pierre: 'yes, yes, I understand that.'

'I cannot help loving the light, it is not my fault. And I am very happy! You understand me? I know you are glad for my sake.'

'Yes, yes,' Pierre assented, looking at his friend with a touched and sad expression in his eyes. The brighter Prince Andrew's lot appeared to him, the gloomier seemed his own.

Chapter 23

Prince Andrew needed his father's consent to his marriage, and to obtain this he started for the country next day.

His father received his son's communication with external composure, but inward wrath. He could not comprehend how anyone could wish to alter his life or introduce anything new into it, when his own life was already ending. 'If only they would let me end my days as I want to,' thought the old man, 'then they might do as they please.' With his son, however, he employed the diplomacy he reserved for important occasions and, adopting a quiet tone, discussed the whole matter.

In the first place the marriage was not a brilliant one as regards birth, wealth, or rank. Secondly, Prince Andrew was no longer as young as he had been and his health was poor (the old man laid special stress on this), while she was very young. Thirdly, he had a son whom it would be a pity to entrust to a chit of a girl. 'Fourthly and finally,' the father said, looking ironically at his son, 'I beg you to put it off for a year: go abroad, take a cure, look out as you wanted to for a German tutor for Prince Nicholas. Then if your love or passion or obstinacy – as you please – is still as great, marry! And that's my last word on it. Mind, the last . . .' concluded the prince, in a tone which showed that nothing would make him alter his decision.

Prince Andrew saw clearly that the old man hoped that his feelings, or his fiancée's, would not stand a year's test, or that he (the old prince himself) would die before then, and he decided to conform to his father's wish – to propose, and postpone the wedding for a year.

Three weeks after the last evening he had spent with the Rostovs, Prince Andrew returned to Petersburg.

Next day after her talk with her mother Natasha expected Bolkonski all day, but he did not come. On the second and third day it was the same. Pierre did not come either and Natasha, not knowing that Prince Andrew had gone to see his father, could not explain his absence to herself.

Three weeks passed in this way. Natasha had no desire to go out anywhere and wandered from room to room like a shadow, idle and listless; she wept secretly at night and did not go to her mother in the evenings. She blushed continually and was irritable. It seemed to her that everybody knew about her disappointment and was laughing at her and pitying her. Strong as was her inward grief, this wound to her vanity intensified her misery.

Once she came to her mother, tried to say something, and suddenly began to cry. Her tears were those of an offended child who does not know why it is being punished.

The countess began to soothe Natasha, who after first listening to her mother's words, suddenly interrupted her:

'Leave off, Mamma! I don't think, and don't want to think about it! He just came and then left off, left off . . .'

Her voice trembled, and she again nearly cried, but recovered and went on quietly:

'And I don't at all want to get married. And I am afraid of him; I have now become quite calm, quite calm.'

The day after this conversation Natasha put on the old dress which she knew had the peculiar property of conducing to cheerfulness in the mornings, and that day she returned to the old way of life which she had abandoned since the ball. Having finished her morning tea she went to the ballroom, which she particularly liked for its loud resonance, and began singing her solfeggio. When she had finished her first exercise she stood still in the middle of the room and sang a musical phrase that particularly pleased her. She listened joyfully (as though she had not expected it) to the charm of the notes reverberating, filling the whole empty ballroom, and slowly dying away; and all at once she felt cheerful. 'What's the good of making so much of it? Things are nice as it is,' she said to herself, and she began walking up and down the room, not stepping simply on the resounding parquet but treading with each step from the heel to the toe (she had on a new and favorite pair of shoes) and listening to the regular tap of the heel and creak of the toe as gladly as she had to the sounds of her own voice. Passing a mirror she glanced into it. 'There, that's me!' the expression of her face seemed to say as she caught sight of herself. 'Well, and very nice too! I need nobody.'

A footman wanted to come in to clear away something in the room but she would not let him, and having closed the door behind him continued her walk. That morning she had returned to her favorite mood – love of, and delight in, herself. 'How charming that Natasha is!' she said again, speaking as some third, collective, male person. 'Pretty, a good voice, young, and in nobody's way if only they leave her in peace.' But however much they left her in peace she could not now be at peace, and immediately felt this.

In the hall the porch door opened, and someone asked, 'At home?' and then footsteps were heard. Natasha was looking at the mirror, but did not see herself. She listened to the sounds in the hall. When she saw herself, her face was pale. It was he. She knew this for certain, though she hardly heard his voice through the closed doors.

Pale and agitated, Natasha ran into the drawing room.

'Mamma! Bolkonski has come!' she said. 'Mamma, it is awful, it is unbearable! I don't want . . . to be tormented? What am I to do? . . .'

Before the countess could answer, Prince Andrew entered the room with an agitated and serious face. As soon as he saw Natasha his face brightened. He kissed the countess' hand and Natasha's, and sat down beside the sofa.

'It is long since we had the pleasure . . .' began the countess, but Prince Andrew interrupted her by answering her intended question, obviously in haste to say what he had to.

'I have not been to see you all this time because I have been at my father's. I had to talk over a very important matter with him. I only got back last night,' he said glancing at Natasha; 'I want to have a talk with you, Countess,' he added after a moment's pause.

The countess lowered her eyes, sighing deeply.

'I am at your disposal,' she murmured.

Natasha knew that she ought to go away, but was unable to do so: something gripped her throat, and regardless of manners she stared straight at Prince Andrew with wide-open eyes.

'At once? This instant! . . . No, it can't be!' she thought.

Again he glanced at her, and that glance convinced her that she was not mistaken. Yes, at once, that very instant, her fate would be decided.

'Go, Natasha! I will call you,' said the countess in a whisper.

Natasha glanced with frightened imploring eyes at Prince Andrew and at her mother and went out.

'I have come, Countess, to ask for your daughter's hand,' said Prince Andrew.

The countess' face flushed hotly, but she said nothing.

'Your offer . . .' she began at last sedately. He remained silent, looking into her eyes. 'Your offer . . .' (she grew confused) 'is agreeable to us, and I accept your offer. I am glad. And my husband . . . I hope . . . but it will depend on her . . .'

'I will speak to her when I have your consent . . . Do you give it to me?' said Prince Andrew.

'Yes,' replied the countess. She held out her hand to him, and with a mixed feeling of estrangement and tenderness pressed her lips to his forehead as he stooped to kiss her hand. She wished to love him as a son, but felt that to her he was a stranger and a terrifying man. 'I am sure my husband will consent,' said the countess, 'but your father . . .'

'My father, to whom I have told my plans, has made it an express condition of his consent that the wedding is not to take place for a year. And I wished to tell you of that,' said Prince Andrew.

'It is true that Natasha is still young, but – so long as that? . . .'

'It is unavoidable,' said Prince Andrew with a sigh.

'I will send her to you,' said the countess, and left the room.

'Lord have mercy upon us!' she repeated while seeking her daughter.

Sonya said that Natasha was in her bedroom. Natasha was sitting on the bed, pale and dry eyed, and was gazing at the icons and whispering something as she rapidly crossed herself. Seeing her mother she jumped up and flew to her.

'Well, Mamma? . . . Well? . . .'

'Go, go to him. He is asking for your hand,' said the countess, coldly it seemed to Natasha. 'Go . . . go,' said the mother, sadly and reproachfully, with a deep sigh, as her daughter ran away.

Natasha never remembered how she entered the drawing room. When she came in and saw him she paused. 'Is it possible that this stranger has now become everything to me?' she asked herself, and immediately answered, 'Yes, everything! He alone is now dearer to me than everything in the world.' Prince Andrew came up to her with downcast eyes.

'I have loved you from the very first moment I saw you. May I hope?'

He looked at her and was struck by the serious impassioned expression of her face. Her face said: 'Why ask? Why doubt what you cannot but know? Why speak, when words cannot express what one feels?'

She drew near to him and stopped. He took her hand and kissed it.

'Do you love me?'

'Yes, yes!' Natasha murmured as if in vexation. Then she sighed loudly and, catching her breath more and more quickly, began to sob.

'What is it? What's the matter?'

'Oh, I am so happy!' she replied, smiled through her tears, bent over closer to him, paused for an instant as if asking herself whether she might, and then kissed him.

Prince Andrew held her hands, looked into her eyes, and did not find in his heart his former love for her. Something in him had suddenly changed; there was no longer the former poetic and mystic charm of desire, but there was pity for her feminine and childish weakness, fear at her devotion and trustfulness, and an oppressive yet joyful sense of the duty that now bound him to her forever. The present feeling, though not so bright and poetic as the former, was stronger and more serious.

'Did your mother tell you that it cannot be for a year?' asked Prince Andrew, still looking into her eyes.

'Is it possible that I – the "chit of a girl," as everybody called me,' thought Natasha – 'is it possible that I am now to be the wife and the equal of this strange, dear, clever man whom even my father looks up to? Can it be true? Can it be true that there can be no more playing with life, that now I am grown up, that on me now lies a responsibility for my every word and deed? Yes, but what did he ask me?'

'No,' she replied, but she had not understood his question.

'Forgive me!' he said. 'But you are so young, and I have already been through so much in life. I am afraid for you, you do not yet know yourself.'

Natasha listened with concentrated attention, trying but failing to take in the meaning of his words.

'Hard as this year which delays my happiness will be,' continued Prince Andrew, 'it will give you time to be sure of yourself. I ask you to make me happy in a year, but you are free: our engagement shall remain a secret, and should you find that you do not love me, or should you come to love . . .' said Prince Andrew with an unnatural smile.

'Why do you say that?' Natasha interrupted him. 'You know that from the very day you first came to Otradnoe I have loved you,' she cried, quite convinced that she spoke the truth.

'In a year you will learn to know yourself . . .'

'A whole year!' Natasha repeated suddenly, only now realizing that the marriage was to be postponed for a year. 'But why a year? Why a year? . . .'

Prince Andrew began to explain to her the reasons for this delay. Natasha did not hear him.

'And can't it be helped?' she asked. Prince Andrew did not reply, but his face expressed the impossibility of altering that decision.

'It's awful! Oh, it's awful! awful!' Natasha suddenly cried, and again burst into sobs. 'I shall die, waiting a year: it's impossible, it's awful!' She looked into her lover's face and saw in it a look of commiseration and perplexity.

'No, no! I'll do anything!' she said, suddenly checking her tears. 'I am so happy.'

The father and mother came into the room and gave the betrothed couple their blessing.

From that day Prince Andrew began to frequent the Rostovs' as Natasha's affianced lover.

THE FAIR SINGER
Andrew Marvell

To make a final conquest of all me,
Love did compose so sweet an enemy,
In whom both beauties to my death agree,
Joining themselves in fatal harmony;
That, while she with her eyes my heart does bind,
She with her voice might captivate my mind.

I could have fled from one but singly fair;
My disentangled soul itself might save,
Breaking the curled trammels of her hair;
But how should I avoid to be her slave,
Whose subtle art invisibly can wreath
My fetters of the very air I breathe?

It had been easy fighting in some plain,
Where victory might hang in equal choice,
But all resistance against her is vain
Who has the advantage both of eyes and voice,
And all my forces needs must be undone
She having gained both the wind and sun.

READING NOTES

After reading this extract, a woman said that she never expected to read *War and Peace*. 'I thought it would be way beyond me, but it seems perfectly easy to understand. When Natasha is singing by herself in the ballroom, it even reminded me of Maria in *West Side Story*, singing "I Feel Pretty".' She was particularly interested in the moment when something in his relationship with Natasha suddenly changes for Prince Andrew. The group talked about the age difference between the couple and what difficulties that might lead to, especially as Natasha seems very young and innocent. Someone noticed the line '"You know that from the very day you first came to Otradnoe I have loved you," she cried, quite convinced that she spoke the truth' – and wondered if this sounded ominous.

At first it seemed to the group as if the speaker in the poem could almost be Prince Andrew – a soldier who is more afraid of love than war and finds himself completely captured by the fair singer. Does the loved one have to be 'the enemy' they wondered, and does this mean that beauty is dangerous, or is it the fatal combination of beauty and voice in this case?

There was also some spirited discussion about freemasonry.

Our Places by the Fireplace

♥

FAR FROM THE MADDING CROWD
(EXTRACT FROM CHAPTER 4)
Thomas Hardy

(approximate reading time 15 minutes)

*Gabriel Oak, a young shepherd, has fallen in love with Bathsheba
Everdene, a spirited, independent woman who has recently come
to live in the area. Here, he has called to see her.*

Bathsheba's aunt was indoors. 'Will you tell Miss Everdene
that somebody would be glad to speak to her?' said Mr Oak.
(Calling one's self merely Somebody, without giving a name, is
not to be taken as an example of the ill-breeding of the rural
world: it springs from a refined modesty, of which townspeople,
with their cards and announcements, have no notion whatever.)

'Will you come in, Mr Oak?'

'Oh, thank 'ee,' said Gabriel, following her to the fireplace.
'I've brought a lamb for Miss Everdene. I thought she might
like one to rear; girls do.'

'She might,' said Mrs Hurst, musingly; 'though she's only
a visitor here. If you will wait a minute Bathsheba will be in.'

'Yes, I will wait,' said Gabriel, sitting down. 'The lamb isn't really the business I came about, Mrs Hurst. In short, I was going to ask her if she'd like to be married.'

'And were you indeed?'

'Yes. Because if she would, I should be very glad to marry her. D'ye know if she's got any other young man hanging about her at all?'

'Let me think,' said Mrs Hurst, poking the fire superfluously . . . 'Yes – bless you, ever so many young men. You see, Farmer Oak, she's so good-looking, and an excellent scholar besides – she was going to be a governess once, you know, only she was too wild. Not that her young men ever come here – but, Lord, in the nature of women, she must have a dozen!'

'That's unfortunate,' said Farmer Oak, contemplating a crack in the stone floor with sorrow. 'I'm only an every-day sort of man, and my only chance was in being the first comer . . . Well, there's no use in my waiting, for that was all I came about: so I'll take myself off home-along, Mrs Hurst.'

When Gabriel had gone about two hundred yards along the down, he heard a 'hoi-hoi!' uttered behind him, in a piping note of more treble quality than that in which the exclamation usually embodies itself when shouted across a field. He looked round, and saw a girl racing after him, waving a white handkerchief.

Oak stood still – and the runner drew nearer. It was Bathsheba Everdene. Gabriel's colour deepened: hers was already deep, not, as it appeared, from emotion, but from running.

'Farmer Oak – I—' she said, pausing for want of breath, pulling up in front of him with a slanted face and putting her hand to her side.

'I have just called to see you,' said Gabriel, pending her further speech.

'Yes – I know that,' she said, panting like a robin, her face red and moist from her exertions, like a peony petal before the sun dries off the dew. 'I didn't know you had come to ask to have me, or I should have come in from the garden instantly. I ran after you to say – that my aunt made a mistake in sending you away from courting me.'

Gabriel expanded. 'I'm sorry to have made you run so fast, my dear,' he said, with a grateful sense of favours to come. 'Wait a bit till you've found your breath.'

'– It was quite a mistake – aunt's telling you I had a young man already,' Bathsheba went on. 'I haven't a sweetheart at all – and I never had one, and I thought that, as times go with women, it was *such* a pity to send you away thinking that I had several.'

'Really and truly I am glad to hear that!' said Farmer Oak, smiling one of his long special smiles, and blushing with gladness. He held out his hand to take hers, which, when she had eased her side by pressing it there, was prettily extended upon her bosom to still her loud-beating heart. Directly he seized it she put it behind her, so that it slipped through his fingers like an eel.

'I have a nice snug little farm,' said Gabriel, with half a degree less assurance than when he had seized her hand.

'Yes; you have.'

'A man has advanced me money to begin with, but still, it will soon be paid off, and though I am only an every-day sort of man I have got on a little since I was a boy.' Gabriel uttered 'a little' in a tone to show her that it was the complacent form of 'a great deal'. He continued: 'When we be married, I am quite sure I can work twice as hard as I do now.'

He went forward and stretched out his arm again. Bathsheba had overtaken him at a point beside which stood a low stunted holly bush, now laden with red berries. Seeing his advance take the form of an attitude threatening a possible enclosure, if not compression, of her person, she edged off round the bush.

'Why, Farmer Oak,' she said over the top, looking at him with rounded eyes, 'I never said I was going to marry you.'

'Well – that *is* a tale!' said Oak, with dismay.' To run after anybody like this, and then say you don't want him!'

'What I meant to tell you was only this,' she said eagerly, and yet half conscious of the absurdity of the position she had made for herself – 'that nobody has got me yet as a sweetheart, instead of my having a dozen, as my aunt said; I *hate* to be thought men's property in that way, though possibly I shall be had some day. Why, if I'd wanted you I shouldn't have run after you like this; 'twould have been the *forwardest* thing! But there was no harm in hurrying to correct a piece of false news that had been told you.'

'Oh, no – no harm at all.' But there is such a thing as being too generous in expressing a judgement impulsively, and Oak added with a more appreciative sense of all the circumstances – 'Well, I am not quite certain it was no harm.'

'Indeed, I hadn't time to think before starting whether I wanted to marry or not, for you'd have been gone over the hill.'

'Come,' said Gabriel, freshening again; 'think a minute or two. I'll wait a while, Miss Everdene. Will you marry me? Do, Bathsheba. I love you far more than common!'

'I'll try to think,' she observed rather more timorously; 'if I can think out of doors; my mind spreads away so.'

'But you can give a guess.'

'Then give me time.' Bathsheba looked thoughtfully into the distance, away from the direction in which Gabriel stood.

'I can make you happy,' said he to the back of her head, across the bush. 'You shall have a piano in a year or two – farmers' wives are getting to have pianos now – and I'll practise up the flute right well to play with you in the evenings.'

'Yes; I should like that.'

'And have one of those little ten-pound gigs for market – and nice flowers, and birds – cocks and hens I mean, because they be useful,' continued Gabriel, feeling balanced between poetry and practicality.

'I should like it very much.'

'And a frame for cucumbers – like a gentleman and lady.'

'Yes.'

'And when the wedding was over, we'd have it put in the newspaper list of marriages.'

'Dearly I should like that!'

'And the babies in the births – every man jack of 'em! And at home by the fire, whenever you look up, there I shall be – and whenever I look up there will be you.'

'Wait, wait, and don't be improper!'

Her countenance fell, and she was silent awhile. He regarded the red berries between them over and over again, to such an extent that holly seemed in his after life to be a cypher signifying a proposal of marriage. Bathsheba decisively turned to him.

'No; 'tis no use,' she said. 'I don't want to marry you.'

'Try.'

'I have tried hard all the time I've been thinking; for a marriage would be very nice in one sense. People would talk about me, and think I had won my battle, and I should feel triumphant, and all that. But a husband—'

'Well!'

'Why, he'd always be there, as you say; whenever I looked up, there he'd be.'

'Of course he would – I, that is.'

'Well, what I mean is that I shouldn't mind being a bride at a wedding, if I could be one without having a husband. But since a woman can't show off in that way by herself, I shan't marry – at least yet.'

'That's a terrible wooden story!'

At this criticism of her statement Bathsheba made an addition to her dignity by a slight sweep away from him.

'Upon my heart and soul, I don't know what a maid can say stupider than that,' said Oak. 'But dearest,' he continued in a palliative voice, 'don't be like it!' Oak sighed a deep honest sigh – none the less so in that, being like the sigh of a pine plantation, it was rather noticeable as a disturbance of the atmosphere. 'Why won't you have me?' he appealed, creeping round the holly to reach her side.

'I cannot,' she said, retreating.

'But why?' he persisted, standing still at last in despair of ever reaching her, and facing over the bush.

'Because I don't love you.'

'Yes, but—'

She contracted a yawn to an inoffensive smallness, so that it was hardly ill-mannered at all. 'I don't love you,' she said.

'But I love you – and, as for myself, I am content to be liked.'

'O Mr Oak – that's very fine! You'd get to despise me.'

'Never,' said Mr Oak, so earnestly that he seemed to be coming, by the force of his words, straight through the bush and into her arms. 'I shall do one thing in this life – one thing certain – that is, love you, and long for you, and *keep wanting you* till I die.' His voice had a genuine pathos now, and his large brown hands perceptibly trembled.

'It seems dreadfully wrong not to have you when you feel so much!' she said with a little distress, and looking hopelessly around for some means of escape from her moral dilemma. 'How I wish I hadn't run after you!' However she seemed to have a short cut for getting back to cheerfulness and set her face to signify archness. 'It wouldn't do, Mr Oak. I want somebody to tame me; I am too independent; and you would never be able to, I know.'

Oak cast his eyes down the field in a way implying that it was useless to attempt argument.

'Mr Oak,' she said, with luminous distinctness and common sense, 'you are better off than I. I have hardly a penny in the world – I am staying with my aunt for my bare sustenance. I am better educated than you – and I don't love you a bit: that's my side of the case. Now yours: you are a farmer just beginning; and you ought in common prudence, if you marry at all (which you should certainly not think of doing at present), to marry a woman with money, who would stock a larger farm for you than you have now.'

Gabriel looked at her with a little surprise and much admiration.

'That's the very thing I had been thinking myself!' he naively said.

Farmer Oak had one-and-a-half Christian characteristics too many to succeed with Bathsheba: his humility, and a superfluous moiety of honesty. Bathsheba was decidedly disconcerted.

'Well, then, why did you come and disturb me?' she said, almost angrily, if not quite, an enlarging red spot rising in each cheek.

'I can't do what I think would be – would be—'

'Right?'

'No: wise.'

'You have made an admission *now*, Mr Oak,' she exclaimed, with even more hauteur, and rocking her head disdainfully. 'After that, do you think I could marry you? Not if I know it.'

He broke in passionately. 'But don't mistake me like that! Because I am open enough to own what every man in my shoes would have thought of, you make your colours come up your face and get crabbed with me. That about your not being good enough for me is nonsense. You speak like a lady – all the parish notice it, and your uncle at Weatherbury is, I have heerd, a large farmer – much larger than ever I shall be. May I call in the evening, or will you walk along with me o' Sundays? I don't want you to make-up your mind at once, if you'd rather not.'

'No – no – I cannot. Don't press me any more – don't. I don't love you – so 'twould be ridiculous,' she said, with a laugh.

No man likes to see his emotions the sport of a merry-go-round of skittishness. 'Very well,' said Oak firmly, with the bearing of one who was going to give his days and nights to Ecclesiastes for ever. 'Then I'll ask you no more.'

THE VIERZIDE[1] CHAIRS
William Barnes

Though days do gaïn upon the night,
An' birds do teäke[2] a leäter[3] flight,
'Tis cwold[4] enough to spread our hands
Oonce now an' then to glowen brands.
Zoo[5] now we two, a-left alwone,
Can meäke a quiet hour our own,
Let's teäke, a-zitten feäce[6] to feäce,
Our pleäces by the vier pleäce,
Where you shall have the window view
Outside, an' I can look on you.

When oonce I brought ye hwome my bride,
In yollow glow o' zummer tide,
I wanted you to teäke a chair
At that zide o' the vier, there,
And have the ground an' sky in zight
Wi' feäce toward the window light;
While I back here should have my brow
In sheäde, an' zit where I do now,
That you mid zee the land outside,
If I could look on you, my bride.

---

[1] Barnes was a Dorset man who wrote in Dorset dialect
[2] teäke: take
[3] leäter: later
[4] cwold: cold
[5] Zoo: so
[6] feäce: face

An' there the water-pool do spread,
Wi' swaÿen elems[7] over head,
An' there's the knap[8] where we did rove
At dusk, along the high-tree'd grove,
The while the wind did whisper down
Our whisper'd words; an' there's the crown
Ov Duncliffe hill, wi' wid'nen sheädes
Ov wood a-cast on slopèn gleädes:
Zoo you injoy the green an' blue
Without, an' I will look on you.

An' there's the copse, where we did all
Goo out a-nutten in the fall,
That now would meäke, a-quiv'ren black,
But little lewth[9] behind your back;
An' there's the tower, near the door,
That we at dusk did meet avore
As we did gather on the green,
An' you did zee, an' wer a-zeen:
All wold zights welcomer than new,
A-look'd on as I look'd on you.

[7] elems: elms
[8] knap: hillock
[9] lewth: lewness, to lew as shelter

READING NOTES

There was much hilarity amongst the group of young women reading the poem aloud and they enjoyed teasing out the meaning of the dialect. They thought it interesting that the subject of Barnes's poem – the chairs on either side of the fire with the fond memories that went with them, should be Gabriel Oak's stumbling block, as Bathsheba evidently could not entertain the thought of a husband *always* being there. The women were surprised at how modern Bathsheba seemed to be – not a bit the strait-laced Victorian. And they liked the moment when she said she would enjoy the wedding if she did not have to end up with a husband. There was some discussion about the future for these two. Could they, would they ever come together? Karen hoped not. 'I think she is too alive for him. He would restrict her and she would run rings around him and make him miserable.'

Once everyone had got used to the dialect, the poem was generally found to be full of warmth, affection and memories. Perhaps Bathsheba is too young to realise what she would be missing, someone said.

The Cry that Soars in Outer Blackness

JANE EYRE

(EXTRACT FROM CHAPTER 23)

Charlotte Brontë

(approximate reading time 25 minutes)

Jane Eyre, small, plain and passionate, has endured a love-less childhood. She is now living at Thornfield Hall where she is governess to Adèle, the ward of Edward Rochester. With no real hope of having her feelings returned, Jane is nevertheless drawn to Rochester. Following an eventful house party, she believes him to be engaged to the beautiful Blanche Ingram. Mrs Fairfax is the housekeeper at Thornfield.

I walked a while on the pavement; but a subtle, well-known scent – that of a cigar – stole from some window; I saw the library casement open a hand-breadth; I knew I might be watched thence; so I went apart into the orchard. No nook in the grounds more sheltered and more Eden-like; a very high wall shut it out from the court on one side; on the other a beech avenue screened it from the lawn. At the bottom was a sunk fence, its sole separation from lonely fields: a winding walk, bordered with laurels and terminating in a giant horse-chestnut, circled at the base by a seat, led down to the fence. Here one could wander unseen. While such honeydew fell, such silence reigned, such gloaming gathered, I felt as if I could haunt such shade for ever; but in threading the flower and fruit parterres at the upper part of the enclosure, enticed there by the light the now rising moon cast on this more open quarter, my step is stayed – not by sound, not by sight, but once more by a warning fragrance.

Sweet-briar and southernwood, jasmine, pink, and rose have long been yielding their evening sacrifice of incense: this new scent is neither of shrub nor flower; it is – I know it well – it is Mr Rochester's cigar. I look round and I listen. I see trees laden with ripening fruit. I hear a nightingale warbling in a wood half a mile off: no moving form is visible, no coming step audible; but that perfume increases: I must flee. I make for the wicket leading to the shrubbery, and I see Mr Rochester entering. I step aside into the ivy recess; he will not stay long: he will soon return whence he came, and if I sit still he will never see me.

But no – eventide is as pleasant to him as to me, and this antique garden as attractive; and he strolls on, now lifting the gooseberry-tree branches to look at the fruit, large as plums, with which they are laden; now taking a ripe cherry from the wall; now stooping towards a knot of flowers, either to inhale their fragrance or to admire the dew-beads on their petals. A great moth goes humming by me; it alights on a plant at Mr Rochester's foot: he sees it, and bends to examine it.

'Now he has his back towards me,' thought I, 'and he is occupied too; perhaps, if I walk softly, I can slip away unnoticed.'

I trod on an edging of turf that the crackle of the pebbly gravel might not betray me: he was standing among the beds at a yard or two distant from where I had to pass; the moth apparently engaged him. 'I shall get by very well,' I meditated. As I crossed his shadow, thrown long over the garden by the moon, not yet risen high, he said quietly, without turning –

'Jane, come and look at this fellow.'

I had made no noise: he had not eyes behind – could his shadow feel? I started at first, and then I approached him.

'Look at his wings,' said he; 'he reminds me rather of a West Indian insect; one does not often see so large and gay a night-rover in England; there! he is flown.'

The moth roamed away. I was sheepishly retreating also; but Mr Rochester followed me, and when we reached the wicket, he said –

'Turn back: on so lovely a night it is a shame to sit in the house; and surely no one can wish to go to bed while sunset is thus at meeting with moonrise.'

It is one of my faults, that though my tongue is sometimes prompt enough at an answer, there are times when it sadly fails me in framing an excuse; and always the lapse occurs at some crisis, when a facile word or plausible pretext is specially wanted to get me out of painful embarrassment. I did not like to walk at this hour alone with Mr Rochester in the shadowy orchard; but I could not find a reason to allege for leaving him. I followed with lagging step, and thoughts busily bent on discovering a means of extrication; but he himself looked so composed and so grave also, I became ashamed of feeling any confusion: the evil – if evil existent or prospective there was – seemed to lie with me only; his mind was unconscious and quiet.

'Jane,' he recommenced, as we entered the laurel walk and slowly strayed down in the direction of the sunk fence and the horse-chestnut, 'Thornfield is a pleasant place in summer, is it not?'

'Yes, sir.'

'You must have become in some degree attached to the house – you who have an eye for natural beauties, and a good deal of the organ of Adhesiveness?'

'I am attached to it, indeed.'

'And though I don't comprehend how it is, I perceive you have acquired a degree of regard for that foolish little child Adèle, too; and even for simple Dame Fairfax?'

'Yes, sir; in different ways, I have an affection for both.'

'And would be sorry to part with them?'

'Yes.'

'Pity!' he said, and sighed and paused.

'It is always the way of events in this life,' he continued presently: 'no sooner have you got settled in a pleasant resting-place, than a voice calls out to you to rise and move on, for the hour of repose is expired.'

'Must I move on, sir?' I asked. 'Must I leave Thornfield?'

'I believe you must, Jane. I am sorry, Janet, but I believe indeed you must.'

This was a blow: but I did not let it prostrate me.

'Well, sir, I shall be ready when the order to march comes.'

'It is come now – I must give it to-night.'

'Then you *are* going to be married, sir?'

'Ex-act-ly – pre-cise-ly: with your usual acuteness, you have hit the nail straight on the head.'

'Soon, sir?'

'Very soon, my – that is, Miss Eyre: and you'll remember, Jane, the first time I, or Rumour, plainly intimated to you that it was my intention to put my old bachelor's neck into the sacred noose, to enter into the holy estate of matrimony – to take Miss Ingram to my bosom, in short (she's an extensive armful: but that's not to the point – one can't have too much of such a very excellent thing as my beautiful Blanche): well, as I was saying – listen to me, Jane! You're not turning your head to look after more moths, are you? That was only a lady-clock, child, "flying away home". I wish to remind you that it was you who first said to me, with that discretion I respect in you – with that foresight, prudence, and humility which befit your responsible and dependent position – that in case I married Miss Ingram, both you and little Adèle had better trot forthwith. I pass over the sort of slur conveyed in this suggestion on the character of my beloved; indeed, when you are far away, Janet, I'll try to forget it: I shall notice only its wisdom; which is such that I have made it my law of action. Adèle must go to school; and you, Miss Eyre, must get a new situation.'

'Yes, sir, I will advertise immediately: and meantime, I suppose–' I was going to say, 'I suppose I may stay here, till I find another shelter to betake myself to': but I stopped, feeling it would not do to risk a long sentence, for my voice was not quite under command.

'In about a month I hope to be a bridegroom,' continued Mr Rochester; 'and in the interim, I shall myself look out for employment and an asylum for you.'

'Thank you, sir; I am sorry to give—'

'Oh, no need to apologise! I consider that when a dependent does her duty as well as you have done yours, she has a sort of claim upon her employer for any little assistance he can conveniently render her; indeed, I have already, through my future mother-in-law, heard of a place that I think will suit: it is to undertake the education of the five daughters of Mrs Dionysius O'Gall of Bitternutt Lodge, Connaught, Ireland. You'll like Ireland, I think: they're such warm-hearted people there, they say.'

'It is a long way off, sir.'

'No matter – a girl of your sense will not object to the voyage or the distance.'

'Not the voyage but the distance: and then the sea is a barrier –'

'From what, Jane?'

'From England and from Thornfield: and—'

'Well?'

'From *you*, sir.'

I said this almost involuntarily, and with as little sanction of free will, my tears gushed out. I did not cry so as to be heard, however; I avoided sobbing. The thought of Mrs O'Gall and Bitternutt Lodge struck cold to my heart; and colder the thought of all the brine and foam, destined, as it seemed, to rush between me and the master at whose side I now walked, and coldest the remembrance of the wider ocean – wealth, caste, custom – intervened between me and what I naturally and inevitably loved.

'It is a long way,' I again said.

'It is, to be sure; and when you get to Bitternutt Lodge, Connaught, Ireland, I shall never see you again, Jane: that's morally certain. I never go over to Ireland, not having myself much of a fancy for the country. We have been good friends, Jane; have we not?'

'Yes, sir.'

'And when friends are on the eve of separation, they like to spend the little time that remains to them close to each other. Come! we'll talk over the voyage and the parting quietly, half an hour or so, while the stars enter into their shining life up in heaven yonder: here is the chestnut tree: here is the bench at its old roots. Come, we will sit there in peace to-night, though we should never more be destined to sit there together.'

He seated me and himself.

'It is a long way to Ireland, Janet, and I am sorry to send my little friend on such weary travels: but if I can't do better, how is it to be helped? Are you anything akin to me, do you think, Jane?'

I could risk no sort of answer by this time: my heart was still.

'Because,' he said, 'I sometimes have a queer feeling with regard to you – especially when you are near me, as now: it is as if I had a string somewhere under my left ribs, tightly and inextricably knotted to a similar string situated in the corresponding quarter of your little frame. And if that bois- terous Channel, and two hundred miles or so of land, come broad between us, I am afraid that cord of communion will be snapped; and then I've a nervous notion I should take to bleeding inwardly. As for you – you'd forget me.'

'That I *never* should, sir: you know –' Impossible to proceed.

'Jane, do you hear that nightingale singing in the wood? Listen!'

In listening, I sobbed convulsively; for I could repress what I endured no longer; I was obliged to yield, and I was shaken from head to foot with acute distress. When I did speak, it was only to express an impetuous wish that I had never been born, or never come to Thornfield.

'Because you are sorry to leave it?'

The vehemence of emotion, stirred by grief and love within me, was claiming mastery, and struggling for full sway, and asserting a right to predominate, to overcome, to live, rise, and reign at last: yes – and to speak.

'I grieve to leave Thornfield: I love Thornfield: I love it, because I have lived in it a full and delightful life – momentarily at least. I have not been trampled on. I have not been petrified. I have not been buried with inferior minds, and excluded from every glimpse of communion with what is bright and energetic and high. I have talked, face to face, with what I reverence, with what I delight in – with an original, a vigorous, an expanded mind. I have known you, Mr Rochester; and it strikes me with terror and anguish to feel I absolutely must be torn from you for ever. I see the necessity of departure; and it is like looking on the necessity of death.'

'Where do you see the necessity?' he asked suddenly.

'Where? You, sir, have placed it before me.'

'In what shape?'

'In the shape of Miss Ingram; a noble and beautiful woman – your bride.'

'My bride! What bride? I have no bride!'

'But you will have.'

'Yes – I will! – I will!' He set his teeth.

'Then I must go – you have said it yourself.'

'No: you must stay! I swear it – and the oath shall be kept.'

'I tell you I must go!' I retorted, roused to something like passion. 'Do you think I can stay to become nothing to you? Do you think I am an automaton? – a machine without feelings? and can bear to have my morsel of bread snatched from my lips, and my drop of living water dashed from my cup? Do you think, because I am poor, obscure, plain, and little, I am soulless and heartless? You think wrong! – I have as much soul as you – and full as much heart! And if God had gifted me with some beauty and much wealth, I should have made it as hard for you to leave me, as it is now for me to leave you. I am not talking to you now through the medium of custom, conventionalities, nor even of mortal flesh: it is my spirit that addresses your spirit; just as if both had passed through the grave, and we stood at God's feet, equal – as we are!'

'As we are!' repeated Mr Rochester – 'so,' he added, enclosing me in his arms, gathering me to his breast, pressing his lips on my lips: 'so, Jane!'

'Yes, so, sir,' I rejoined: 'and yet not so; for you are a married man – or as good as a married man, and wed to one inferior to you – to one with whom you have no sympathy – whom I do not believe you truly love; for I have seen and heard you sneer at her. I would scorn such a union: therefore I am better than you – let me go!'

'Where, Jane? To Ireland?'

'Yes – to Ireland. I have spoken my mind, and can go anywhere now.'

'Jane, be still; don't struggle so, like a wild frantic bird that is rending its own plumage in its desperation.'

'I am no bird; and no net ensnares me; I am a free human being with an independent will, which I now exert to leave you.'

Another effort set me at liberty, and I stood erect before him.

'And your will shall decide your destiny,' he said. 'I offer you my hand, my heart, and a share of all my possessions.'

'You play a farce, which I merely laugh at.'

'I ask you to pass through life at my side – to be my second self, and best earthly companion.'

'For that fate you have already made your choice, and must abide by it.'

'Jane, be still a few moments: you are over-excited: I will be still too.'

A waft of wind came sweeping down the laurel walk, and trembled through the boughs of the chestnut: it wandered away – away – to an indefinite distance – it died. The nightin-gale's song was then the only voice of the hour: in listening to it I again wept. Mr Rochester sat quiet, looking at me gently and seriously. Some time passed before he spoke; he at last said –

'Come to my side, Jane, and let us explain and understand one another.'

'I will never again come to your side: I am torn away now, and cannot return.'

'But, Jane, I summon you as my wife: it is you only I intend to marry.'

I was silent: I thought he mocked me.

'Come, Jane – come hither.'

'Your bride stands between us.'

He rose, and with a stride reached me.

'My bride is here,' he said, again drawing me to him, 'because my equal is here, and my likeness. Jane, will you marry me?'

Still I did not answer, and still I writhed myself from his grasp: for I was still incredulous.

'Do you doubt me, Jane?'

'Entirely.'

'You have no faith in me?'

'Not a whit.'

'Am I a liar in your eyes?' he asked passionately. 'Little sceptic, you *shall* be convinced. What love have I for Miss Ingram? None: and that you know. What love has she for me? None: as I have taken pains to prove: I caused a rumour to reach her that my fortune was not a third of what was supposed, and after that I presented myself to see the result; it was coldness both from her and her mother. I would not – I could not – marry Miss Ingram. You – you strange, you almost unearthly thing! – I love as my own flesh. You – poor and obscure, and small and plain as you are – I entreat to accept me as a husband.'

'What, me!' I ejaculated, beginning in his earnestness – and especially in his incivility – to credit his sincerity: 'me who have not a friend in the world but you – if you are my friend: not a shilling but what you have given me?'

'You, Jane, I must have you for my own – entirely my own. Will you be mine? Say yes, quickly.'

'Mr Rochester, let me look at your face: turn to the moonlight.'

'Why?'

'Because I want to read your countenance – turn!'

'There! you will find it scarcely more legible than a crumpled, scratched page. Read on: only make haste, for I suffer.'

His face was very much agitated and very much flushed, and there were strong workings in the features, and strange gleams in the eyes

'Oh, Jane, you torture me!' he exclaimed. 'With that searching and yet faithful and generous look, you torture me!'

'How can I do that? If you are true, and your offer real, my only feelings to you must be gratitude and devotion – they cannot torture.'

'Gratitude!' he ejaculated; and added wildly – 'Jane, accept me quickly. Say, Edward – give me my name – Edward – I will marry you.'

'Are you in earnest? Do you truly love me? Do you sincerely wish me to be your wife?'

'I do; and if an oath is necessary to satisfy you, I swear it.'

'Then, sir, I will marry you.'

'Edward – my little wife!'

'Dear Edward!'

'Come to me – come to me entirely now,' said he; and added, in his deepest tone, speaking in my ear as his cheek was laid on mine, 'Make my happiness – I will make yours.'

'God pardon me!' he subjoined ere long; 'and man meddle not with me: I have her, and will hold her.'

'There is no one to meddle, sir. I have no kindred to interfere.'

'No – that is the best of it,' he said. And if I had loved him less I should have thought his accent and look of exultation savage; but, sitting by him, roused from the nightmare of parting – called to the paradise of union – I thought only of the bliss given me to drink in so abundant a flow. Again and again he said, 'Are you happy, Jane?' And again and again I answered, 'Yes.' After which he murmured, 'It will atone – it will atone. Have I not found her friendless, and cold, and comfortless? Will I not guard, and cherish, and solace her? Is there not love in my heart, and constancy in my resolves? It will expiate at God's tribunal. I know my Maker sanctions what I do. For the world's judgement – I wash my hands thereof. For man's opinion – I defy it.'

But what had befallen the night? The moon was not yet set, and we were all in shadow: I could scarcely see my master's face, near as I was. And what ailed the chestnut tree? it writhed and groaned; while wind roared in the laurel walk, and came sweeping over us.

'We must go in,' said Mr Rochester: 'the weather changes. I could have sat with thee till morning, Jane.'

'And so,' thought I, 'could I with you.' I should have said so, perhaps, but a livid, vivid spark leapt out of a cloud at which I was looking, and there was a crack, a crash, and a close rattling peal; and I thought only of hiding my dazzled eyes against Mr Rochester's shoulder.

The rain rushed down. He hurried me up the walk, through the grounds, and into the house; but we were quite wet before we could pass the threshold. He was taking off my shawl in the hall, and shaking the water out of my loosened hair, when Mrs Fairfax emerged from her room. I did not observe her at first, nor did Mr Rochester. The lamp was lit. The clock was on the stroke of twelve.

'Hasten to take off your wet things,' said he; 'and before you go, good-night – good-night, my darling!'

He kissed me repeatedly. When I looked up, on leaving his arms, there stood the widow, pale, grave, and amazed. I only smiled at her, and ran upstairs. 'Explanation will do for another time,' thought I. Still, when I reached my chamber, I felt a pang at the idea she should even temporarily misconstrue what she had seen. But joy soon effaced every other feeling; and loud as the wind blew, near and deep as the thunder crashed, fierce and frequent as the lightning gleamed, cataract-like as the rain fell during a storm of two hours' duration, I experienced no fear and little awe. Mr Rochester came thrice to my door in the course of it, to ask if I was safe and tranquil: and that was comfort, that was strength for anything.

Before I left my bed in the morning, little Adèle came running in to tell me that the great horse-chestnut at the bottom of the orchard had been struck by lightning in the night, and half of it split away.

SICK LOVE
Robert Graves

O Love, be fed with apples while you may,
And feel the sun and go in royal array,
A smiling innocent on the heavenly causeway,

Though in what listening horror for the cry
That soars in outer blackness dismally,
The dumb blind beast, the paranoiac fury:

Be warm, enjoy the season, lift your head,
Exquisite in the pulse of tainted blood,
That shivering glory not to be despised.

Take your delight in momentariness,
Walk between dark and dark – a shining space
With the grave's narrowness, though not its peace.

READING NOTES

It is hard to talk of *Jane Eyre* without spoilers. Although
many know the story from the book or the several films and
TV versions, some do not. In most groups, people want to
talk about Rochester with the knowledge that at this point
in the story he is not free to marry Jane. Opinion is often
divided between those who sympathise with him to a certain
extent and those who believe his behaviour is selfish and
immoral. The argument for the former is often weighted
by the teasing way he leads Jane on to believe that he is to
marry Blanche and she to be sent away from Thornfield. The
latter camp will say that he has done everything right by his
wife but the law is against him. People usually want to talk
about Jane's declaration, 'I grieve to leave Thornfield . . .'
and a little later her wonderful assertion of individual
spirit, 'I have as much soul as you . . .' The ominous ending
of the scene often leads people into the poem. 'I haven't a
clue what this really means,' said a woman in a community
group, 'but to me, the poem seems to be saying love is
fleeting, grab it while you can – but there is something dark
and threatening going on.' 'Yes,' said another, 'this love is
like Rochester's, real but threatened and tainted from the
start.' Everyone talked of how the poem was beautiful and
terrible at once – especially the last verse.

The Wedding-Days

♥

THE ROAD TO NAB END

(EXTRACT FROM CHAPTER 17, LIVINGSTON ROAD)

William Woodruff

(approximate reading time 15 minutes)

William Woodruff was born in 1916 in the carding room of a cotton mill where his mother was a factory worker. The Road to Nab End is his evocative account of growing up in Blackburn, Lancashire during the depression. Jenny and Brenda are his sisters.

Soon after we moved to Livingston Road, Jenny married Gordon Weall. That was when I got my first pair of long pants. Father took me to a shop called Weaver to Wearer where I was measured for a suit of dark brown worsted wool. Weaver to Wearer was the cheapest tailor in town. Their cloth was thought to be better than that sold by the workers' Cooperative Store. Also, Weaver to Wearer gave me two fittings, at the Co-op I'd have only got one.

When I took the suit home in a big cardboard box, I felt like a millionaire. At last, I had stopped being a boy and had become a man. I explored all the pockets and found the sixpence, which the tailor always hid in a boy's first suit. That night I put the suit on and paraded before the family. There were many 'ooohs' and 'aaaahs.' It was the first time in my life that I had ever worn anything over my knees. It made them itch.

The wedding itself was the most elaborate affair in the family's history. Mother was not prepared to settle for second best, not in Livingston Road. It was one of the high points of her life. That's how she thought life should be.

At great expense, we went the whole way. Everybody had new clothes. Mother was in her seventh heaven deciding what everyone should wear. Jenny wore white. Her dress had a low neck with a tight waist and sleeves all puffed up. She had a veil and carried lilies of the valley. Beautiful she looked. She also had two little girls as train bearers. Gordon wore a hired frock coat, pin striped trousers and a special grey waistcoat with a watch chain. He looked like the Lord Mayor. Nobody would have guessed he was a painter's apprentice. Like the rest of us, he got a new suit and new shoes for the wedding but kept them for going away on his honeymoon.

As it was a June wedding and the weather was kind, family and friends stood outside the church for a moment to say hello and wave greetings before going in. It's amazing what clothes will do to people when they are wearing their best. Everybody held themselves stiffly and spoke in funny voices. I never saw such a change; they weren't the same folk at all.

When we went in, the organ was playing quietly. We had organ, choir and soloist. There were six little flower girls. Gordon and a fellow-painter were waiting near the altar rail – white gardenias in their buttonholes. There were a lot of people there whom I'd never seen before. All the Wealls were present, Mrs Weall constantly wiping her eyes. Mr Weall, a little red-nosed man, who looked as if he had just stepped out of a hot bath, steadily supplied his wife with clean handkerchiefs. Mother put our neighbours, the Peeks, including Millicent, well up front. 'Savages, we are!' I could hardly recognize mother and Brenda in their flowing pink dresses and enormous wide-brimmed hats.

Then father arrived with Jenny and the train-bearers in a shining limousine. What agony father must have suffered having to pay for that car with its chauffeur and its white ribbons and orange blossom! Jenny looked an angel; she glided down the aisle with her tiny toes peeping out of her white slippers. She had the easy motions of a good dancer. Mother had seen to it that Jenny wore 'Something old, something new, something borrowed, something blue.' Father walked at her side as if he had just fallen off a wall. It was one of the few times I ever saw him wearing a tie. If the organ hadn't been thundering, 'Here comes the bride,' we could have heard his new suit creaking.

Then Jenny joined Gordon. We all stood and sang: 'Rejoice and be glad.' Then we sat down while a young woman sang, 'Love divine, all love excelling.' Then the preacher came forward and talked about matrimony, and what a serious business it was. He went on and on about loving and being faithful to each other, and bringing up children. 'The fear of the Lord,' he stressed, 'is the beginning of all wisdom.'

Then they got on with the marriage, with Bertha Weall crying so hard that she could be heard throughout the church.

Then the preacher asked Gordon if he would marry Jenny, and Jenny if she would marry Gordon – which is what I thought we'd come for. You could hardly hear Jenny's reply, but Gordon's 'I do' was strong. Then the preacher gave them his blessing. 'What God had joined together, let no man put asunder.'

While Jenny and Gordon were in the vestry, the choir sang, 'Blessed be the tie that binds.' Then everybody together, including the married couple and the choir, sang, 'God the creator, God the good.'

After pictures had been taken outside the church, Jenny and Gordon and the parents of both sides went off in the limousine. The rest of us – relatives, friends, and those who hung on in the hope of a free meal – walked down town to Harper's where the reception was to be held. It wasn't that far, the weather was good, and we made fun all the way.

Jenny told me later that both mothers cried in the limousine. Mrs Weall blubbered most. She kept saying, 'I've lost my only son, Maggie, I've lost my only child.'

In response to which mother sobbingly replied, 'Aye, but tha's got a good daughter, Bertha.'

'Hisht, women,' father had scolded.

At Harper's we first had family pictures taken and then sat down to a proper ham and tongue wedding breakfast. Trifle followed, and there was lots to drink. Gordon made a speech in which he couldn't help being a clown.

While everyone was stuffing themselves and having a good time, Jenny and Gordon changed to go away. Then we all got up in our best clothes and trooped off behind the married couple, who went hand in hand, across town to the railway station. Gordon had already dropped off a suitcase there. We were a happy, laughing throng of about twenty or thirty people. Several excited children brought up the tail end.

'God bless you,' passers-by called to the bride and groom.

'All the best.'

'Never grow old.'

'Here's to your health and wealth.'

On reaching the platform we rained confetti and streamers upon the happy couple. The women hugged and kissed the bride. The men were more restrained. They patted the bride-groom on the shoulder as if he was going to war. Father stood stiffly to one side, preoccupied with his thoughts. I'm sure he was still worrying about the cost of the ribbon-bedecked limousine that awaited him in the street.

It must have taken father a long time to pay for that wedding. He must have spent the family's savings on it, and gone into debt. It will always remain a mystery to me how a man who resented paying a penny on the tram, and who was not known for giving his children anything, could suddenly spend like a profligate. The money for all the clothes must have come out of his pocket, for none of us belonged to a clothing club in which garments were bought by payments made over time.

I can only think that marrying off a daughter was something special. Of course, mother was the driving force. She didn't let price interfere. Besides the Wealls were a cut about the Woodruffs and it was up to us not to let the side down. Pride demanded that we should impress them. Also, we lived in Livingston Road. A threadbare marriage from such an address would have been unthinkable.

In any event, money was never better spent. We had a wonderful time, we all got stuffed with food and drink; and everybody finished up with new clothes. Father's suit lasted him the rest of his life. We'd never spent like that before, and we never did again. 'Everybody's entitled to go mad once,' mother said. Mother saw to it that the wedding got into the paper. She kept asking father to read it to her over and over again. I think she often relived Jenny's wedding in her dreams.

Several months after Jenny's wedding, Brenda became engaged to Harry Entwistle. They were both members of the Salvation Army. The Army thought the world of them. Harry was a Derbyshire man. Twice the size of Brenda, he had a ruddy, well-weathered face, a mass of blond hair combed back, hands like shovels, and a body like an ox. He was one of the boil-ermen at Dougdale's mill. He'd been in Blackburn about a year. Not much was known about him. He didn't seem to have any family. When I first met him, he had two passions: Brenda and the Salvation Army. Brenda at this time was about twenty.

With all the tenderness of possession, Brenda brought him home one night to show him off to the family. Harry's big, bright eyes and his infectious, happy laugh exuded warmth. We took to him at once. He was so open, friendly and genuine that we were drawn to him instinctively. In an ox-like way he was also good-looking; handsome would be the right word. There were not many young men in town with as rich a blond beard as Harry's; his eyebrows were equally splendid.

Mother thought them a good match. Harry was four years older than Brenda. He had a job, and he obviously loved her.

Brenda couldn't have enough of him. Without a dissenting word, the family came down on Harry's side.

Henceforth, Harry became a member of the Woodruff household. He was always coming up to Livingston Road; always eating with us, always engaging us in jolly laughter. Brenda and he often went off to Salvation Army meetings, their faces glowing.

One night they came back and announced to the family that they were going to get married. Harry didn't formally ask father for Brenda's hand, but then members of the working class rarely did. The couple just said they'd made up their mind.

Everybody was delighted. The date was set. According to Salvation Army tradition, they were to be married under the flag, which meant that the Army took responsibility for the service and the reception. The wedding breakfast had all been arranged; two bands had agreed to play. Brenda and Harry were to lead a short demonstration march, to be followed by prayers and massed singing. Nothing was going to be left out for the couple who had won everybody's heart.

None of us will ever forget the wedding day. There was such hustle and bustle in the house on Livingston Road. Other than Brenda, who wore her Salvation Army uniform, we all put on the new clothes we'd obtained for Jenny's wedding and hurried down to the Salvation Army headquarters where the marriage was to take place. We took umbrellas because the weather looked bad. Father and Brenda were to follow in a taxi. The Army captain received us and made us all real welcome. Scrubbed, glowing faces, black hats and red bands were every-where. Resting against the wall in the hall were the flags to be used in the march. Harry stood waiting with a Soldier of Christ as best man.

While one of the bands was playing, Brenda and father arrived. They were just walking up to Harry when a young woman hurried toward them from one of the side doors and blocked their path. Her face was grey and drawn. Brenda stopped. She looked flummoxed. Everybody stared at the intruder.

'What can I do for you?' Brenda asked the stranger who seemed distraught.

'It's more what I can do for you,' the intruder gasped.

'Who are you?' said Brenda, her face darkening.

'Mrs Harry Entwistle,' the woman sobbed. 'Thank God I got here in time.'

Brenda's face became distorted; her lips quivered and throbbed. She looked at the woman with stony eyes.

Mother pushed past me and threw her arms around Brenda. 'Come home child,' she pleaded. Everybody in the hall was so still, they might have been struck by lightning.

Brenda turned on Harry. 'Harry Entwistle,' she asked, 'is this your wife?'

Harry shifted his feet uneasily; he was trembling; his face was flushed; he was staring at the floor. After a moment or two he looked up. 'Yis,' he stammered.

Snatching the umbrella from father's hand, Brenda struck Harry across the face. A red weal appeared. 'You scum!' she screamed, as she delivered blow after blow. Harry didn't move. Didn't flinch. Nor did anybody else. The crowd just stared. 'You rotten devil!' Brenda went on hitting him until the umbrella broke. So did her spirit. With a sob she collapsed onto a chair. With all the women weeping, the family somehow managed to get her home.

For days, Brenda didn't speak to anyone. When she did come downstairs her face was a frightful sight. She looked twenty years older. A vague sadness had replaced her distress.

She never wore the Salvation Army uniform again.

In time the wounds healed. She married a good man called Richard Paden. He was a clerk at a store in town with little money and fewer prospects. In contrast to Jenny's wedding – it was an in-and-out-of-church affair with no trimmings. Nobody said it, but I think everybody felt that the ghost of Harry Entwistle was there, mocking us with hearty laughter.

THE WHITSUN WEDDINGS
Philip Larkin

That Whitsun, I was late getting away:
    Not till about
One-twenty on the sunlit Saturday
Did my three-quarters-empty train pull out,
All windows down, all cushions hot, all sense
Of being in a hurry gone. We ran
Behind the backs of houses, crossed a street
Of blinding windscreens, smelt the fish-dock; thence
The river's level drifting breadth began,
Where sky and Lincolnshire and water meet.

All afternoon, through the tall heat that slept
    For miles inland,
A slow and stopping curve southwards we kept.
Wide farms went by, short-shadowed cattle, and
Canals with floatings of industrial froth;
A hothouse flashed uniquely: hedges dipped
And rose: and now and then a smell of grass
Displaced the reek of buttoned carriage-cloth
Until the next town, new and nondescript,
Approached with acres of dismantled cars.

At first, I didn't notice what a noise
    The weddings made
Each station that we stopped at: sun destroys
The interest of what's happening in the shade,

And down the long cool platforms whoops and skirls
I took for porters larking with the mails,
And went on reading. Once we started, though,
We passed them, grinning and pomaded, girls
In parodies of fashion, heels and veils,
All posed irresolutely, watching us go,

As if out on the end of an event
    Waving goodbye
To something that survived it. Struck, I leant
More promptly out next time, more curiously,
And saw it all again in different terms:
The fathers with broad belts under their suits
And seamy foreheads; mothers loud and fat;
An uncle shouting smut; and then the perms,
The nylon gloves and jewellery-substitutes,
The lemons, mauves, and olive-ochres that

Marked off the girls unreally from the rest.
    Yes, from cafés
And banquet-halls up yards, and bunting-dressed
Coach-party annexes, the wedding-days
Were coming to an end. All down the line
Fresh couples climbed aboard: the rest stood round;
The last confetti and advice were thrown,
And, as we moved, each face seemed to define
Just what it saw departing: children frowned
At something dull; fathers had never known

Success so huge and wholly farcical;
    The women shared
The secret like a happy funeral;
While girls, gripping their handbags tighter, stared
At a religious wounding. Free at last,
And loaded with the sum of all they saw,
We hurried towards London, shuffling gouts of steam.
Now fields were building-plots, and poplars cast
Long shadows over major roads, and for
Some fifty minutes, that in time would seem

Just long enough to settle hats and say
    I nearly died,
A dozen marriages got under way.
They watched the landscape, sitting side by side
—An Odeon went past, a cooling tower,
And someone running up to bowl—and none
Thought of the others they would never meet
Or how their lives would all contain this hour.
I thought of London spread out in the sun,
Its postal districts packed like squares of wheat:

There we were aimed. And as we raced across
    Bright knots of rail
Past standing Pullmans, walls of blackened moss
Came close, and it was nearly done, this frail
Travelling coincidence; and what it held
Stood ready to be loosed with all the power

That being changed can give. We slowed again,
And as the tightened brakes took hold, there swelled
A sense of falling, like an arrow-shower
Sent out of sight, somewhere becoming rain.

READING NOTES

'Reading that poem left me feeling tearful,' said a woman in a library group. 'I am not sure why because weddings are happy occasions, aren't they?' The group tried to find what, in the poem, had made her feel that way. Someone else thought the closing lines felt rather like a blessing. One man was interested in the picture of a vanished England: the steam trains, Pullmans, Whitsun outings and weddings. Another likened the line 'The women shared/ The secret like a happy funeral' to the scene in the story in which the sobbing mother cries, 'I've lost my only son.' People talked of their own weddings and how the rather rushed affairs of the 1950s were so different from the lavish, spread-out events of today.

Most people had only good things to say about the Salvation Army, but the moment when the real wife turned up came as a shock, especially since Brenda's family had all liked Harry so much. They talked about the man in the train watching all the weddings getting under way; how couples make promises, for better or worse, never really imagining there would be any worse. 'Perhaps that is what made me sad,' said the first woman.

I Know Not if
I Sink or Swim

OUR MUTUAL FRIEND

(EXTRACT FROM BOOK 4, CHAPTER 6)

Charles Dickens

(approximate reading time 30 minutes)

Eugene Wrayburn, an idle, disaffected barrister who is bored with life, has become attracted to Lizzie Hexam. She knows he has no intention of marriage since she is poor and the daughter of a common waterman who makes a living robbing the dead bodies he finds in the River Thames. Lizzie is herself an experienced oars-woman and an honourable, intelligent young woman. She has left London to get away from Wrayburn, but he has come after her and is waiting on a riverbank. Mortimer is a friend of Wrayburn.

Turning again at the water-lilies, he saw her coming, and advanced to meet her.

'I was saying to myself, Lizzie, that you were sure to come, though you were late.'

'I had to linger through the village as if I had no object before me, and I had to speak to several people in passing along, Mr Wrayburn.'

'Are the lads of the village – and the ladies – such scandal-mongers?' he asked, as he took her hand and drew it through his arm.

She submitted to walk slowly on, with downcast eyes. He put her hand to his lips, and she quietly drew it away.

'Will you walk beside me, Mr Wrayburn, and not touch me?' For, his arm was already stealing round her waist.

She stopped again, and gave him an earnest supplicating look. 'Well, Lizzie, well!' said he, in an easy way though ill at ease with himself, 'don't be unhappy, don't be reproachful.'

'I cannot help being unhappy, but I do not mean to be reproachful. Mr Wrayburn, I implore you to go away from this neighbourhood, to-morrow morning.'

'Lizzie, Lizzie, Lizzie!' he remonstrated. 'As well be reproachful as wholly unreasonable. I can't go away.'

'Why not?'

'Faith!' said Eugene in his airily candid manner. 'Because you won't let me. Mind! I don't mean to be reproachful either. I don't complain that you design to keep me here. But you do it, you do it.'

'Will you walk beside me, and not touch me;' for, his arm was coming about her again; 'while I speak to you very seriously, Mr Wrayburn?'

'I will do anything within the limits of possibility, for you, Lizzie,' he answered with pleasant gaiety as he folded his arms. 'See here! Napoleon Buonaparte at St Helena.'

'When you spoke to me as I came from the Mill the night before last,' said Lizzie, fixing her eyes upon him with the look of supplication which troubled his better nature, 'you told me that you were much surprised to see me, and that you were on a solitary fishing excursion. Was it true?'

'It was not,' replied Eugene composedly, 'in the least true. I came here, because I had information that I should find you here.'

'Can you imagine why I left London, Mr Wrayburn?'

'I am afraid, Lizzie,' he openly answered, 'that you left London to get rid of me. It is not flattering to my self-love, but I am afraid you did.'

'I did.'

'How could you be so cruel?'

'O Mr Wrayburn,' she answered, suddenly breaking into tears, 'is the cruelty on my side! O Mr Wrayburn, Mr Wrayburn, is there no cruelty in your being here to-night!'

'In the name of all that's good – and that is not conjuring you in my own name, for Heaven knows I am not good' – said Eugene, 'don't be distressed!'

'What else can I be, when I know the distance and the difference between us? What else can I be, when to tell me why you came here, is to put me to shame!' said Lizzie, covering her face.

He looked at her with a real sentiment of remorseful tenderness and pity. It was not strong enough to impell him to sacrifice himself and spare her, but it was a strong emotion.

'Lizzie! I never thought before, that there was a woman in the world who could affect me so much by saying so little. But don't be hard in your construction of me. You don't know what my state of mind towards you is. You don't know how you haunt me and bewilder me. You don't know how the cursed carelessness that is over-officious in helping me at every other turning of my life, WON'T help me here. You have struck it dead, I think, and I sometimes almost wish you had struck me dead along with it.'

She had not been prepared for such passionate expressions, and they awakened some natural sparks of feminine pride and joy in her breast. To consider, wrong as he was, that he could care so much for her, and that she had the power to move him so!

'It grieves you to see me distressed, Mr Wrayburn; it grieves me to see you distressed. I don't reproach you. Indeed I don't reproach you. You have not felt this as I feel it, being so different from me, and beginning from another point of view. You have not thought. But I entreat you to think now, think now!'

'What am I to think of?' asked Eugene, bitterly.

'Think of me.'

'Tell me how *not* to think of you, Lizzie, and you'll change me altogether.'

'I don't mean in that way. Think of me, as belonging to another station, and quite cut off from you in honour. Remember that I have no protector near me, unless I have one in your noble heart. Respect my good name. If you feel towards me, in one particular, as you might if I was a lady, give me the full claims of a lady upon your generous behaviour. I am removed from you and your family by being a working girl. How true a gentleman to be as considerate of me as if I was removed by being a Queen!'

He would have been base indeed to have stood untouched by her appeal. His face expressed contrition and indecision as he asked:

'Have I injured you so much, Lizzie?'

'No, no. You may set me quite right. I don't speak of the past, Mr Wrayburn, but of the present and the future. Are we not here now, because through two days you have followed me so closely where there are so many eyes to see you, that I consented to this appointment as an escape?'

'Again, not very flattering to my self-love,' said Eugene, moodily; 'but yes. Yes. Yes.'

'Then I beseech you, Mr Wrayburn, I beg and pray you, leave this neighbourhood. If you do not, consider to what you will drive me.'

He did consider within himself for a moment or two, and then retorted, 'Drive you? To what shall I drive you, Lizzie?'

'You will drive me away. I live here peacefully and respected, and I am well employed here. You will force me to quit this place as I quitted London, and – by following me again – will force me to quit the next place in which I may find refuge, as I quitted this.'

'Are you so determined, Lizzie – forgive the word I am going to use, for its literal truth – to fly from a lover?'

'I am so determined,' she answered resolutely, though trembling, 'to fly from such a lover. There was a poor woman died here but a little while ago, scores of years older than I am, whom I found by chance, lying on the wet earth. You may have heard some account of her?'

'I think I have,' he answered, 'if her name was Higden.'

'Her name was Higden. Though she was so weak and old, she kept true to one purpose to the very last. Even at the very last, she made me promise that her purpose should be kept to, after she was dead, so settled was her determination. What she did, I can do. Mr Wrayburn, if I believed – but I do not believe – that you could be so cruel to me as to drive me from place to place to wear me out, you should drive me to death and not do it.'

He looked full at her handsome face, and in his own handsome face there was a light of blended admiration, anger, and reproach, which she – who loved him so in secret – whose heart had long been so full, and he the cause of its overflowing – drooped before. She tried hard to retain her firmness, but he saw it melting away under his eyes. In the moment of its dissolution, and of his first full knowledge of his influence upon her, she dropped, and he caught her on his arm.

'Lizzie! Rest so a moment. Answer what I ask you. If I had not been what you call removed from you and cut off from you, would you have made this appeal to me to leave you?'

'I don't know, I don't know. Don't ask me, Mr Wrayburn. Let me go back.'

'I swear to you, Lizzie, you shall go directly. I swear to you, you shall go alone. I'll not accompany you, I'll not follow you, if you will reply.'

'How can I, Mr Wrayburn? How can I tell you what I should have done, if you had not been what you are?'

'If I had not been what you make me out to be,' he struck in, skilfully changing the form of words, 'would you still have hated me?'

'O Mr Wrayburn,' she replied appealingly, and weeping, 'you know me better than to think I do!'

'If I had not been what you make me out to be, Lizzie, would you still have been indifferent to me?'

'O Mr Wrayburn,' she answered as before, 'you know me better than that too!'

There was something in the attitude of her whole figure as he supported it, and she hung her head, which besought him to be merciful and not force her to disclose her heart. He was not merciful with her, and he made her do it.

'If I know you better than quite to believe (unfortunate dog though I am!) that you hate me, or even that you are wholly indifferent to me, Lizzie, let me know so much more from yourself before we separate. Let me know how you would have dealt with me if you had regarded me as being what you would have considered on equal terms with you.'

'It is impossible, Mr Wrayburn. How can I think of you as being on equal terms with me? If my mind could put you on equal terms with me, you could not be yourself. How could I remember, then, the night when I first saw you, and when I went out of the room because you looked at me so attentively? Or, the night that passed into the morning when you broke to me that my father was dead? Or, the nights when you used to come to see me at my next home? Or, your having known how uninstructed I was, and having caused me to be taught better? Or, my having so looked up to you and wondered at you, and at first thought you so good to be at all mindful of me?'

'Only "at first" thought me so good, Lizzie? What did you think me after "at first"? So bad?'

'I don't say that. I don't mean that. But after the first wonder and pleasure of being noticed by one so different from any one who had ever spoken to me, I began to feel that it might have been better if I had never seen you.'

'Why?'

'Because you *were* so different,' she answered in a lower voice. 'Because it was so endless, so hopeless. Spare me!'

'Did you think for me at all, Lizzie?' he asked, as if he were a little stung.

'Not much, Mr Wrayburn. Not much until to-night.'

'Will you tell me why?'

'I never supposed until to-night that you needed to be thought for. But if you do need to be; if you do truly feel at heart that you have indeed been towards me what you have called yourself to-night, and that there is nothing for us in this life but separation; then Heaven help you, and Heaven bless you!'

The purity with which in these words she expressed something of her own love and her own suffering, made a deep impression on him for the passing time. He held her, almost as if she were sanctified to him by death, and kissed her, once, almost as he might have kissed the dead.

'I promised that I would not accompany you, nor follow you. Shall I keep you in view? You have been agitated, and it's growing dark.'

'I am used to be out alone at this hour, and I entreat you not to do so.'

'I promise. I can bring myself to promise nothing more to-night, Lizzie, except that I will try what I can do.'

'There is but one means, Mr Wrayburn, of sparing your-
self and of sparing me, every way. Leave this neighbourhood
to-morrow morning.'

'I will try.'

As he spoke the words in a grave voice, she put her hand in
his, removed it, and went away by the river-side.

'Now, could Mortimer believe this?' murmured Eugene,
still remaining, after a while, where she had left him. 'Can I
even believe it myself?'

He referred to the circumstance that there were tears upon
his hand, as he stood covering his eyes. 'A most ridiculous
position this, to be found out in!' was his next thought. And
his next struck its root in a little rising resentment against the
cause of the tears.

'Yet I have gained a wonderful power over her, too, let her
be as much in earnest as she will!'

The reflection brought back the yielding of her face and
form as she had drooped under his gaze. Contemplating the
reproduction, he seemed to see, for the second time, in the
appeal and in the confession of weakness, a little fear.

'And she loves me. And so earnest a character must be very
earnest in that passion. She cannot choose for herself to be
strong in this fancy, wavering in that, and weak in the other.
She must go through with her nature, as I must go through
with mine. If mine exacts its pains and penalties all round, so
must hers, I suppose.'

'And yet,' said Eugene, 'I should like to see the fellow who
would undertake to tell me that this was not a real sentiment
on my part, won out of me by her beauty and her worth, in

spite of myself, and that I would not be true to her. I should particularly like to see the fellow to-night who would tell me so, or who would tell me anything that could he construed to her disadvantage; for I am wearily out of sorts with one Wrayburn who cuts a sorry figure, and I would far rather be out of sorts with somebody else. "Eugene, Eugene, Eugene, this is a bad business.""

Strolling on, he thought of something else to take himself to task for. 'Where is the analogy, Brute Beast,' he said impatiently, 'between a woman whom your father coolly finds out for you and a woman whom you have found out for yourself, and have ever drifted after with more and more of constancy since you first set eyes upon her? Ass! Can you reason no better than that?'

But, again he subsided into a reminiscence of his first full knowledge of his power just now, and of her disclosure of her heart. To try no more to go away, and to try her again, was the reckless conclusion it turned uppermost. And yet again, 'Eugene, Eugene, Eugene, this is a bad business!'

Looking above, he found that the young moon was up, and that the stars were beginning to shine in the sky from which the tones of red and yellow were flickering out, in favour of the calm blue of a summer night. He was still by the river-side. Turning suddenly, he met a man, so close upon him that Eugene, surprised, stepped back, to avoid a collision. The man carried something over his shoulder which might have been a broken oar, or spar, or bar, and took no notice of him, but passed on.

'Halloa, friend!' said Eugene, calling after him, 'are you blind?'

The man made no reply, but went his way.

Eugene Wrayburn went the opposite way, with his hands behind him and his purpose in his thoughts. He passed the sheep, and passed the gate, and came within hearing of the village sounds, and came to the bridge. The inn where he stayed, like the village and the mill, was not across the river, but on that side of the stream on which he walked. However, knowing the rushy bank and the backwater on the other side to be a retired place, and feeling out of humour for noise or company, he crossed the bridge, and sauntered on: looking up at the stars as they seemed one by one to be kindled in the sky, and looking down at the river as the same stars seemed to be kindled deep in the water. A landing-place overshadowed by a willow, and a pleasure-boat lying moored there among some stakes, caught his eye as he passed along. The spot was in such dark shadow, that he paused to make out what was there, and then passed on again.

The rippling of the river seemed to cause a correspondent stir in his uneasy reflections. He would have laid them asleep if he could, but they were in movement, like the stream, and all tending one way with a strong current. As the ripple under the moon broke unexpectedly now and then, and palely flashed in a new shape and with a new sound, so parts of his thoughts started, unbidden, from the rest, and revealed their wickedness. 'Out of the question to marry her,' said Eugene, 'and out of the question to leave her. The crisis!'

He had sauntered far enough. Before turning to retrace his steps, he stopped upon the margin, to look down at the reflected night. In an instant, with a dreadful crash, the reflected night turned crooked, flames shot jaggedly across the air, and the moon and stars came bursting from the sky.

Was he struck by lightning? With some incoherent half-formed thought to that effect, he turned under the blows that were blinding him and mashing his life, and closed with a murderer, whom he caught by a red neckerchief — unless the raining down of his own blood gave it that hue.

Eugene was light, active, and expert; but his arms were broken, or he was paralysed, and could do no more than hang on to the man, with his head swung back, so that he could see nothing but the heaving sky. After dragging at the assailant, he fell on the bank with him, and then there was another great crash, and then a splash, and all was done.

Lizzie Hexam, too, had avoided the noise, and the Saturday movement of people in the straggling street, and chose to walk alone by the water until her tears should be dry, and she could so compose herself as to escape remark upon her looking ill or unhappy on going home. The peaceful serenity of the hour and place, having no reproaches or evil intentions within her breast to contend against, sank healingly into its depths. She had meditated and taken comfort. She, too, was turning homeward, when she heard a strange sound.

It startled her, for it was like a sound of blows. She stood still, and listened. It sickened her, for blows fell heavily and cruelly on the quiet of the night. As she listened, undecided, all was silent. As she yet listened, she heard a faint groan, and a fall into the river.

Her old bold life and habit instantly inspired her. Without vain waste of breath in crying for help where there were none to hear, she ran towards the spot from which the sounds had come. It lay between her and the bridge, but it was more removed from her than she had thought; the night being so very quiet, and sound travelling far with the help of water.

At length, she reached a part of the green bank, much and newly trodden, where there lay some broken splintered pieces of wood and some torn fragments of clothes. Stooping, she saw that the grass was bloody. Following the drops and smears, she saw that the watery margin of the bank was bloody. Following the current with her eyes, she saw a bloody face turned up towards the moon, and drifting away.

Now, merciful Heaven be thanked for that old time, and grant, O Blessed Lord, that through thy wonderful workings it may turn to good at last! To whomsoever the drifting face belongs, be it man's or woman's, help my humble hands, Lord God, to raise it from death and restore it to some one to whom it must be dear!

It was thought, fervently thought, but not for a moment did the prayer check her. She was away before it welled up in her mind, away, swift and true, yet steady above all – for without steadiness it could never be done – to the landing-place under the willow-tree, where she also had seen the boat lying moored among the stakes.

A sure touch of her old practised hand, a sure step of her old practised foot, a sure light balance of her body, and she was in the boat. A quick glance of her practised eye showed her, even through the deep dark shadow, the sculls in a rack against the red-brick garden-wall. Another moment, and she had cast off (taking the line with her), and the boat had shot out into the moonlight, and she was rowing down the stream as never other woman rowed on English water.

Intently over her shoulder, without slackening speed, she looked ahead for the driving face. She passed the scene of the struggle – yonder it was, on her left, well over the boat's stern – she passed on her right, the end of the village street, a hilly street that almost dipped into the river; its sounds were growing faint again, and she slackened; looking as the boat drove, everywhere, everywhere, for the floating face.

She merely kept the boat before the stream now, and rested on her oars, knowing well that if the face were not soon visible, it had gone down, and she would overshoot it. An untrained sight would never have seen by the moonlight what she saw at the length of a few strokes astern. She saw the drowning figure rise to the surface, slightly struggle, and as if by instinct turn over on its back to float. Just so had she first dimly seen the face which she now dimly saw again.

Firm of look and firm of purpose, she intently watched its coming on, until it was very near; then, with a touch unshipped her sculls, and crept aft in the boat, between kneeling and crouching. Once, she let the body evade her, not being sure of her grasp. Twice, and she had seized it by its bloody hair.

It was insensible, if not virtually dead; it was mutilated, and streaked the water all about it with dark red streaks. As it could not help itself, it was impossible for her to get it on board. She bent over the stern to secure it with the line, and then the river and its shores rang to the terrible cry she uttered.

But, as if possessed by supernatural spirit and strength, she lashed it safe, resumed her seat, and rowed in, desperately, for the nearest shallow water where she might run the boat aground. Desperately, but not wildly, for she knew that if she lost distinctness of intention, all was lost and gone.

She ran the boat ashore, went into the water, released him from the line, and by main strength lifted him in her arms and laid him in the bottom of the boat. He had fearful wounds upon him, and she bound them up with her dress torn into strips. Else, supposing him to be still alive, she foresaw that he must bleed to death before he could be landed at his inn, which was the nearest place for succour.

This done very rapidly, she kissed his disfigured forehead, looked up in anguish to the stars, and blessed him and forgave him, 'if she had anything to forgive.' It was only in that instant that she thought of herself, and then she thought of herself only for him.

Now, merciful Heaven be thanked for that old time, enabling me, without a wasted moment, to have got the boat afloat again, and to row back against the stream! And grant, O Blessed Lord God, that through poor me he may be raised from death, and preserved to some one else to whom he may be dear one day, though never dearer than to me!

She rowed hard – rowed desperately, but never wildly – and seldom removed her eyes from him in the bottom of the boat. She had so laid him there, as that she might see his disfigured face; it was so much disfigured that his mother might have covered it, but it was above and beyond disfigurement in her eyes.

The boat touched the edge of the patch of inn lawn, sloping gently to the water. There were lights in the windows, but there chanced to be no one out of doors. She made the boat fast, and again by main strength took him up, and never laid him down until she laid him down in the house.

Surgeons were sent for, and she sat supporting his head. She had oftentimes heard in days that were gone, how doctors would lift the hand of an insensible wounded person, and would drop it if the person were dead. She waited for the awful moment when the doctors might lift this hand, all broken and bruised, and let it fall.

The first of the surgeons came, and asked, before proceeding to his examination, 'Who brought him in?'

'I brought him in, sir,' answered Lizzie, at whom all present looked.

'You, my dear? You could not lift, far less carry, this weight.'

'I think I could not, at another time, sir; but I am sure I did.'

The surgeon looked at her with great attention, and with some compassion. Having with a grave face touched the wounds upon the head, and the broken arms, he took the hand.

O! would he let it drop?

He appeared irresolute. He did not retain it, but laid it gently down, took a candle, looked more closely at the injuries on the head, and at the pupils of the eyes. That done, he replaced the candle and took the hand again. Another surgeon then coming in, the two exchanged a whisper, and the second took the hand. Neither did he let it fall at once, but kept it for a while and laid it gently down.

'Attend to the poor girl,' said the first surgeon then. 'She is quite unconscious. She sees nothing and hears nothing. All the better for her! Don't rouse her, if you can help it; only move her. Poor girl, poor girl! She must be amazingly strong of heart, but it is much to be feared that she has set her heart upon the dead. Be gentle with her.'

THE WATER IS WIDE
Anon

The water is wide, I can't swim o'er
Nor do I have wings to fly
Give me a boat that can carry two
And both shall row, my love and I

A ship there is and she sails the sea
She's loaded deep as deep can be
But not so deep as the love I'm in
I know not if I sink or swim

I leaned my back against an oak
Thinking it was a trusty tree
But first it swayed and then it broke
So did my love prove false to me

Oh love is handsome and love is kind
Sweet as a flower when first it is new
But love grows old and waxes cold
And fades away like the morning dew

Must I go bound while you go free
Must I love a man who doesn't love me
Must I be born with so little art
As to love a man who'll break my heart

READING NOTES

In a library group, someone knew a tune to the poem and was even persuaded to sing. They talked about the repetition of the word 'must': how it meant that you have no choice when it comes to falling in love, and felt sympathy for the person who said she could relate to the third verse.

Eugene Wrayburn was not admired. 'He may be rich and posh but he's not a gentleman in the true sense.' People often note the moment when Eugene realises his power over Lizzie and could do the right thing but Dickens says abruptly 'He was not merciful with her, and he made her do it,' as if this decision contains a threat of the real violence that comes afterwards.

Eugene's shallowness; Lizzie's deep feeling and her honour; the way good is shown to come from bad, as Lizzie's knowledge of boatmanship learned from her father is put to good use; the way the landscape feels treacherous or untrustworthy, like Eugene himself; the tenderness of the doctors – were all points in the story that were thought about by the group.

Loneliness Like This

♥

LADY'S DREAM
Tobias Wolff

(approximate reading time 16 minutes)

Lady's suffocating. Robert can't stand to have the windows down because the air blowing into the car bothers his eyes. The fan is on but only at the lowest speed, as the sound annoys him. Lady's head is getting heavy, and when she blinks she has to raise her eyelids by an effort of will. The heat and dampness of her skin give her the sensation of a fever. She's beginning to see things in the lengthening moments when her eyes are closed, things more distinct and familiar than the dipping wires and blur of trees and the silent staring man she sees when they're open.

'Lady?' Robert's voice calls her back, but she keeps her eyes closed.

That's him to the life. Can't stand her sleeping when he's not. He'd have some good reason to wake her, though. Never a mean motive. Never. When he's going to ask somebody for a favor he always calls first and just passes the time, then calls back the next day and says how great it was talking to them, he enjoyed it so much he forgot to ask if they'd mind doing something for him. Has no idea he does this. She's never heard him tell a lie, not even to make a story better. Tells the most boring stories. Just lethal. Considers every word. Considers everything. Early January he buys twelve vacumn cleaner bags and writes a different month on each one so she'll remember to change them. Of course she goes as long as she can on every bag and throws away the extras at the end of the year, because otherwise he'd find them and know. Not say anything – just know. Once she threw away seven. Sneaked them outside through the snow and stuffed them in the garbage can.

Considerate. Everything a matter of principle. Justice for all, yellow brown black or white they are precious in his sight. Can't say no to any charity but always forgets to send the money. Asks her questions about his own self. *Who's that actress I like so much? What's my favorite fish?* Is calm in every circumstance. Polishes his glasses all the time. They gleam so you can hardly see his eyes. Has to sleep on the right side of the bed. The sheets have to be white. Any other color gives him nightmares, forget about patterns. Patterns would kill him. Wears a hardhat when he works around the house. Says her name a hundred times a day. Always has. Any excuse.

He loves her name. Lady. Married her name. Shut her up in her name. Shut her up.

'Lady?'

Sorry, sir. Lady's gone.

She knows where she is. She's back home. Her father's away but her mother's home and her sister Jo. Lady hears their voices. She's in the kitchen running water into a glass, letting it overflow and pour down her fingers until it's good and cold. She lifts the glass and drinks her fill and sets the glass down, then walks slow as a cat across the kitchen and down the hall to the bright doorway that opens onto the porch where her mother and sister are sitting. Her mother straightens up and settles back again as Lady goes to the railing and leans on her elbows and looks down the street then out to the fields beyond.

Lordalmighty it's hot.

Isn't it hot, though.

Jo is slouched in her chair, rolling a bottle of Coke on her forehead. I could just die.

Late again, Lady?

He'll be here.

Must have missed his bus again.

I suppose.

I bet those stupid cornpones were messing with him like they do, Jo says. I wouldn't be a soldier.

He'll be here. Else he'd call.

I wouldn't be a soldier.

Nobody asked you.

Now, girls.

I'd like to see you a soldier anyway, sleeping all day and laying in bed eating candy. Mooning around. Oh, General, don't make me march, that just wears me out. Oh, do I have to wear that old green thing, green just makes me look sick, haven't you got one of those in red? Why, I can't eat lima beans, don't you know about me and lima beans?

Now, Lady . . .

But her mother's laughing and so is Jo, in spite of herself. Oh, the goodness of that sound. And of her own voice. Just like singing. General, honey, you know I can't shoot that nasty thing, how about you ask one of those old boys to shoot it for me, they just love to shoot off their guns for Jo Kay.

Lady!

The three of them on the porch, waiting but not waiting. Sufficient unto themselves. Nobody has to come.

But Robert is on his way. He's leaning his head against the window of the bus and trying to catch his breath. He missed the first bus and had to run to catch this one because his sergeant found fault with him during inspection and stuck him on a cleanup detail. The sergeant hates his guts. He's an ignorant cracker and Robert is an educated man from Vermont, an engineer just out of college, quit Shell Oil in Louisiana to enlist the day North Korea crossed the parallel. The only Yankee in his company. Robert says when they get overseas there won't be any more Yankees and Southerners, just Americans. Lady likes him for believing that, but she gives him the needle because she knows it isn't true.

He changed uniforms in a hurry and didn't check the mirror before he left the barracks. There's a smudge on his right cheek. Shoe polish. His face is flushed and sweaty, his shirt soaked through. He's watching out the window and reciting a poem to himself. He's a great one for poems, this Robert. He has poems for running and poems for drill and poems for going to sleep, and poems for when the rednecks start getting him down.

> *Out of the night that covers me,*
> *Black as the Pit from pole to pole,*
> *I thank whatever Gods may be*
> *For my unconquerable soul.*

That's the poem he uses to fortify himself. He thinks it over and over even when they're yelling in his face. It keeps him strong. Lady laughs when he tells her things like this, and he always looks at her a little surprised and then he laughs too, to show he likes her sass, though he doesn't. He thinks it's just her being young and spoiled and that it'll go away if he can get her out of that house and away from her family and among sensible people who don't think everything's a joke. In time it'll wear off and leave her quiet and dignified and respectful of life's seriousness – leave her pure Lady.

That's what he thinks some days. Most days he sees no hope at all. He thinks of taking her home, into the house of his father, and when he imagines what she might say to his father he starts hearing his own excuses and apologies. Then he knows that it's impossible. Robert has picked up some psychology here and there, and he believes he understands how he got himself into this mess. It's rebellion. Subconscious, of course. A subconscious rebellion against his father, falling in love with a girl like Lady. Because you don't fall in love. No. Life isn't a song. You choose to fall in love. And there are reasons for that choice, just as there's a reason for every choice, if you get to the bottom of it. Once you figure out your reasons, you master your choices. It's as simple as that.

Robert is looking out the window without really seeing anything.

It's impossible. Lady is just a kid, she doesn't know anything about life. There's a rawness to her that will take years to correct. She's spoiled and wilful and half-wild, except for her tongue, which is all wild. And she's Southern, not that there's anything wrong with that per se, but a particular kind of Southern. Not trash, as she would put it, but too proud of not being trash. Irrational. Superstitious. Clannish.

And what a clan it is, clan Cobb. Mr Cobb a suspender-snapping paint salesman always on the road, full of drummer's banter and jokes about nigras and watermelon. Mrs Cobb a morning-to-night gossip, weepily religious, content to live on her daughters' terms rather than raise them to woman's estate with discipline and right example. And the sister. Jo Kay. You can write that sad story before it happens.

All in all, Robert can't imagine a better family than the Cobbs to beat his father over the head with. That must be why he's chosen them, and why he has to undo that choice. He's made up his mind. He meant to tell her last time, but there was no chance. Today. No matter what. She won't understand. She'll cry. He will be gentle about it. He'll say she's a fine girl but too young. He'll say that it isn't fair to ask her to wait for him when who knows what might happen, and then to follow him to a place she's never been, far from family and friends.

He'll tell Lady anything but the truth, which is that he's ashamed to have picked her to use against his father. That's his own fight. He's been running from it for as long as he can remember, and he knows he has to stop. He has to face the man.

He will, too. He will, after he gets home from Korea. His father will have to listen to him then. Robert will make him listen. He will tell him, he will face his father and tell him . . .

Robert's throat tightens and he sits up straight. He hears himself breathing in quick shallow gasps and wonders if anyone else has noticed. His heart is kicking. His mouth is dry. He closes his eyes and forces himself to breathe more slowly and deeply, imitating calm until it becomes almost real.

They pass the power company and the Greyhound station. Red-faced soldiers in shiny shoes stand around out front smoking. The bus stops on a street lined with bars and the other men get off, hooting and pushing one another. There's just Robert and four women left on board. They turn off Jackson and bump across the railroad tracks and head east past the lumberyard. Black men are throwing plants into a truck, their shirts off, skin gleaming in the hazy light. Then they're gone behind a fence. Robert pulls the cord for his stop, waits behind a wide woman in a flowered dress. The flesh swings like hammocks under her arms. She takes forever going down the steps.

The sun dazzles his eyes. He pulls down the visor of his cap and walks to the corner and turns right. This is Arsenal Street. Lady lives two blocks down where the street runs into fields. There's no plan to the way it ends – it just gives out. From here on there's nothing but farms for miles. At night Lady and Jo Kay steal strawberries from the field behind their house, dish them up with thick fresh cream and grated chocolate. The strawberries have been stewing in the heat all day and burst open at the first pressure of the teeth. Robert disapproves of reaping another man's harvest, though he eats his share and then some. The season's about over. He'll be lucky if he gets any tonight.

He's thinking about strawberries when he sees Lady on the porch, and at that moment the sweetness of that taste fills his mouth. He stops as if he just remembered something, then comes toward her again. Her lips are moving but he can't hear her, he's aware of nothing but the taste in his mouth, and the closer he comes the stronger it gets. His pace quickens, his hand goes out for the railing. He takes the steps as if he means to devour her.

No, she's saying, no. She's talking to him and to the girl whose life he seeks. She knows what will befall her if she lets him have it. Stay here on this porch with your mother and your sister, they will soon have need of you. Gladden your father's eye yet awhile. This man is not for you. He will patiently school you half to death. He will kindly take you among unbending strangers to watch him fail to be brave. To suffer his careful-ness, and to see your children writhe under it and fight it off with every kind of self-hurting recklessness. To be changed. To hear yourself, and not know who is speaking. Wait, young Lady. Bide your time.

'Lady?'

It's no good. The girl won't hear. Even now she's bending toward him as he comes up the steps. She reaches for his cheek, to brush away the smudge he doesn't know is there. He thinks it is something else that makes her do it, and his fine lean face confesses everything, asks everything. There's no turning back from this touch. She can't be stopped. She has a mind of her own, and she knows something Lady doesn't. She knows how to love him.

Lady hears her name again.

Wait, sir.

She blesses the girl. Then she turns to the far-rolling fields she used to dream an ocean, this house the ship that ruled it. She takes a last good look, and opens her eyes.

SOLITUDE
Babette Deutsch

There is the loneliness of peopled places:
Streets roaring with their human flood; the crowd
That fills bright rooms with billowing sounds and faces,
Like foreign music, overshrill and loud.
There is the loneliness of one who stands
Fronting the waste under the cold sea-light,
A wisp of flesh against the endless sands,
Like a lost gull in solitary flight.
Single is all up-rising and down-lying;
Struggle or fear or silence none may share;
Each is alone in bearing and in dying;
Conquest is uncompanioned as despair.
Yet I have known no loneliness like this,
Locked in your arms and bent beneath your kiss.

READING NOTES

There is so much to talk about in this story: choices, wrong love, fathers and sons, loneliness in marriage, responsibility, poems for life. People have expressed strong opinions about this husband's control of his wife; wondered what it would be like to be married to him; thought about their own pedantic habits and questioned why Lady stays with Robert. They have talked about the way the story changes its point of view and how that alters your perception of the characters. Someone wondered if there would be anyone in the UK called Lady and this led to a conversation about American names.

People frequently talk of the difference between solitude and loneliness and many admit to sometimes feeling lonely in a crowd. A man, new to a breakfast group, pointed out the line 'Each is alone in bearing and in dying', and there was a conversation about what the word 'bearing' would mean or involve in this context. He said he had experienced a lot of loneliness in his life and the poem meant a lot to him.

One Spirit Within Two Frames

WUTHERING HEIGHTS

(EXTRACT FROM CHAPTER 15)

Emily Brontë

(approximate reading time 18 minutes)

When a boy, Heathcliff was discovered roaming the streets of Liverpool and taken to Wuthering Heights where he grew up with the daughter of the house, Catherine Earnshaw. They became inseparable, although Cathy later chose marriage to the wealthy Edgar Linton. Having given birth to a daughter she has now become dangerously ill and her old nurse, Nelly, after informing Heathcliff, narrates the consequences.

Mrs Linton sat in a loose, white dress, with a light shawl over her shoulders, in the recess of the open window, as usual. Her thick, long hair had been partly removed at the beginning of her illness; and now she wore it simply combed in its natural tresses over her temples and neck. Her appearance was altered, as I had told Heathcliff, but when she was calm, there seemed unearthly beauty in the change. The flash of her eyes had been succeeded by a dreamy and melancholy softness: they no longer gave the impression of looking at the objects around here; they appeared always to gaze beyond, and far beyond – you would have said out of this world. Then, the paleness of her face – its haggard aspect having vanished as she recovered flesh – and the peculiar expression arising from her mental state, though painfully suggestive of their causes, added to the touching interest which she awakened; and – invariably to me, I know, and to any person who saw her, I should think – refuted more tangible proofs of convalescence and stamped her as one doomed to decay.

A book lay spread on the sill before her, and the scarcely perceptible wind fluttered its leaves at intervals. I believe Linton had laid it there, for she never endeavoured to divert herself with reading, or occupation of any kind; and he would spend many an hour in trying to entice her attention to some subject which had formerly been her amusement. She was conscious of his aim, and in her better moods endured his efforts placidly, only showing their uselessness by now and then suppressing a wearied sigh, and checking him at last, with the saddest of smiles and kisses. At other times, she would turn petulantly away, and hide her face in her hands, or even push him off angrily; and then he took care to let her alone, for he was certain of doing no good.

Gimmerton chapel bells were still ringing; and the full, mellow flow of the beck in the valley came soothingly on the ear. It was a sweet substitute for the yet absent murmur of the summer foliage, which drowned that music about the Grange, when the trees were in leaf. At Wuthering Heights it always sounded on quiet days, following a great thaw or a season of steady rain – and, of Wuthering Heights, Catherine was thinking as she listened; that is, if she thought, or listened at all; but she had the vague, distant look I mentioned before, which expressed no recognition of material things either by ear or eye.

'There's a letter for you, Mrs Linton,' I said, gently inserting it in one hand that rested on her knee. 'You must read it immediately, because it wants an answer. Shall I break the seal?'

'Yes,' she answered, without altering the direction of her eyes. I opened it – it was very short. 'Now,' I continued, 'read it.' She drew away her hand, and let it fall. I replaced it in her lap, and stood waiting till it should please her to glance down; but that movement was so long delayed that at last I resumed –

'Must I read it, ma'am? It is from Mr Heathcliff.'

There was a start and a troubled gleam of recollection, and a struggle to arrange her ideas. She lifted the letter, and seemed to peruse it; and when she came to the signature she sighed; yet still I found she had not gathered its import, for upon my desiring to hear her reply, she merely pointed to the name, and gazed at me with mournful and questioning eagerness.

'Well, he wishes to see you,' said I, guessing her need of an interpreter. 'He's in the garden by this time, and impatient to know what answer I shall bring.'

As I spoke, I observed a large dog, lying on the sunny grass beneath, raise its ears as if about to bark, and then smoothing them back, announce, by a wag of the tail that some one approached whom it did not consider a stranger.

Mrs Linton bent forward, and listened breathlessly. The minute after a step traversed the hall; the open house was too tempting for Heathcliff to resist walking in: most likely he supposed that I was inclined to shirk my promise, and so resolved to trust to his own audacity. With straining eagerness Catherine gazed towards the entrance of her chamber. He did not hit the right room directly; she motioned me to admit him; but he found it out, ere I could reach the door, and in a stride or two was at her side, and had her grasped in his arms.

He neither spoke, nor loosed his hold for some five minutes, during which period he bestowed more kisses than ever he gave in his life before, I dare say; but then my mistress had kissed him first, and I plainly saw that he could hardly bear, for downright agony, to look into her face! The same conviction had stricken him as me, from the instant he beheld her, that there was no prospect of ultimate recovery there – she was fated, sure to die.

'O, Cathy! Oh, my life! how can I bear it?' was the first sentence he uttered, in a tone that did not seek to disguise his despair. And now he stared at her so earnestly that I thought the very intensity of his gaze would bring tears into his eyes; but they burned with anguish, they did not melt.

'What now?' said Catherine, leaning back, and returning his look with a suddenly clouded brow – her humour was a mere vane for constantly varying caprices. 'You and Edgar have broken my heart, Heathcliff! And you both come to bewail the deed to me, as if you were the people to be pitied! I shall not pity you, not I. You have killed me – and thriven on it, I think. How strong you are! How many years do you mean to live after I am gone?'

Heathcliff had knelt on one knee to embrace her; he attempted to rise, but she seized his hair, and kept him down.

'I wish I could hold you,' she continued, bitterly, 'till we were both dead! I shouldn't care what you suffered. I care nothing for your sufferings. Why shouldn't you suffer? I do! Will you forget me – will you be happy when I am in the earth? Will you say twenty years hence, "That's the grave of Catherine Earnshaw? I loved her long ago, and was wretched to lose her; but it is past. I've loved many others since – my children are dearer to me than she was, and, at death, I shall not rejoice that I am going to her; I shall be sorry that I must leave them!" Will you say so, Heathcliff?'

'Don't torture me till I'm as mad as yourself,' cried he, wrenching his head free, and grinding his teeth.

The two, to a cool spectator, made a strange and fearful picture. Well might Catherine deem that heaven would be a land of exile to her, unless, with her mortal body, she cast away her mortal character also. Her present countenance had a wild vindictiveness in its white cheek, and a bloodless lip, and scintillating eye; and she retained, in her closed fingers, a portion of the locks she had been grasping. As to her companion, while raising himself with one hand, he had taken her arm with the other; and so inadequate was his stock of gentleness to the requirements of her condition, that on his letting go I saw four distinct impressions left blue in the colourless skin.

'Are you possessed with a devil,' he pursued, savagely, 'to talk in that manner to me, when you are dying? Do you reflect that all those words will be branded in my memory, and eating deeper eternally, after you have left me? You know you lie to say I have killed you; and, Catherine, you know that I could as soon forget you, as my existence! Is it not sufficient for your infernal selfishness, that while you are at peace I shall writhe in the torments of hell?'

'I shall not be at peace,' moaned Catherine, recalled to a sense of physical weakness by the violent, unequal throbbing of her heart, which beat visibly, and audibly, under this excess of agitation. She said nothing further till the paroxysm was over; then she continued, more kindly –

'I'm not wishing you greater torment than I have, Heathcliff. I only wish us never to be parted – and should a word of mine distress you hereafter, think I feel the same distress under-ground, and for my own sake, forgive me! Come here and kneel down again! You never harmed me in your life. Nay, if you nurse anger, that will be worse to remember than my harsh words! Won't you come here again? Do!'

Heathcliff went to the back of her chair, and leant over, but not so far as to let her see his face, which was livid with emotion. She bent round to look at him; he would not permit it; turning abruptly, he walked to the fireplace, where he stood, silent, with his back towards us. Mrs Linton's glance followed him suspiciously: every movement woke a new sentiment in her. After a pause, and a prolonged gaze, she resumed, addressing me in accents of indignant disappointment.

'Oh, you see, Nelly! he would not relent a moment to keep me out of the grave. *That* is how I'm loved! Well, never mind. That is not *my* Heathcliff. I shall love mine yet; and take him with me – he's in my soul. And,' added she, musingly, 'the thing that irks me most is this shattered prison, after all. I'm tired, tired of being enclosed here. I'm wearying to escape into that glorious world, and to be always there; not seeing it dimly through tears, and yearning for it through the walls of an aching heart; but really with it, and in it. Nelly, you think you are better and more fortunate than I; in full health and strength – you are sorry for me – very soon that will be altered. I shall be sorry for *you*. I shall be incomparably beyond and above you all. I *wonder* he won't be near me!' She went on to herself. 'I thought he wished it. Heathcliff, dear! you should not be sullen now. Do come to me, Heathcliff.'

In her eagerness she rose, and supported herself on the arm of the chair. At that earnest appeal, he turned to her, looking absolutely desperate. His eyes wide, and wet, at last, flashed fiercely on her; his breast heaved convulsively. An instant they held asunder; and then how they met I hardly saw, but Catherine made a spring, and he caught her, and they were locked in an embrace from which I thought my mistress would never be released alive. In fact, to my eyes, she seemed directly insensible. He flung himself into the nearest seat, and on my approaching hurriedly to ascertain if she had fainted, he gnashed at me, and foamed like a mad dog, and gathered her to him with greedy jealousy. I did not feel as if I were in the company of a creature of my own species; it appeared that he would not understand, though I spoke to him; so I stood off, and held my tongue, in great perplexity.

A movement of Catherine's relieved me a little presently: she put up her hand to clasp his neck, and bring her cheek to his, as he held her: while he, in return, covering her with frantic caresses, said wildly –

'You teach me now how cruel you've been – cruel and false. *Why* did you despise me? *Why* did you betray your own heart, Cathy? I have not one word of comfort – you deserve this. You have killed yourself. Yes, you may kiss me, and cry; and wring out my kisses and tears. They'll blight you – they'll damn you. You loved me – then what *right* had you to leave me? What right – answer me – for the poor fancy you felt for Linton? Because misery, and degradation, and death, and nothing that God or Satan could inflict would have parted us, *you*, of your own will, did it. I have not broken your heart – *you* have broken it – and in breaking it, you have broken mine. So much the worse for me, that I am strong. Do I want to live? What kind of living will it be when you – oh, God! would *you* like to live with your soul in the grave?'

'Let me alone. Let me alone,' sobbed Catherine. 'If I've done wrong, I'm dying for it. It is enough! You left me too: but I won't upbraid you! I forgive you. Forgive me!'

'It is hard to forgive, and to look at those eyes, and feel those wasted hands,' he answered. 'Kiss me again; and don't let me see your eyes! I forgive what you have done to me. I love *my* murderer – but *yours*! How can I?'

They were silent – their faces hid against each other, and washed by each other's tears. At least, I suppose the weeping was on both sides; as it seemed Heathcliff *could* weep on a great occasion like this.

I grew very uncomfortable, meanwhile; for the afternoon wore fast away, the man whom I had sent off returned from his errand, and I could distinguish, by the shine of the westering sun up the valley, a concourse thickening outside Gimmerton chapel porch.

'Service is over,' I announced. 'My master will be here in half an hour.'

Heathcliff groaned a curse, and strained Catherine closer – she never moved.

Ere long I perceived a group of the servants passing up the road towards the kitchen wing. Mr Linton was not far behind; he opened the gate himself, and sauntered slowly up, probably enjoying the lovely afternoon that breathed as soft as summer.

'Now he is here,' I exclaimed. 'For Heaven's sake, hurry down! You'll not meet any one on the front stairs. Do be quick; and stay among the trees till he is fairly in.'

'I must go, Cathy,' said Heathcliff, seeking to extricate himself from his companion's arms. 'But, if I live, I'll see you again before you are asleep. I won't stray five yards from your window.'

'You must not go!' she answered, holding him as firmly as her strength allowed. 'You shall not, I tell you.'

'For one hour,' he pleaded earnestly.

'Not for one minute,' she replied.

'I *must* – Linton will be up immediately,' persisted the alarmed intruder.

He would have risen, and unfixed her fingers by the act – she clung fast, gasping: there was mad resolution in her face.

'No!' she shrieked. 'Oh, don't, don't go. It is the last time! Edgar will not hurt us. Heathcliff, I shall die! I shall die!'

'Damn the fool! There he is,' cried Heathcliff, sinking back into his seat. 'Hush, my darling! Hush, hush, Catherine! I'll stay. If he shot me so, I'd expire with a blessing on my lips.'

And there they were fast again. I heard my master mounting the stairs – the cold sweat ran from my forehead; I was horrified.

'Are you going to listen to her ravings?' I said, passionately. 'She does not know what she says. Will you ruin her, because she has not wit to help herself? Get up! You could be free instantly. That is the most diabolical deed that ever you did. We are all done for – master, mistress, and servant.'

I wrung my hands, and cried out; and Mr Linton hastened his step at the noise. In the midst of my agitation, I was sincerely glad to observe that Catherine's arms had fallen relaxed, and her head hung down.

'She's fainted or dead,' I thought; 'so much the better. Far better that she should be dead, than lingering a burden and a misery-maker to all about her.'

Edgar sprang to his unbidden guest, blanched with aston-ishment and rage. What he meant to do, I cannot tell; however, the other stopped all demonstrations, at once, by placing the lifeless-looking form in his arms.

'Look there!' he said. 'Unless you be a fiend, help her first – then you shall speak to me!'

He walked into the parlour, and sat down. Mr Linton summoned me, and with great difficulty, and after resorting to many means, we managed to restore her to sensation; but she was all bewildered; she sighed, and moaned, and knew nobody. Edgar, in his anxiety for her, forgot her hated friend. I did not. I went, at the earliest opportunity, and besought him to depart; affirming that Catherine was better, and he should hear from me in the morning how she passed the night.

'I shall not refuse to go out of doors,' he answered; 'but I shall stay in the garden; and, Nelly, mind you keep your word tomorrow. I shall be under those larch trees, mind! or I pay another visit, whether Linton be in or not.'

He sent a rapid glance through the half-open door of the chamber, and, ascertaining that what I stated was apparently true, delivered the house of his luckless presence.

from EPIPSYCHIDION
Percy Bysshe Shelley

Our breath shall intermix, our bosoms bound,
And our veins beat together; and our lips
With other eloquence than words, eclipse
The soul that burns between them, and the wells
Which boil under our being's inmost cells,
The fountains of our deepest life, shall be
Confused in passion's golden purity,
As mountain-springs under the morning Sun.
We shall become the same, we shall be one
Spirit within two frames, oh! wherefore two?
One passion in twin-hearts, which grows and grew,
Till, like two meteors of expanding flame,
Those spheres instinct with it become the same,
Touch, mingle, are transfigured; ever still
Burning, yet ever inconsumable:
In one another's substance finding food,
Like flames too pure and light and unimbued
To nourish their bright lives with baser prey,
Which point to Heaven and cannot pass away:
One hope within two wills, one will beneath
Two overshadowing minds, one life, one death,
One Heaven, one Hell, one immortality,
And one annihilation!

READING NOTES

People are always interested in the kind of love Cathy talks about and how sustainable or desirable it would be in everyday life. Some group members expressed a desire to be loved with such intensity and wondered what it would be like, whilst others were much more fearful of the dangers of such an all-consuming passion. Some spoke about the difference between first love and the sort of love that makes for a lasting, steady relationship. Heathcliff was like Marmite, someone said: you either love him or you loathe him. An older member of the group remembered her hair being cut, like Cathy's, when she had scarlet fever as a child.

A woman was interested in the lines from the poem 'We shall become the same, we shall be one/Spirit within two frames'. She wondered if this was what the term 'soulmate' might mean. In general, people thought that however much we might want to be at one with someone we love, there is always a separating distance.

Two Poems: All the Heart?

♥

LOVE IS NOT ALL
Edna St. Vincent Millay

Love is not all: it is not meat nor drink
Nor slumber nor a roof against the rain;
Nor yet a floating spar to men that sink
And rise and sink and rise and sink again;
Love can not fill the thickened lung with breath,
Nor clean the blood, nor set the fractured bone;
Yet many a man is making friends with death
Even as I speak, for lack of love alone.
It well may be that in a difficult hour,
Pinned down by pain and moaning for release,
Or nagged by want past resolution's power,
I might be driven to sell your love for peace,
Or trade the memory of this night for food.
It well may be. I do not think I would.

NEVER GIVE ALL THE HEART
W. B. Yeats

Never give all the heart, for love
Will hardly seem worth thinking of
To passionate women if it seem
Certain, and they never dream
That it fades out from kiss to kiss;
For everything that's lovely is
But a brief, dreamy, kind delight.
O never give the heart outright,
For they, for all smooth lips can say,
Have given their hearts up to the play.
And who could play it well enough
If deaf and dumb and blind with love?
He that made this knows all the cost,
For he gave all his heart and lost.

READING NOTES

The poems generated a lot of discussion, some of it quite heated, when someone resented what she saw as Yeats's anti-feminist stand. One of the men in the group said he thought that the scenario could just as easily play out the other way round, that is to say with a woman losing to a man. We talked about unconditional love – could that be the same as giving 'all the heart'? Perhaps it is just human nature, someone suggested, to take for granted something that is freely and wholly given but to want more of what you only half have. If love is a game, the stakes are high, as this poet knows to his cost, and how could he play well if he was so incapacitated by love? There was more heated discussion about the idea of love as a game to play.

What would a person give up for love, was the question that came out of the reading of 'Love Is Not All'. In dire circumstances would you choose to sell love for peace or the memory of love for food? A woman who really liked the poem said she wanted to talk about how she felt the poem kept coming up to the brink, or dangerous edge of something: the sensation of drowning in the third and fourth lines; the proximity of death 'even as I speak', and how near the poem comes to selling love before pulling back at the last minute. We were divided about whether the last sentence felt doubtful or not. Jim said: 'If someone once said to me, "I love you with *all* my heart," I would die a happy man.'

Wonder and Wealth

THE GREAT GATSBY

(EXTRACT FROM CHAPTER 5)

F. Scott Fitzgerald

(approximate reading time 14 minutes)

Jay Gatsby's whole life has been directed towards winning the love of Daisy, whom he first met when they were young and he too poor to support her. He has since become a man of great wealth, and though no one quite knows his background or how he made his money, they are happy to enjoy his famous parties and lavish hospitality. Daisy is now pretty, flighty, and married to Tom Buchanan. Gatsby has befriended the narrator of the novel, Nick Carraway, and persuaded him to arrange a meeting with Daisy at Nick's house. Gatsby is terribly nervous; the meeting goes badly at first and so Nick leaves the couple on their own for a while.

I went in – after making every possible noise in the kitchen, short of pushing over the stove – but I don't believe they heard a sound. They were sitting at either end of the couch, looking at each other as if some question had been asked, or was in the air, and every vestige of embarrassment was gone. Daisy's face was smeared with tears, and when I came in she jumped up and began wiping at it with her handkerchief before a mirror. But there was a change in Gatsby that was simply confounding. He literally glowed; without a word or a gesture of exultation a new well-being radiated from him and filled the little room.

'Oh, hello, old sport,' he said, as if he hadn't seen me for years. I thought for a moment he was going to shake hands.

'It's stopped raining.'

'Has it?' When he realized what I was talking about, that there were twinkle-bells of sunshine in the room, he smiled like a weather man, like an ecstatic patron of recurrent light, and repeated the news to Daisy. 'What do you think of that? It's stopped raining.'

'I'm glad, Jay.' Her throat, full of aching, grieving beauty, told only of her unexpected joy.

'I want you and Daisy to come over to my house,' he said, 'I'd like to show her around.'

'You're sure you want me to come?'

'Absolutely, old sport.'

Daisy went up stairs to wash her face – too late I thought with humiliation of my towels – while Gatsby and I waited on the lawn.

'My house looks well, doesn't it?' he demanded. 'See how the whole front of it catches the light.'

I agreed that it was splendid.

'Yes.' His eyes went over it, every arched door and square tower. 'It took me just three years to earn the money that bought it.

'I thought you inherited your money.'

'I did, old sport,' he said automatically, 'but I lost most of it in the big panic – the panic of the war.'

I think he hardly knew what he was saying, for when I asked him what business he was in her answered: 'That's my affair,' before he realized that it wasn't an appropriate reply.

'Oh, I've been in several things,' he corrected himself. 'I was in the drug business and then I was in the oil business. But I'm not in either one now.' He looked at me with more attention. 'Do you mean you've been thinking over what I proposed the other night?'

Before I could answer, Daisy came out of the house and two rows of brass buttons on her dress gleamed in the sunlight.

'That huge place *there*?' she cried pointing.

'Do you like it?'

'I love it, but I don't see how you live there all alone.'

'I keep it always full of interesting people, night and day. People who do interesting things. Celebrated people.'

Instead of taking the short cut along the Sound we went down the road and entered by the big postern. With enchanting murmurs Daisy admired this aspect or that of the feudal silhouette against the sky, admired the gardens, the sparkling odour of jonquils and the frothy odour of hawthorn and plum blossoms and the pale gold odour of kiss-me-at-the-gate. It was strange to reach the marble steps and find no stir of bright dresses in and out the door, and hear no sound but bird voices in the trees.

And inside, as we wandered through Marie Antoinette music-rooms and Restoration Salons, I felt that there were guests concealed behind every couch and table, under orders to be breathlessly silent until we had passed through. As Gatsby closed the door of 'the Merton College Library' I could have sworn I heard the owl-eyed man break into ghostly laughter.

We went upstairs, through period bedrooms swathed in rose and lavender silk and vivid with new flowers, through dressing-rooms and poolrooms, and bath-rooms with sunken baths – intruding into one chamber where a dishevelled man in pyjamas was doing liver exercises on the floor. It was Mr Klipspringer, the 'boarder'. I had seen him wandering hungrily about the beach that morning. Finally we came to Gatsby's own apartment, a bedroom and a bath, and an Adam's study, where we sat down and drank a glass of some Chartreuse he took from a cupboard in the wall.

He hadn't once ceased looking at Daisy, and I think he revalued everything in his house according to the measure of response it drew from her well-loved eyes. Sometimes, too, he stared around at his possessions in a dazed way, as though in her actual and astounding presence none of it was any longer real. Once he nearly toppled down a flight of stairs.

His bedroom was the simplest of all – except where the dresser was garnished with a toilet set of pure dull gold. Daisy took the brush with delight, and smoothed her hair, where-upon Gatsby sat down and shaded his eyes and began to laugh.

'It's the funniest thing, old sport,' he said hilariously. 'I can't – When I try to—'

He had passed visibly through two states and was entering upon a third. After his embarrassment and his unreasoning joy he was consumed with wonder at her presence. He had been full of the idea so long, dreamed it right through to the end, waited with his teeth set, so to speak, at an inconceivable pitch of intensity. Now, in the reaction, he was running down like an over-wound clock.

Recovering himself in a minute he opened for us two hulking patent cabinets which held his massed suits and dressing-gowns and ties, and his shirts, piled like bricks in stacks a dozen high.

'I've got a man in England who buys me clothes. He sends over a selection of things at the beginning of each season, spring and fall.'

He took a pile of shirts and began throwing them, one by one, before us, shirts of sheer linen and thick silk and fine flannel, which lost their folds as they fell and covered the table in many coloured disarray. While we admired he brought more and the soft rich heap mounted higher – shirts with stripes and scrolls and plaids in coral and apple-green and lavender and faint orange, with monograms of indian blue. Suddenly, with a strained sound, Daisy bent her head into the shirts and began to cry stormily.

'They're such beautiful shirts,' she sobbed, her voice muffled in the thick folds. 'It makes me sad because I've never seen such – such beautiful shirts before.'

After the house, we were to see the grounds and the swimming-pool, and the hydroplane and the mid-summer flowers – but outside Gatsby's window it began to rain again, so we stood in a row looking at the corrugated surface of the Sound.

'If it wasn't for the mist we could see your home across the bay,' said Gatsby. 'You always have a green light that burns all night at the end of your dock.'

Daisy put her arm through his abruptly, but he seemed absorbed in what he had just said. Possibly it had occurred to him that the colossal significance of that light had now vanished forever. Compared to the great distance that had separated him from Daisy it had seemed very near to her, almost touching her. It had seemed as close as a star to the moon. Now it was again a green light on a dock. His count of enchanted objects had diminished by one.

I began to walk about the room, examining various indefinite objects in the half darkness. A large photograph of an elderly man in a yachting costume attracted me, hung on the wall over his desk.

'Who's this?'

'That? That's Mr Dan Cody, old sport.'

The name sounded faintly familiar.

'He's dead now. He used to be my best friend years ago.'

There was a small picture of Gatsby, also in yachting costume, on the bureau – Gatsby with his head thrown back defiantly – taken apparently when he was about eighteen.

'I adore it,' exclaimed Daisy. 'The pompadour! You never told me you had a pompadour – or a yacht.'

'Look at this,' said Gatsby quickly. 'Here's a lot of clippings – about you.'

They stood side by side examining it. I was going to ask to see the rubies when the phone rang, and Gatsby took up the receiver.

'Yes . . . Well, I can't talk now . . . I can't talk now, old sport . . . I said a *small* town . . . He must know what a small town is . . . Well, he's no use to us if Detroit is his idea of a small town . . .'

He rang off.

'Come here *quick*!' cried Daisy at the window.

The rain was still falling, but the darkness had parted in the west, and there was a pink and gold billow of foamy clouds above the sea.

'Look at that,' she whispered, and then after a moment: 'I'd like to just get one of those pink clouds and put you in it and push you around.'

I tried to go then, but they wouldn't hear of it; perhaps my presence made them feel more satisfactorily alone.

'I know what we'll do,' said Gatsby, 'we'll have Klipspringer play the piano.'

He went out of the room calling 'Ewing!' and returned in a few minutes accompanied by an embarrassed, slightly worn young man, with shell-rimmed glasses and scanty blond hair. He was now decently clothed in a 'sport shirt', open at the neck, sneakers, and duck trousers of a nebulous hue.

'Did we interrupt your exercise?' inquired Daisy politely.

'I was asleep,' cried Mr Klipspringer, in a spasm of embarrassment. 'That is, I'd *been* asleep. Then I got up . . .'

'Klipspringer plays the piano,' said Gatsby, cutting him off. 'Don't you, Ewing, old sport?'

'I don't play well. I don't – hardly play at all. I'm all out of prac—'

'We'll go downstairs,' interrupted Gatsby. He flipped a switch. The grey windows disappeared as the house glowed full of light.

In the music-room Gatsby turned on a solitary lamp beside the piano. He lit Daisy's cigarette from a trembling match, and sat down with her on a couch far across the room, where there was no light save what the gleaming floor bounced in from the hall.

When Klipspringer had played 'The Love Nest' he turned around on the bench and searched unhappily for Gatsby in the gloom.

'I'm all out of practice, you see. I told you I couldn't play. I'm all out of prac—'

'Don't talk so much, old sport,' commanded Gatsby. 'Play!'

'In the morning,
In the evening,
        Ain't we got fun –'

Outside the wind was loud and there was a faint flow of thunder along the Sound. All the lights were going on in West Egg now; the electric trains, men-carrying, were plunging home through the rain from New York. It was the hour of a profound human change, and excitement was generating through the air.

'One thing's sure and nothing's surer
The rich get richer and the poor get – children.
        In the meantime,
        In between time –'

As I went over to say good-bye I saw that the expression of bewilderment had come back into Gatsby's face, as though a faint doubt had occurred to him as to the quality of his present happiness. Almost five years! There must have been moments even that afternoon when Daisy tumbled short of his dreams – not through her own fault, but because of the colossal vitality of his illusion. It had gone beyond her, beyond everything. He had thrown himself into it with a creative passion, adding to it all the time, decking it out with every bright feather that drifted his way. No amount of fire or freshness can challenge what a man can store up in his ghostly heart.

As I watched him he adjusted himself a little, visibly. His hand took hold of hers, and as she said something low in his ear he turned toward her with a rush of emotion. I think that voice held him most, with its fluctuating, feverish warmth, because it couldn't be over-dreamed – that voice was a deathless song.

They had forgotten me, but Daisy glanced up and held out her hand; Gatsby didn't know me now at all. I looked once more at them and they looked back at me, remotely, possessed by intense life. Then I went out of the room and down the marble steps into the rain, leaving them there together.

SUMMUM BONUM
Robert Browning

All the breath and the bloom of the
    year in the bag of one bee:
All the wonder and wealth of the mine in
    the heart of one gem:
In the core of one pearl all the shade and the
    shine of the sea:
    Breath and bloom, shade and shine,—wonder,
    wealth and—how far above them—
      Truth, that's brighter than gem,
      Trust, that's purer than pearl,—
Brightest truth, purest trust in the universe—
    all were for me
      In the kiss of one girl.

READING NOTES

In a book at breakfast group, the discussion of the book centred on Gatsby's obsession with Daisy. People thought she would not be able to live up to his expectation of her. Kim was appalled at his wealth – 'Fancy having a solid gold hairbrush!' But others speculated about just what his wealth actually meant to him. The chapter demanded so many questions: who is Gatsby; what is the meaning of the mysterious phone call; why is he evasive about his business? Why does he take all his shirts out for show, and why should this move Daisy to tears? There was talk of the brightness and purity of truth and trust in the poem which people contrasted with the story. Here was brightness, certainly, but how could there be truth and trust in their situation? No one felt confident that Gatsby and Daisy faced a bright future. As no one knew Latin, the title of the poem remained a mystery, although there were some good guesses. How to describe a kiss? After the group had had a go they awarded Browning full marks.

Tell Me the Truth
About Love

♥

PUPPY
George Saunders

(approximate reading time 22 minutes)

Twice already Marie had pointed out the brilliance of the autumnal sun on the perfect field of corn, because the brilliance of the autumnal sun on the perfect field of corn put her in mind of a haunted house – not a haunted house she had ever actually seen but the mythical one that sometimes appeared in her mind (with adjacent graveyard and cat on a fence) whenever she saw the brilliance of the autumnal sun on the perfect etc., etc. – and she wanted to make sure that, if the kids had a corresponding mythical haunted house that appeared in their minds whenever they saw the brilliance of the etc., etc., it would come up now, so that they could all experience it together, like friends, like college friends on a road trip, sans pot, ha ha ha!

But no. When she, a third time, said, 'Wow, guys, check that out,' Abbie said, 'Okay, Mom, we get it, it's corn,' and Josh said, 'Not now, Mom, I'm Leavening my Loaves,' which was fine with her; she had no problem with that, Noble Baker being preferable to Bra Stuffer, the game he'd asked for.

Well, who could say? Maybe they didn't even have any mythical vignettes in their heads. Or maybe the mythical vignettes they had in their heads were totally different from the ones she had in her head. Which was the beauty of it, because, after all, they were their own little people! You were just a caretaker. They didn't have to feel what *you* felt; they just had to be supported in feeling what *they* felt.

Still, wow, that cornfield was such a classic.

'Whenever I see a field like that, guys?' she said, 'I somehow think of a haunted house!'

'Slicing Knife! Slicing Knife!' Josh shouted. 'You nimrod machine! I chose that!'

Speaking of Halloween, she remembered last year, when their cornstalk column had tipped their shopping cart over. Gosh, how they'd laughed at that! Oh, family laughter was golden; she'd had none of that in her childhood, Dad being so dour and Mom so ashamed. If Mom and Dad's cart had tipped, Dad would have given the cart a despairing kick and Mom would have stridden purposefully away to reapply her lipstick, distancing herself from Dad, while she, Marie, would have nervously taken that horrid plastic army man she'd named Brady into her mouth.

Well, in this family laughter was encouraged! Last night, when Josh had goosed her with his Game Boy, she'd shot a spray of toothpaste across the mirror and they'd all cracked up, rolling around the floor with Goochie, and Josh had said, such nostalgia in his voice, 'Mom, remember when Goochie was a puppy?' Which was when Abbie had burst into tears, because, being only five, she had no memory of Goochie as a puppy.

Hence this Family Mission. And as far as Robert? Oh, God bless Robert! There was a man. He would have no problem whatsoever with this Family Mission. She loved the way he had of saying 'Ho HO!' whenever she brought home something new and unexpected.

'Ho HO!' Robert had said, coming home to find the iguana. 'Ho HO!' he had said, coming home to find the ferret trying to get into the iguana cage. 'We appear to be the happy operators of a menagerie!'

She loved him for his playfulness – you could bring home a hippo you'd put on a credit card (both the ferret and the iguana had gone on credit cards) and he'd just say, 'Ho HO!' and ask what the creature ate and what hours it slept and what the heck they were going to name the little bugger.

In the backseat, Josh made the *git-git-git* sound he always made when his Baker was in Baking Mode, trying to get his Loaves into the oven while fighting off various Hungry Denizens, such as a Fox with a distended stomach; such as a fey Robin that would improbably carry the Loaf away, speared on its beak, whenever it had succeeded in dropping a Clonking Rock on your Baker – all of which Marie had learned over the summer by studying the Noble Baker manual while Josh was asleep.

And it had helped, it really had. Josh was less withdrawn lately, and when she came up behind him now while he was playing and said, like, 'Wow, honey, I didn't know you could do Pumpernickel,' or 'Sweetie, try Serrated Blade, it cuts quicker.

Try it while doing Latch the Window,' he would reach back with his noncontrolling hand and swat at her affectionately, and yesterday they'd shared a good laugh when he'd accidentally knocked off her glasses.

So her mother could go right ahead and claim that she was spoiling the kids. These were not spoiled kids. These were *well-loved* kids. At least she'd never left one of them standing in a blizzard for two hours after a junior-high dance. At least she'd never drunkenly snapped at one of them, 'I hardly consider you college material.' At least she'd never locked one of them in a closet (a closet!) while entertaining a literal ditchdigger in the parlor.

Oh, God, what a beautiful world! The autumn colors, that glinting river, that lead-colored cloud pointing down like a rounded arrow at that half-remodeled McDonald's standing above I-90 like a castle.

This time it would be different, she was sure of it. The kids would care for this pet themselves, since a puppy wasn't scaly and didn't bite. ('Ho HO!' Robert had said the first time the iguana bit him. 'I see you have an opinion on the matter!')

Thank you, Lord, she thought, as the Lexus flew through the cornfield. You have given me so much: struggles and the strength to overcome them; grace, and new chances every day to spread that grace around. And in her mind she sang out, as she sometimes did when feeling that the world was good and she had at last found her place in it, 'Ho HO, ho HO!'

Callie pulled back the blind.

Yes. Awesome. It was solved so *perfect*.

There was plenty for him to do back there. A yard could be a whole world. Like her yard when she was a kid had been a whole world. From the three holes in their wood fence she'd been able to see Exxon (Hole One) and Accident Corner (Hole Two), and Hole Three was actually two holes that if you lined them up right your eyes would do this weird crossing thing and you could play Oh My God I Am So High by staggering away with your eyes crossed, going 'Peace, man, peace.'

When Bo got older, it would be different. Then he'd need his freedom. But now he just needed not to get killed. Once they'd found him way over on Testament. And that was across I-90. How had he crossed I-90? She knew how. Darted. That's how he crossed streets. Once a total stranger had called them from Hightown Plaza. Even Dr Brile had said it: 'Callie, this boy is going to end up dead if you don't get this under control. Is he taking the medications?'

Well, he was and he wasn't. The meds made him grind his teeth and his fist would suddenly pound down. He'd broken plates that way, and once a glass tabletop and got four stitches in his wrist.

Today he didn't need the meds because he was safe in the yard, because she'd fixed it so *perfect*.

He was out there practicing pitching by filling his Yankees helmet with pebbles and winging them at the tree.

He looked up and saw her and did the thing where he blew a kiss.

Sweet little man.

Now all she had to worry about was the pup. She hoped the lady who'd called would actually show up. It was a nice pup.

White, with brown round one eye. Cute. If the lady showed up, she'd definitely want it. And if she took it, Jimmy was off the hook. He'd hated doing it that time with the kittens. But if no one took that pup he'd do it. He'd have to. Because his feeling was, when you said you were going to do a thing and didn't do it, that was how kids got into drugs. Plus he'd been raised on a farm, or near a farm anyways, and anybody raised on a farm knew you had to do what you had to do in terms of sick animals or extra animals – the being not sick, just extra.

That time with the kittens, Brianna and Jessi had called him a murderer, getting Bo all worked up, and Jimmy had yelled, 'Look, you kids, I was raised on a farm and you got to do what you got to do!' Then he'd cried in bed, saying how the kittens had mewed in the bag all the way to the pond, and how he wished he'd never been raised on a farm, and she'd almost said, 'You mean near a farm' (his dad had run a car wash outside Cortland), but sometimes when she got too smart-assed he would do this hard pinching thing on her arm while waltzing her around the bedroom, as if the place where he was pinching her was like her handle, going, 'I'm not sure I totally heard what you just said.'

So, that time after the kittens, she'd only said, 'Oh, honey, you did what you had to do.'

And he'd said, 'I guess I did, but it's sure not easy raising the kids the right way.'

And then, because she hadn't made his life harder by being a smart-ass, they had lain there making plans, like why not sell this place and move to Arizona and buy a car wash, why not buy the kids Hooked on Phonics, why not plant tomatoes, and then they'd got to wrestling around and (she had no idea why she remembered this) he'd done this thing of, while holding her close, bursting this sudden laugh/despair-snort into her hair, like a sneeze, or like he was about to start crying.

Which had made her feel special, him trusting her with that.

So what she'd love, for tonight? Was getting the pup sold, putting the kids to bed early, and then, Jimmy seeing her as all organized in terms of the pup, they could mess around and afterward lie there making plans, and he could do that laugh/ snort thing in her hair again.

Why that laugh/snort meant so much to her she had no freaking idea. It was just one of the weird things about the Wonder That Was Her, ha ha ha.

Outside, Bo hopped to his feet, suddenly curious, because (here we go) the lady who'd called had just pulled up?

Yep, and in a nice car, too, which meant too bad she'd put 'Cheap' in the ad.

Abbie squealed, 'I love it, Mommy, I want it!' as the puppy looked up dimly from its shoebox and the lady of the house went trudging away and one-two-three-four plucked up four *dog turds* from the rug.

Well, wow, what a super field trip for the kids, Marie thought, ha ha (the filth, the mildew smell, the dry aquarium holding the single encyclopedia volume, the pasta pot on the bookshelf with an inflatable candy cane inexplicably sticking out of it), and although some might have been disgusted (by the spare tire on the *dining-room table*, by the way the glum mother dog, the presumed in-house pooper, was now dragging her rear over the pile of clothing in the corner, in a sitting position, splay-legged, moronic look of pleasure on her face), Marie realized (resisting the urge to rush to the sink and wash her hands, in part because the sink had a *basketball* in it) that what this really was, was deeply sad.

Please do not touch anything, please do not touch, she said to Josh and Abbie, but just in her head, wanting to give the children a chance to observe her being democratic and accepting, and afterward they could all wash up at the half-remodeled McDonald's, as long as they just please please kept their hands out of their mouths, and God forbid they should rub their eyes.

The phone rang, and the lady of the house plodded into the kitchen, placing the daintily held, paper-towel-wrapped turds *on the counter*.

'Mommy, I want it,' Abbie said.

'I will definitely walk him like twice a day,' Josh said.

'Don't say "like,"' Marie said.

'I will definitely walk him twice a day,' Josh said.

Okay, then, all right, they would adopt a white-trash dog. Ha ha. They could name it Zeke, buy it a little corncob pipe and a straw hat. She imagined the puppy, having crapped on the rug, looking up at her, going, *Cain't hep it*. But no. Had she come from a perfect place? Everything was transmutable. She imagined the puppy grown up, entertaining some friends, speaking to them with a British accent: *My family of origin was, um, rather not, shall we say, of the most respectable . . .*

Ha ha, wow, the mind was amazing, always cranking out these—

Marie stepped to the window and, anthropologically pulling the blind aside, was shocked, so shocked that she dropped the blind and shook her head, as if trying to wake herself, shocked to see a young boy, just a few years younger than Josh, harnessed and chained to a tree, via some sort of doohickey by which – she pulled the blind back again, sure that she could not have seen what she thought she had—

When the boy ran, the chain spooled out. He was running now, looking back at her, showing off. When he reached the end of the chain, it jerked and he dropped as if shot.

He rose to a sitting position, railed against the chain, whipped it back and forth, crawled to a bowl of water, and, lifting it to his lips, took a drink: a drink *from a dog's bowl.*

Josh joined her at the window.

She let him look.

He should know that the world was not all lessons and iguanas and Nintendo. It was also this muddy simple boy tethered like an animal.

She remembered coming out of the closet to find her mother's scattered lingerie and the ditchdigger's metal hanger full of orange flags. She remembered waiting outside the junior high in the bitter cold, the snow falling harder, as she counted over and over to two hundred, promising herself each time that when she reached two hundred she would begin the long walk back—

God, she would have killed for just one righteous adult to confront her mother, shake her, say, 'You idiot, this is your child, your child you're—'

'So what were you guys thinking of naming him?' the woman said, coming out of the kitchen.

The cruelty and ignorance just radiated from her fat face, with its little smear of lipstick.

'I'm afraid we won't be taking him after all,' Marie said coldly.

Such an uproar from Abbie! But Josh – she would have to praise him later, maybe buy him the Italian Loaves Expansion Pak – hissed something to Abbie, and then they were moving out through the trashed kitchen (past some kind of *crankshaft* on a cookie sheet, past a partial red pepper afloat *in a can of green paint*) while the lady of the house scuttled after them, saying, wait, wait, they could have it free, please take it – she just really wanted them to have it.

No, Marie said, it would not be possible for them to take it at this time, her feeling being that one really shouldn't possess something if one wasn't up to properly caring for it.

'Oh,' the woman said, slumping in the doorway, the scrambling pup on one shoulder.

Out in the Lexus, Abbie began to cry softly, saying, 'Really, that was the perfect pup for me.'

And it was a nice pup, but Marie was not going to contribute to a situation like this in even the smallest way.

Simply was not going to do it.

The boy came to the fence. If only she could say to him, with a single look, *Life will not necessarily always be like this. Your life could suddenly blossom into something wonderful. It can happen. It happened to me.*

But secret looks, looks that conveyed a world of meaning with their subtle blah blah blah – that was all bullshit. What was not bullshit was a call to Child Welfare, where she knew

Linda Berling, a very no-nonsense lady who would snatch this poor kid away so fast it would make that fat mother's thick head spin.

Callie shouted, 'Bo, back in a sec!' and, swiping the corn out of the way with her non-pup arm, walked until there was nothing but corn and sky.

It was so small it didn't move when she set it down, just sniffed and tumped over.

Well, what did it matter, drowned in a bag or starved in the corn? This way Jimmy wouldn't have to do it. He had enough to worry about. The boy she'd first met with hair to his waist was now this old man shrunk with worry. As far as the money, she had sixty hidden away. She'd give him twenty of that and go, 'The people who bought the pup were super-nice.'

Don't look back, don't look back, she said in her head as she raced away through the corn.

Then she was walking along Teallback Road like a sport-walker, like some lady who walked every night to get slim, except that she was nowhere near slim, she knew that, and also knew that when sportwalking you did not wear jeans and unlaced hiking boots. Ha ha. She wasn't stupid. She just made bad choices. She remembered Sister Lynette saying, 'Callie, you are bright enough but you incline toward that which does not benefit you.' *Yep, well, Sister, you got that right*, she said to the nun in her mind. But what the hell. What the heck. When things got easier moneywise, she'd get some decent tennis shoes and start walking and get slim. And start night school. Slimmer. Maybe medical technology. She was never going to be really slim. But Jimmy liked her the way she was. And she liked him the way the way he was. Which maybe that's what love was: liking someone how he was and doing things to help him get even better.

Like right now she was helping Jimmy by making his life easier by killing something so he – no. All she was doing was walking, walking away from—

What had she just said? That had been good. *Love was liking someone how he was and doing things to help him get even better.*

Like Bo wasn't perfect, but she loved him how he was and tried to help him get better. If they could keep him safe, maybe he'd mellow out as he got older. If he mellowed out, maybe he could someday have a family. Like there he was now in the yard, sitting quietly, looking at flowers. Tapping with his bat, happy enough. He looked up, waved the bat at her, gave her that smile. Yesterday he'd been stuck in the house, all miserable. He'd ended the day screaming in bed, so frustrated. Today he was looking at flowers. Who was it that thought up that idea, the idea that had made today better than yesterday? Who loved him enough to think that up? Who loved him more than anyone else in the world loved him?

Her.

She did.

O TELL ME THE TRUTH ABOUT LOVE
W. H. Auden

Some say love's a little boy,
    And some say it's a bird,
Some say it makes the world go round,
    And some say that's absurd,
And when I asked the man next door,
    Who looked as if he knew,
His wife got very cross indeed,
    And said it wouldn't do.

Does it look like a pair of pyjamas,
    Or the ham in a temperance hotel?
Does its odour remind one of llamas,
    Or has it a comforting smell?
Is it prickly to touch as a hedge is,
    Or soft as eiderdown fluff?
Is it sharp or quite smooth at the edges?
    O tell me the truth about love.

Our history books refer to it
    In cryptic little notes,
It's quite a common topic on
    The Transatlantic boats;
I've found the subject mentioned in
    Accounts of suicides,
And even seen it scribbled on
    The backs of railway guides.

Does it howl like a hungry Alsatian,
    Or boom like a military band?
Could one give a first-rate imitation
    On a saw or a Steinway Grand?
Is its singing at parties a riot?
    Does it only like Classical stuff?
Will it stop when one wants to be quiet?
    O tell me the truth about love.

I looked inside the summer-house;
    It wasn't ever there;
I tried the Thames at Maidenhead,
    And Brighton's bracing air,
I don't know what the blackbird sang,
    Or what the tulip said;
But it wasn't in the chicken-run,
    Or underneath the bed.

Can it pull extraordinary faces?
    Is it usually sick on a swing?
Does it spend all its time at the races,
    Or fiddling with pieces of string?
Has it views of its own about money?
    Does it think Patriotism enough?
Are its stories vulgar but funny?
    O tell me the truth about love.

When it comes, will it come without warning,
    Just as I'm picking my nose?

Will it knock on my door in the morning,
    Or tread in the bus on my toes?
Will it come like a change in the weather?
    Will its greeting be courteous or rough?
Will it alter my life altogether?
    O tell me the truth about love.

READING NOTES

'When we first read this story,' said Lee, 'I struggled to keep up with what was happening. The second time it made much more sense; it's not really like anything I have read before.' The group stopped often during the reading of the story to try and sort out what was happening. People talked about Marie's bad childhood experience and how important it was to her that she could call *her* children 'well-loved'. Jez said, 'Marie is never going to see that Callie loves her husband and her poor son. Social Services are going to get in there and take the boy away, that's for sure.' He went on, 'Callie is so right when she thinks, "maybe that's what love was: liking someone how he was and doing things to help him get even better." ' There was much discussion about whether it was right to take the boy out of the dangerously filthy house where he was chained up but sincerely loved.

What is the truth about love? Is there a truth to be told? The poem appears to be light-hearted and yet it asks one huge question by asking dozens of smaller ones, most of them ridiculous – why? Can you answer any of them? The group tried with mixed results but much enthusiasm.

Where You Go, I Will Go Too

THE BOOK OF RUTH

(EXTRACT FROM CHAPTER 1)

The Bible

(approximate reading time 4 minutes)

1: Now it came to pass in the days when the judges ruled, that there was a famine in the land. And a certain man of Beth-lehem-judah went to sojourn in the country of Moab, he, and his wife, and his two sons.

2: And the name of the man was Elimelech, and the name of his wife Naomi, and the name of his two sons Mahlon and Chilion, Ephrathites of Beth-lehem-judah. And they came into the country of Moab, and continued there.

3: And Elimelech Naomi's husband died; and she was left, and her two sons.

4: And they took them wives of the women of Moab; the name of the one was Orpah, and the name of the other Ruth: and they dwelled there about ten years.

5: And Mahlon and Chilion died also both of them; and the woman was left of her two sons and her husband.

6: Then she arose with her daughters in law, that she might return from the country of Moab: for she had heard in the country of Moab how that the Lord had visited his people in giving them bread.

7: Wherefore she went forth out of the place where she was, and her two daughters in law with her; and they went on the way to return unto the land of Judah.

8: And Naomi said unto her two daughters in law, Go, return each to her mother's house: the Lord deal kindly with you, as ye have dealt with the dead, and with me.

9: The Lord grant you that ye may find rest, each of you in the house of her husband. Then she kissed them; and they lifted up their voice, and wept.

10: And they said unto her, Surely we will return with thee unto thy people.

11: And Naomi said, Turn again, my daughters: why will ye go with me? are there yet any more sons in my womb, that they may be your husbands?

12: Turn again, my daughters, go your way; for I am too old to have an husband. If I should say, I have hope, if I should have an husband also to night, and should also bear sons;

13: Would ye tarry for them till they were grown? would ye stay for them from having husbands? nay, my daughters; for it grieveth me much for your sakes that the hand of the Lord is gone out against me.

14: And they lifted up their voice, and wept again: and Orpah kissed her mother in law; but Ruth clave unto her.

15: And she said, Behold, thy sister in law is gone back unto her people, and unto her gods: return thou after thy sister in law.

16: And Ruth said, Intreat me not to leave thee, or to return from following after thee: for whither thou goest, I will go; and where thou lodgest, I will lodge: thy people shall be my people, and thy God my God:

17: Where thou diest, will I die, and there will I be buried: the Lord do so to me, and more also, if ought but death part thee and me.

18: When she saw that she was stedfastly minded to go with her, then she left speaking unto her.

19: So they two went until they came to Beth-lehem. And it came to pass, when they were come to Beth-lehem, that all the city was moved about them, and they said, *Is* this Naomi?

THE BOOK OF RUTH AND NAOMI
Marge Piercy

When you pick up the Tanakh and read
the Book of Ruth, it is a shock
how little it resembles memory.
It's concerned with inheritance,
lands, men's names, how women
must wiggle and wobble to live.

Yet women have kept it dear
for the beloved elder who
cherished Ruth, more friend than
daughter. Daughters leave. Ruth
brought even the baby she made
with Boaz home as a gift.

Where you go, I will go too,
your people shall be my people,
I will be a Jew for you,
for what is yours I will love
as I love you, oh Naomi
my mother, my sister, my heart.

Show me a woman who does not dream
a double, heart's twin, a sister
of the mind in whose ear she can whisper,
whose hair she can braid as her life

twists its pleasure and pain and shame.
Show me a woman who does not hide
in the locket of bone that deep
eye beam of fiercely gentle love
she had once from mother, daughter,
sister; once like a warm moon
that radiance aligned the tides
of her blood into potent order.

At the season of first fruits, we recall
two travellers, co-conspirators, scavengers
making do with leftovers and mill ends,
whose friendship was stronger than fear,
stronger than hunger, who walked together,
the road of shards, hands joined.

READING NOTES

This combination has been read with both young members of reading groups and with care-home groups. A woman in her eighties remembered this Bible story from Sunday school and said she agreed with the first verse of the poem. 'I have forgotten many parts of Bible stories I once knew so well.' She repeated the vow of verse 16 softly to herself during the session. Most of the members of this group were themselves mothers-in-law and talked about that experience fondly – for the most part. Someone thought the word 'cherished' a lovely, underused word. Often people remark on the strength of the loving bond between the women and in a group of students, the line of the poem 'fiercely gentle love' was picked out, thought about and well-liked. This group liked the juxtaposition of ancient and modern and one said she would never have thought of reading a story from the Bible for pleasure. The closeness of love and friendship was discussed particularly in relation to the poem's description of 'friendship . . . stonger than fear, stronger than hunger'.

The Right Human Face

♥

ADAM BEDE

(THE MEETING ON THE HILL, CHAPTER 54)

George Eliot

(approximate reading time 14 minutes)

Adam Bede, a carpenter, has previously been in love with pretty Hetty Sorrel, but her life ended in tragedy. Now, as the novel draws to its conclusion in 1799, he has realised his enduring love for Dinah Morris, a Methodist lay preacher. He has proposed marriage, but Dinah, who has always loved Adam, has asked him to wait for an answer. After everything that has happened, she needs time to think about what she should do.

Adam understood Dinah's haste to go away, and drew hope rather than discouragement from it. She was fearful lest the strength of her feeling towards him should hinder her from waiting and listening faithfully for the ultimate guiding voice from within.

'I wish I'd asked her to write to me, though,' he thought. 'And yet even that might disturb her a bit, perhaps. She wants to be quite quiet in her old way for a while. And I've no right to be impatient and interrupting her with my wishes. She's told me what her mind is; and she's not a woman to say one thing and mean another. I'll wait patiently.'

That was Adam's wise resolution, and it throve excellently for the first two or three weeks on the nourishment it got from the remembrance of Dinah's confession that Sunday afternoon. There is a wonderful amount of sustenance in the first few words of love. But towards the middle of October the resolution began to dwindle perceptibly, and showed dangerous symptoms of exhaustion. The weeks were unusually long: Dinah must surely have had more than enough time to make up her mind. Let a woman say what she will after she has once told a man that she loves him, he is a little too flushed and exalted with that first draught she offers him to care much about the taste of the second. He treads the earth with a very elastic step as he walks away from her, and makes light of all difficulties. But that sort of glow dies out: memory gets sadly diluted with time, and is not strong enough to revive us. Adam was no longer so confident as he had been. He began to fear that perhaps Dinah's old life would have too strong a grasp upon her for any new feeling to triumph. If she had not felt this, she would surely have written to him to give him some comfort; but it appeared that she held it right to discourage him. As Adam's confidence waned, his patience waned with it, and he thought he must write himself; he must ask Dinah not to leave him in painful doubt longer than was needful. He sat up late one night to write her a letter, but the next morning he burnt it, afraid of its effect. It would be worse to have a discouraging answer by letter than from her own lips, for her presence reconciled him to her will.

You perceive how it was: Adam was hungering for the sight of Dinah, and when that sort of hunger reaches a certain stage, a lover is likely to still it though he may have to put his future in pawn.

But what harm could he do by going to Snowfield? Dinah could not be displeased with him for it: she had not forbidden him to go: she must surely expect that he would go before long. By the second Sunday in October this view of the case had become so clear to Adam, that he was already on his way to Snowfield, on horseback this time, for his hours were precious now, and he had borrowed Jonathan Burge's good nag for the journey.

What keen memories went along the road with him! He had often been to Oakbourne and back since that first journey to Snowfield, but beyond Oakbourne the grey-stone walls, the broken country, the meagre trees, seemed to be telling him afresh the story of that painful past which he knew so well by heart. But no story is the same to us after a lapse of time; or rather, we who read it are no longer the same interpreters; and Adam this morning brought with him new thoughts through that grey country – thoughts which gave an altered significance to its story of the past.

That is a base and selfish, even a blasphemous spirit, which rejoices and is thankful over the past evil that has blighted or crushed another, because it has been made a source of unfore-seen good to ourselves. Adam could never cease to mourn over that mystery of human sorrow which had been brought so close to him; he could never thank God for another's misery. And if I were capable of that narrow-sighted joy in Adam's behalf, I should still know he was not the man to feel it for himself.

He would have shaken his head at such a sentiment and said, 'Evil's evil, and sorrow's sorrow, and you can't alter it's nature by wrapping it up in other words. Other folks were not created for my sake, that I should think all square when things turn out well for me.'

But it is not ignoble to feel that the fuller life which a sad experience has brought us is worth our own personal share of pain: surely it is not possible to feel otherwise, any more than it would be possible for a man with a cataract to regret the painful process by which his dim blurred sight of men as trees walking had been exchanged for clear outline and effulgent day. The growth of higher feeling within us is like the growth of faculty, bringing with it a sense of added strength: we can no more wish to return to a narrower sympathy, than a painter or a musician can wish to return to his cruder manner, or a philosopher to his less complete formula.

Something like this sense of enlarged being was in Adam's mind this Sunday morning, as he rode along in vivid recollection of the past. His feeling towards Dinah, the hope of passing his life with her, had been the distant unseen point towards which that hard journey from Snowfield eighteen months ago had been leading him. Tender and deep as his love for Hetty had been – so deep that the roots of it would never be torn away – his love for Dinah was better and more precious to him; for it was the outgrowth of that fuller life which had come to him from his acquaintance with deep sorrow. 'It's like as if it was a new strength to me,' he said to himself, 'to love her, and know as she loves me. I shall look t' her to help me to see things right. For she's better than I am – there's less o' self in her, and pride. And it's a feeling as gives you a sort o' liberty, as if you could walk more fearless, when you've more trust in another than y' have in yourself. I've always been thinking I knew better than them as belonged to me, and that's a poor sort o' life, when you can't look to them nearest to you t' help you with a bit better thought than what you've got inside you a'ready.'

It was more than two o'clock in the afternoon when Adam came in sight of the grey town on the hill-side, and looked searchingly towards the green valley below, for the first glimpse of the old thatched roof near the ugly red mill. The scene looked less harsh in the soft October sunshine than it had in the eager time of early spring; and the one grand charm it possessed in common with all wide-stretching woodless regions – that it filled you with a new consciousness of the overarching sky – had a milder, more soothing influence than usual, on this almost cloudless day. Adam's doubts and fears melted under this influence, as the delicate web-like clouds had gradually melted away into the clear blue above him. He seemed to see Dinah's gentle face assuring him, with its looks alone, of all he longed to know.

He did not expect Dinah to be at home at this hour, but he got down from his horse and tied it at the little gate, that he might ask where she was gone to-day. He had set his mind on following her and bringing her home. She was gone to Sloman's End, a hamlet about three miles off, over the hill, the old woman told him: had set off directly after morning chapel, to preach in a cottage there, as her habit was. Anybody at the town would tell him the way to Sloman's End. So Adam got on his horse again and rode to the town, putting up at

the old inn and taking a hasty dinner there in the company
of the too chatty landlord, from whose friendly questions and
reminiscences he was glad to escape as soon as possible and
set out towards Sloman's End. With all his haste, it was nearly
four o'clock before he could set off, and he thought that as
Dinah had gone so early, she would perhaps already be near
returning. The little grey, desolate-looking hamlet, unscreened
by sheltering trees, lay in sight long before he reached it, and
as he came near he could hear the sound of voices singing a
hymn. 'Perhaps that's the last hymn before they come away,'
Adam thought. 'I'll walk back a bit and turn again to meet
her, further off the village.' He walked back till he got nearly
to the top of the hill again, and seated himself on a loose stone,
against the low wall, to watch till he should see the little black
figure leaving the hamlet and winding up the hill. He chose
this spot, almost at the top of the hill, because it was away
from all eyes – no house, no cattle, not even a nibbling sheep
near – no presence but the still lights and shadows, and the
great embracing sky.

She was much longer coming than he expected: he waited
an hour at least, watching for her and thinking of her, while
the afternoon shadows lengthened and the light grew softer. At
last he saw the little black figure coming from between the grey
houses, and gradually approaching the foot of the hill. Slowly,
Adam thought, but Dinah was really walking at her usual pace,
with a light quiet step. Now she was beginning to wind along
the path up the hill, but Adam would not move yet: he would
not meet her too soon: he had set his heart on meeting her
in this assured loneliness. And now he began to fear lest he

should startle her too much, 'Yet,' he thought, 'she's not one to be overstartled; she's always so calm and quiet, as if she was prepared for anything.'

What was she thinking of as she wound up the hill? Perhaps she had found complete repose without him, and had ceased to feel any need of his love. On the verge of a decision we all tremble: hope pauses with fluttering wings.

But now at last she was very near, and Adam rose from the stone wall. It happened that just as he walked forward, Dinah had paused and turned round to look back at the village: who does not pause and look back in mounting a hill? Adam was glad: for, with the fine instinct of a lover, he felt that it would be best for her to hear his voice before she saw him. He came within three paces of her and then said, 'Dinah!' She started without looking round, as if she connected the sound with no place. 'Dinah!' Adam said again. He knew quite well what was in her mind. She was so accustomed to think of impressions as purely spiritual monitions that she looked for no material visible accompaniment of the voice.

But this second time she looked round. What a look of yearning love it was that the mild grey eyes turned on the strong dark-eyed man! She did not start again at the sight of him; she said nothing, but moved towards him so that his arm could clasp her round.

And they walked on so in silence, while the warm tears fell. Adam was content, and said nothing. It was Dinah who spoke first.

'Adam,' she said, 'it is the Divine Will. My soul is so knit with yours that it is but a divided life I live without you. And this moment, now you are with me, and I feel that our hearts are filled with the same love, I have a fulness of strength to bear and do our heavenly Father's will, that I had lost before.'

Adam paused and looked into her sincere loving eyes.

'Then we'll never part any more, Dinah, till death parts us.'

And they kissed each other with a deep joy.

What greater thing is there for two human souls, than to feel that they are joined for life – to strengthen each other in all labour, to rest on each other in all sorrow, to minister to each other in all pain, to be one with each other in silent unspeakable memories at the moment of the last parting?

THE CONFIRMATION
Edwin Muir

Yes, yours, my love, is the right human face.
I in my mind had waited for this long,
Seeing the false and searching for the true,
Then found you as a traveller finds a place
Of welcome suddenly amid the wrong
Valleys and rocks and twisting roads. But you,
What shall I call you? A fountain in a waste,
A well of water in a country dry,
Or anything that's honest and good, an eye
That makes the whole world seem bright. Your open heart,
Simple with giving, gives the primal deed,
The first good world, the blossom, the blowing seed,
The hearth, the steadfast land, the wandering sea
Not beautiful or rare in every part,
But like yourself, as they were meant to be.

READING NOTES

Two passages in particular interested a breakfast reading group. The first, 'Evil's evil, and sorrow's sorrow, and you can't alter its nature by wrapping it up in other words.' The second, 'Tender and deep as his love for Hetty had been – so deep that the roots of it would never be torn away – his love for Dinah was better and more precious to him; for it was the outgrowth of that fuller life which had come to him from his acquaintance with deep sorrow.' Ted said he liked the idea of growing into a fuller life through experience. A woman told how she had thought she would never be able to love another man after her first husband died but she had, and therefore welcomed the words of Adam's experience. Someone said she did not like women vicars and then the discussion became heated.

A group leader notes: 'People have an initial reaction that the poem is beautiful without understanding why. The idea of the "right human face" is often discussed: how do you know the right face? Is there a right face for everyone? Is there only one right face . . .? How do you know if you are "seeing the false" – how can you tell? Someone talked about thinking they had found the right face and then subsequently divorcing, so it's not necessarily an easy thing to know. When we talk about the last two lines, the idea of being "like yourself, as they were meant to be", people often really like the idea that it is enough to simply be yourself with the right person. Adam loved Hetty but she was the wrong person for him. Dinah was the "true", and with each other they could be fully themselves.'

The Ring So Worn

♥

HOMESTEAD

(LAURA: BENT ELBOW HOMESTEAD 1977, CHAPTER 12)

Rosina Lippi

(approximate reading time 22 minutes)

Homestead is a novel of twelve linked stories set in a remote Austrian village and spanning the years 1907–77. The lives of the people are governed by farming and family and each story focuses on a moment in the life of a particular woman of the three clans of Rosenau. As well as a legal surname, most people are known by a clan name. This is the story of Bent Elbow's Martin's Laura and is the final story in the novel.

On the day Bent Elbow's Martin's Laura, once known as Kasparle's Laura, started the sixth month of her fourth pregnancy, two things happened: she stopped thinking all the time about the last baby, the lost one, and her wedding ring broke.

It was early evening when she took the children to pick up the milk cans from the stand at the side of the road, Annile scooting ahead down the narrow scythe of path that cut through the hayfields. Laura shifted Jakob on her hip and trudged after her daughter: her muscles twitched and her neck was slick with sweat, her hair heavy and damp under a kerchief shot through with hay dust. Once at the stand, she was glad to load the boy, heavy as he was, into the cart with the empty canisters.

They began to work their way back up the hill to the cowshed. Annile and Laura pushed steadily, heads bowed close together over the cart, bare feet splayed against the warmth of the road. At the top, where the path leveled out, Annile insisted that she could do it herself, so Laura stepped away, trying not to hover.

Annile leaned into the task, her small brown face screwed down upon itself in concentration, and in one good shove the cart tipped smartly sideways.

Laura reached in quick to right it before Jakob could tumble out; stepping back, she felt an odd sharpness against her palm. She looked down and there it was: her wedding ring broken in two against an angry welt on her finger. And she remembered the first summer they were married, how this very ring had flashed in the sunlight as it rose and fell with the rhythm of the hay rake. Now she put it in her pocket, dull and thin and rent beyond repair.

'Moved it pretty far that time,' Laura said to Annile. 'Run on now and get the cows in, your daddy's almost ready to start milking.'

Then she paused to look westward at the sky, wanting rain, thinking of how much housework she could get done on a cool, wet day with no fieldwork, thinking of a trip to town and of the watchmaker's little collection of rings. But on the western horizon, where the mountains gave reluctant way to the Rhine and the Rhine fed into the warm water of Lake

Constance, Laura saw deep blues seeping away into shades of rose. She reconciled herself to another afternoon in the hayfield.

Her mother-in-law would come to hay. She would bring the brothers with her. She would wield her rake like a sword, a dour slip of a woman moving in fits and starts among the five silent men who sailed through the field with great, generous motions. She would set them working faster with a sigh, a nod, a lifted eyebrow. All afternoon she would work like a demon beside Laura and never say a word, but when they were done she would stay behind to talk. She would stand in the middle of the kitchen and she would tell Laura about what was going on in the village, about the dinner she had cooked the pastor, her eyes darting here and there constantly: fly-specked window-panes, weeds in the garden, dust in the corners, runny noses, gray diapers.

A bare ring finger.

'You'll see,' Mikatrin had said to her before the wedding as she was moving out and Laura was moving in. 'You'll see how this place wears things down.'

Martin had brought Laura home on a rainy Sunday and said it straight out in the crowded kitchen where his younger brothers hunched over pork roast and dumplings, cabbage, apple salad, fresh tomatoes: they wanted to get married. The brothers turned to Laura, and she held up her head and met their looks, eye for eye. Rudi was the first to look away; the others dropped their heads too.

Then Mikatrin took Laura to see the third-floor apartment.

'A home inside a home,' Mikatrin said as they looked through the two rooms and a bath.

'Snug,' she added when they stood on the little balcony under the eaves where two lawn chairs had been set up cheek to jowl.

Mikatrin had made up the apartment for the tourists who wandered over the border from Germany for long weekends: dried flowers in a vase and a sheet of plastic over the red-checked tablecloth. Green flowered curtains with cows on the hem, a cookstove with two electric rings.

'You'll eat with us,' Mikatrin went on, flapping her handker-chief at a bit of dust on the dresser.

Laura looked out the window over the vegetable garden and the herd grazing on the wet slope of the mountain. Now she understood how things were ordered in this family: patched shoes but triple-A fodder; five brothers in one room, but an apartment for the tourists.

Mikatrin turned away from Laura and licked her finger to rub it against a fleck in the linoleum counter top. 'Martin's father was a good farmer,' she told Laura. 'A hard worker.'

Later, Laura drew on something hard and strong in herself and turned down the arrangement: she understood that there would be no sharing this household with her mother-in-law, that when she looked at herself in the mirror Mikatrin had hung in the little bathroom, she would see a woman who was becoming, day by day, more of a daughter and less of a wife.

'Times you'll wonder why,' was all Mikatrin said when Laura made her position known.

To her son, Mikatrin had more to say. But in the end Martin wanted Laura more than he needed to please his mother, and so they waited. They waited two years until each of the brothers had learned a trade: the twins went to apprentice with the cabinetmaker in Ackenau; Rudi built a shop where he could sell radios and tape players, mixers and electric meat slicers; Jok learned how to fix them. All four of them moved with Mikatrin into the little house that she had inherited from Miss Martha. Mikatrin learned to sleep late in the mornings and waited on customers in Rudi's shop when the mood took her, when she wasn't busy in her garden or tending the family graves. Mostly she made it her business to stay away from Bent Elbow, but when the haying was more than Martin and Laura could handle, she would gather the boys together and come for an afternoon.

The third-floor apartment was empty now; sometimes they rented it to skiers when the snow was good.

Laura had got what she wanted.

Now Laura watched her daughter sprint toward the grazing cows, whooping her own call to them, scolding in a high voice: 'Hi-ya, hi-ya, mind now! hi-ya!'

The baby laughed, his hands fluttering around his face, and Laura laughed with him, hefting him out of the cart to set him down among the chickens while she carried the milk cans to the barn door. Martin came out to meet her, still pulling himself into his milking gear. Together they watched Jakob crawl after a banty hen.

'Do you think he'll walk before the next one gets here?' he asked, leaning down over her shoulder to chafe her cheek with his stubble.

'Maybe,' Laura answered. She put her hand with its red welt against his cheek

'Look,' she said finally.

He took her hand and turned it palm up. 'Ma went through four rings, I think it was, before she stopped wearing them altogether,' he said.

Jakob squawked suddenly and Laura ran to scoop him up, and in that time Martin disappeared into the cowshed. She put the baby to her hip again and headed for the house.

'Laura!' Martin called after her, leaning out from the doorway.

She stopped, her fingers working the sharp edges of the ring in her apron pocket.

'Do you have time to look in on the sow?'

She nodded, feeling tears tangle in her eyelashes. Now what did you expect, she asked herself. Just what did you expect of him?

The pigpen was large because the sow was large, and growing larger: that was her function, to grow and produce the piglets that brought so much trouble and profit. There were two boxes, her big one with its trough and a smaller one with a warming lamp, connected by a sliding door that would only be opened at scheduled intervals to let the piglets in to suckle; they were not left in the large pen until they were old enough and smart enough to get out of the sow's way. Even so, one of them would get caught now and then and would have to be hauled out, limp and cold, from under the sleepy sow. If there seemed to be some spark left, the piglet would be put under the warming lamp to recover, because as Mikatrin liked to point out, pigs were tough animals and could stand a lot.

Laura leaned over the rail to have a closer look. The pen was quiet, removed from the constantly shifting weight of the cows, the nervous skittering of the calves: the sow at the height of her term was the heavy heart of the barn. She rested uneasily, grumbling softly when Laura rubbed a hand over the small bright eyes. The animal could go into labor at any time; tonight Laura would alternate between bed and barn, relieving Martin every few hours to keep watch.

In the front hall the wildflowers she had arranged so carefully in a pottery case on the oak chest were drooping, shedding petals in a lazy arc over the floor. Laura watched them fall, then turned and went into the kitchen, warm in the late afternoon sun and buzzing with flies. There were piles of dishes on the washboard, toys scattered everywhere, a basket of ironing and another of mending. From the open window came the sounds of sheets snapping in the breeze and a soft, full thud as a pear fell to the ground.

A little more of the brightness went out of her.

'Come on,' she said suddenly to Annile, who watched from the door. 'There's more than an hour of sun left, we're going for a walk.' She settled Jakob more firmly on her hip and took his sun hat from the peg on the wall.

They played hooky, hurrying up the old stone path that led through the homestead pasture, then into the woods and up to Hutla Meadow and beyond to the rough cliffs of the Praying Hands.

'Can I help when the piglets come, Mama?'

'A-yo,' Laura said slowly. 'If they come in the daylight.'

On a cold March morning the old sow had started to farrow her last litter before sunrise. Annile had been put on duty fresh out of bed; Laura went out with her to see her settled into the pen. The sow shifted and growled, and a shiny packet slid out: the piglet in its birth sac. It was an early one and strong; it fought its way out on its own. Those to come after might not be so keen: when one appeared, Annile was to yell for her father and Martin would come leaping over animals and milking stools to peel the sac away. Laura showed Annile how to lift the sow's tail to check for progress, and then she went back to the kitchen and her baking.

When they came in to breakfast together, Martin was carrying a cold, limp piglet. The oven had cooled down some, and Laura put him on a tray and slid him in. They might have forgotten him if he hadn't started squealing as they sat down to breakfast. Martin took him back to the litter fully recovered.

'How'd that happen?' Laura asked him when he returned to the table.

'Just one of those things.' He never even looked at the child hanging her head over her milk cup.

Laura saw this. She imagined Annile asleep in the warm, steamy stall: the windows streaky with the moisture of animal respiration; the heavy, sweet smells of hay and dung and hot milk thick in the air; Annile's head propped against the wall of the pigpen; Annile lulled away to sleep by the rhythmic rush of milk onto metal. Getting up to fill the jug from the bucket Martin had brought in that morning, Laura paused to run her hand through his hair.

She was thinking about this, about the feel of Martin's hair, when they came to a wire fence. Laura lifted it so that the child could shimmy under, stepping over it herself. The ground grew marshy, and then there was a spring.

They settled themselves on a log propped across the small expanse of water, and Laura eased her swollen feet in, hiccupping at the shock and trying to balance the struggling baby on her lap. He fussed at her until she set him down on the bank. Working his bottom and fists into the mud, he rewarded her with a smile and a grunt.

'Look at the mess,' Annile complained. 'Old muddy-butt Jakob.'

'What d'you want him, muddy or cranky?'

Annile shrugged.

Laura reached down into the spring to let a tadpole slip into her palms; she felt the tentative life shivering there as she had once felt these children who were now irreversibly, inexplicably distant from her tremble within her; as she felt life there now, strong and growing stronger every day.

With both the children labor had come down hard on her while Martin rushed to finish the morning milking. With Jakob things had moved too fast, and she had waited for Martin bent double to keep herself from pushing. Then they had raced all the way to the midwife, Martin pressing the car into an arthritic and reluctant gallop, slowing down only once as they drove through the church square to yell out the window to Rudi, who was sweeping the walk in front of his shop, that he should send Mikatrin out to Bent Elbow, where they had left Annile asleep in her crib and the cows impatient to get to pasture.

And when they got to Ackenau and the midwife's, Laura hadn't been able to get out of the car. Martin had seen how it was with her and leaned in to snatch her up. Taking the steps two at a time, never breathing hard, he put her down gently as he stepped across the doorsill, where she bent into a bow just in time to catch the child herself, hot and wet and reeking of the womb. The midwife had stood there with her hands outspread, torn between distress and irritation.

It had put a scare into both of them; at the time, Laura couldn't imagine ever being so scared again. Then, the following winter, she woke in the middle of the night, the bedclothes sticky with her own blood, and she learned better. The day she got home from the hospital with the picture of her fragile, pale curl of a baby still burning in her mind, Mikatrin had been waiting.

'I lost my first when she was four,' she reminded Laura. 'Lost two more after that, both early, like yours.' She busied herself folding towels.

'Three times,' Laura whispered, waiting for her to say more.

With her back to Laura, Mikatrin said, 'It's what you wanted, isn't it? It's the life you wanted.'

Laura held out her hands to show her daughter the tadpole: a gift, a vision. Annile wanted to drink from her cupped palms.

'No, he'll jump out,' Laura said, but she tilted her hands toward the small red mouth. The tadpole leapt frantically, striking the startled child in the cheek, and fell back into the spring.

The water rippled and danced; Laura saw her reflection shift. She looked into the water and watched it draw the picture of a younger woman, a woman in a dark green dress edged with white lace at the throat, her hair long and glossy and well kept, her hands smooth and white, her nails clean and even.

'Who's that?' her daughter asked, following her mother's gaze, wanting to play this old game, to hear her mother's dreams.

'Why, that's a young woman I know,' Laura answered. 'A teacher.'

'Tell me about her, Mama.'

She pulled the child up closer to her on the log, cast an eye at the baby digging in the mud. 'Well, let's see. She's just started teaching. She found a little apartment all to herself with a view of the Three Sisters, way off. Sometimes she just reads away the evenings in a big comfortable chair. She likes to sew, she sewed a dress to wear to a dance. Her beau comes on Friday nights in a dark gray suit and sometimes they go out to eat. Once in a while she takes a trip. Greece, to swim in the sea.'

Annile thought for a good time.

'Have you ever been there?'

'No, I haven't. Bought a book about Greece, though. I gave it to your great-great-aunt Johanna when I was a girl.'

'Is the teacher lady you?'

Laura stroked the child's hair away from her face and looked back into the depths of the spring.

'No, that was never me. But maybe it'll be you, sometime. Maybe you can take up where your great-aunt Martha left off. She was a fine teacher.'

'Gran says I'll be a farmer's wife,' Annile volunteered.

Mikatrin.

I never took off and left a kitchen full of work to be done, Laura imagined Mikatrin saying.

But they're little for such a short time, she answered, even as she gathered her children to her to start back.

The day ebbed, but they walked slowly. At the turn of the path where it left the woods, Laura hesitated. Annile sat down in a patch of wildflowers, spotty now as the summer wore away. Laura looked at the Three Sisters, the meadows, the busy expanse of their small homestead, an oasis in an eternity of trees and hills, green layer upon layer in shades of the coming night. And in the shadows lengthening on the vegetable garden she saw children playing: the child she had lost, grown sturdy and up to mischief, peeking out from leafy corners in an endless game of hide-and-seek; the other children she would bear or lose before she was forty; the grandchildren who would come soon after.

From this good distance Laura watched Martin as he loaded the cans, now filled with fresh milk, onto the tractor to take them down to the stand for pickup. She knew that he was ticking off chores to himself, counting the time until he could put aside the work and come in to the house to sit with her in the circle of light in the kitchen.

If only he would look up, he would see them there, watching him.

He bent over the tractor hitch.

I wish my mother had took us walking in the evening, she imagined him saying.

So do I, she answered him.

And a sea of wanting him washed over her, left her shaking: he must come looking for her, he must put his arms around her and see what she saw. Laura wanted him to climb the path to them in his long, quick stride; she saw him smiling, reaching out to take their sleeping, muddy boy, pausing to run a hand over the growing curve of her belly.

Let me, she heard him say. *Rest your arms.*

And: *Tomorrow we'll just go see about a new wedding ring.*

What about the hay? she asked him.

It can wait, he said.

After a time, she knew that it could not, that he could not, and she shook herself, and went down to him.

HIS LATE WIFE'S WEDDING-RING
George Crabbe

The ring so worn, as you behold,
So thin, so pale, is yet of gold:
The passion such it was to prove;
Worn with life's care, love yet was love.

READING NOTES

'It seems to me that the pregnant pig is going to get more attention than the pregnant woman,' said one reader; 'I love it when she just says sod it to the dishes and goes for a walk.' The women's group talked about how hard Laura's life seemed to be and how difficult it is to get by without affection. The strong silent type of man was not much admired. There was discussion about Mikatrin's question, 'It's the life you wanted', and about mothers-in-law in general, and people thought hard about whether Laura was happy or not. 'She knows him', said another reader, 'well enough to know that he would never say the hay can wait. I think she would have known that before they were married. It is like the poem says, the ring is worn with life's care but that proves the strength and endurance of love. I think she loves him still.' There was discussion about being loved and how it might not always be in the way we might want. The poem prompted people's stories and memories about their rings or their mothers' rings. The group was delighted with the piglet put into the oven but concerned that it might be bacon when it came out.

All You Have Lost

UNDER STORM'S WING
(EXTRACT FROM WORLD WITHOUT END, CHAPTER 17)
Helen Thomas with Myfanwy Thomas

(approximate reading time 12 minutes)

Helen Thomas was the wife of the poet Edward Thomas. He enlisted in the British army in 1915 and was killed in action, aged thirty-nine, during the Battle of Arras, 9 April, Easter Monday, 1917. In the first extract he has been home on leave and this is his last night before returning to France.

We lay, all night, sometimes talking of our love and all that had been, and of the children, and what had been amiss and what right. We knew the best was that there had never been untruth between us. We knew all of each other, and it was right. So talking and crying and loving in each other's arms we fell asleep as the cold reflected light of the snow crept through the frost-covered windows.

Edward got up and made the fire and brought me some tea, and then got back into bed, and the children clambered in, too, and sat in a row sipping our tea. I was not afraid of crying any more. My tears had been shed, my heart was empty, stricken with something that tears would not express or comfort. The gulf had been bridged. Each bore the other's suffering. We concealed nothing, for all was known between us. After breakfast, while he showed me where his account books were and what each was for, I listened calmly, and unbelievingly he kissed me when I said I, too, would keep accounts. 'And here are my poems. I've copied them all out in this book for you, and the last of all is for you. I wrote it last night, but don't read it now . . . It's still freezing. The ground is like iron, and more snow has fallen. The children will come to the station with me; and now I must be off.'

We were alone in my room. He took me in his arms, holding me tightly to him, his face white, his eyes full of a fear I had never seen before. My arms were round his neck. 'Beloved, I love you,' was all I could say. 'Helen, Helen, Helen,' he said, 'remember that, whatever happens, all is well between us for ever and ever.' And hand in hand we went downstairs and out to the children, who were playing in the snow.

A thick mist hung everywhere, and there was no sound except, far away in the valley, a train shunting. I stood at the gate watching him go; he turned back to wave until the mist and hill hid him. I heard his old call coming up to me: 'Coo-ee!' he called. 'Coo-ee!' I answered, keeping my voice strong to call again. Again through the muffled air came his 'Coo-ee'. And again went my answer like an echo. 'Coo-ee' came fainter next time with the hill between us, but my 'Coo-ee' went out of my lungs strong enough to pierce to him as he strode away from me. 'Coo-ee!' So faint now, it might only be my own call flung back from the thick air and muffling snow. I put my hands up to my mouth to make a trumpet, but no sound came. Panic seized me, and I ran through the mist and the snow to the top of the hill, and stood there a moment dumbly, with straining eyes and ears. There was nothing but the mist and snow and the silence of death.

Then with leaden feet which stumbled in a sudden darkness that overwhelmed me I groped my way back to the empty house.

Extracts from letters from Helen Thomas to her friend Janet Hooton:

4 April 1917

High Beech nr. Loughton

. . . I hear very often from Edward, splendid letters full of his work and his life and also of that absolute assurance that all is so well between us that that is all that really matters come what may. And I write long cheery letters to him, all about our little doings and interests, and the children and the country, and for both of us the post is the event of the day.

I think he is just wonderful, doing his soldier's work as well as ever he can, and yet still the poet too delighting in what beauty there is there, and *he* finds beauty where no one else would find it and it's good for his soul and he needs it. He gets little time for depression, and so do I. That awful fear is always clutching at my heart, but I put it away time after time, and keep at my work and think of his homecoming. The real thing that matters is eternal, but Oh tho' my soul is perfectly content, my poor old body does want him. My eyes and ears and hands long for him, and nearly every night I dream he has come and we are together once again. But I can wait easily enough if only my beloved will come to me at last. If I knew he would come how easy would be this interval! Oh Janet how lucky you and Mary and all the other women I know are who have got their men safe and sound, I can't imagine what the war means to them. And yet I know how we do feel it all those fine young lives and all the terror and horror and vileness of it. And then too our pockets. We just scramble along somehow, I just making ends meet and wondering how I can do it next month when things are still dearer and what I can cut out next of our already so very simple menu and general expenditure. Isn't it difficult? But nothing matters to me I don't care how I have to work and manage and scrimp and scrape in fact I'm glad I have to do it, I'm glad I, like my dear man, have material troubles as well as those others, and if at the end he comes back to me safe and sound and we can start life again how worth while it will all have been.

And it will be a new start for him you know. The army at least provides a small income, not enough but something anyway. When he's out of it we shall have nothing and he will have to make a place for himself and all the old struggle over again.

Well surely the end is in sight.

Thank you dear for thinking of me and Myfanwy. Give me another chance sometime. I get *so* tired for I do everything here, washing and all and never have a bit of help, and I'm not quite the untirable horse I used to be. Still, I'm game for a good bit more.

My dear love to Harry and the children and your dear old self from

Helen

On the morning of Easter Day, Edward added a brief line to a letter to Helen written the night before: 'Sunday: I slept jolly well and now it is sunshine and wind and we are in for a long day and I must post this when I can. All and always yours, Edwy'.

In England it had been a hard winter and spring came late that year in a sudden burst of flowers and warm clear skies. Just a few days after her previous letter, Helen wrote again to her friend Janet and her husband, Harry. She wanted to tell them, before they saw it in the newspapers, that her beloved Edwy had been killed on Easter Monday. He had been their loving friend and she knew what the news would mean to them. Helen wrote that she was trying to 'hold steadfastly to life' in the hope that this would bring peace to her soul, just as Edward must now be at peace.

14 May 1917

c/o Mrs Lock Ellis
Selsfield House, East Grinstead

My dear old Janet,

It's only quite lately that I've felt able to write to any of the numerous friends who have written to me and helped me through these terrible days that so nearly were utter despair.

Here is country that he knew and loved and among friends in whose lives he made an unfillable place a great peace has come to me. His great strong tender arms have lifted my soul out of despair, and he and I are one again, our love unchanged and eternal. Sometimes the pain comes back, terrible, soul rending, but it is as if he took my hand in his dear one and gave me fresh courage to live again the life he would have me live, happy and carefree with the children. I try to remember how rich I am in his love and his spirit and in all those wonderful years, and so forget that I am poor in not having his voice and touch and help. I *am* rich. What a man is mine, above all other men. How little he guessed dear boy what a place he had in the very hearts of his friends. He exacted all or nothing, and those who knew him loved him with a love surpassing anything I have ever known of. All kinds – men and women, great and small, rich and poor, clever and simple, they loved him as very few men are loved. And now because of their love for him it is poured on me. I am enfolded by it, Oh it is wonderful. I send you a copy of the letter his commanding officer wrote to me. It is above all letters precious to me in its simple sincerity and the characteristic picture it gives of my beloved. The very last letter I had from him was written the day before death came, and it was bubbling with happiness and eagerness and love. My God how rich I am in such love. 'He has awakened from the dream of life' and someday like the prince in the story he will kiss me to waking and we shall be together again as we never conceived, closer closer than ever we have been, one in body and soul, one in essence.

Janet dear I can't undertake the children. A great weakness came to my body, it failed me as it never had before, and I don't feel able yet to face my own little affairs and cannot think of taking on more than I have. Thank you for thinking of it, later perhaps I could but not yet.

I shall be in town before long, and will come and see you and old Hallow. May I? I want to keep in touch with all that he loved and that loved him, people and places and things, and you are our old friends.

I'll write no more now dear. Goodnight to you both my two dear friends. Pray for me for indeed sometimes my courage goes and the way seems too far and lonely. Only sometimes because I get tired and full of pain, really he is so near me we speak to each other and I have but to put out my hand and he takes it. He is my all, my life, all all to me.

Helen

AND YOU, HELEN
Edward Thomas

And you, Helen, what should I give you?
So many things I would give you
Had I an infinite great store
Offered me and I stood before
To choose. I would give you youth,
All kinds of loveliness and truth,
A clear eye as good as mine,
Lands, waters, flowers, wine,
As many children as your heart
Might wish for, a far better art
Than mine can be, all you have lost
Upon the travelling waters tossed,
Or given to me. If I could choose
Freely in that great treasure-house
Anything from any shelf,
I would give you back yourself,
And power to discriminate
What you want and want it not too late,
Many fair days free from care
And heart to enjoy both foul and fair,
And myself, too, if I could find
Where it lay hidden and it proved kind.

READING NOTES

These letters and memories are terribly sad. But despite the sadness, people have found a real sense of comfort in them for the powerful love they demonstrate and the courage and strength to go on with life. A breakfast group talked about the trenches on the western front and were amazed that people could write poetry in such conditions. They also admired the bravery involved in having to go back to France after a leave, when you knew exactly what you were going back to. In a one-to-one reading, a man newly in residential care thought very highly of Helen's continuing feeling of richness and her determination to honour her husband's memory by believing he was ever with her. He was touched by Edward's showing his wife the accounts and her listening unbelieving. 'She knew he was really saying, "In case I am killed".'

People frequently like that we hear Edward's voice in return. They usually think the poem anticipates his death as if he knew it would happen. The final lines make people wonder about the character of the man. Was he lacking in confidence, afraid or simply resigned, and why does he say 'if . . . it proved kind'? What does he mean by 'kind' and how might Helen take it?

Two Poems: If I Should Go Away

SONG
John Donne

Sweetest love, I do not go
    For weariness of thee,
Nor in hope the world can show
    A fitter love for me;
        But since that I
Must die at last, 'tis best
To use myself in jest
    Thus by fained deaths to die.

Yesternight the sun went hence,
    And yet is here today,
He hath no desire nor sense,
    Nor half so short a way:
        Then fear not me,
But believe that I shall make
Speedier journeys, since I take
    More wings and spurs than he.

O how feeble is man's power,
   That if good fortune fall,
Cannot add another hour,
    Nor a lost hour recall!
      But come bad chance,
And we join to it our strength,
And we teach it art and length,
   Itself o'er us to advance.

When thou sigh'st, thou sigh'st not wind,
   But sigh'st my soul away,
When thou weep'st, unkindly kind,
   My life's blood doth decay.
     It cannot be
That thou lov'st me, as thou say'st,
If in thine my life thou waste,
   That art the best of me.

Let not thy divining heart
   Forethink me any ill;
Destiny may take thy part,
   And may thy fears fulfil;
    But think that we
Are but turned aside to sleep;
They who one another keep
   Alive, ne'er parted be.

POSTSCRIPT: FOR GWENO
Alun Lewis

If I should go away,
Beloved, do not say
'He has forgotten me'.
For you abide,
A singing rib within my dreaming side;
You always stay.
And in the mad tormented valley
Where blood and hunger rally
And Death the wild beast is uncaught, untamed,
Our soul withstands the terror
And has its quiet honour
Among the glittering stars your voices named.

READING NOTES

Alun Lewis was a soldier in the Second World War. In a lunchtime reading group Phil said he had read several poems from the First World War but nothing from the Second, and we wondered why that should be. There was a conversation about the difference it would make to our reading and understanding of the poem if we had not known Lewis's history. People liked and thought about the line: 'you abide,/a singing rib within my dreaming side'. But the last line was a puzzle: why 'voices' and not 'voice'?

We took the John Donne poem very slowly as it felt quite hard at first but Phil supposed that the person in 'Song' was going away out of duty, perhaps even to war as in 'Postscript', and not because he wanted to end the relationship. There was real recognition of the truth of the third verse. When we are happy we hardly take the time to say to ourselves 'I am really happy', but some of us can make the bad times last longer than need be by dwelling on them or feeling sorry for ourselves. The fourth verse was the hardest for us. We talked about the term 'unkindly kind' and thought he was probably saying that he sees that she cries because she wants to be with him, but that it hurts him to see her upset. The group admired the skilful way he turned things round – it can't be you really love me as you say you do. At the end of the session Alison said that this poem had really stumped her at first but that she had thoroughly enjoyed teasing out the meaning with the group. 'I would never have done that on my own.'

The Rest of What We Do

♥

YOURS
Mary Robison

(approximate reading time 6 minutes)

Allison struggled away from her white Renault, limping with the weight of the last of the pumpkins. She found Clark in the twilight on the twig- and-leaf-littered porch, behind the house. He wore a tan wool shawl. He was moving up and back in a cushioned glider, pushed by the ball of his slippered foot.

Allison lowered a big pumpkin and let it rest on the porch floor.

Clark was much older than she – seventy-eight to Allison's thirty-five. They had been married for four months. They were both quite tall, with long hands, and their faces looked something alike. Allison wore a natural-hair wig. It was a thick blonde hood around her face. She was dressed in bright-dyed denims today. She wore durable clothes, usually, for she volunteered afternoons at a children's day-care center.

She put one of the smaller pumpkins on Clark's long lap. 'Now, nothing surreal,' she told him. 'Carve just a *regular* face. These are for the kids.'

In the foyer, on the Hepplewhite desk, Allison found the maid's chore list, with its cross-offs, which included Clark's supper. Allison went quickly through the day's mail: a garish coupon packet, a flyer advertising white wines at Jamestown Liquors, November's pay-TV program guide, and – the worst thing, the funniest – an already opened, extremely unkind letter from Clark's married daughter, up North. 'You're an old fool,' Allison read, and, 'You're being cruelly deceived.' There was a gift check for Clark, enclosed – his birthday had just passed – but it was uncashable. It was signed 'Jesus H. Christ.'

Late, late into this night, Allison and Clark gutted and carved the pumpkins together, at an old table set on the back porch. They worked over newspaper after soggy newspaper, using paring knives and spoons and a Swiss Army knife Clark liked for the exact shaping of teeth and eyes and nostrils. Clark had been a doctor – an internist – but he was also a Sunday watercolor painter. His four pumpkins were expressive and artful. Their carved features were suited to the sizes and shapes of the pumpkins. Two looked ferocious and jagged. One registered surprise. The last was serene and beaming.

Allison's four faces were less deftly drawn, with slits and areas of distortion. She had cut triangles for noses and eyes. The mouths she had made were all just wedges – two turned up and two turned down.

By one A.M., they were finished. Clark, who had bent his long torso forward to work, moved over to the glider again and looked out sleepily at nothing. All the neighbors' lights were out across the ravine. For the season and time, the Virginia night was warm. Most of the leaves had fallen and blown away already, and the trees stood unbothered. The moon was round, above them.

Allison cleaned up the mess.

'Your jack-o'-lanterns are much much better than mine,' Clark said to her.

'Like hell,' Allison said.

'Look at me,' Clark said, and Allison did. She was holding a squishy bundle of newspapers. The papers reeked sweetly with the smell of pumpkin innards. 'Yours are *far* better,' he said.

'You're wrong. You'll see when they're lit,' Allison said.

She went inside, came back with yellow vigil candles. It took her a while to get each candle settled into a pool of its own melted wax inside the jack-o'-lanterns, which were lined up in a row on the porch railing. Allison went along and relit each candle and fixed the pumpkin lids over the little flames. 'See?' she said. They sat together a moment and looked at the orange faces.

'We're exhausted. It's good-night time,' Allison said. 'Don't blow out the candles. I'll put in new ones tomorrow.'

In her bedroom, a few weeks earlier in her life than had been predicted, she began to die. 'Don't look at me if my wig comes off,' she told Clark. 'Please.' Her pulse cords were fluttering under his fingers. She raised her knees and kicked away the comforter. She said something to Clark about the garage being locked.

At the telephone, Clark had a clear view out back and down to the porch. He wanted to get drunk with his wife once more. He wanted to tell her, from the greater perspective he had, that to own only a little talent, like his, was an awful, plaguing thing;

that being only a little special meant you expected too much, most of the time, and liked yourself too little. He wanted to assure her that she had missed nothing.

Clark was speaking into the phone now. He watched the jack-o'-lanterns. The jack-o'-lanterns watched him.

LOVE POEM WITH TOAST
Miller Williams

Some of what we do, we do
to make things happen,
the alarm to wake us up, the coffee to perc,
the car to start.

The rest of what we do, we do
trying to keep something from doing something,
the skin from aging, the hoe from rusting,
the truth from getting out.

With yes and no like the poles of a battery
powering our passage through the days,
we move, as we call it, forward,
wanting to be wanted,
wanting not to lose the rain forest,
wanting the water to boil,
wanting not to have cancer,
wanting to be home by dark,
wanting not to run out of gas,

as each of us wants the other
watching at the end,
as both want not to leave the other alone,
as wanting to love beyond this meat and bone,
we gaze across breakfast and pretend.

READING NOTES

After reading the story, people have talked about Halloween, cancer, breakfast, sons and daughters who can't accept their parents' second marriages, and even aging skin, but mostly people want to talk about truth. In such a short, short story, so much detail is revealed. There are glimpses of things but the truth of the whole is tantalisingly elusive. The moment when the husband makes his wife look at him when he repeats that her pumpkins are better than his seems for many to be an important moment of truth between them, even if it is superficially about pumpkins. There is usually some puzzlement and disagreement about the ending of both the poem and the story. Sam said he found the poem very thought-provoking, particularly the way the big wants went side by side with the trivial. He said he thought the pretending in the last line of the poem was pretending that everything would be all right – 'because the poem is titled "Love Poem"'. Not everyone agreed with him.

Always This Infinity Between Us

♥

THE AGE OF GRIEF

(EXTRACT)

Jane Smiley

(approximate reading time 12 minutes)

Dave and Dana are dentists. They live a good life with three young children, Lizzie, Stephanie and Leah, until Dave begins to suspect that Dana is having an affair. He decides that to challenge her would mean the certain end of their marriage and so he keeps silent. Meanwhile day-to-day family and working life must go on. Dave recounts their story in the novella and at this point they are all staying in their weekend house in the country.

For someone who has been married so long, I remember what it was like to be single quite well. It was like riding a little moped down a country road, hitting every bump, laboring up every hill. Marriage is like a semi, or at least a big pickup truck jacked up on fat tires. It barrels over everything in its path, zooming with all the purpose of great weight and importance into the future. When I was single, it seemed to me that I made up my future every time I registered for classes. After I paid my fees, I looked down at that little $4,000 card in my hand and felt the glow of relief. It was not that I was closer to being a dentist. That was something I couldn't imagine. It was that four more months of the future were visible, if only just. At the end of every term, the future dropped away, leaving me gasping.

Dana, however, always had plans. She would talk about them in bed after we had made love. She talked so concretely about each one, whether it was giving up dentistry and going to Mazatlán, or whether it was having Belgian waffles for breakfast if only we could get up two hours hence, at five thirty, in time to make it to the pancake house before our early classes, that it seemed to me that all I had to do was live and breathe. The future was a scene I only had to walk into. What a relief. And that is what it has been like for thirteen years now. I had almost forgotten that old vertigo. I think I must have thought I had grown out of it.

The day after I stayed up all night, which I spent working around the country house, clearing up dead tree limbs and other trash, pruning back this and that, the future dropped away entirely, and I could not even have said whether I would be at my stool, picking up my tools, the next morning. The very biological inertia that propelled me around the property, and from meal to meal, was amazing to me. I was terrified. I was like a man who keeps totting up the days that the sun has risen and making odds on whether it will rise again, who can imagine only too well the deepening cold of a sunless day. I gather that I was rather forbidding, to boot, because everyone stayed away from me except Leah, who clambered after me, dragging sticks and picking up leaves, and keeping up a stream of talk in her most man-pleasing tones.

Dana supported her spirits, and theirs, with a heroic and visible effort. They drove to one of the bigger supermarkets, about twenty miles away, and brought everything back from the deli that anyone could possibly have wanted – bagels, cream cheese mixed with lox, cream cheese mixed with walnuts and raisins, French doughnuts, croissants with chocolate in them, swordfish steaks for later, to be grilled with basil, heads of Buttercrunch lettuce, raspberry vinegar and olive oil, bottles of seltzer for Lizzie's stomach, *The New York Times*, the Chicago *Tribune*, for the funny papers. She must have thought she could lose herself in service, because she was up and down all day, getting one child this and another child that, dressing them so that they could go out for five minutes, complain of the cold, and be undressed again. She read them about six books and fiddled constantly with the TV reception. She sat on the couch and lured them into piling on top of her, as if the warmth of human flesh could help her. She was always smiling at them, and there was the panting of effort about everything she did. I wondered what he had done to her, to give her this desperation. Even so, I stayed out of the way. Any word would be like a spark in a dynamite factory. I kept Leah out of her hair. That is what I did for her, that is the service I lost myself in.

At dinner, when we sat across from each other at the old wooden table, she did not lift her eyes to my face. The portions she served me were generous, and they rather shamed me, as they reminded me of my size and my lifelong greed for food.

I complained about the fish. It was a little undercooked. Well, it *was* a little undercooked, but I didn't have to say it. That was the one time she looked at me, and it was a look of concentrated annoyance, to which I responded with an aggressive stare. About eight we drove back to town. I remember that drive perfectly, too. Leah was sleeping in her car seat beside me, Lizzie was in the back, and Dana had Stephanie in her car. At stoplights, my glances in the rearview mirror gave me a view of her unyielding head. At one point, when I looked at her too long and missed the turning of the light, she beeped her horn. Lizzie said that her stomach hurt. I said, 'You can stand it until we get home,' and Lizzie fell silent at once, hearing the hardness in my voice. It was one of those drives that you remember from your own childhood and swear you will never have, so frightening, that feeling of everything wrong but nothing visibly different, of no future. But of course, there is a future, plenty of future for the results of this drive to reveal themselves, like a long virus that visits the child as a simple case of chicken pox and returns over and over to the adult as a painful case of shingles.

I should say that what I do remember about Dana, from the beginning, is a long stream of talk. I don't, as a rule, like to talk. That's why I preferred those rubber dams.[1] That is why I like Laura. Dana is right, people who don't talk and rarely smile seem threatening. I am like my mother in this, not my father, whose hardware store was a place where a lot of men talked. They wandered among the bins of traps and U joints and washers and caulk, and they talked with warmth and

[1]   a latex sheet used in dentistry

enthusiasm, but also with cool expertise, about the projects they were working on. My father walked with them, drawing them out about the details, then giving advice about products. When my father was sick or out of town, my mother worked behind the counter and receipts plummeted. 'I don't know' – that's what she answered to every question. And she didn't. She didn't know what there was or where it might be or how you might do something. It was not that she didn't want to know, but you would think it was from the way she said it: 'Sorry, I don't know.' Snap. Her eyelids dropped and her lips came together. I suspect that 'I don't know' is the main sentiment of most people who don't talk. Maybe 'I don't know, please tell me.' That was my main sentiment for most of my boyhood. And Dana did. She told me everything she was thinking, and bit by bit I learned to add something here and there. I didn't know, for example, until the other night that I don't smile as much as most people. She told me. Now I know.

What is there to say about her voice. It is hollow. There is a vibration in it, as of two notes, one slightly higher than the other, sounding at the same time. This makes her singing voice very melodious, but the choir director doesn't often let her sing solo. He gives someone with purer tones the solo part, and has Dana harmonize. These small groups of two or three are often complimented after the choir concerts. It is in this hollow in her voice that I imagine the flow of that thirteen-year stream of talk. She is a talker. I suppose she is talking now to him, since I won't let her talk to me.

Monday night, after a long, silent day in the office to the accompaniment of extra care by the office staff that made me very uncomfortable, we went to bed in silence. She woke up cursing. 'Oh,' she said, 'oh shit. Ouch.' I could feel her reaching for her feet. When we were first married, she used to get cramps in her insteps from pointing her toes in her sleep. Some say this is a vitamin deficiency. I don't know. Anyway, I slithered under the covers and grabbed her feet. What you do is bend the toes and ankles back, and then massage the instep until the knot goes away. Massage by itself doesn't work at all; you have to hold on to the toes so that they don't point by mistake, for about five minutes. I did. She let me. While I was holding on to her feet I felt such a welling up of desire and pain and grief that I began to heave with dry sobs. 'Dave,' she said. 'Dave.' Her hollow voice was regretful and full of sorrow. In the hot dark under the covers, I ran my thumbs over her insteps and pushed back her toes with my fingers. Your wife's feet are not something, as a rule, that you are tactilely familiar with, and I hadn't had much to do with her feet for eight or nine years, so maybe I was subject to some sort of sensual memory, but it seemed to me that I was twenty-five years old and ragingly greedy for this darling person whom I had had the luck to fool into marrying me. Except that I wasn't, and I knew I wasn't, and that ten minutes encompassed ten years, and I was about to be lost. When the cramps were out of her feet, I knelt up and threw off the covers, and said, 'Oh, God! Dana, I'm sorry I'm me!' That's what I said. It just came out. She grabbed me by the shoulders and pulled me down on top of her and hugged me tightly, and said in a much evener voice, 'I'm not sorry you're you.'

And so, how could she tell me then? She couldn't, and didn't. I think she was sorry I was me, sorry that I wasn't him in bed with her. But when husbands express grief and fear, wives automatically comfort them, and they are automatically comforted. Years ago, such an exchange of sorrow would have sent us into a frenzy of lovemaking. It did not this time. She held me and kissed my forehead, and I was comforted but not reassured. We went back to sleep and got up at seven to greet the daily round that is family life. Zap, she used to say, there goes another one.

BETWEEN
Micheal O'Siadhail

As we fall into step I ask a penny for your thoughts.
'Oh, nothing,' you say, 'well, nothing so easily bought.'

Sliding into the rhythm of your silence, I almost forget
how lonely I'd been until that autumn morning we met.

At bedtime up along my childhood's stairway, tongues
of fire cast shadows. Too earnest, too highstrung.

My desire is endless: others ended when I'd only started.
Then, there was you: so whole-hog, so wholehearted.

Think of the thousands of nights and the shadows fought.
And the mornings of light. I try to read your thought.

In the strange openness of your face, I'm powerless.
Always this love. Always this infinity between us.

READING NOTES

People frequently pick up on how it is that when couples most need to talk to each other, they are, for a variety of reasons, or maybe no understandable reason, unable to do so. They have talked of Dave's fear of the future as a single man and how hard it is to be single after being a couple. They also talked about personal, old fears and how they never seem to completely go away but feel worse after long absence. People spoke of children getting caught up in marital quarrels; of Dana's observation, 'people who don't talk and rarely smile seem threatening', and whether Dave should confront Dana or not. Other topics that come up have been dentists, waffles, choirs and remedies for cramp.

Although the poem does not give up its meaning on a first reading, it is the last line that people both recognise as true but also have trouble explaining exactly why this should be. Someone said that to her, the line meant being human. 'We are first and foremost separate beings, no matter how close we might be.' The fourth verse is often mulled over. By 'others ended when I'd only started', is he referring to relationships or to something else? The suggestion of being powerless before 'the strange openness of your face' reminded some of the story and the moment when, over supper, the couple finally look at each other, not with openness but with so much hidden, and are equally powerless.

Love Rises Through Us

♥

UNRAVISHED BRIDE
Edith Pearlman

(approximate reading time 13 minutes)

'Tell me about yourself,' Marlene chattered to this Rafferty fellow. The wedding was going to her head, as all weddings did. There was nothing majestic about the suburban parish church, but the late September day was beautiful, and the bride, Marlene's cousin's daughter, was certainly pretty – she resembled Marlene's grandmother. The groom was a salesman for the Raffertys. He was handsome in an untrustworthy way: hair too abundant, eyes too calculating, smile erupting with teeth. He might have passed for a young Kennedy. His name, however, was O'Riordan.

Somehow during the reception Marlene had become sepa-rated from her husband and their children. At these family affairs Paul and the kids always looked so interesting, or just so Jewish, that they got snapped up like savories. So she had begun to move alone through the receiving line, like a widow – no: like a maiden. Then this Hugh Rafferty materialized at her side. Marlene kissed the bride, Peggy Ann, and told the groom she hoped he'd be very happy. Hugh did the same. They drifted together into the swirl, and Hugh grabbed two champagnes from a passing tray.

'Tell me about yourself.' Not the most sophisticated of openings. But sophistication would leave this man cold – she knew that just by looking at him. She knew, too, that he had been gently bred and properly educated (Harvard, it turned out); he was respectful and observant; his wife was the sort who gets things done (she was director of publicity at a local college, he told Marlene with pride); he loved his many kids. He sailed and skied and played tennis, but a paunch was rising anyway.

His eyes were bright blue and his smile was the turned-up kind that children put on cookies. She meant to slip away as she often did at parties, fearful that she was restraining people ambitious to be elsewhere. But Hugh pleasantly stood fast, telling Marlene about himself. He managed the family lumber business and lived on the South Shore. He was the third gener-ation to do both; love of work and pleasure in home were strong in him. His smile must once have haunted the dreams of virgins . . .

'You were at Wellesley?' he said. 'You'd think we'd have met.'

'I was a fireman's daughter, on scholarship, from Detroit. It's my mother's relatives at this wedding, though she's gone, so's my father. My sisters are scattered,' she babbled.

Paul came up. Marlene introduced the men, then said to her husband, 'You've been a trooper with Aunt Tess. I was watching you. Is it her gout this time?'

'It's her gums.'

'Are you a dentist?' Hugh asked.

'I'm a radiologist.'

'It's all the same to Aunt Tess,' Marlene said, and they laughed, and then Hugh excused himself, shaking hands first.

That should have been that. Meeting again seemed unlikely – Hugh halfway to the Cape, Marlene near to town; his crowd rich, hers high-minded. If O'Riordan were to take an ax to Peggy Ann, they might see each other at the funeral, or the trial. Otherwise, no.

They saw each other five days later. Marlene's avocation – she was an amateur biographer – sometimes took her to the Boston Public Library. Hugh's work demanded his presence at the company's Prudential Center office twice a week. He was headed there at quarter past twelve that Thursday; she was about to enter the library.

'Hello!' he called.

The usual flurries. And then – he so easily might not have said it – 'Have you had lunch yet?'

'I . . . don't have lunch, usually.'

'Then you can't have had it yet. Have it with me.'

Once in a while at a college party some tall handsome boy, caught by her alert face, had danced with her . . . She walked next to Hugh, along Boylston Street, along Clarendon. She wished her friends could see her.

They talked so easily. Neither liked to worry a subject to death. They passed up wine and shared a dessert. Afterward they retraced their steps. At the entrance to the library she turned and shook hands.

'Thank you very much,' she said, looking up at him. 'You've reminded me of the pleasures of having lunch.'

'Let me do it again,' he said relinquishing her hand and putting his own in his pocket. Don't make too much of this, his attitude said.

'I'm here every Thursday,' she lied.

'Next Thursday, then? Tell me where you usually work.'

'I drift from section to section,' she said. 'I could arrange to be in bound periodicals. Near *Fortune*, say.'

'Fine. At about one?'

So it began – Thursday lunches. They feasted at taverns and went hungry at salad bars. They ate raw fish wrapped in seaweed. One Thursday when Hugh was in a hurry they sat at a doughnut counter. The next week he insisted on several courses at the Ritz.

At Christmastime they took an enforced break while Hugh and his family went south. In February, Marlene had a week-long flu; that Thursday morning, trembling, she called his office.

'Mr Rafferty, please,' she said to the secretary, who sounded gorgeous. 'Ms Winokaur calling.'

'Marlene?' he said when he picked up. She had never before heard his voice on the telephone. Her bowels turned to water; but that was probably the flu. 'Oh, I'm sorry,' he said, when she told him she was too ill to come out. 'Feel better.' His voice was frank and unashamed. Anyone hearing the conversation would have assumed that they were merely two friends canceling a luncheon appointment.

And were they anything else? Their weekly meetings couldn't have been more blameless if some Sister made them a threesome. They were as public as statues. They talked about politics, basketball, first communions they had lived through, the lives she investigated, the trees he loved. They talked about the few people they knew in common (the young O'Riordans were expecting a baby already). They were like college boy and college girl on that outmoded, rule-bound thing: a date. But dates were only the beginning, weren't they – the slow beginning of a series that became hurried, became precipitous, came to a head, and ended in either a broken heart or a ceremony in a stone church. 'How did I get here?' more than one panicky bride had said to Marlene. How did *we* get here? Marlene wondered now. Where are we going?

On the first warm Thursday in May, they bought a bag of pretzels and ate them on the bank of the Charles. They sat on Hugh's raincoat. He loosened his tie. Hundreds of men all over the city were loosening their ties in the spring warmth. Yet she had to look away until she felt her flush recede.

They spent most summer Thursdays picnicking on the river or watching swan boats in the public garden. If it rained they sat at a sidewalk café under an umbrella. Their vacations happened to coincide – temporally, not geographically; the Raffertys went camping in Wyoming, the Winokaurs exchanged houses with a family in Hampstead. September found them both back in town. It was almost a year since they'd first met.

The Thursday after vacation, they took a noontime cruise on the harbor. The boat was crowded and noisy. The ladies' room was out of order. Hugh spilled coffee on Marlene's skirt. He apologized, but his annoyance seemed to be directed at her.

'Sorry to be in your way,' she said stiffly.

'Hey!'

And the boat returned so late that they had to take a cab across town. She huddled in the backseat corner and watched his profile. Many a college romance had not survived the summer vacation. As if you could call this romance! *How did we get here?* she echoed herself. *Where are we going? Suppose Paul found out?*

Suppose Paul found out what? She and Hugh had never kissed. They had never held hands. Once his knuckles had burned hers as he handed a menu across the table. Once, on the riverbank, he had flipped over onto his stomach beside her and she had placed her hand briefly on his blue-and-white striped back. He'd shuddered and turned his face away . . .

'Would you like to visit a hotel together?' he was saying now.

Her skirt was still soaked with coffee. 'Are you inviting me or the cab driver?'

So he had to look at her. He was unsmiling, and his face flamed like a boy's.

'Yes,' she said. 'I would. I would.'

They knew where to go. Twice they had lunched in the lobby café at the Orlando, a lively salesman's hotel, and they watched couples without luggage – handsome, well-dressed couples – checking in.

'Next Thursday, then' Hugh said.

'Next Thursday,' Marlene agreed.

She had never stopped loving Paul. During the week that followed she loved him tenderly, gratefully – loved his short, muscular body, his preoccupied manner, his kindness to their children. One love had nothing to do with the other. Paul was the man she would contentedly grow old with. But though she and Hugh were both past forty, theirs was the brief happy fling of youth. Everything proved it: their indifference to the future, their bright news-of-the-week conversation. He was her boyfriend. She was his girl.

She wore a new dress – silk, with a dropped waist. It was the color of Hugh's eyes. She looked beautiful, she hoped . . . even though her cheeks were a little too round and her slate-colored eyes disappeared when she laughed. Her headful of curls was in fashion. At a distance she could pass for a femme fatale.

And it was at a distance that they saw each other, that next Thursday. She was standing at the rear of the lobby when he came through the revolving door. The lobby café separated them. He made his way among the tables, lumbering a bit, bigger than most men, handsomer than all. The smile curved. It curved, it curved . . . but falsely; she could tell that at once. 'You don't have to,' she said, under her breath. Then his face was close to hers, so close that she could have kissed him, and who would have thought anything of that? – two old friends kissing, people did it all the time, Paul was always complaining that women he hardly knew embraced him at parties like tango dancers. She said it again. 'You don't have to. Dear.'

'I cannot,' he told her.

She probably could have talked him into it. 'I've put on my diaphragm,' she could have said, and he would have understood that by that act she had already betrayed her marriage. Or she could have allowed her eyes to fill with chagrined tears. Or her enthusiasm, her delight, might have carried him along. But she didn't use those wiles.

'You don't have to,' she said for the third time. 'Although,' she couldn't help adding, 'everybody else does.'

He took her arm and led her toward a table. 'We're not everybody else,' he said.

No, they were not everybody else, she thought while pretending to eat her salad. Everybody else – in Boston, in Paris, in Tel Aviv; Protestants, Catholics, Jews; black and white, young and old and rich and poor – everybody else played by today's rules. Young O'Riordan would turn up in this hotel within a decade. And Marlene's children, when the time came; and Hugh's children . . . Everybody else was up-to-date. But she and Hugh were throwbacks. They were bound to the code of their youth – self-denial and honor and fidelity – an inconvenient code that would keep them, she realized with a pang, forever chaste, and forever in love.

IN DEFENCE OF ADULTERY
Julia Copus

We don't fall in love: it rises through us
the way that certain music does –
whether a symphony or ballad –
and it is sepia-coloured,
like spilt tea that inches up
the tiny tube-like gaps inside
a cube of sugar lying by a cup.
Yes, love's like that: just when we least
needed or expected it
a part of us dips into it
by chance or mishap and it seeps
through our capillaries, it clings
inside the chambers of the heart.
We're victims, we say: mere vessels,
drinking the vanilla scent
of this one's skin, the lustre
of another's eyes so skilfully
darkened with bistre. And whatever
damage might result we're not
to blame for it: love is an autocrat
and won't be disobeyed.
Sometimes we manage
to convince ourselves of that.

READING NOTES

This story usually generates a good deal of debate. People have discussed whether Hugh and Marlene are in a moral, if not physical, adulterous relationship, with some insisting that the story suggests they know they are already cheating. 'Marlene says they are boyfriend and girlfriend, but you can't just pretend like that.' Someone else said that perhaps they could not admit to themselves that what they were doing was not as innocent as they might have wanted it to be. Others have said that until the end they do not seem to know whether they are simply friends or whether it is more than that. Why do they not tell their spouses? The story says, 'One love had nothing to do with the other,' but can you love two people? At the end the story says they were 'bound to the code of their youth – self-denial and honor and fidelity.' Group members have not always agreed that the couple have stuck to this code.

A man in a community reading group was angry with the lines in the poem 'whatever damage might result we're not to blame for it': 'It's true that we can't help falling in love, but of course we are to blame if we cause damage as a result.' Someone else pointed out that they thought the poem agreed with him.

There has often been talk about weddings and a woman said she liked Marlene's remark that at the reception, she was 'fearful she was restraining people ambitious to be elsewhere'. 'I often feel like that at social occasions,' she said. 'I never thought that other people would too.'

A Need to Reach Out Sometimes

♥

BED AMONG THE LENTILS

(FROM *TALKING HEADS*)

Alan Bennett

(approximate reading time 30 minutes)

Susan is a vicar's wife. She is thin and nervous and probably smokes. She sits on an upright chair in the kitchen. It is evening.

Geoffrey's bad enough but I'm glad I wasn't married to Jesus. The lesson this morning was the business in the Garden of Gethsemane when Jesus prays and the disciples keep falling asleep. He wakes them up and says, 'Could you not watch with me one hour?' It's my mother.

I overslept this morning, flung on a cardigan and got there just as everybody was standing up. It was Holy Communion so the militants were out in force, the sub-zero temperature in the side-chapel doubtless adding to the attraction.

Geoffrey kicks off by apologising for his failure to de-frost the church. (Subdued merriment.) Mr Medlicott has shingles,

Geoffrey explains, and, as is well known, has consistently refused to initiate us lesser mortals into the mysteries of the boiler. (Helpless laughter).

Mrs Belcher read the lesson. Mr Belcher took the plate round. 'Big day for you,' I said to them afterwards.

The sermon was about sex. I didn't actually nod off, though I have heard it before. Marriage gives the OK to sex is the gist of it, but while it is far from being the be all and end all (you can say that again) sex is nevertheless the supreme joy of the married state and a symbol of the relationship between us and God. So, Geoffrey concludes, when we put our money on the plate it is a symbol of everything in our lives we are offering to God and that includes our sex. I could only find 10p.

Thinking about the sermon during the hymn I felt a pang of sympathy for the Deity, gifted with all this sex. No fun being made a present of the rare and desiccated conjuctions that take place between Geoffrey and me. Or the frightful collisions that presumably still occur between the Belchers. Not to mention whatever shamefaced fumblings go on between Miss Budd and Miss Bantock. 'It's all right if we offer it to God, Alice.' 'Well, if you say so, Pauline.'

Amazing scenes at the church door. Geoffrey has announced that after Easter the bishop would be paying a visit so the fan club were running around in small circles, Miss Frobisher even going so far as to squeeze my elbow. Meanwhile, Geoffrey stands there the wind billowing out his surplice and ruffling his hair, what 'Who's Who in the Diocese of Ripon' calls 'his schoolboy good looks'. I helped put away the books while he did his 'underneath this cassock I am but a man like anybody else' act. 'Such a live wire,' said Mrs Belcher, 'really putting the parish on the map.' 'That's right,' burbles Mrs Shrubsole, looking at me. 'We must cherish him.'

We came back and I cherished him with some chicken wings in a tuna fish sauce. He said, 'That went down well.' I said, 'The chicken wings?' He said, 'My sermon. I felt it hit the nail on the head.' He put his hand on mine, hoping, I suppose, that having hit one nail he might hit another, but I said I had to go round with the parish magazine. 'Good girl,' he said. 'I can attack my paperwork instead.'

Roads busy. Sunday afternoon. Families having a run out. Wheeling the pram, walking the dog. Living. Almighty God unto whom all hearts be open, and from whom no secrets are hid, cleanse the thoughts of our hearts by the inspiration of thy holy spirit that we may perfectly love thee and worthily magnify thy glorious name and not spend our Sunday after-noons parked in a lay-by on the Ring Road wondering what happened to our life.

When I got back Geoffrey was just off to Evensong, was I going to come? When I said 'No' he said, 'Really? Then I'd better pretend you have a headache.'

Why? One of the unsolved mysteries of life, or the unsolved mysteries of my life, is why the vicar's wife is expected to go to church at all. A barrister's wife doesn't have to go to court, an actor's wife isn't at every performance, so why have I always got to be on parade? Not to mention the larger question of whether one believes in God in the first place. It's assumed that being the vicar's wife one does but the question has never actually come up, not with Geoffrey anyway. I can understand why, of course. To look at me, the hair, the flat chest, the wan smile, you'd think I was just cut out for God. And maybe I am. I'd just like to have been asked that's all. Not that it matters of course. So long as you can run a tight jumble sale you can believe in what you like.

It could be that Geoffrey doesn't believe in God either. I've always longed to ask him only God never seems to crop up. 'Geoffrey,' I'd say. 'Yes, Susan?' 'Do you really believe in God? I mean, cards on tables, you don't honestly, do you? God's just a job like any other. You've got to bring home the bacon somehow.' But no. Not a word. The subject's never discussed.

After he'd gone I discovered we were out of sherry so I've just been round to the off-licence. The woman served me. Didn't smile. I can't think why. I spend enough.

Go to black.
Come up on Susan on the steps of the side-chapel, polishing a candlestick. Afternoon.

We were discussing the ordination of women. The bishop asked me what I thought. Should women take the services? So long as it doesn't have to be me, I wanted to say, they can be taken by a trained gorilla. 'Oh yes,' Geoffrey chips in, 'Susan's all in favour. She's keener than I am, aren't you, darling?' 'More sprouts anybody?' I said.

On the young side for a bishop, but he's been a prominent sportsman at university so that would explain it. Boxing or rugby. Broken nose at some stage anyway. One of the 'Christianity is common sense' brigade. Hobby's bricklaying apparently and refers to me throughout as 'Mrs Vicar'. Wants beer with his lunch and Geoffrey says he'll join him so this leaves me with the wine. Geoffrey's all over him because the rumour is he's shopping round for a new Archdeacon. Asks Geoff how outgoing I am. Actually says that. 'How outgoing is Mrs Vicar?' Mr Vicar jumps in with a quick rundown of my accomplishments and an outline of my punishing schedule. On a typical day, apparently, I kick off by changing the wheel on the Fiesta, then hasten to the bedside of a dying pensioner, after which, having done the altar flowers and dispensed warmth and appreciation to sundry parishioners en route, I top off a thrill-packed morning by taking round Meals on Wheels . . . somehow – 'and this to me is the miracle,' says Geoffrey – 'somehow managing to rustle up a delicious lunch in the interim', the miracle somewhat belied by the flabby lasagne we are currently embarked on. 'The ladies,' says the bishop. 'Where would we be without them?'

Disaster strikes as I'm doling out the tinned peaches: the jug into which I've decanted the Carnation milk gets knocked over, possibly by me. Geoffrey, for whom turning the other cheek is part of the job, claims it caught his elbow and his lordship takes the same line, insisting he gets doused in Carnation milk practically every day of his life. Still, when I get a dishcloth and sponge off his gaiters I catch him giving me a funny look. It's Mary Magdalen and the Nivea cream all over again. After lunch Geoffrey's supposed to be taking him on a tour of the parish but while we're having a cup of instant he claps his hand to his temple because he's suddenly remembered he's supposed to be in Keighley blessing a steam engine.

We're stacking the dishwasher and I ask Geoffrey how he thinks it's gone. Doesn't know. 'Fingers crossed,' I say. 'I think there are more constructive things we could do than that,' he says crisply, and goes off to mend his inner tube. I sit by the Aga for a bit and as I doze off it comes to me that by 'constructive things' he perhaps means prayer.

When I wake up there's a note from Geoffrey. 'Gone to talk to the Ladies Bright Hour. Go to bed.' I'm not sleepy and anyway we're running low on sherry so I drive to Leeds. I've stopped going round the corner now as I owe them a bit on the side and she's always so surly. There's a little Indian shop behind the Infirmary I've found. It's a newsagents basically but it sells drink and anything really, the way they do. Open last thing at night, Sundays included, my ideal. Ramesh he's called. Mr Ramesh I call him, though Ramesh may be his Christian name. Only not Christian of course. I've been once or twice now, only this time he sits me in the back place on a sack of something and talks. Little statuette of a god on the wall. A god. Not The God. Not the definite article. One of several thousand apparently. 'Safety in numbers,' I said but he didn't understand. Looks a bit more fun than Jesus anyway. Shows me pictures of other gods, getting up to all sorts. I said, 'She looks a very busy lady. Is that yoga?' He said, 'Well, it helps.' He's quite athletic himself apparently, married, but his wife's only about fourteen so they won't let her in. He calls me Mrs Vicar too, only it's different. He has lovely teeth.

Go to black.
Come up on Susan in the kitchen near the Aga. Morning.

Once upon a time I had my life planned out . . . or half of it at any rate. I wasn't clear about the first part, but at the stroke of fifty I was all set to turn into a wonderful woman . . . the wife to a doctor, or a vicar's wife, Chairman of the Parish Council, a pillar of the WI. A wise, witty and ultimately white-haired old lady, who's always stood on her own two feet until one day at the age of eighty she comes out of the County Library, falls under the weight of her improving book, breaks her hip and dies peacefully, continently and without fuss under a snowy coverlet in the cottage hospital. And coming away from her funeral in a country churchyard on a bright winter's afternoon people would say, 'Well, she was a wonderful woman.'

Had this been a serious ambition I should have seen to it I was equipped with the skills necessary to its achievement. How to produce jam which, after reaching a good, rolling boil, successfully coats the spoon; how to whip up a Victoria sponge that just gives to the fingertips; how to plan, execute and carry through a successful garden fête. All weapons in the armoury of any upstanding Anglican lady. But I can do none of these things. I'm even a fool at the flower arrangement. I ought to have a PhD in the subject the number of classes I've been to but still my efforts show as much evidence of art as walking sticks in an umbrella stand. Actually it's temperament. I don't have it. If you think squash is a competitive activity try flower arrangement.

On this particular morning the rota has Miss Frobisher and Mrs Belcher down for the side aisles and I'm paired with Mrs Shrubsole to do the altar and the lectern. My honest opinion, never voiced needless to say, is that if they were really sincere about religion they'd forget flower arrangement altogether, invest in some permanent plastic jobs and put the money towards the current most popular famine. However, around mid-morning I wander over to the church with a few dog-eared chrysanthemums. They look as if they could do with an immediate drink so I call in at the vestry and root out a vase or two from the cupboard where Geoffrey keeps the communion wine.

It not looming very large on my horizon, I assume I am doing the altar and Mrs Shrubsole the lectern, but when I come out of the vestry Mrs S is at the altar well embarked on her arrangement. I said, 'I thought I was doing the altar.' She said, 'No. I think Mrs Belcher will bear me out. I'm down to do the altar. You are doing the lectern. Why?' She smiled sweetly. 'Do you have a preference?' The only preference I have is to shove my chrysanthemums up her nose but instead I practise a bit of Christian forbearance and go and stick them in a vase by the lectern. In the best tradition of my floral arrangements they look like the poles of a wigwam, so I go and see if I can cadge a bit of backing from Mrs Belcher. 'Are you using this?' I say, picking up a bit of mouldy old fern. 'I certainly am. I need every bit of my spiraea. It gives it body.' I go over and see if Miss Frobisher has any greenery going begging only she's doing some Japanese number, a vase like a test-tube half filled with gravel, in which she's throttling a lone carnation. So I retire to the vestry for a bit to calm my shattered nerves, and when I come out ready to tackle my chrysanths again Mrs Shrubsole has apparently finished and fetched the other two up to the altar to admire her handiwork. So I wander up and take a look.

Well, it's a brown job, beech leaves, teazles, grass, that school of thought. Mrs Shrubsole is saying, 'It's called Forest

Murmurs. It's what I did for my Highly Commended at Harrogate last year. What do you think?' Gert and Daisy are of course speechless with admiration, but when I tentatively suggest it might look a bit better if she cleared up all the bits and pieces lying around she said, 'What bits and pieces?' I said, 'All these acorns and fir-cones and what not. What's this conker in aid of?' She said, 'Leave that. The whole arrangement pivots on that.' I said, 'Pivots?' 'When the adjudicator was commenting on my arrangement he particularly singled out the hint I gave of the forest floor.' I said, 'Mrs Shrubsole. This is the altar of St Michael and All Angels. It is not The Wind in the Willows.' Mrs Belcher said, 'I think you ought to sit down.' I said, 'I do not want to sit down.' I said, 'It's all very well to transform the altar into something out of Bambi but do not forget that for the vicar the altar is his working surface. Furthermore,' I added, 'should the vicar sink to his knees in prayer, which since this is the altar he is wont to do, he is quite likely to get one of these teazle things in his eye. This is not a flower arrangement. It is a booby trap. A health hazard. In fact,' I say in a moment of supreme inspiration, 'it should be labelled HAZFLOR. Permit me to demonstrate.' I begin getting down on my knees just to prove how lethal her bloody Forest Murmurs is. Only I must have slipped because the next thing I know I'm rolling down the altar steps and end up banging my head on the communion rail.

Mrs Shrubsole, who along with every other organisation known to man has been in the St John's Ambulance Brigade, wants me left lying down, whereas Mrs Belcher is all for getting me on to a chair. 'Leave them lying down,' says Mrs Belcher, 'and they inhale their own vomit. It happens all the time, Veronica.' 'Only, Muriel,' says Mrs Shrubsole, 'when they have vomited. She hasn't vomited.' 'No,' I say, 'but I will if I have to listen to any more of this drivel,' and begin to get up. 'Is that blood, Veronica?' says Mrs Belcher pointing to my head. 'Well,' says Mrs Shrubsole, reluctant to concede to Mrs B on any matter remotely touching medicine, 'it could be, I suppose. What we need is some hot sweet tea.' 'I thought that theory had been discredited,' says Mrs Belcher. Discredited or not it sends Miss Frobisher streaking off to find a teabag, and also, it subsequently transpires, to telephone all and sundry in an effort to locate Geoffrey. He is in York taking part in the usual interdenominational conference on the role of the church in a hitherto uncolonised department of life, underfloor central heating possibly. He comes haring back thinking I'm at death's door, and finding I'm not has nothing more constructive to offer than I take a nap.

This gives the fan club the green light to invade the vicarage, making endless tea and the vicar his lunch and, as he puts it, 'spoiling him rotten'. Since this also licenses them to conduct a fact-finding survey of all the housekeeping arrangements or absence of same ('Where does she keep the Duroglit, vicar?'), a good time is had by all. Meanwhile Emily Brontë is laid out on the sofa in a light doze.

I come round to hear Geoffrey saying, 'Mrs Shrubsole's going now, darling.' I don't get up. I never even open my eyes. I just wave and say, 'Goodbye, Mrs Shrubsole.' Only thinking about it as I drift off again I think I may have said, 'Goodbye, Mrs Subsoil.' Anyway I meant the other. Shrubsoil.

When I woke up it was dark and Geoffrey'd gone out. I couldn't find a thing in the cupboard so I got the car out and drove into Leeds. I sat in the shop for a bit, not saying much. Then I felt a bit wanny and Mr Ramesh let me go into the back place to lie down. I must have dozed off because when I woke up Mr Ramesh has come in and started taking off his clothes. I said, 'What are you doing? What about the shop?' He said, 'Do not worry about the shop. I have closed the shop.' I said, 'It's only nine. You don't close till eleven.' 'I do tonight,' he said. I said, 'What's tonight?' He said, 'A chance in a million. A turn-up for the books. Will you take your clothes off please.' And I did.

Go to black.
Come up on Susan sitting in the vestry having a cigarette.
Afternoon.

You never see pictures of Jesus smiling, do you? I mentioned this to Geoffrey once. 'Good point, Susan,' is what he said, which made me wish I'd not brought it up in the first place. Said I should think of Our Lord as having an inward smile, the doctrine according to Geoffrey being that Jesus was made man so he smiled, laughed and did everything else just like the rest of us. 'Do you think he ever smirked?' I asked, whereupon Geoffrey suddenly remembered he was burying somebody in five minutes and took himself off.

If Jesus *is* all man I just wish they'd put a bit more of it into the illustrations. I was sitting in church yesterday, wrestling with this point of theology, when it occurred to me that something seemed to have happened to Geoffrey. The service should have kicked off ages ago but he's still in the vestry. Mr Bland is filling in with something uplifting on the organ and Miss Frobisher, never one to let an opportunity slip, has slumped to her knees for a spot of unscheduled silent prayer. Mrs Shrubsole is lost in contemplation of the altar, still adorned with Forest Murmurs, a trail of ivy around the cross the final inspired touch. Mr Bland now ups the volume but still no sign of Geoff. 'Arnold,' says Mrs Belcher, 'there seems to be some hiatus in the proceedings,' and suddenly the fan club is on red alert. She's just levering him to his feet when I get in first and nip in there to investigate.

His reverence is there, white-faced, every cupboard open and practically in tears. He said, 'Have you seen it?' I said, 'What?' He said, 'The wine. The communion wine. It's gone.' I said, 'That's no tragedy,' and offer to pop out and get some ordinary. Geoffrey said, 'They're not open. Besides, what does it look like?' I said, 'Well, it looks like we've run out of communion wine.' He said, 'We haven't run out. There was a full bottle here on Friday. Somebody has drunk it.'

It's on the tip of my tongue to say that if Jesus is all he's cracked up to be why doesn't he use tap-water and put it to the test when I suddenly remember that Mr Bland keeps a bottle of cough mixture in his cupboard in case any of the choirboys gets chesty. At the thought of celebrating the Lord's Supper in Benylin Geoffrey now has a complete nervous breakdown but, as I point out, it's red and sweet and nobody is going to notice. Nor do they. I see Mr Belcher licking his lips a bit thoughtfully as he walks back down the aisle but that's all. 'What was the delay?' asks Mrs Shrubsole. 'Nothing,' I said, 'just a little hiccup.'

Having got it right for once I'm feeling quite pleased with myself, but Geoffrey obviously isn't and never speaks all afternoon so I bunk off Evensong and go into Leeds.

Mr Ramesh has evidently been expecting me because there's a bed made up in the storeroom upstairs. I go up first and get in. When I'm in bed I can put my hand out and feel the lentils running through my fingers. When he comes up he's put on his proper clothes. Long white shirt, sash and what not. Loincloth underneath. All spotless. Like Jesus. Only not. I watch him undress and think about them all at Evensong and Geoffrey praying in that pausy way he goes, giving you time to mean each phrase. And the fan club lapping it up, thinking they love God when they just love Geoffrey. Lighten our darkness we beseech thee O Lord and by thy great mercy defend us from all perils and dangers of this night. Like Mr Ramesh who is twenty-six with lovely legs, who goes swimming every morning at Merrion Street Baths and plays hockey for Horsforth. I ask him if they offer their sex to God. He isn't very interested in the point but with them, so far as I can gather, sex is all part of God anyway. I can see why too. It's the first time I really understand what all the fuss is about. There among the lentils on the second Sunday after Trinity.

I've just popped into the vestry. He's put a lock on the cupboard door.

Go to black.
Come up on Susan sitting in the drawing-room of the
vicarage. Much smarter than in previous scenes, she has
had her hair done and seems a different woman. Evening.

I stand up and say, 'My name is Susan. I am a vicar's wife and
I am an alcoholic.' Then I tell my story. Or some of it anyway.
'Don't pull any punches,' says Clem, my counsellor. 'Nobody's
going to be shocked, believe me love, we've all been there.' But
I don't tell them about Mr Ramesh because they've not been
there. 'Listen, people. I was so drunk I used to go and sleep
with an Asian grocer. Yes, and you won't believe this. I loved
it. Loved every minute.' Dear oh dear. This was a real drunken
lady.

So I draw a veil over Mr Ramesh who once, on the feast of
St Simon and St Jude (Choral Evensong at six, daily services at
the customary hour), put make-up on his eyes and bells on his
ankles, and naked except for his little belt danced in the back
room of the shop with a tambourine.

'So how did you come to AA,' they ask. 'My husband,' I
say. 'The vicar. He persuaded me.' But I lie. It was not my
husband, it was Mr Ramesh, the exquisitely delicate and polite
Mr Ramesh who one Sunday night turned his troubled face
towards me with its struggling moustache and asked if he
might take the bull by the horns and enquire if intoxication
was a prerequisite for sexual intercourse, or whether it was only
when I was going to bed with him, the beautiful Mr Ramesh,
twenty-six, with wonderful legs, whether it was only with him
I had to be inebriated. And was it, asked this slim, flawless

and troubled creature, was it perhaps his colour? Because if not he would like to float the suggestion that sober might be even nicer. So the credit for the road to Damascus goes to Mr Ramesh, whose first name turns out also to be Ramesh. Ramesh Ramesh, a member of the community council and the Leeds Federation of Trade.

But none of this I say. In fact I never say anything at all. Only when it becomes plain to Geoffrey (and it takes all of three weeks) that Mrs Vicar is finally on the wagon, who is it gets the credit? Not one of Mr Ramesh's jolly little gods, busy doing everything under the sun to one another, much like Mr Ramesh. Oh no. It's full marks to Geoffrey's chum, the Deity, moving in his well-known mysterious way.

So now everything has changed. For the moment I am a new woman and Geoffrey is a new man. And he brings it up on the slightest pretext. 'My wife's an alcoholic, you know. Yes. It's a great challenge to me and to the parish as extended family.' From being a fly in the ointment I find myself transformed into a feather in his cap. Included it in his sermon on Prayers Answered when he reveals that he and the fan club have been having these jolly get togethers in which they'd all prayed over what he calls 'my problem'. It practically sent me racing back to the Tio Pepe even to think of it. The fans, of course, never dreaming that their prayers would be answered, are furious. They think it's brought us closer together. Geoffrey thinks that too. We were at some doleful diocesan jamboree last week and I'm stuck there clutching my grapefruit juice as Geoffrey's telling the tale to some bearded cleric. Suddenly he seizes my hand. 'We met it with love,' he cries, as if love were some all-purpose antibiotic, which to Geoffrey it probably is.

And it goes on, the mileage in it endless. I said to Geoffrey that when I stood up at AA I sometimes told the story about the flower arranging. Result: he starts telling it all over the diocese. The first time was at a conference on The Supportive Parish. Gales of deep, liberated, caring laughter. He's now given it a new twist and tells the story as if he's talking about a parishioner, then at the end he says, 'Friends I want to tell you something. (Deep hush.) That drunken flower-arranger was my wife.' Silence . . . then the applause, *terrific*.

I've caught the other young, upwardly mobile parsons sneaking looks at me now and again and you can see them thinking why weren't they smart enough to marry an alcoholic or better still a drug addict, problem wives whom they could do a nice redemption job on, right there on their own doorstep. Because there's no stopping Geoffrey now. He grips my hand in public, nay *brandishes* it. 'We're a team,' he cries. Looks certain to be rural dean and that's only the beginning. As the bishop says, 'Just the kind of man we're looking for on the bench . . . someone with a seasoned compassion, someone who's looked life in the face. Someone who's been there.'

Mr Ramesh sold his shop. He's gone back to India to fetch his wife. She's old enough now apparently. I went down there on Sunday. There was a boy writing Under New Management on the window. Spelled wrong. And something underneath in Hindi, spelled right probably. He said he thought Mr Ramesh would be getting another shop, only in Preston.

They do that, of course, Asians, build something up, get it going nicely, then take the profit and move on. It's a good thing. We ought to be more like that, more enterprising.

My group meets twice a week and I go. Religiously. And that's what it is, of course. The names are different, Frankie and Steve, Susie and Clem. But it's actually Miss Frobisher and Mrs Shrubsole all over again. I never liked going to one church so I end up going to two. Geoffrey would call that the wonderful mystery of God. I call it bad taste. And I wouldn't do it to a dog. But that's the thing nobody ever says about God . . . he has no taste at all.

Fade out.

NOT LOVE PERHAPS
A. S. J. Tessimond

This is not Love perhaps – Love that lays down
Its life, that many waters cannot quench, nor the floods
　　drown –
But something written in lighter ink, said in a lower tone:
Something perhaps especially our own:
A need at times to be together and talk –
And then the finding we can walk
More firmly through dark narrow places
And meet more easily nightmare faces:
A need to reach out sometimes hand to hand –
And then find Earth less like an alien land:
A need for alliance to defeat
The whisperers at the corner of the street:
A need for inns on roads, islands in seas, halts for
　　discoveries to be shared,
Maps checked and notes compared:
A need at times of each for each
Direct as the need of throat and tongue for speech.

READING NOTES

Someone said that it was extraordinary how the monologue could make you laugh out loud and yet feel sad at the same time, so we looked for places where this happened. Lots of issues were raised: the Church of England, underage marriage, AA and alcoholism, loneliness. Everyone was concerned about what happened next. Ramesh was her saviour, not God or the vicar, so what would become of her resolve without him? The group spent some time on the lines of the poem: 'A need to reach out sometimes hand to hand/ And then find Earth less like an alien land'. Susan has a kind of love for Ramesh; not just the sex, his feelings matter to her.

A project worker who has read the poem with many groups adds: 'People often talk about how important relationships like that are – to help us get through hard times. Often I've asked about whether this is love or not, and groups are often divided – some feel that it is absolutely love, a truly supportive loving relationship, but others feel that it is more like friendship. Either way, the closeness suggested by the phrase "Something perhaps especially our own" feels important.' Another group leader said, 'A new lady in the group was so taken aback about how much she connected to it. "I just never thought that reading a poem would bring so much to me – personally." She liked the lines where it talks about a need for "inns on roads, islands in seas" and spoke about how important it was to have meeting places in life – places where you could go to meet, stop and talk to other people.'

Why Do I Love?

HE
Doris Lessing

(approximate reading time 17 minutes)

'Goodness! You gave me a start, Mary . . .'

Mary Brooke was quietly knitting beside the stove. 'Thought I'd drop in,' she said.

Annie Blake pulled off her hat, and flopped a net of bread and vegetables on the table; at the same time her eyes were anxiously inspecting her kitchen: there was an unwashed dish in the sink, a cloth over a chair. 'Everything's in such a mess,' she said irritably.

Mary Brooke, eyes fixed on her knitting, said: 'Eh, sit down. It's clean as can be.'

After a hesitation Annie flopped herself into the chair, and shut her eyes. 'Those stairs. . . .' she panted. Then: 'Like a cuppa tea, Mary?'

Mary quickly pushed her knitting away, and said: 'You sit still. I'll do it.' She heaved up her large tired body, filled a kettle from the tap, and set it on the flame. Then, following her friend's anxious glance, she hung the dish-cloth where it belonged and shut the door. The kitchen was so clean and neat it could have gone on exhibition. She sat down, reached for her knitting and knitted without looking at it, contemplating the wall across the room. 'He was carrying on like anything last night,' she observed.

Annie's drooping lids flew open, her light body straightened. 'Yes?' she murmured casually. Her face was tense.

'What can you expect with that type? She doesn't get the beds made before dinner-time. There's dirt everywhere. He was giving it to her proper. Dirty slut, he called her.'

'She won't do for him what I did, that's for certain,' said Annie bitterly.

'Shouting and banging until nearly morning – we all heard it.' She counted purl, plain, purl, and added: 'Don't last long, do it? Six months he's been with her now?'

'He never lifted his hand to me *that's* certain,' said Annie victoriously, 'Never. I've got my pride if others haven't.'

'That's right love. Two purl. One plain.'

'Nasty temper he's got. I'd be up summer and winter at four, cleaning those offices till ten, then cleaning for Mrs Lynd till dinner-time. Then if he got home and found his dinner not ready, he'd start, shout and carry-on – well, I'd say, if you can't wait five minutes, get home and cook it yourself, I'd say. I bring in as much money as you, don't I? But he never lifted a finger. Bone lazy. Men are all the same.'

Mary gave her friend a swift searching glance, then murmured: 'Eh, you can't tell *me* . . .'

'I'd have the kids and the cleaning and the cooking, and working all day – sometimes when he was unemployed I'd bring in all the money . . . and he wouldn't even put the kettle on for me. Women's work, he said.'

'Two purl, one plain.' But Mary's kindly face seemed to suggest that she was waiting to say something else. 'We all know what it is,' she agreed at last, patiently.

Annie rose lightly, pulled the shrieking kettle off the flame and reached for the teapot. Seen from the back she looked twenty, slim and erect. When she turned with the steaming pot, she caught a glimpse of herself – she set down the pot, and went to the mirror. She stood touching her face anxiously. 'Look at me!' She pushed a long sagging curl into position, then shrugged: 'Well, who's to care what I look like anyway?'

She began setting out the cups. She had a thin face, sharpened by worry, small sharp blue eyes. As she sat down, she nervously felt her hair. 'I must get the curlers on to my hair,' she muttered.

'Heard from the boys?'

Annie's hand fell and clenched itself on the table. 'Not a word from Charlie for months. They don't think . . . he'll turn up one fine day and expect his place laid, if I know my Charlie. Tommy's after a job in Manchester, Mrs Thomas said. But I had a nice letter from Dick . . .' Her face softened; her eyes were soft and reminiscent. 'He wrote about his father. Should he come down and speak to the old so and so for me, he said. I wrote back and said that was no way to speak of his father. He should respect him, I said, no matter what he's done. It's not his place to criticize his father, I said.'

'You're lucky in your boys, Annie.'

'They're good workers, no one can say they aren't. And they've never done anything they shouldn't. They don't take after their dad, *that's* certain.'

At this, Mary's eyes showed a certain tired irony. 'Eh, Annie – but we all do things we shouldn't.' This gaining no response from the bitter Annie, she added cautiously: 'I saw him this morning in the street.'

Annie's cup clattered down into the saucer. 'Was he alone?'

'No. But he took me aside – he said I could give you a message if I was passing this way – he might be dropping in this evening instead of tomorrow with your money, he said. Thursday *she* goes to her mother's – I suppose he thinks while the cat's away . . .'

Annie had risen, in a panic. She made herself sit down again, and stirred her tea. The spoon tinkled in the cup with the quivering of her hand. 'He's a regular with the money, anyway,' she said heavily. 'I didn't need to take him to court. He offered. And I suppose he needn't, now the boys are out keeping themselves.'

'He still feels for you, Annie . . .' Mary was leaning forward, speaking in direct appeal. 'He does, really.'

'He never felt for anyone but himself,' snapped Annie. 'Never.'

Mary let a sigh escape her. 'Oh well . . .' she murmured. 'Well, I'll be getting along to do the supper.' She stuffed her knitting into her carry-all, and said consolingly: 'You're lucky. No one to get after you if you feel like sitting a bit. No one to worry about but yourself . . .'

'Oh don't think I'm wasting my tears over *him*. I'm taking it easy for the first time in my life. You slave your life out for your man and your kids. Then off they go, with not so much as a thank-you. Now I can please myself.'

'I wouldn't mind being in your place,' said Mary loyally. At the door she remarked, apparently at random: 'Your floor's so clean you could eat off it.'

The moment Mary was gone, Annie rushed into her apron, and began sweeping. She got down to her knees to polish the floor, and then took off her dress and washed herself at the sink. She combed her dragging wisps of pale hair; and did each one up neatly with a pin till her face was surrounded by a ring of little sausages. She put back her dress and sat down at the table. Not a moment too soon. The door opened, and Rob Blake stood there.

He was a thin, rather stooping man, with an air of apology. He said politely: 'You busy, Annie?'

'Sit down,' she commanded sharply. He stooped loosely in the doorway for a moment, then came forward, minding his feet. Even so she winced as she saw the dusty marks on the gleaming linoleum. 'Take it easy,' he said with friendly sarcasm. 'You can put up with my dust once a week, can't you?'

She smiled stiffly, her blue eyes fastened anxiously on him, while he pulled out a chair and sat down. 'Well, Annie?'

To this conciliatory opening she did not respond. After a moment she remarked: 'I heard from Dick. He's thinking of getting married.'

'Getting married now? That puts us on the shelf, don't it?'

'*You're* not on any shelf that I can see,' she snapped.

'Now – Annie . . .' he deprecated, with an appealing smile. She showed no signs of softening. Seeing her implacable face, his smile faded, and he took an envelope from his pocket and pushed it over.

'Thanks,' she said, hardly glancing at it. Then that terrible bitterness came crowding up, and he heard the words: 'If you can spare it from *her.*'

He let that one pass; he looked steadily at his wife, as if seeking a way past that armour of anger. He watched her, passing the tip of his tongue nervously over his lips.

'Some women know how to keep themselves free from kids and responsibilities. They just do this and that, and take up with anyone they please. None of the dirty work for *them.*'

He gave a sigh, and was on the point of getting up, when she demanded: 'Like a cuppa tea?'

'I wouldn't mind.' He let himself sink back again.

While she worked at the stove, her back to him, he was looking around the kitchen: his face had a look of tired, disappointed irony. An ageing man, but there was a dogged set to his shoulders. Trying to find the right words, he remarked: 'Not so much work for you now, Annie.'

But she did not answer. She returned with the two cups, and put the sugar into his for him. This wifely gesture encouraged him. 'Annie,' he began, 'Annie – can't we talk this over . . .' He was stirring the tea clumsily, not looking at it, leaning forward. The cup knocked over. 'Oh look what you've done,' she cried out, 'just look at the mess.' She snatched up a cloth and wiped the table.

'It's only a drop of tea, Annie,' he protested at last, shrinking a little aside from her furious energy.

'Only a drop of tea – I can polish and clean half the day, and then in a minute the place is like a pig-sty.'

His face darkened with remembered irritation.

'Yes, I've heard,' she went on accusingly, 'she lets the beds lie until dinner, and the place isn't cleaned from one week to the next.'

'At least she cares more for me than she does for a clean floor,' he shouted. Now they looked at each other with hatred.

At this delicate moment there came a shout: 'Rob. Rob!'

She laughed angrily. 'She's got you where she wants you – waits and spies on you and now she comes after you.'

'Rob! You there, Rob?' It was a loud, confident, female voice.

'She sounds just what she is, a proper . . .'

'Shut up,' he interrupted. He was breathing heavily. 'You keep that tongue of yours quiet, now.'

Her eyes were full of tears, but the blue shone through bright and vengeful. 'Rob, Rob – and off you trot like a little dog.'

He got up from the table heavily, as a loud knock came at the door.

Annie's mouth quivered at the insult of it. And *his* first instinct was to stand by her – she could see that. He looked apologetically at her, then went to the door, opened it an inch and said in a low furious voice: 'Don't you do that now. Do you hear me!' He shut the door, leaned against it facing Annie. 'Annie,' he said again, in an awkward appeal. 'Annie . . .'

But she sat at her table, hands folded in a trembling knot before her, her face tight and closed against him.

'Oh all right!' he said at last despairingly, angry. 'You've always got to be in the right about everything, haven't you? That's all that matters to you, if you're in the right. Bloody plaster saint, you are.' He went out quickly.

She sat quite still, listening until it was quiet. Then she drew a deep breath, and put her two fists to her cheeks, as if trying to keep them still. She was sitting thus when Mary Brooke came in. 'You let him go?' she said incredulously.

'And good riddance, too.'

Mary shrugged. Then she suggested bravely: 'You shouldn't be so hard on him, Annie – give him a chance.'

'I'd see him dead first,' said Annie through shaking lips. Then: 'I'm forty-five, and I might as well be on the dust-heap.' And then, after a pause, in a remote, cold voice: 'We've been together twenty-five years. Three kids. And then he goes off with that . . . with that . . .'

'You're well rid of him, and that's a fact,' agreed Mary swiftly.

'Yes I am, and I know it . . .' Annie was swaying from side to side in her chair. Her face was stony, but the tears were trickling steadily down, following a path worn from nose to chin. They rolled off and splashed on to her white collar.

'Annie,' implored her friend. 'Annie . . .'

Annie's face quivered, and Mary was across the room and had her in her arms. 'That's right, love, that's right, that's right, love,' she crooned.

'I don't know what gets into me,' wept Annie, her voice coming muffled from Mary's large shoulder. 'I can't keep my wicked tongue still. He's fed up and sick of that – cow, and I drive him away. I can't help it. I don't know what gets into me.'

'There now, love, there now, love.' The big fat comfortable woman was rocking the frail Annie like a baby. 'Take it easy, love. He'll be back, you'll see.'

'You think he will?' asked Annie, lifting her face up to see if her friend was lying to comfort her.

'Would you like me to go and see if I can fetch him back for you now?'

In spite of her longing, Annie hesitated. 'Do you think it'll be all right?' she said doubtfully.

'I'll go, and slip in a word when *she's* not around.'

'Will you do that, Mary?'

Mary got up, patting at her crumpled dress. 'You wait here, love,' she said imploringly. She went to the door and said as she went out: 'Take it easy now, Annie. Give him a chance.'

'I go running after him to ask him back?' Annie's pride spoke out of her in a wail.

'Do you want him back or don't you?' demanded Mary, patient to the last, although there was a hint of exasperation now. Annie did not say anything, so Mary went running out.

Annie sat still, watching the door tensely. But vague rebellious angry thoughts were running through her head: 'If I want to keep him, I can't ever say what I think, I can't ever say what's true – I'm nothing to him but a convenience, but if I say so he'll just up and off . . .'

But that was not the whole truth; she remembered the affection in his face, and for a moment the bitterness died. Then she remembered her long hard life, the endless work, work, work – she remembered, all at once, as if she were feeling it now, her aching back when the children were small; she could see him lying on the bed reading the newspaper when she could hardly drag herself . . . 'It's all very well,' she cried out to herself, 'it's not right, it just isn't right . . .' A terrible feeling of injustice was gripping her; and it was just this feeling she must push down, keep under, if she wanted him. For she knew finally, and this was stronger than anything else, that without him there would be no meaning in her life at all.

TO ONE THAT ASKED ME WHY I LOVED J.G.
Ephelia

Why do I Love? go ask the glorious sun
Why every day it round the world doth run:
Ask Thames and Tiber, why they ebb and flow:
Ask damask roses why in June they blow:
Ask ice and hail the reason why they're cold:
Decaying beauties, why they will grow old:
They'll tell thee, Fate, that everything doth move,
Inforces them to this, and me to love.
There is no reason for our love or hate,
'Tis irresistible, as Death or Fate;
'Tis not his face; I've sense enough to see,
That is not good, though doated on by me:
Nor is't his tongue, that has this conquest won,
For that at least is equalled by my own:
His carriage can to none obliging be,
'Tis rude, affected, full of vanity:
Strangely ill natured, peevish and unkind,
Unconstant, false, to jealousy inclin'd;
His temper could not have so great a power,
'Tis mutable, and changes every hour:
Those vigorous years that women so adore
Are past in him: he's twice my age and more;
And yet I love this false, this worthless man,
With all the passion that a woman can;
Doat on his imperfections, though I spy
Nothing to love; I love, and know not why.
Sure 'tis decreed in the dark Book of Fate,
That I should love, and he should be ingrate.

READING NOTES

A group of young mothers thought the poem sounded 'old-fashioned' but were interested that it nevertheless said something they all understood today. They looked specifically at the lines 'And yet I love this false, this worthless man' and 'Nothing to love; I love, and know not why', which made them think of women who are physically and emotionally abused by their partners and yet stay with them. This subject came up again at the end of the story, at the point when Annie says her life has no meaning without her husband. They talked about Annie's terrible bitterness and her obsession with housework versus Rob's chauvinistic behaviour. They wondered, as he wouldn't even put the kettle on, when the story was written. They thought about Mary's part in the story – whether she could have done more or differently, and speculated about what could happen next, and there was talk about how impossible it is to judge a marriage from the outside. There was quite a spirited discussion on whether or not we can say why we love, and even if it is possible to love without really liking.

Two Poems: Considering My Love

MY LOVER
Wendy Cope

For I will consider my lover, who shall remain nameless.

For at the age of 49 he can make the noise of five different kinds of lorry changing gear on a hill.

For he sometimes does this on the stairs at his place of work.

For he is embarrassed when people overhear him.

For he can also imitate at least three different kinds of train.

For these include the London tube train, the steam engine, and the Southern Rail electric.

For he supports Tottenham Hotspur with joyful and unswerving devotion.

For he abhors Arsenal, whose supporters are uncivilized and rough.

For he explains that Spurs are magic, whereas Arsenal are boring and defensive.

For I knew nothing of this six months ago, nor did I want to.

For now it all enchants me.

For this he performs in ten degrees.

For first he presents himself as a nice, serious, liberated
person.

For secondly he sits through many lunches, discussing life
and love and never mentioning football.

For thirdly he is careful not to reveal how much he
dislikes losing an argument.

For fourthly he talks about the women in his past, acknowl-
edging that some of it must have been his fault.

For fifthly he is so obviously reasonable that you are
inclined to doubt this.

For sixthly he invites himself round for a drink one evening.

For seventhly you consume two bottles of wine between
you.

For eighthly he stays the night.

For ninthly you cannot wait to see him again.

For tenthly he does not get in touch for several days.

For having achieved his object he turns again to his other
interests.

For he will not miss his evening class or his choir practice
for a woman.

For he is out nearly all of the time.

For you cannot even get him on the telephone.

For he is the kind of man who has been driving women
round the bend for generations.

For, sad to say, this thought does not bring you to your
senses.

For he is charming.

For he is good with animals and children.

For his voice is both reassuring and sexy.

For he drives an A-registration Vauxhall Astra estate.

For he goes at 80 miles per hour on the motorways.

For when I plead with him he says, 'I'm not going any slower than *this*.'

For he is convinced he knows his way around better than anyone else on earth.

For he does not encourage suggestions from his passengers.

For if he ever got lost there would be hell to pay.

For he sometimes makes me sleep on the wrong side of my own bed.

For he cannot be bossed around.

For he has this grace, that he is happy to eat fish fingers or Chinese takeaway or to cook the supper himself.

For he knows about my cooking and is realistic.

For he makes me smooth cocoa with bubbles on the top.

For he drinks and smokes at least as much as I do.

For he is obsessed with sex.

For he would never say it is overrated.

For he grew up before the permissive society and remembers his adolescence.

For he does not insist it is healthy and natural, nor does he ask me what I would like him to do.

For he has a few ideas of his own.

For he has never been able to sleep much and talks with me late into the night.

For we wear each other out with our wakefulness.

For he makes me feel like a light-bulb that cannot switch itself off.

For he inspires poem after poem.

For he is clean and tidy but not too concerned with his
  appearance.
For he lets the barber cut his hair too short and goes
  round looking like a convict for a fortnight.
For when I ask if this necklace is all right he replies, 'Yes,
  if no means looking at three others.'
For he was shocked when younger team-mates began
  using talcum powder in the changing-room.
For his old-fashioned masculinity is the cause of continual
  merriment on my part.
For this puzzles him.

LOVE POEM
John Frederick Nims

My clumsiest dear, whose hands shipwreck vases,
At whose quick touch all glasses chip and ring,
Whose palms are bulls in china, burs in linen,
And have no cunning with any soft thing

Except all ill-at-ease fidgeting people:
The refugee uncertain at the door
You make at home; deftly you steady
The drunk clambering on his undulant floor.

Unpredictable dear, the taxi drivers' terror,
Shrinking from far headlights pale as a dime
Yet leaping before apopleptic streetcars—
Misfit in any space. And never on time.

A wrench in clocks and the solar system. Only
With words and people and love you move at ease,
In traffic of wit expertly manoeuvre
And keep us, all devotion, at your knees.

Forgetting your coffee spreading on our flannel,
Your lipstick grinning on our coat,
So gaily in love's unbreakable heaven
Our souls on glory of spilt bourbon float.

Be with me, darling, early and late. Smash glasses—
I will study wry music for your sake.
For should your hands drop white and empty
All the toys of the world would break.

READING NOTES

In a home for the elderly, the group made their own versions of 'My Lover' by choosing the three lines they thought most applicable to them and adding at least five lines of their own. Some wrote several more. Ron said he did not think it was a real poem, which prompted debate of what a poem should be.

 People have liked the idea that a love poem does not have to be hearts and flowers and souls to be loving or even romantic. Often the discussion of 'Love Poem' is about how it is best to have a clear-eyed view of someone you love so that you can love them warts and all, so to speak. One woman said she appreciated the way the poet loved his dear one's clumsiness and untidiness because if he didn't, he would soon find them irritating and what would that turn into? The line 'Only with words and people and love you move at ease' is a favourite. Readers note the word 'Only' and have decided that the poet is not downgrading anything, rather he is singling out these three big things as the most important.

Love's Integrity

♥

VALLEY OF DECISION
(EXTRACT FROM CHAPTER 16)
Stanley Middleton

(approximate reading time 11 minutes)

Mary and David Blackwell were enjoying a happy marriage until Mary's blossoming career as an opera singer took her to America where she began an affair with her producer. David, a music teacher, stayed in England and at this point in the novel, Mary's work has now run out; she has returned to England and come to see her husband.

'Why didn't you phone me, Mary?'

'How could I? After the way I'd treated . . .'

Subdued anger was directed away from him, towards the hearth.

'Tell you what,' he said. 'Come and help me get the tea ready.'

'You do it.'

He grasped it then, the extent of her effort. She was the husk of herself. This hour and a quarter had killed her beyond all politeness.

'You can have salmon sandwiches or ham,' he said.

'You choose.'

'I will.'

David felt glad to be in the kitchen, trembling, doing tasks not beyond him, cutting bread thin, making sure the best china was spotless. When he brought in the crockery, the cutlery, he noted she had not moved, that she sat, eyes wide open, in her chair, staid and stable. He arranged Mrs Stiles's saffron buns on a doyley on a plate. Twenty minutes had passed by the time he finally carried in the teapot.

'At long last,' he said. 'It's salmon. Made to your taste.' He carried over a stool which he placed in front of her, and lifted her feet on to it. She allowed the advance. Next he arranged a small table by her chair, handed her napkin, plate and knife, poured out her tea. She accepted a sandwich, moistened her lips, gave no thanks.

'Eat up,' he ordered.

She smiled, thin as water, across at him, tried a small bite.

'To your satisfaction?'

She nodded, incapable of speech. When she had masticated the sandwich, slowly, without appetite, in misery, he, watching her covertly, gave her a minute's grace before he carried the plate across. When she refused, he pressed her, and she yielded.

'We've got to build you up,' he said, and went unanswered.

Mary drank a second cup of tea, crumbled and ate one of her mother's cakes. David had lapsed into bleak, uncompanionable silence and was glad in the end to ask if she wanted more. She had removed her legs from the stool.

'No, thanks. That was lovely.'

Small victory sounded in the two sentences. While he was outside washing the dishes he heard her go upstairs, presumably to the lavatory, and then almost immediately come down. He had hoped she would look about, in and out of the bedrooms, but she disappointed him. Clearing the kitchen put off his return to the dining room.

He found her again at the window.

'Those bulbs have done well,' he said. 'Those you set in the tubs. Narcissi'

She returned to her seat and he opposite.

'I've not asked you a word about yourself,' she said. 'It's been nothing but me and my foolery.' She skirmished with the last word.

'First things first.'

'Tell me.' Her voice lacked power, powerfully.

He described his time with the Trent Quartet, delineating the characters, making her smile at Barton's old womanliness, Wilkinson's domestic yoke, Fred's dignified homosexuality. From time to time she threw in a question as she would have done in the old days, and he relaxed, but she would then reassume the complicated stiffness of pose which kept him uncertain. He did not give up; he outlined technical difficulties in the Shostakovich, in Britten's Third, then sketched concert organizers, discomfort in dressing rooms, audiences, the chances of the Trent's becoming professional.

'How did you manage for white shirts for the concerts?' she asked so feebly he wondered if he were inventing the conversation for himself.

'My mother bought me three, and kept them laundered.'

That seemed a confession of weakness.

'I did the rest. Honestly. Washing machine on every Wednesday and every weekend. I'm quite an expert with the iron.'

She dismissed the trivialities with a short sweep of the arm, violently energetic within the context of her immobility.

'How have you been?' she asked.

'Pretty healthy really. Usual coughs and colds.'

'I didn't mean like that.'

As soon as she had posed the first question he knew intensely how he had been. This afternoon he had hedged himself, disciplined himself to be her friend and host and now she came out with this demand. Depression winded him like a kick.

'Pretty bloody,' he answered.

'But you kept working?'

'To the best of my ability. I was lucky in that I had interesting things to do. If I'd been at a factory bench . . .' He rubbed his chin. 'Sometimes, even so, it was so painful it stopped me practising, but mostly I could stagger on, not very fast, not very straight.' He tried to keep his voice light. 'I wished sometimes I had an animal, a cat to sit on my knee, or a dog to take out for a walk. Of course, for weeks I kept hoping, looking out for the postman, telling myself the transatlantic mail service had slipped up.'

'You must have . . .?' she faltered.

'In the end. Yes. I realized something was seriously wrong.'

'I'm sorry. It was awful, David.' She groped outwards. She was crying, soundlessly.

'Come back to me, Mary,' he said, off balance.

The imperative passed without effect. He had decided that she was not going to answer, that he must toss his cap again into the fearful ring, when she spoke.

'Do you mean that?'

He did not know; on his dizzy distress he had no landmarks expect for this central pointer: he must take her.

'Yes. I wouldn't say it otherwise.' That sounded weakly, unconvincing even to him. 'I want you back.'

She said nothing, but her posture hinted of hope. She did not deny him, repel him with stiffness. She was listening.

'Come home,' he said. He remembered a catchword of his father's from some radio show. His was all subsumed under ham acting, comedians' foolery, half-forgotten ephemerality. The gaiety of nations.

'I have,' she said.

'For good?'

'You don't want me.' Silent crying began again; rolling of tears etched her grief into him.

'I do.'

'Why?'

'Because I love you.'

'But look what I've done to you.' Her voice was strong, letting him get away with nothing, checking his banalities.

'I want you here.'

'David.' She stopped, as if to make sure her argument was clear before she put it. 'You'll never be able to forget what I've done to you. It'll always be there, in your mind, whether you say anything or not. It will fester. I acted abominably. How can you say . . .?'

'I've said it.' Strongly, upstanding.

'That's sentimental.'

The schoolmaster answered, on top of his class.

'Expressing more emotion than the situation warrants,' he said, mock-pedantically. 'Allow me to think otherwise.' He checked her with his hand. 'Argument is not going to change my mind. Do you want to come back?'

'Yes. If you'll . . . I think so.'

Her face, tear-stricken, was turned away from him. Was this wholehearted? He did not know, but he crouched, on his right heel like a miner again, by her chair.

'You won't be able to forget what I've done, will you?'

'I'm not perfect. No. I expect what you say is right enough, but it hardly seems worth wasting energy on just now.'

'It's no use starting off forgetting these things.'

'You'll be telling me next,' he said, flaring, 'that I only took you back because I didn't much care one way or the other about what had happened.'

'I didn't say that.'

'I know you didn't. But what you don't realize is how glad I am to see you sitting in this room, telling me you're going to stay.'

As soon as he established it in words it became the truth. A powerful sensation of, at present, satisfaction rather than exhilaration gripped him, expressed by his monosyllable 'glad'. He could not define it, or defend it. Perhaps, these disclaimers darted, flitted at him sharp, resisted temptations, his pride had been temporarily bandaged, in so far that he had no longer to go about saying 'My wife has left me for another man.' It did not feel like this. He could not quite disturb the universe, even shake the street and his bent legs were beginning to hurt, but his conviction grew, strong, huge, deepening, not over-whelming yet, but near flood level. Dangerous, yes, all that. But right, right. Correct. Just.

THE WEAVERS
Jan Struther

Keenness of heart and brain,
Deftness of hand and lip –
All these are not enough
To weave a perfect stuff
Out of the difficult skein
Of this relationship.

A passionate patience we
Must also bring to bear:
Be tireless to smooth out
Coil, caffle, or knot
Before time's shuttles weave it
Into the stuff, and leave it,
A lasting blemish, there.

Thus only can we keep
Ice-clear, rock-fast, sea-deep,
Our love's integrity;
Thus only can we make
A fine and flawless cloak
To wrap us round, and cover
From wind and rain our linked lives for ever.

READING NOTES

'I felt I could completely picture this scene,' said a reader. 'More than that, I felt I could sense the atmosphere in the room.' We talked of how a cup of tea in time of trouble is so much more than just a cup of tea; of the little ordinary trivialities – the sandwiches, the footstool, the washing-up – the polite, formal behaviour behind which deep and powerful feelings were barely contained. Someone pointed out the moment near the end when David is so exhilarated his feelings almost disturb the universe and yet, at the same time, he feels uncomfortable from crouching down. 'It seems so real.'

In the second verse, the poem seems to present the argument as if from Mary's point of view: 'You'll never be able to forget what I've done to you. It'll always be there, in your mind.' Is David being truthful with himself? Can sweeping the past under the carpet preserve love's integrity? Is his conviction honestly right and correct? All these ideas were seriously talked over and the group expressed a wish to read on to find out what would happen.

Marriage Is

♥

AMONGST WOMEN

(EXTRACT)

John McGahern

(approximate reading time 18 minutes)

Michael Moran, former IRA member and Republican guerilla fighter, is getting older and feels his days of glory are now regrettably behind him. Although he loves his five grown children (Luke, Maggie, Mona, Sheila and Michael) in his way, he retains strict and sometimes tyrannical control over them. He has very recently married for the second time and his new wife, Rose, undoubtedly loves him and tries always to keep an uneasy peace. Luke Moran is estranged from the family and lives in London.

Often when talking with the girls she had noticed that whenever Moran entered the room silence and deadness would fall on them; and if he was eating alone or working in the room – setting the teeth of a saw, putting a handle in a broken spade on a wet day, taking apart the lighting plant that never seemed to run properly for long – they always tried to slip away. If they had to stay they moved about the place like shadows. Only when they dropped or rattled something, the startled way they would look towards Moran, did the nervous tension of what it took to glide about so silently show. Rose had noticed this and she had put it down to the awe and respect in which the man she so loved was held, and she was loath to see differently now. She had chosen Moran, had married him against convention and her family. All her vanity was in question. The violence Moran had turned on her she chose to ignore, to let her own resentment drop and to join the girls as they stole about so that their presences would never challenge his.

He came in very late, wary, watchful. The cheerfulness with which Rose greeted him he met with a deep reserve. She was unprepared for it and her nervousness increased tenfold as she bustled about to get his tea. Sheila and Mona were writing at side tables; Michael was kneeling at the big armchair, a book between his elbows, as if in prayer, a position he sometimes used for studying. All three looked up gravely to acknowledge their father's presence; but, sensing his mood at once, they buried themselves again in their schoolwork.

'Where's Maggie?' he demanded.

'She went to visit some friends in the village.'

'She seems always to be on the tramp these days.'

'She's going around mostly saying goodbye to people.'

'I'm sure she'll be missed,' he said acidly.

Rose poured him his tea. The table was covered with a spotless cloth. As he ate and drank she found herself chattering away to him out of nervousness, a stream of things that went through her head, the small happenings of a day. She talked out of confusions: fear, insecurity, love. Her instinct told her she should not be talking but she could not stop. He made several brusque, impatient movements at the table but still she could not stop. Then he turned round the chair in a fit of hatred. The children were listening though they kept their eyes intently fixed on their school books.

'Did you ever listen carefully to yourself, Rose?' he said. 'If you listened a bit more carefully to yourself I think you might talk a lot less.'

She looked like someone who had been struck without warning but she did not try to run or cry out. She stood still for a long moment that seemed to the others to grow into an age. Then, abjectly, as if engaged in reflection that gave back only its own dullness, she completed the tasks she had been doing and, without saying a word to the expectant children, left the room.

'Where are you going, Rose?' he asked in a tone that told her that he knew he had gone too far but she continued on her way.

It galled him to have to sit impotently in silence; worse still, that it had been witnessed. They kept their heads down in their books though they had long ceased to study, unwilling to catch his eye or even to breathe loudly. All they had ever been able to do in the face of violence was to bend to it.

Moran sat for a long time. When he could stand the silence no longer he went briskly into the other room. 'I'm sorry, Rose,' they heard him say. They were able to hear clearly though he had closed the door. 'I'm sorry, Rose,' he had to say again. 'I lost my temper.' After a pause they thought would never end they heard, 'I want to be alone,' clear as a single bell note, free of all self-assertiveness. He stayed on in the room but there was nothing he could do but withdraw.

When he came back he sat beside the litter of his meal on the table among the three children not quite knowing what to do with himself. Then he took a pencil and paper and started to tot up all the monies he presently held against the expenses he had. He spent a long time over these calculations and they appeared to soothe him.

'We might as well say the Rosary now,' he announced when he put pencil and paper away, taking out his beads and letting them dangle loudly. They put away their exercises and took out their beads.

'Leave the doors open in case Rose wants to hear,' he said to the boy. Michael opened both doors to the room. He paused at the bedroom door but the vague shape amid the bedclothes did not speak or stir.

At the Second Glorious Mystery Moran paused. Sometimes if there was an illness in the house the sick person would join in the prayers through the open doors but when the silence was not broken he nodded to Mona and she took up Rose's Decade. After the Rosary, Mona and Sheila made tea and they all slipped away early.

Moran sat on alone in the room. He was so engrossed in himself that he was startled by the sound of the back door opening just after midnight. Maggie was even more startled to find him alone when she came in and instantly relieved that she hadn't allowed the boy who had seen her home from the village further than the road gate.

'You're very late,' he said.

'The concert wasn't over till after eleven.'

'Did you say your prayers on the way home?'

'No, Daddy. I'll say them as soon as I go upstairs.'

'Be careful not to wake the crowd that has to go to school in the morning.'

'I'll be careful. Good night, Daddy.' As on every night, she went up to him and kissed him on the lips.

He sat on alone until all unease was lost in a luxury of self-absorption. The fire had died. He felt stiff when he got up from the chair and turned out the light and groped his way through the still open doorway to the bed, shedding his clothes on to the floor. When he got into bed he turned his back energetically to Rose.

She rose even earlier than usual next morning. Usually she enjoyed the tasks of morning but this morning she was grateful above all mornings for the constancy of the small demanding chores: to shake out the fire, scatter the ashes on the grass outside, to feel the stoked fire warm the room. She set the table and began breakfast. When the three appeared for school they were wary of her at first but she was able to summon sufficient energy to disguise her lack of it and they were completely at ease before they left for school. When Moran eventually appeared he did not speak but fussed excessively as he put on socks and boots. She did not help him.

'I suppose I should be sorry,' he said at length.

'It was very hard what you said.'

'I was upset over that telegram my beloved son sent. It was as if I didn't even exist.'

'I know, but what you said was still hard.'

'Well then, I'm sorry.'

It was all she demanded and immediately she brightened. 'It's all right, Michael. I know it's not easy.' She looked at him with love. Though they were alone they did not embrace or kiss. That belonged to darkness and the night.

'Do you know what I think, Rose? We get too cooped up here sometimes. Why don't we just go away for the day?'

'Where would we go to?'

'We can drive anywhere we want to drive to. That's the great thing about having a car. All we have to do is back it out of the shed and *go*.'

'Do you think you can spare the day?' She was still careful.

'It's bad if we can't take one day off,' he said laughingly. He was happy now, relieved, pleased with himself, ready to be indulgent.

He backed the Ford out of the shed and faced it to the road. Maggie had risen and was taking breakfast when he came in.

'Is there anything you want, Daddy?'

'Not a thing in the wide world, thanks be to God.' She was relieved to hear the tone. 'You'll have the whole place to yourself today. Rose and myself are away for the day.'

'When do you think you'll be back, Daddy?'

Rose had left out his brown suit and shirt and tie and socks and he had started to dress.

'We'll be back when you see us. We'll be back before night anyhow,' he said as he tucked his shirt into his trousers, hoisting them round his hips.

'I'm holding everybody up,' Rose fussed self-effacingly. She looked well, even stylish in a discreet way, in her tweed suit and white blouse.

'Daddy looks wonderful. I hope I'm not too much of a disgrace,' she laughed nervously, moving her hands and features in one clear plea to please.

'You look lovely, Rose. You look like a lady.' Maggie said.

'I'm bound to be taken for the chauffeur,' he laughed out, mispronouncing the word with relish but he was not corrected as he hoped.

'There'd never be a fear of that,' she said with feeling.

They set off together in the small car, Rose's girlish smiles and waves only accentuating the picture of the happy couple going on a whole day's outing alone together. Maggie watched the car turn carefully out into the main road and then she went and closed the gate under the big yew tree.

Moran drove purposefully. The car crossed the shallow racing river in Boyle, passed the grey walls of the roofless monastery, and it kept on the main road leading across the Curlews. Rose hadn't asked him where they were driving to; she didn't care anyhow: it was enough to be with him in the day.

'O'Neill and O'Donnell crossed here with cannon and horses on the way to Kinsale in one night,' he told her as the car was climbing into the low mountains. 'They were able to cross because the black frost made the ground hard as rock that night.'

He seemed to relax more after he had spoken, to be less fixedly focused on the empty road.

'I suppose some of your own nights when you were on the run were not unlike that,' she ventured into what they had never spoken of.

'No. They were different,' he said not unkindly but it was clear he didn't want to talk about those nights.

'Would you like to go to Strandhill? When the children were young we went there every year.'

'I'd love to see the ocean,' she said. She didn't care where she went or what she saw as long as he was pleased and she was with him. Now most of her pleasure and all of her pain flowed through him. For her there was always a strange excitement in his presence of something about to happen. Nothing was ever still. She felt inordinately grateful when he behaved normally.

'That's the calm sea,' he pointed out the inlet that ran to Ballysadare as they came along the narrow twisting road into Strandhill. 'We all used to swim there. It's more private and safe. The rough sea at the front is dangerous. There was hardly a summer that three or four weren't drownded.'

'It was very good of you to take them to the sea. Hardly anybody else about except the schoolteachers ever thought of taking their children to the sea.'

'I always tried to do the best or what I thought was best. It is not easy to know sometimes. When you think you're right that is the time it'll fly back in your teeth. Luke wouldn't come to the sea in the finish.'

'All boys growing up get that way,' she said.

'We had to stop selling the turf then,' he said.

'What turf?' she asked.

'We took a lorry load of turf for our own fire and sold the rest in bags door to door.' He pointed out the pebbled street in front of Park's Guest House where they had first stayed and a bungalow they had taken between the church and the golf links. 'We sold the turf from there. It paid for the entire holiday. There was a great take on it. That whole summer was wet. Everybody wanted a fire because of the rain. We made money on that holiday.'

There were only two other cars at the front and they rolled to a stop alongside the plinth on which the antique cannon stood pointing out to sea like some deep-chested mongrel. They sat for a long time in silence watching the Atlantic crash down on the empty shore.

'We haven't come to the sea in three years. I suppose that's how you get old. You find yourself not doing a whole lot of things you once did without a thought.'

'You're not old,' Rose said.

'The mileage is up,' he said. 'You can't turn it back.'

'I wasn't sure what you'd want to do,' Rose said with the utmost caution, 'and I brought a flask of tea and sandwiches just in case.'

'That's great.' He had been dreading having to look for a place for lunch. He knew no cheap place here any more and he would have to search one out like a blind man. 'We can go anywhere we want to afterward,' he added in case he was appearing stingy.

Rose opened the flask, spreading the sandwiches on the dashboard. 'Bless us, O Lord, and these Thy gifts . . .' He ate and drank with relish, pointing out a fishing boat leaving Sligo harbour, remarking how Rosses Point across the bay had safe bathing while here you couldn't stand in the water without feeling the currents pushing the sand out from under your feet. 'But it's dull at the old Point, Rose. The waves there are small even in a storm. Here you get the real feel of the ocean. That's what I always used to say to the troops.'

'It's a wonderful place,' she said.

'I feel like a new man,' he said as she put the flask away and combed the crumbs from the dashboard into her cupped hand.

They both took up together, 'We give Thee thanks, O Almighty God, for Thy bounty which we have received through Christ Our Lord who liveth and reigneth world without end, amen.' Cheerfully they got out of the car into the open day and went down the rocks to the strand and then out to the tideline. They walked along the tide's edge for a mile. Rose picked some sea shells and rounded stones and Moran put bits of dilsk in his pocket. They turned back before reaching the roofless church in the middle of the old graveyard out on the edge of land.

'The locals still bury there,' he told her.

They came back along the path that threaded a way between the sand dunes. Some bees where already crawling on the early clover.

'This place will have a lot of tents and caravans and people in a month's time.'

'It's nicer walking here than on the strand. There's a lovely spring in the turf.'

'Except you have to watch for the rabbit holes. You could twist an ankle like nobody's business.'

'Aren't we lucky to have met and to have this whole day to ourselves and the sea and the sky,' Rose said enthusiastically.

'It's our life,' he said harshly. She looked at him carefully. He was changing less predictably than the tide. Soon he would need to vent the anger she felt already gathering, and she was the nearest person. Her life was bound up completely with this man she so loved and whose darkness she feared. They should go home before the whole day was about them in ruins.

'Maybe we should go to one of the hotels for tea or ice-cream?' he asked fretfully, as if somehow sensing her withdrawal.

As if to point out that they were not entirely alone, a man with a white terrier came towards them from behind the sand-hills. He carried a pale bone which he kept throwing out into the dune for the terrier to retrieve. Without speaking he lifted his cap as they passed.

'No,' she said firmly. 'I think we should go home. It's easy to spoil the day by trying to do too much.'

'Are you sure, Rose?'

'I'm certain.'

'We must do this more often, Rose,' he said as he backed the Ford out from the ornamental cannon. There were now four people on the long wide stretch of strand. They looked small and black against the width of rushing water and pale sand.

'We can but of course it won't be as easy for us to get away once Maggie is gone,' she said it in a pleasant way that sometimes humoured him and sometimes could put his teeth on edge. This time it seemed to please him. He would not have liked it if she seemed to be saying that they could get away any time they wanted to. Anything easy and pleasant aroused deep suspicion and people enjoying themselves were usually less inclined to pay attention to others.

HABITATION
Margaret Atwood

Marriage is not
a house or even a tent

it is before that, and colder:

the edge of the forest, the edge
of the desert
        the unpainted stairs
at the back where we squat
outside, eating popcorn

the edge of the receding glacier

where painfully and with wonder
at having survived even
this far

we are learning to make fire

READING NOTES

An afternoon reading group thought hard about the last line of the poem. Some said they thought it was implying that fire is dangerous, others that a fire is not always easy to get started and then it has to be looked after if you want it to stay alight. Alice noticed that the word 'edge' is used three times. Is it saying that marriage is a dangerous edge? Not everyone agreed with this. Someone else noticed that the poem begins 'Marriage is not' which immediately begs the question what *is* marriage?

Having read the story, the group went back to the poem and Alice said she thought that Rose's marriage seemed to be constantly on a dangerous edge. 'If she didn't really love him, it would be a cold and painful affair, as the poem suggests.' The group talked about Moran's character and someone said he reminded her of her father whose moods dominated her childhood. At one point, Rose talks 'out of confusions: fear, insecurity, love' and people thought about how those feelings could go on together – how love could survive fear and insecurity. Other things people were interested in were the IRA, the Troubles, Rose's ability to read Moran's mood when they were at the sea, and the effect of Moran's behaviour on his children.

I Cannot Look on Thee

MIDDLEMARCH

(EXTRACT FROM CHAPTER 74)

George Eliot

(approximate reading time 15 minutes)

Nicholas Bulstrode, a wealthy banker, has an ignoble past which he is keen to keep hidden. However, his misdeeds involving an old business partner, John Raffles, were brought to light at a town meeting and the news has spread through Middlemarch. Bulstrode has taken to his bed, pleading illness. His honest and upright wife has yet to know about his shame, and, sensing trouble, she goes to see the doctor, Lydgate.

'Mr Lydgate, pray be open with me: I like to know the truth. Has anything happened to Mr Bulstrode?'

'Some little nervous shock,' said Lydgate, evasively. He felt that it was not for him to make the painful revelation.

'But what brought it on?' said Mrs Bulstrode, looking directly at him with her large dark eyes.

'There is often something poisonous in the air of public rooms,' said Lydgate. 'Strong men can stand it, but it tells on people in proportion to the delicacy of their systems. It is often impossible to account for the precise moment of an attack – or rather, to say why the strength gives way at a particular moment.'

Mrs Bulstrode was not satisfied with this answer. There remained in her the belief that some calamity had befallen her husband, of which she was to be kept in ignorance; and it was in her nature strongly to object to such concealment. She begged leave for her daughters to sit with their father, and drove into the town to pay some visits, conjecturing that if anything were known to have gone wrong in Mr Bulstrode's affairs, she should see or hear some sign of it.

She called on Mrs Thesiger, who was not at home, and then drove to Mrs Hackbutt's on the other side of the churchyard. Mrs Hackbutt saw her coming from an up-stairs window, and remembering her former alarm lest she should meet Mrs Bulstrode, felt almost bound in consistency to send word that she was not at home; but against that, there was a sudden strong desire within her for the excitement of an interview in which she was quite determined not to make the slightest allusion to what was in her mind.

Hence Mrs Bulstrode was shown into the drawing-room, and Mrs Hackbutt went to her, with more tightness of lip and rubbing of her hands than was usually observable in her, these being precautions adopted against freedom of speech. She was resolved not to ask how Mr Bulstrode was.

'I have not been anywhere except to church for nearly a week,' said Mrs Bulstrode, after a few introductory remarks. 'But Mr Bulstrode was taken so ill at the meeting on Thursday that I have not liked to leave the house.'

Mrs Hackbutt rubbed the back of one hand with the palm of the other held against her chest, and let her eyes ramble over the pattern on the rug.

'Was Mr Hackbutt at the meeting?' persevered Mrs Bulstrode.

'Yes, he was,' said Mrs Hackbutt, with the same attitude. 'The land is to be bought by subscription, I believe.'

'Let us hope that there will be no more cases of cholera to be buried in it,' said Mrs Bulstrode. 'It is an awful visitation. But I always think Middlemarch a very healthy spot. I suppose it is being used to it from a child; but I never saw the town I should like to live at better, and especially our end.'

'I am sure I should be glad that you always should live at Middlemarch, Mrs Bulstrode,' said Mrs Hackbutt, with a slight sigh. 'Still, we must learn to resign ourselves, wherever our lot may be cast. Though I am sure there will always be people in this town who will wish you well.'

Mrs Hackbutt longed to say, 'if you take my advice you will part from your husband,' but it seemed clear to her that the poor woman knew nothing of the thunder ready to bolt on her head, and she herself could do no more than prepare her a little. Mrs Bulstrode felt suddenly rather chill and trembling: there was evidently something unusual behind this speech of Mrs Hackbutt's; but though she had set out with the desire to be fully informed, she found herself unable now to pursue her brave purpose, and turning the conversation by an inquiry about the young Hackbutts, she soon took her leave saying that she was going to see Mrs Plymdale. On her way thither she tried to imagine that there might have been some unusually warm sparring at the meeting between Mr Bulstrode and some of his frequent opponents – perhaps Mr Hackbutt might have been one of them. That would account for everything.

But when she was in conversation with Mrs Plymdale that comforting explanation seemed no longer tenable. 'Selina' received her with a pathetic affectionateness and a disposition to give edifying answers on the commonest topics, which could hardly have reference to an ordinary quarrel of which the most important consequence was a perturbation of Mr Bulstrode's health. Beforehand Mrs Bulstrode had thought that she would sooner question Mrs Plymdale than any one else; but she found to her surprise that an old friend is not always the person whom it is easiest to make a confidant of: there was the barrier of remembered communication under other circumstances – there was the dislike of being pitied and informed by one who had been long wont to allow her the superiority. For certain words of mysterious appropriateness that Mrs Plymdale let fall about her resolution never to turn her back on her friends, convinced Mrs Bulstrode that what had happened must be some kind of misfortune, and instead of being able to say with her native direct-ness, 'What is it that you have in your mind?' she found herself anxious to get away before she had heard anything more explicit. She began to have an agitating certainty that the misfortune was something more than the mere loss of money, being keenly sensitive to the fact that Selina now, just as Mrs Hackbutt had done before, avoided noticing what she said about her husband, as they would have avoided noticing a personal blemish.

She said good-bye with nervous haste, and told the coachman to drive to Mr Vincy's warehouse. In that short drive her dread gathered so much force from the sense of darkness, that when she entered the private counting-house where her brother sat at his desk, her knees trembled and her usually florid face was deathly pale. Something of the same effect was produced in him by the sight of her: he rose from his seat to meet her, took her by the hand, and said, with his impulsive rashness –

'God help you, Harriet! you know all.'

That moment was perhaps worse than any which came after. It contained that concentrated experience which in great crises of emotion reveals the bias of a nature, and is prophetic of the ultimate act which will end an intermediate struggle. Without that memory of Raffles she might still have thought only of monetary ruin, but now along with her brother's look and words there darted into her mind the idea of some guilt in her husband – then, under the working of terror came the image of her husband exposed to disgrace – and then, after an instant of scorching shame in which she felt only the eyes of the world, with one leap of her heart she was at his side in mournful but unreproaching fellowship with shame and isolation. All this went on within her in a mere flash of time – while she sank into the chair, and raised her eyes to her brother, who stood over her. 'I know nothing, Walter. What is it?' she said, faintly.

He told her everything, very inartificially, in slow fragments, making her aware that the scandal went much beyond proof, especially as to the end of Raffles.

'People will talk,' he said. 'Even if a man has been acquitted by a jury, they'll talk, and nod and wink – and as far as the world goes, a man might often as well be guilty as not. It's a breakdown blow, and it damages Lydgate as much as Bulstrode. I don't pretend to say what is the truth. I only wish we had never heard the name of either Bulstrode or Lydgate. You'd better have been a Vincy all your life.'

Mrs Bulstrode made no reply.

'But you must bear up as well as you can, Harriet. People don't blame *you*. And I'll stand by you whatever you make up your mind to do,' said the brother, with rough but well-meaning affectionateness.

'Give me your arm to the carriage, Walter,' said Mrs Bulstrode. 'I feel very weak.'

And when she got home she was obliged to say to her daughter, 'I am not well, my dear; I must go and lie down. Attend to your papa. Leave me in quiet. I shall take no dinner.'

She locked herself in her room. She needed time to get used to her maimed consciousness, her poor lopped life, before she could walk steadily to the place allotted her. A new searching light had fallen on her husband's character, and she could not judge him leniently: the twenty years in which she had believed in him and venerated him by virtue of his concealments came back with particulars that made them seem an odious deceit. He had married her with that bad past life hidden behind him, and she had no faith left to protest his innocence of the worst that was imputed to him. Her honest ostentatious nature made the sharing of a merited dishonour as bitter as it could be to any mortal.

But this imperfectly-taught woman, whose phrases and habits were an odd patchwork, had a loyal spirit within her. The man whose prosperity she had shared through nearly half a life, and who had unvaryingly cherished her – now that punishment had befallen him it was not possible to her in any sense to forsake him. There is a forsaking which still sits at the same board and lies on the same couch with the forsaken soul, withering it the more by unloving proximity. She knew, when she locked her door, that she should unlock it ready to go down to her unhappy husband and espouse his sorrow, and say of his guilt, I will mourn and not reproach. But she needed time to gather up her strength; she needed to sob out her fare-well to all the gladness and pride of her life. When she had resolved to go down, she prepared herself by some little acts which might seem mere folly to a hard onlooker; they were her way of expressing to all spectators visible or invisible that she had begun a new life in which she embraced humiliation. She took off all her ornaments and put on a plain black gown, and instead of wearing her much-adorned cap and large bows of hair, she brushed her hair down and put on a plain bonnet-cap, which made her look suddenly like an early Methodist.

Bulstrode, who knew that his wife had been out and had come in saying that she was not well, had spent the time in an agitation equal to hers. He had looked forward to her learning the truth from others, and had acquiesced in that probability, as something easier to him than any confession. But now that he imagined the moment of her knowledge come, he awaited the result in anguish. His daughters had been obliged to consent to leave him, and though he had allowed some food to be brought to him, he had not touched it. He felt himself perishing slowly in unpitied misery. Perhaps he should never see his wife's face with affection in it again. And if he turned to God there seemed to be no answer but the pressure of retribution.

It was eight o'clock in the evening before the door opened and his wife entered. He dared not look up at her. He sat with his eyes bent down, and as she went towards him she thought he looked smaller – he seemed so withered and shrunken. A movement of new compassion and old tenderness went through her like a great wave, and putting one hand on his which rested on the arm of the chair, and the other on his shoulder, she said, solemnly but kindly –

'Look up, Nicholas.'

He raised his eyes with a little start and looked at her half amazed for a moment: her pale face, her changed, mourning dress, the trembling about her mouth, all said, 'I know;' and her hands and eyes rested gently on him. He burst out crying and they cried together, she sitting at his side. They could not yet speak to each other of the shame which she was bearing with him, or of the acts which had brought it down on them. His confession was silent, and her promise of faithfulness was silent. Open-minded as she was, she nevertheless shrank from the words which would have expressed their mutual consciousness, as she would have shrunk from flakes of fire. She could not say, 'How much is only slander and false suspicion?' and he did not say, 'I am innocent.'

LOVE (III)
George Herbert

Love bade me welcome: yet my soul drew back,
    Guilty of dust and sin.
But quick-ey'd Love, observing me grow slack
    From my first entrance in,
Drew nearer to me, sweetly questioning,
    If I lack'd any thing.

A guest, I answer'd, worthy to be here:
    Love said, you shall be he.
I the unkind, ungrateful? Ah my dear,
    I cannot look on thee.
Love took my hand, and smiling did reply,
    Who made the eyes but I?

Truth Lord, but I have marr'd them: let my shame
    Go where it doth deserve.
And know you not, says Love, who bore the blame?
    My dear, then I will serve.
You must sit down, says Love, and taste my meat:
    So I did sit and eat.

READING NOTES

A project worker on Merseyside writes: 'This extract is a particular favourite of mine to read with groups. Together with Herbert's poem they are two of the most powerful pieces of literature I know. Everyone has experienced shame at some point in their lives and everyone has thoughts on the nature of forgiveness. People empathise with poor Mrs Bulstrode as she goes about the town, not daring to ask directly, yet aware that everyone knows something about her husband. The moments in the story that provoke the most discussion are her dislike of being pitied; the thought that the eyes of the town are on her; her realisation that a friend is not always the best confidant, and the moment when, not knowing what he has done, she instinctively takes his side – "with one leap of her heart". But most powerful of all is the ending of the chapter. From Mrs Bulstrode's putting off of her old self, to the couple crying *together*, there is so much here to admire, to empathise with and to pity.

'Although the poem is obviously religious, people always see that it has much to say about our human experience of shame and forgiveness. Bulstrode can hardly bear his wife to see his shame, "I cannot look on thee", yet she persists: "Look up, Nicholas." People often talk about whether it is harder to forgive or be forgiven and although it is a difficult poem, they have really grappled with it and felt the benefit.'

Two Poems: Holding Up

♥

ATLAS
U. A. Fanthorpe

There is a kind of love called maintenance
Which stores the WD40 and knows when to use it;

Which checks the insurance, and doesn't forget
The milkman; which remembers to plant bulbs;

Which answers letters; which knows the way
The money goes; which deals with dentists

And Road Fund Tax and meeting trains,
And postcards to the lonely; which upholds

The permanently rickety elaborate
Structures of living, which is Atlas.

And maintenance is the sensible side of love,
Which knows what time and weather are doing
To my brickwork; insulates my faulty wiring;
Laughs at my dryrotten jokes; remembers
My need for gloss and grouting; which keeps
My suspect edifice upright in air,
As Atlas did the sky.

A MARRIAGE
Michael Blumenthal

You are holding up a ceiling
with both arms. It is very heavy,
but you must hold it up, or else
it will fall down on you. Your arms
are tired, terribly tired,
and, as the day goes on, it feels
as if either your arms or the ceiling
will soon collapse.

But then,
unexpectedly,
something wonderful happens:
Someone,
a man or a woman,
walks into the room
and holds their arms up
to the ceiling beside you.

So you finally get
to take down your arms.
You feel the relief of respite,
the blood flowing back
to your fingers and arms.
And when your partner's arms tire,

you hold up your own
to relieve him again.

And it can go on like this
for many years
without the house falling.

READING NOTES

'Atlas' is always a favourite. We have often debated romantic love vs practical love. People like the idea that both poems are about holding something up whether it be your partner or your marriage or your life. In a library group people talked about the need to work on a relationship and about who in the family knows where the WD40 is kept and who looks after the bills or builds the flat-pack furniture or puts the bins out. They frequently note that while 'Atlas' is like a tribute to a loved one and 'A Marriage' celebrates partnership, both poems speak of frailty. The poems made people think about what makes for a successful marriage or loving partnership, and a man who was a full-time carer for his wife said that when he read the lines in 'A Marriage' 'You feel the relief of respite,/ the blood flowing back/ to your fingers and arms' it made him think not so much of his wife (much as he loved her) but the relief he experienced when he got help with her care.

In Wars and Peaces

♥

WITNESS
David Constantine

(approximate reading time 30 minutes)

The school itself had belonged to an industrialist. It was his home. He moved smartly west before the Russians arrived and died many years later in the bosom of his family, before the bad things about him became known. His children and their children had a harder time. The eldest son very determinedly, through much hostile bureaucracy, went back to see the house he had spent his childhood in, and saw it full of schoolchildren, Grete being one of them perhaps. Had he come back a few years later he would have found the place empty, he might have gone from room to room, tried to put himself together. The school had moved, under a new dispensation.

Before passing to the industrialist the big house had been in one family for nearly a hundred years. They were well liked locally, in a respectful sort of way. Their land near the city, most of it forest, was a remnant of the many thousands of acres that, until 1919, they had held in Mecklenburg. They lost that remnant, the house and the forest, in the mid-1930s, to the industrialist, whose interests coincided with the Party's.

When Sam and Grete met – end of May 1990, on the terrace at Stratford, during the interval of *Richard III* – they did not begin with that history. Grete liked the look of him (he was staring into the river) and came over to ask, in very clear English, could he explain to her where Gloucester had come from, so to speak, in the dynastic struggle. She knew Brecht's version, of course, but had only once read Shakespeare's, in German, years ago, too early. And she added that she could not afford a programme. Sam did his best. She thanked him; and said in a matter-of-fact voice that she had sat all afternoon by the Avon and not since she was a little girl had she been so happy. They met up afterwards and continued talking. He was at university in Manchester but had friends he could stay with in Warwick, she had a B&B in Stratford. In the event, they ignored these possibilities and wandered around till very late, then hid behind the church and dozed there chastely. By then he had confessed that he was writing a Ph.D. on forced labour under the Nazis. But all of the East interested him greatly, he said. And how people managed under one regime or another. So here I am, she said: the word made flesh. And she added, My mother was a Christian, it was her way of answering back. My father's was Esperanto. I see, he said. But you musn't like me just for things like that, she said. I don't, he answered. I won't. He liked her for her intensity and candour. His eyes had never looked into eyes as darkly bright as hers. Her thin body felt concentrated keenly on a purpose.

At first when they slept together they scarcely slept at all. The occasions were rare and their hunger for the pleasures of one another felt insatiable. But almost as keen was their hunger to talk. West and East they were new-found-land. And when she worried – or pretended to worry – that he loved her because she was living history, he answered that he was too, whether she cared for that in him or no, he was citizen of a land of failure, betrayal and numerous enslavements. She agreed, but countered that in her land the betrayals, failures and oppression had been worse, far worse; and that its future looked only differently unpromising. Their own future, on the other hand, looked boundless and abundant.

On Grete's second visit to Manchester Sam promised her better accommodation for the few days, in his new bedsit. But when they came back from the airport together, the place had been burgled, burgled and trashed. He stood with her in the wreckage. The wreckers had ignored the stereo, worth very little, but had cleaned out the CDs – jazz, blues, world music, much it would be hard to find again, for years the gaps would strike him with a little recurrence of grief. His books and papers were all over the floor. They had come in through the window, stepping down on to his desk. The page he had written last – on Russians worked to death by I.G. Farben – had a bootprint on it, large and very dirty. I ought to frame that, Sam said. Frame it and put it on the wall. It might keep me real. But the worst was when he turned to the bed. He saw Grete's framed photograph flung down there. The thought that they had touched it made him sick. Then he saw that they had stolen her gift to him, a little Chinese good-luck charm, an old man in wood with a fish slung over his shoulder, they had taken it from the bedside table. Grete had not seen a man so hurt, not since her father had stood before her finally and admitted that her mother was dead. Remembering that occasion, feeling the difference in degrees of loss, she was kind to Sam, but brisk. You don't need a charm, she said. Whoever did this does. And I'll find you another one. And as for the music, did you not promise me we'd travel the world?

Instead of going to bed, they cleaned up together thoroughly, he fixed the broken window lock, and soon, but for the losses, there was no sign of any violation. Then they went out, to see more of the city. He showed her the room in Chetham's Library, where Engels had worked, by the foul river. Then the place of the Peterloo Massacre. After that they crossed the river into Salford, where his family were from. They got bombed out, he said. The planes came up the canal and the railway line. In all that area only one named street remained, all the rest had gone, long since gone, in the clearances, under the Thatcher new enterprises, themselves now already derelict. Grete and Sam walked in the sun, talking, talking. The vanished past was itself a territory, they felt rich, in a free exchange.

That night, speaking softly in German, Grete told Sam about her school, the big house that had belonged to one of Hitler's industrialists and before him to a landowner from Mecklenburg. And that when the weather was kind her mother would sometimes be waiting for her after school and they would walk away together into the forest for an hour or so. Her mother carried a picnic in a wicker basket, under a blue or red check cloth. It might be apples or small sweet plums in the season, and always a slice of cake, lemon or chocolate, just made, and a drink in a special bottle. They walked through the forest to a clearing, in which there was a house, quite a substantial house, all of wood, and empty. And they sat on the wooden steps of the verandah, and had their picnic. The removal of the check cloth, the laying of it down, the setting of the things upon it, all was performed in silence. Then they might talk, but never very much. There was birdsong, there were fiery-black squirrels, now and then a deer. But Grete particularly remembered the stillness, nobody else ever came. Once she asked her mother why the house was empty. Who had it belonged to? But her mother shook her head, to mean that she did not know, or did not want to be asked. After a gap of years, after the death of her mother, Grete went back there on her own. She had trouble finding the place. The clearing was scarcely a clearing any more. The house had been broken into and had begun to tumble down. Grete turned and walked very definitely away. Then she asked her father who the house had belonged to. He was evasive, but she insisted. Altogether, after the death of her mother, Grete *insisted*. Jews, he said at last. They lived there, or went and hid there. They thought they might live out the bad years, I daresay. But somebody told the Gestapo. Or so I was told when I was growing up.

Soon after this admission by Grete's father, the forest itself began to disappear. Mile after mile it was felled and transported. Then the scraping for brown coal began. The house in the clearing went away with the topsoil. Where did the birds and animals go? And the stillness over the picnics in the clearing? Mile after mile, deeper and deeper, the mining pushed. It came within earshot of the school. Soon there was only a poor cordon of forest between the children and the excavation.

They could hear the machines. They became accustomed to the noise as dwellers by the surf cease hearing even that. Instead of the forest where I walked with my mother, there was a hole, said Grete softly in the dark. The biggest and ugliest hole in the world, spreading from my schooldays, further and further, deeper and deeper down. And still? Sam asked. Of course still. Except there's no work now, only wreckage in the hole.

At the end of the year Sam went to visit Grete in Leipzig. He arrived by train from Berlin. The station amazed him, so vast, dirty, purposeful, bustling, the travellers, the arrivals and departures, all the business seeming filmed in a hurried black and white. Don't get to love it, said Grete. Next time you come it will be a shopping mall. But there'll still be trains? A shopping mall, with trains offstage somewhere. Sam told her about Berlin. He had walked the corridor of trees and ruins along the broken wall. There were still rabbits in the Potsdamerplatz. Rabbits and gypsies. And in the middle of it all he saw a man painting the ironwork of the old U-Bahn exit. The exit reminded the world of tunnels that still existed. There in the very middle of a savage park, the reminder! Like a spring, surviving, about to be unstopped. Nice way to think about it, said Grete. But also they've found the old Gestapo cellars, Sam continued. There's a sort of archaeological dig going on. It was a torture place. People can visit. I didn't. I wanted to see the decades of ruins and trees, before they vanish.

Grete loved her city and wanted to show him. They walked miles across it and rode its trams to and fro in brilliant cold sunlight. Water and forest ran through the heart of it, such a healthful vein, surviving, indeed growing in strength. She took him to the Nikolaikirche, where she had stood in the crowds every Monday, all leaning their quiet force against the untenable state. And the broad boulevard, the inner ring, where they had processed in thousands under the Stasi windows and in the end, growing bolder, stormed the place, believing it defended, expecting violence, finding it abandoned. When Grete recounted these things Sam stared like a child at her. And he thought again: The creature hath a purpose, its eyes are bright with it. He asked was her father ever with her on these big occasions. In spirit he was. I'm with you in spirit, he would say to me, she answered. He was working. He is an anxious man. My mother would have been there in the spirit and in the flesh, at the Nikolaikirche week after week and in the Stasi corridors. So I was there for her as well as for me, in the body and in spirit.

Grete's father still lived in the family flat. One Sunday she and Sam crossed town from her student bedsit, to visit him and stay the night. He was indeed an anxious man. The *Wende* had thrown him out of work at once. He was in his fifties and looked to have little chance. But he re-trained, working almost maniacally at it, and got a job programming and fixing computers with a firm in Munich. Every Sunday afternoon he set off down the motorways; spent the week in a hostel with men half his age. Sam liked him. He put his heels together and bowed when they shook hands, almost giggling with nervousness. My English is very poor, he said. But your German is very good. Then he said something that made both the children blush. You and Grete, he said. It is the coming of the brotherhood of man. He said the sentence first in German, then in

Esperanto: Vi kaj Grete, vi estas la alveno de la kongregacio de la homaro! Grete will have told you about my Esperanto. It was my dissidence. And he smiled a little smile that on a less anxious face would have looked like smugness. Sam said it was strange – then he corrected himself – it was *sad* that a regime professing fraternity should have been so unfriendly towards Esperanto. Indeed, said Grete's father. They spied on us. They spied on everyone, said Grete. Where two or three are gathered together in my name, there shall the Stasi be in the midst of them. So my mother said. Her father excused himself. He must get ready for his drive to Munich.

That night Sam said, Your father is a lovable man. You think so? said Grete. Really, you think so? Of course I think so. For a while she was silent in the dark. Then she said, I don't like him driving so far every week. And to the young men he works with he must seem very strange and stand-offish. He has nothing in common with them. Then she laughed. We are the coming of the brotherhood of man, you and I, Sam. So we are, said Sam. The coming of the sister- and brotherhood of humans beneath the visiting moon. Then she told him another thing about her mother. There's such a lot still to tell you. She worked in the community creche. There was one black baby. All the years there was only one black baby. He was the son of a pair of students from Mozambique, about the only place in Africa we were allowed to have fraternal dealings with. But his mother and father disappeared. Perhaps they went back to Africa, perhaps they went West. So my mother looked after him. In the end she brought him home, he was my little foster-brother. He was called Tobias, or my mother called him that. And when she pushed him in the pram through our neighbourhood the neighbours looked away, they would not speak to her. Except that once a man came close and spat into the pram. I was there. My mother slapped his face. There on the public street she slapped that big man's face.

Grete had no idea that her mother might die. On the morning in question she said goodbye to her as usual but came home from school to an empty house. When her father appeared after an hour or so, with Tobias, who had been left at the police station, he said it was nothing to worry about, she had to spend a night in hospital, she would be home next day, or they would all go and visit her. In fact she had died in the ambulance. It was years before Grete could forgive her father his evasion. He said she would understand it one day.

Sam was silent in the dark, thinking of that. Perhaps he slept. But then, perhaps after a while, perhaps in no time at all, he felt Grete clinging to him very tightly and heard her say, Sam, you do love me, don't you? I'll never get a job here. I'll come to England and train as a teacher and we'll live together. You do want that, don't you? He assured her that he did. Good, she said. Good. Because I have heard of something and I want to go and see is it true or not. There's only you in the world I'd go and see it with. I'd have gone with my mother if she hadn't died and I hadn't met you. But she's dead and I love you so tomorrow we'll go and see whether this thing that sounds unbelievable is true or not. I think it will be true if we go and look together.

Next morning Grete took Sam first to her old school. It was playtime, the children were running and yelling around the yard like enchanted animals. They're the last year, Grete said, the place shuts next summer. Then she led him the way she had walked with her mother, from the school gates into what was left of the forest. They could see the light ahead where the trees gave out. They passed a square settlement of low huts and houses, some derelict, others quite cheerful with gnomes and geraniums. Tobias lived out here for a while, said Grete. To think, he said. It was a satellite of Sachsenhausen, said Sam. Foreign women, communists mainly. They worked for the industrialist who owned your school. You find things out, said Grete. Then the trees finished and they saw the wasteland. Grete had described it more than once, but the reality, even to her, was a shock.

The hole was terraced along the contours, further and further, deeper and deeper, year after year. It, and the air around it and above it, had filled with silence, the silence of afterwards, of what continues and must be contemplated after the thing has been done. Absence; fact of the deed; the long thereafter. Terracing is a lovely art, so clever, so caring, so tuned to the slopes of a terrain. Terracers want to make platforms to plant on, build on, live on, and ways of going along and up and down between them. They work tactfully and the hills allow it. But this was a working of the land to death, it was the will to barrenness unleashed to run its course. The tools of it lay on the finished ground, rusting. Take it in, said Grete. Look and look. As far and deep and wide as you can see. Indeed it went further than eyesight. Mournfully the spirit supposed it must last for ever.

Grete took a paper out of her pocket. Sam saw a rough map. She was concentrating hard, glancing from the map to the land

and to the map again, narrowing her black eyes, shielding her sight from the brilliant sun. I think I see where, she said. I think I see how we get there. She took Sam's hand. Who gave you the map? he asked. Tobias, she answered. Who else?

All around the rim, snaking for miles, were concrete posts and wire. They carried notices of prohibition and death. Left, said Grete, seventeen along from that leaning one. The wire was vandalized or rusted through in many places, but at the seventeenth post there was a welcoming gap. And really it's to show us where to start, she said. They had to get down, vast step by step, and the stepping down took them further in, so that they were crossing as well as fathoming the hole. The map gave them the start and the general direction, but the connections from level to level had to be discovered, the old routes having fallen in or having been blocked by the machines that had made them. Roughly the way was zig-zag. Grete seemed to be trusting her instinct, almost remembering, and it was Sam who first noticed the cairns: small mounds of stone or some arranged wreckage of iron, wood, rubber, glass, either the earth's body itself or the machinery of its violation that had been used to make small waymarkers at the head of each new diagonal down. Tobias, said Grete. That's his doing. He is guiding us. And she made a sort of greeting and acknowledgement with the fist of her left hand.

The coal had been near the surface, their descent through the strata of sand and gravel did not take long. Two hundred and fifty million years in no time at all! The ledges were rather like shelves on which specimens of the strata – abandoned diggers, broken trucks, futilely lifted conveyor-belts – were beached and displayed. Or it was a battlefield, a rout of tanks, guns, transport and soldiers' paraphernalia. Or a camp, its workplace and its pit, big enough to enslave and disappear the world. Wire, concrete and wire. Hideous however you looked at it, dead-planet and spectral. But their descent was not in the least like tunnelling. They were not leaving the sunlight and the sky. The heavens seemed amplified by the vastness of the dead excavation. Going down was eerie because of their own smallness. They had a troubling sense of what they must look like viewed from high above. Step by step diminishing, degree by degree going down and further in, all by their own locomotion, on legs, with an occasional steadying by hands, spying ahead with eyes, thinking and wondering, they magnified the feeling of their own going out of sight. At the same time, if they shook off that perspective and fixed wholly on their own purpose, they felt a bud- and seedlike concentration of individual life.

They reached the floor, the last wide level. Here there was nothing. The machinery of work had been hauled up and out. They could see now that, entering and descending, they had come into the sealed end of a vast horseshoe. Most of the excavation stretched away north and, because of the extending sky above it, looked to go on for ever. The stepped walls either side made a long embrace. For the first time they felt fearful. Is this it? Sam asked. Is this what you wished to show me? Not yet, Grete answered, whispering, afraid she might echo and the giant open-ended theatre overhear. She looked again at the sketchy map. Two hundred metres. Then Sam noticed the coal itself, the undug floor of it, ridged up into an arrow-shaped cicatrice, man-sized and pointing. Tobias, he said. Only think of him down here on his own. I suppose he was on his own? He was, said Grete. They began counting their strides but could soon make out their objective and hand in hand ran towards it. Here we are, Grete said. This is what I believed would be here.

It was another horseshoe, about thirty yards long, about ten yards across, an image in extreme miniature of the colossal shape at whose southern end it lay, the ground around it rising in a lip. And the small horseshoe held a crystal-clear water. This is the start, said Grete. Or one of the starts. According to Tobias there may be dozens of them. But this is the one he found and told me about and that I wanted to see the truth of with you. The water was icy clear and still, but with a trembling in it, a thrill of continuous quivering, and that was the spring, rising, donating, becoming a well and a pool. Grete kneeled down, leaned over. Hold me, she said. Sam held her at the hips, she leaned over and in and down and extended her hands, put out her long fingers, immersed their tips, he brought her up wetted, and kissed the cold water on her nails. Then, sitting on the brim, they ate the bread, cheese and apples of their picnic.

Think of my mother and me, said Grete, up there some-where, on a forest floor, in a clearing, on the wooden steps of an empty house, in the upper air and the roots of trees feeling down for a water like this one. Tobias says that in not many years the entire excavation will fill from springs like this. There will be a weight of clear water where there was a weight of topsoil, sand, gravel, rock and coal. Tobias works for the mapmakers. They are marking these waters in, as already arrived. There is one in Mecklenburg as large as a town, with sailing boats already on it. Breezes and sails and thousands of clamorous visiting birds. They know Tobias by now. They give him the future parts of their maps to do. He is very thorough in his researches. He promises only what he truly believes the earth can deliver. There will be several such lakes under the skies. The waiting shapes of them are on the maps, attested by Tobias, my black foster-brother.

Grete's whispering voice excited Sam. It was the voice she told him her history in, at nights. He wanted to make love there and then, on the lips of the rising spring, in the vast derelict and replenishing horseshoe, under the infinite cold bright sky. But she was sensible, said they would freeze, said they would go to bed at home as soon as they got back.

They began the climb, which looked infinitely arduous. Sam babbled his thoughts, though he needed his breath for climbing. If it was full already we'd go up naked hand in hand and very fast in a stream of bubbles. When it is full we'll come again, we'll find a rowing boat, we'll row out to where the house was in the forest in the upper air. We'll be over the horseshoe which will be as far below us as the clearing in the forest is above us now. He felt the life of water, all the seeding it contains, all the beauties it draws to it, the mirrorings of trees, of rainbows, of moon, of a dizzying number of cold bright stars, of their dust falling in showers whenever the turning of the year desires it.

UNDER THE WATERFALL
Thomas Hardy

'Whenever I plunge my arm, like this,
In a basin of water, I never miss
The sweet sharp sense of a fugitive day
Fetched back from its thickening shroud of gray.
      Hence the only prime
      And real love-rhyme
      That I know by heart,
      And that leaves no smart,
Is the purl of a little valley fall
About three spans wide and two spans tall
Over a table of solid rock,
And into a scoop of the self-same block;
The purl of a runlet that never ceases
In stir of kingdoms, in wars, in peaces;
With a hollow boiling voice it speaks
And has spoken since hills were turfless peaks.'

'And why gives this the only prime
Idea to you of a real love-rhyme?
And why does plunging your arm in a bowl
Full of spring water, bring throbs to your soul?'

'Well, under the fall, in a crease of the stone,
Though where precisely none ever has known,
Jammed darkly, nothing to show how prized,
And by now with its smoothness opalized,
      Is a drinking-glass:

>   For, down that pass,
>   My lover and I
>   Walked under a sky
> Of blue with a leaf-wove awning of green,
> In the burn of August, to paint the scene,
> And we placed our basket of fruit and wine
> By the runlet's rim, where we sat to dine;
> And when we had drunk from the glass together,
> Arched by the oak-copse from the weather,
> I held the vessel to rinse in the fall,
> Where it slipped, and sank, and was past recall,
> Though we stooped and plumbed the little abyss
> With long bared arms. There the glass still is.
> And, as said, if I thrust my arm below
> Cold water in basin or bowl, a throe
> From the past awakens a sense of that time,
> And the glass we used, and the cascade's rhyme.
> The basin seems the pool, and its edge
> The hard smooth face of the brook-side ledge,
> And the leafy pattern of china-ware
> The hanging plants that were bathing there.

> 'By night, by day, when it shines or lours,
> There lies intact that chalice of ours,
> And its presence adds to the rhyme of love
> Persistently sung by the fall above.
> No lip has touched it since his and mine
> In turns therefrom sipped lovers' wine.'

READING NOTES

There is so much to think about in this story which revisits Germany's past. People have said it is a story to keep re-reading and certainly it is one that benefits from being read aloud, slowly, stopping often to talk about what is happening. We have thought about stillness and silence: 'the air around it and above it, had filled with silence, the silence of afterwards, of what continues and must be contemplated after the thing is done.' We have thought about the barriers of language and of the strange nature of Esperanto; the Gestapo, the Stasi – the legacy of evil. We have wondered about Grete's mother and her brother Tobias. Someone said they wanted to follow their paths in and out of the story, there seemed to be so much more to know about them. The end of the story is tremendously uplifting and, as someone said, 'when, in time, things are covered over and forgotten, it is Love that knows and remembers. We have to trust in Love.'

The poem prompted lots of discussion about the things that trigger memories and how the past can sometimes seem vividly present. In both the poem and the story the couple reach down into the water plunging their arms into the water of life and we noticed how the poem says explicitly what the story shows, even 'in wars and peaces', love is constant and persistent.

What of the Heart Without Her?

THE CAR
Jennifer O'Hagan

(approximate reading time 13 minutes)

'Bastard', John muttered as the red Volvo in front of him swerved without warning into the neighbouring lane. 'Idiotic bastard', he said, louder this time, feeling the hot and ugly release that comes with thrashing the whip at your temper instead of holding firmly on to the reins. He let the fury peal out steadily now; flinging his hand out of the window; his aging, infirm voice jerking every few syllables into deeper tones – like a sad second try at adolescence: 'fucking son of a bitch driving like a bloody lunatic could have bloody killed someone. BASTARD!'

Val would be heartbroken to see him like this; but she was gone, and he no longer saw why he should hold back a single angry impulse. He missed her everywhere, but particularly when he was in the car. Why had no one taken away that passenger seat when they took away the body, he wondered, trying to refocus on the road ahead. Why had they not buried that bloody thing with her? It never stopped: it sat smugly beside him, prodding at him each time he made a journey, flaunting its emptiness all the way from every A to every B and back again.

They had been particularly strong in the car. Driving along the motorway with his wife at his side and the little ones in the back, John had often felt that he and Val were the joint captains of a winning team. It had seemed to him the perfect arrangement for a family: the mother and father up ahead organising the route; the children, freed from decisions, behind them; everybody strapped in safely; the road straight; the speed constant; the destination certain. Val would arrange the toilet stops, and John would locate the service stations. John would quietly curse the traffic, and Val would calmly turn up the radio.

Even when the children had grown up and the tight, well-knotted bonds of the family had begun to fray, John and his wife had been at their closest in the car. After every argument, they would be brought back to each other here: the silence eased by the hum of tyres against the road, and the resentment softened by their two inner elbows knocking together occasionally when he would reach across for the gear stick, and she would adjust her seatbelt. Marriage was about compromise, they both knew this, and here in the car was where their compromises most often took place – two people, one on the left and one on the right, both with a destination in mind, and manoeuvring their opinions back and forth until they got there.

He looked over at the glove compartment and remembered the journey home from a friend's wedding anniversary a few years ago. He couldn't remember exactly what he had said to cause it. She had wanted to leave the party early, and he had said something flippant to his friends about her feet not being able to cope with wearing heels anymore. She had taken it as a slight. She had thought he was saying something about her age, or her weight, or her tendency to prefer evenings at home. John was almost certain he hadn't meant anything unkind by it, but it had led, in any case, to an angry drive home. She had slammed the door after climbing into the car, pulled off her shoes, and crammed them into the glove compartment. Right into this very glove compartment! He smiled to think of it. He had thought it incredibly bold at the time, but knew that what she had done also contained the promise of an argument. She had turned her face to the window. He had had to go first.

'What did you do that for?'

'Oh, you know, my feet aren't cut out for heels anymore. Best put those shoes away!'

'Don't be like that. It was a joke – it was just a joke.'

'Yes, I know it was a joke – I could hear everyone laughing!'

'Love, please, I didn't mean anything by it.'

'Then why say it?'

At that point, John had decided to take a longer route home. He knew that if they didn't manage to clear the air in the car, the argument would follow them into the house, up the stairs, and through to tomorrow. He indicated off the main road, into a residential area. They would have to keep going. They shouldn't let the silences last too long.

'You looked great tonight, Val.'

It hadn't been what she wanted to hear, but he noticed it had eased the tension. They could steer themselves out of this. After a short pause, she said, 'The music was a bit loud in there wasn't it?' He agreed. And so they had gone on, side-stepping the issue, but both keen to keep talking. It had not been a conversation, it had been more an exchange of isolated comments – each comment another sideways step in the right direction. And the whole time, with John driving more slowly than he had wanted to, weaving irritatingly in and out of the untidy, fiddly back roads. He tried to remember how they had resolved it. They had stopped at a red light. He must have yawned or said something about being tired, and she had nodded and said that maybe he was the one who couldn't take these late nights anymore. She had meant it kindly.

John remembered how she had hobbled across the driveway that night, her stockinged feet wincing over the pebbles. He could tell she wanted to retrieve her shoes from the glove compartment, but knew she was too stubborn to do so. She could hardly take them out now, and undermine how angry she had been when she had thrown them in there. She would get them back out when John wasn't around, even if it meant waiting a few days. John had wanted to pick her up and carry her into the house. He had swallowed down the urge for fear of making the mood too merry. He didn't want her to think he had forgotten about upsetting her. And so they had walked from the vehicle to the front door, both holding back the small pleasures they might have had, and, for that, holding on ever tighter to what they had gained, like clutching a smooth banister on a narrow staircase.

There was nothing to steady John now. He was driving without her. He pulled at his tie and loosened his collar. He edged over the speed limit, keeping his eyes on the Volvo, directing his stock of vile feelings at this tidy red target. He wanted to follow it. He wanted to stamp down on the accelerator and surge forward. Faster. He wanted to steer the rage and the wrenching, excruciating sadness right into the back of that car, loudly and recklessly.

The traffic lights snapped to red, and John watched the Volvo slip through in front of him. He pressed down on the brakes. 'What a bastard', he muttered. The car was out of sight now.

The pause was lasting too long. The distractions were too few. The empty passenger seat was vying for his attention. What do other people do when they are at a red light and driving alone? He put his hand out to the radio. He could see his fingers trembling as he pushed one of the buttons randomly. A burst of noise. This will not do, he thought, willing his eyes to focus on what was in front of him. That blasted chair. That awful, blasted chair.

As soon as he had made it past the traffic lights, John looked for a place to pull over. He turned into a residential street. He turned off the engine and drew up his stiff legs as best he could onto his seat. He tried to bend his torso over the gear stick so that he could lean his head onto the empty seat next to him. He wanted to put his head on that seat and close his eyes for a while. He wanted to be done with it all for a while. But it was too awkward: the gear stick interfered with every clumsy movement he made. Feeling defeated, John got out of the car. He hovered around the vehicle restlessly. What do other people do, he wondered, when everything inside of them hurts?

He walked around the car and opened the door on the passenger side. He knelt down to smell the worn fabric, desperate for something of her to bring him back to himself. But there was nothing. He thought how unfair it was that a car should retain that new-car smell for weeks, while the scent of a person who had sat inside it almost every day for close to seventeen years should disappear so abruptly.

This had been her seat. It was intolerable that it had lasted longer than she had. He pressed his face into the bottom of the seat. It was intolerable. Where was the damage? Where were the rips and tears and gaping holes? Where was the loss; where was the grief? It had to stop looking so damned okay. It had to look like she was gone.

It was a three-door car. Both of the front seats could be moved forward to allow people to climb into the back. John wrapped his fingers around the metal lever at the side of the chair. He pulled it, listening for the click as the chair was released. He stood up and gently tipped it forward as far as it would go. He knew that the chair wouldn't stay in this position, and that it would jerk back if he stopped suddenly or drove quickly around sharp corners. He took the seatbelt, and guided it around the back of the chair, stooping down to fasten it into place. It wasn't a perfect solution – the belt was old and had slackened somewhat over the years, but it would prevent the chair from falling back into its normal position. It was an alteration, at least.

He stood back to look at the car. It looked obscure and sad. With the back of the seat so broad and square, and the head-rest perched on top, John thought how it resembled a suited man. He took another step back. It looked like a suited man slumped over, or a suited man taking a bow.

John got back into the car. Before starting the engine again, he placed his hand on the seatbelt clasp to check that it was secure. Yes, that will hold, he thought. He realised then that the seat would obstruct his view through the left-hand window. He noticed how the car felt crooked and off-balance, and wondered if that would interfere with his driving. Probably. So be it, he thought.

He resumed his journey with his wife's seat bent forward and strapped down, craning his neck occasionally to see through the window on the other side of it.

WITHOUT HER

(FROM *THE HOUSE OF LIFE*, SECTION 53)

Dante Gabriel Rossetti

What of her glass without her? The blank gray
    There where the pool is blind of the moon's face.
    Her dress without her? The tossed empty space
Of cloud-rack whence the moon has passed away.
Her paths without her? Day's appointed sway
    Usurped by desolate night. Her pillowed place
    Without her? Tears, ah me! for love's good grace,
And cold forgetfulness of night or day.

What of the heart without her? Nay, poor heart,
    Of thee what word remains ere speech be still?
    A wayfarer by barren ways and chill,
Steep ways and weary, without her thou art,
Where the long cloud, the long wood's counterpart,
    Sheds doubled darkness up the labouring hill.

READING NOTES

A project worker wrote the following: 'I've read "The Car" quite a few times in groups. Very frequently people are confused about what has happened to the wife and think she might have been killed in a car accident. One person (in a prison group) was even certain her husband had killed her! People are struck by the depth of the man's grief and how much of an influence his wife has been in his life – she used to act as a sort of handbrake for him and now she has gone, he has no reason to not be aggressive and angry any more. We usually also talk about their relationship having been sustained over many, many years through the children growing up and on into probable old age, and what it must feel like to have that person ripped away from you. People find the story very sad and I do too but I also feel that the sadness is directly in proportion to the depth of love and companionship they have experienced, and that is a precious thing so it makes me feel glad for him too that he got to have that.'

Most Near, Most Dear

♥

CIDER WITH ROSIE

(EXTRACT FROM MOTHER, CHAPTER 7)

Laurie Lee

(approximate reading time 22 minutes)

This is Laurie Lee's memoir of growing up in a remote village in the Cotswolds in the early twentieth century. Here he lovingly tells his mother's story.

My mother was born near Gloucester, in the village of Quedgeley, sometime in the early 1880s. On her own mother's side she was descended from a long line of static Cotswold farmers who had been deprived of their lands through a monotony of disasters in which drink, simplicity, gambling, and robbery played more or less equal parts. Through her father, John Light, the Berkeley coachman, she had some mysterious connexion with the Castle, something vague and intimate, half-forgotten, who knows what? but implying a blood-link somewhere. Indeed, it was said that a retainer called Lightly led the murder of Edward II – at least, this was a local scholar's opinion. Mother accepted the theory with both shame and pleasure – as it has similarly confused me since.

But whatever the illicit grandeurs of her forebears, Mother was born to quite ordinary poverty, and was the only sister to a large family of boys, a responsibility she discharged somewhat wildly. The lack of sisters and daughters was something Mother had always regretted; brothers and sons being her lifetime's lot.

She was a bright and dreamy child, it seems, with a curious, hungry mind; and she was given to airs of incongruous elegance which never quite suited her background. She was the pride, none the less, of the village schoolmaster, who did his utmost to protect and develop her. At a time when country schooling was little more than a cane-whacking interlude in which boys picked up facts like bruises and the girls scarcely counted at all, Mr Jolly, the Quedgeley schoolmaster, found this solemn child and her ravenous questioning both rare and irresistible. He was an elderly man who had battered the rudiments of learning into several generations of farm-hands. But in Annie Light he saw a freak of intelligence which he felt bound to nurture and cherish.

'Mr Jolly was really educated,' Mother told us; 'and the pains he took with poor me.' She giggled. 'He used to stop after school to put me through my sums – I was never any good at figures. I can see him now, parading up and down, pulling at his little white whiskers. "Annie," he used to say, "you've got a lovely fist. You write the best essay in class. But you can't do sums . . ." And I couldn't, either; they used to tie me in knots inside. But he was patience itself; he *made* me learn; and he used to lend me all his beautiful books. He wanted me to train to be a teacher, you see. But of course Father wouldn't hear of it . . .'

When she was about thirteen years old her mother was taken ill, so the girl had to leave school for good. She had her five young brothers and her father to look after, and there was no one else to help. So she put away her books and her modest ambitions as she was naturally expected to do. The school-master was furious and called her father a scoundrel, but was helpless to interfere. 'Poor Mr Jolly,' said Mother, fondly. 'He never seemed to give up. He used to come round home when I was doing the washing and lecture me on Oliver Cromwell. He used to sit there so sad, saying it was a sinful shame, till Father used to dance and swear . . .'

There was probably no one less capable of bringing up five husky brothers than this scatter-brained, half-grown girl. But she did what she could, at least. Meanwhile, she grew into tumble-haired adolescence, slap-dashing the housework in fits of abstractions and sliding into trances over the vegetables. She lived by longing rather than domestic law: Mr Jolly and his books had ruined her. During her small leisure hours she would put up her hair, squeeze her body into a tight-boned dress, and either sit by the window, or walk in the fields – getting poetry by heart, or sketching the landscape in a delicate snowflake scribble.

To the other village girls Mother was something of a case, yet they were curiously drawn towards her. Her strain of fantasy, her deranged sense of fun, her invention, satire, and elegance of manner, must have intrigued and perplexed them equally. One gathered that there were also quarrels at times, jealousies, name-callings, and tears. But there existed a coterie among the Quedgeley girls of which Mother was the exasperating centre. Books were passed round, excursions arranged, boys confounded by witty tongues. 'Beatie Thomas, Vi Phillips – the laughs we used to have. The things we did. We were *terrible*.'

When her brothers were big enough to look after themselves, Mother went into domestic service. Wearing her best straw hat and carrying a rope-tied box, seventeen and shapely, half-wistful, half-excited, she set out alone for that world of great houses which in those days absorbed most of her kind. As scullery-maid, housemaid, nursemaid, parlour-maid, in large manors all over the west, she saw luxuries and refinements she could never forget, and to which in some way she naturally belonged.

The idea of the Gentry, like love or the theatre, stayed to haunt her for the rest of her life. It haunted us too, through her. 'Real Gentry wouldn't hear of it,' she used to say; 'the Gentry always do it like this.' Her tone of voice, when referring to their ways, was reverent, genteel, and longing. It proclaimed standards of culture we could never hope to attain and mourned their impossible perfections.

Sometimes, for instance, faced by a scratch meal in the kitchen, Mother would transform it in a trance of memory. A gleam would come to her hazy eyes and a special stance to her body. Lightly she would deploy a few plates on the table and curl her fingers airily . . .

'For dining, they'd have every place just *so*; personal cruets for every guest . . .' Grimly we settled into our greens and bacon: there was no way to stop her now. 'The silver and napery must be arranged in order, a set for each separate dish . . .' Our old bent forks would be whisked into line, helter-skelter along the table. 'First of all, the butler would bring in the soup (scoop-scoop) and begin by serving the ladies. There'd be river-trout next, or fresh salmon (flick-flick) lightly sprinkled with herbs and sauces. Then some woodcock perhaps, or a guinea-fowl – oh, yes, and a joint as well. And a cold ham on the sideboard, too, if you wished. For the gentlemen only, of course. The ladies never did more than pick at their food –' 'Why not?' '– Oh, it wasn't thought proper. Then Cook would send in some violet cakes, and there'd be walnuts and fruit in brandy. You'd have wine, of course, with every dish, each served with a different glass . . .' Stunned, we would listen, grinding our teeth and swallowing our empty hungers. Meanwhile Mother would have completely forgotten about our soup, which then boiled over, and put out the fire.

But there were other stories of Big House life which we found somewhat less affronting. Glimpses of balls and their shimmering company, the chandeliers loaded with light. ('We cleared a barrel of candle-ends next morning.') And then Miss Emily's betrothal. ('What a picture she was – we were allowed a peep from the stairs. A man came from Paris just to do her hair. Her dress had a thousand pearls. There were fiddlers in black perched up in the gallery. The gentlemen all wore uniform. Then the dances – the Polka, the Two-Step, the Schottische – oh dear, I was carried away. We were all of us on the top landing, listening; I was wicked in those days, I know. I seized hold of the pantry-boy and said, "Come on Tom", and we danced up and down the passage. Then the Butler found us and boxed our ears. He was a terrible man, Mr Bee . . .')

The long hard days the girls had of it then: rising before dawn, all feathered with sleep, to lay twenty or thirty fires; the sweeping, scrubbing, dusting, and polishing that was done but to be done again; the scouring of pyramids of glass and silver; the scampering up and down stairs; and those irritable little bells that began ringing in tantrums just when you'd managed to put up your feet.

There was a £5-a-year wage, a fourteen-hour day, and a small attic for ravenous sleep: for the rest, the sub-grandees of the servants' hall with a caste-system more rigid than India's.

All the same, below-stairs was a lusty life, an underworld of warmth and plenty, huge meals served cosily cheek-by-jowl, with roast joints and porter for all. Ruled by a despotic or gin-mellow Butler and a severe or fun-fattened Cook, the young country girls and the grooms and the footmen stirred a seething broth together. There were pursuits down the passages, starched love in the laundry, smothered kisses behind green-baize doors – such flights and engagements filled the scrambling hours when the rows of brass bells were silent.

How did mother fit into all this, I wonder? And those neat-fingered parlour-queens, prim over-housemaids, reigning Cooks, raging Nannies, who ordered her labours – what could they have made of her? Mischievous, muddle-headed, full of brilliant fancies, half witless, half touched with wonder; she was something entirely beyond their ken and must often have been their despair. But she was popular in those halls, a kind of mascot or clown; and she was beautiful, most beautiful at that time. She may not have known it, but her pictures reveal it; she herself seemed astonished to be noticed.

Two of her stories which reflect this astonishment I remember very well. Each is no more than an incident, but

when she told them to us they took on a poignancy which
prevented us from thinking them stale. I must have heard them
many times, right on into her later years, but at each re-telling
she flushed and shone, and looked down at her hands in amaze-
ment, recalling again those two magic encounters which raised
her for a moment from Annie Light the housemaid to a throne
of enamelled myrtles.

The first one took place at the end of the century, when
Mother was at Gaviston Court. 'It was an old house, you know;
very rambling and dark; a bit primitive too in some ways. But
they entertained a lot – not just Gentry, but all sorts, even black
men too at times. The Master had travelled all round the world
and he was a very distinguished gentleman. You never quite knew
what you were going to run into – it bothered us girls at times.

'Well, one winter's night they had this big house-party and
the place was packed right out. It was much too cold to use the
outside privy, and there was one just along the passage. The
staff wasn't supposed to use it, of course; but I thought, oh,
I'll take a chance. Well, I'd just got me hand on the privy door
when suddenly it flew wide open. And there, large as life, stood
an Indian prince, with a turban, and jewels in his beard. I felt
awful, you know – I was only a girl – I wished the ground to
swallow me up. I just bobbed him a curtsy and said, "Pardon,
your Highness" – I was paralysed, you see. But he only smiled,
and then folded his hands, and bowed low, and said "Please
madame to enter." So I held up my head, and went in, and sat
down. Just like that. I felt like a Queen . . .'

The second encounter Mother always described as though it
had never happened – in that special, morning, dream-telling

voice that set it apart from all ordinary life. 'I was working at the time in a big red house at a place called Farnhamsurrey. On my Sundays off I used to go into Aldershot to visit my friend Amy Frost – Amy Hawkins that was, from Churchdown you know, before she got married, that is. Well, this particular Sunday I'd dressed up as usual, and I do think I looked a picture. I'd my smart lace-up boots, striped blouse and choker, a new bonnet, and crochet-work gloves. I got into Aldershot far too early so I just walked about for a bit. We'd had rain in the night and the streets were shining, and I was standing quite alone on the pavement. When suddenly round the corner, without any warning, marched a full-dress regiment of soldiers. I stood transfixed; all those men and just me; I didn't know where to look. The officer in front – he had beautiful whiskers – raised his sword and cried out "Eyes right!" Then, would you believe, the drums started rolling, and the bagpipes started to play, and all those wonderful lads as they went swinging by snapped to attention and looked straight in my eyes. I stood all alone in my Sunday dress, it quite took my breath away. All those drums and pipes, and that salute just for me – I just cried, it was so exciting . . .'

Later, our grandfather retired from his horses and went into the liquor business. He became host at The Plough, a small Sheepscombe inn, and when Grandmother died, a year or two afterwards, Mother left service to help him. Those were days of rough brews, penny ales, tuppenny rums, home-made cider, the staggers, and violence. Mother didn't altogether approve of the life, but she entered the calling with spirit. 'That's where I learned the frog-march,' she'd say; 'and there were plenty of those who got it! Pug Sollars, for instance; the biggest bully in Sheepscombe – cider used to send him mad. He'd pick up the tables and lay about him like an animal while the chaps hid behind the piano. "Annie!" they'd holler, "for the Lord's sake save us!" I was the only one who could handle Pug. Many's the time I've caught him by the collar and run him along the passage. Others, too – if they made me wild, I'd just throw them out in the road. Dad was too easy, so it was me had to do it . . . They smirk when they see me now.'

The Plough Inn was built as one of the smaller stages on the old coach road to Birdlip; but by Mother's time the road had decayed and was no longer the main route to anywhere. One or two carters, impelled by old habits, still used the lane and the inn, and Mother gave them ale and bacon suppers and put them to sleep in the stables. Otherwise, few travellers passed that way, and the lane was mostly silent. So through the long afternoons Mother fell into dreams of idleness, would dress in her best and sit out on the terrace, reading, or copying flowers. She was a lonely young woman, mysteriously detached, graceful in face and figure. Most of the village boys were afraid of her, of her stormy temper, her superior wit, her unpredictable mental exercises.

Mother spent several odd years in that village pub, living her double life, switching from bar-room rages to terrace medi-tations, and waiting while her twenties passed. Grandfather, on the other hand, spent his time in the cellars playing the fiddle across his boot. He held the landlordship of an inn to be the same as Shaw's definition of marriage – as something combining the maximum of temptation with the maximum of opportunity. So he seldom appeared except late in the evening, when he'd pop up through a hole in the floor, his clothes undone, his face streaming with tears, singing 'The Warrior's Little Boy'.

Mother stuck by him faithfully, handled the drunks, grew older, and awaited deliverance. Then one day she read in a local paper: 'Widower (4 Children) Seeks Housekeeper.' She had had enough of Pug Sollars by now, and of fiddle-tunes in the cellar. She changed into her best, went out on to the terrace, sat down, and answered the advertisement. A reply came back, an appointment was made; and that's how she met my father.

When she moved into his tiny house in Stroud, and took charge of his four small children, Mother was thirty and still quite handsome. She had not, I suppose, met anyone like him before. This rather priggish young man, with his devout gentility, his airs and manners, his music and ambitions, his charm, bright talk, and undeniable good looks, overwhelmed her as soon as she saw him. So she fell in love with him immediately, and remained in love for ever. And herself being comely, sensitive, and adoring, she attracted my father also. And so he married her. And so later he left her – with his children and some more of her own.

When he'd gone, she brought us to the village and waited. She waited for thirty years. I don't think she even knew what had made him desert her, though the reasons seemed clear enough. She was too honest, too natural for this frightened man; too remote from his tidy laws. She was, after all, a country girl; disordered, hysterical, loving. She was muddled and mischievous as a chimney-jackdaw, she made her nest of rags and jewels, was happy in the sunlight, squawked loudly at danger, pried and was insatiably curious, forgot when to eat or ate all day, and sang when sunsets were red. She lived by the easy laws of the hedgerow, loved the world, and made no plans, had a quick holy eye for natural wonders and couldn't have kept a neat house for her life. What my father wished for was something quite different, something she could never give him – the protective order of an unimpeachable suburbia, which was what he got in the end.

The three or four years Mother spent with my father she fed on for the rest of her life. Her happiness at that time was something she guarded as though it must ensure his eventual return. She would talk about it almost in awe, not that it had ceased but that it had happened at all.

'He was proud of me then. I could make him laugh. "Nance, you're a killer," he'd say. He used to sit on the doorstep quite helpless with giggles at the stories and things I told him. He admired me too; he admired my looks; he really loved me, you know. "Come on, Nance," he'd say. "Take out your pins. Let your hair down – let's see it shine!" He loved my hair; it had gold lights in it then and it hung right down my back. So I'd sit in the window and shake it over my shoulders – it was so heavy you wouldn't believe – and he'd twist and arrange it so that it caught the sun, and then sit and just gaze and gaze . . .

'Sometimes, when you children were all in bed, he'd clear all his books away – "Come one, Nance," he'd say, "I've had enough of them. Come and sing us a song!" We'd go to the piano, and I'd sit on his lap, and he'd play with his arms around me. And I'd sing him "Killarney" and "Only a Rose". They were both his favourites then . . .'

When she told us these things it was yesterday and she held him again in her enchantment. His later scorns were stripped away and the adored was again adoring. She'd smile and look up the weed-choked path as though she saw him coming back for more.

But it was over all right, he'd gone for good, we were alone and that was that.

TO MY MOTHER
George Barker

Most near, most dear, most loved and most far,
Under the window where I often found her
Sitting as huge as Asia, seismic with laughter,
Gin and chicken helpless in her Irish hand,
Irresistible as Rabelais, but most tender for
The lame dogs and hurt birds that surround her,—
She is a procession no one can follow after
But be like a little dog following a brass band.

She will not glance up at the bomber, or condescend
To drop her gin and scuttle to a cellar,
But lean on the mahogany table like a mountain
Whom only faith can move, and so I send
O all my faith and all my love to tell her
That she will move from mourning into morning.

READING NOTES

A group of young mothers was amazed that Laurie Lee's mother stayed in love with her husband 'for ever', even though he walked out and left her with four of his children and three more of her own. They thought it was dreadfully sad that a bright girl should have to leave school at thirteen to look after her family. 'She sounds really special,' said Katie. 'I love her untidiness and her hysterics and the fact that she waited for her man for thirty years.' Everyone felt that Laurie Lee must have truly loved his mother and this led to talk of people's relationships with their mothers and hopes that their own children would stay close and love them as much as they grew older.

The poem too is a celebration of a son's love for his larger-than-life mother. The group enjoyed the poem's vibrant portrait of the mother and thought imaginatively of her character; shrugged their shoulders at Rabelais, and wondered about the sadness in the last line.

In a group of older readers, people told of their grandparents being 'in service' and some remembered having to go to air-raid shelters during the war, though someone said she had been more afraid of the unpleasant shelter than the threat of bombs.

Two Poems: Wheresoe'er You Are

I CARRY YOUR HEART
e e cummings

i carry your heart with me(i carry it in
my heart)i am never without it(anywhere
i go you go,my dear;and whatever is done
by only me is your doing,my darling)
                                        i fear
no fate(for you are my fate,my sweet)i want
no world(for beautiful you are my world,my true)
and it's you are whatever a moon has always meant
and whatever a sun will always sing is you

here is the deepest secret nobody knows
(here is the root of the root and the bud of the bud
and the sky of the sky of a tree called life;which grows
higher than soul can hope or mind can hide)
and this is the wonder that's keeping the stars apart

i carry your heart(i carry it in my heart)

LOVE'S OMNIPRESENCE
Joshua Sylvester

Were I as base as is the lowly plain,
And you, my Love, as high as heaven above,
Yet should the thoughts of me your humble swain
Ascend to heaven in honour of my Love.
Were I as high as heaven above the plain,
And you, my Love, as humble and as low
As are the deepest bottoms of the main,
Wheresoe'er you were, with you my love should go.
Were you the earth, dear Love, and I the skies,
My Love should shine on you like to the sun,
And look upon you with ten thousand eyes,
Till heaven waxed blind, and till the world were done.
Wheresoe'er I am, below or else above you,
Wheresoe'er you are, my heart shall truly love you.

READING NOTES

People usually comment on the strange grammar: no capital letters, not much punctuation and lots of brackets. 'When you read it slowly, out loud,' said Paul, 'it makes sense.' Someone else said that the poem was beautifully read at her daughter's wedding and made everyone cry. We have wondered why the words 'I fear' are stuck out all by themselves at the end of the line; thought about the ways in which the poem is romantic but also considered that the poem could be addressed to a baby. Paul said he liked the way that the word 'true' stood by itself – 'you are my world, my true'.

Joshua Sylvester's poem caused a young woman to reflect that when we are in love, we always want to measure love – how much do I love you? This much, or that much? Someone else wondered if the poet would still be as passionate after twenty years of marriage. 'Never mind the poems, she'll be lucky then if she gets a bunch of garage flowers on their anniversary.'

Hand in Hand We'll Go

WALK TWO MOONS

(EXTRACT FROM THE MARRIAGE BED, CHAPTER 12)

Sharon Creech

(approximate reading time 10 minutes)

Salamanca Hiddle is driving across America with her grandparents. They are bound for Lewiston, Idaho, where she hopes to be reunited with her mother who inexplicably left home some months previously.

That night we stayed in Injun Joe's Peace Palace Motel. On a sign in the lobby, someone had crossed out 'Injun' and written 'Native American' so the whole sign read: 'Native American Joe's Peace Palace Motel.' In our room, the 'Injun Joe's' embroidered on the towels had been changed with black marker to 'Indian Joe's'. I wished everybody would just make up their minds.

By now, I was used to staying in a room with Gram and Gramps. They did exactly the same things in the same order each night. Gramps brought in the suitcases and tossed them on the beds. Gram opened up their suitcase and fished out their pajamas. She handed Gramps' small black shaving bag to him and he flung it on the sink in the bathroom. She took out her own blue make-up bag and carried it to the bathroom, where she set it on the sink next to Gramps' black bag.

Returning to the suitcase, she removed a clean shirt and clean underwear for Gramps, and a clean dress and clean underwear for herself. Gramps stuffed hangers into the shirt and the dress while Gram placed the underwear in a dresser drawer. Then Gram straightened the shirt and dress that Gramps had rammed into the closet.

The first night, I watched them and then I repeated everything they had done: I opened my suitcase, took out what I needed, put it away. After the first night, I just followed along behind them, doing everything they did.

Every night, when they climbed into bed, they lay right beside each other on their backs and Gramps said, every single night, 'Well, this ain't our marriage bed, but it will do.'

Probably the most precious thing in the whole world to Gramps – beside Gram – was their marriage bed. This is what he called their bed back home in Bybanks, Kentucky. One of the stories that Gramps liked to tell was about how he and all his brothers had been born in that bed, and all Gram's and Gramps' own children had been born in that same bed.

When Gramps tells this story, he starts with when he was seventeen-years-old and living with his parents in Bybanks. That's when he met Gram. She was visiting her aunt who lived over the meadow from where Gramps lived.

'I was a wild thing, then,' Gramps said, 'and I didn't stand still for any girl, I can tell you that. They had to try to catch me on the run. But, when I saw your grandmother running in the meadow, with her long hair silky as a filly's, I was the one who was trying to do the catching. Talk about wild things! Your grandmother was the wildest, most untamed, most ornery and beautiful creature ever to grace this earth.'

Gramps said he followed her like a sick, old dog for twenty-two days, and on the twenty-third day, he marched up to her father and asked if he could marry her.

Her father said, 'If you can get her to stand still long enough and if she'll have you, I guess you can.'

When Gramps asked Gram to marry him, she said, 'Do you have a dog?'

Gramps said that yes, as a matter of fact, he had a fat old beagle, named Sadie.

Gram said, 'And, where does she sleep?'

Gramps stumbled around a bit and said, 'To tell you the truth, she sleeps right next to me, but if we was to get married, I—'

'When you come in the door at night,' Gram said, 'what does that dog do?'

Gramps couldn't figure what she was getting at, so he just told the truth. 'She jumps all over me, a-lickin and a-howlin.'

'And, then, what do *you* do?' Gram asked.

'Well, gosh!' Gramps said. He did not like to admit it, but he said, 'I take her in my lap and pet her till she calms down, and sometimes I sing her a song. You're making me feel foolish,' he said to Gram.

'I don't mean to,' she said. 'You've told me all I need to know. I figure if you treat a dog that good, you'll treat me better. I figure if that old beagle Sadie loves you so much, I'll probably love you better. Yes, I'll marry you.'

They were married three months later. During that time between his proposal and their wedding day, Gramps and his father and brothers built a small house in the clearing behind the first meadow.

'We didn't have time,' Gramps said, 'to completely finish it, and there wasn't a single stick of furniture in it, but that didn't matter. We were going to sleep there on our wedding night, all the same.'

They were married in an aspen grove on a clear July day, and afterwards they and all their friends and relatives had a wedding supper on the banks of the river. During the supper, Gramps noticed that his father and two of his brothers were absent. He thought maybe they were planning a wet cheer, which is when the men kidnap the groom for an hour or so and they all go out to the woods and share a bottle of whiskey. Before the end of the supper, his father and brothers came back, but they did not kidnap him for a wet cheer. Gramps was just as glad, he said, because he needed his wits about him that evening.

After supper, Gramps picked up Gram in his arms and carried her across the meadow. Behind them, everyone was singing, 'Oh meet me, in the tulips, when the tulips do blooom . . .' This is what they always sing at weddings when the married couple leaves. It is supposed to be a joke, as if Gram and Gramps were going away by themselves and might not reappear until the following spring when the tulips were in bloom.

Gramps carried Gram all the way across the meadow and through the trees and into the clearing where their little house stood. He carried her in through the door, and took one look around and started to cry.

'In my life,' Gram once told me, 'I only saw your grand-
father cry five times. Once was when he carried me into that
house. The only other times were when each of our four babies
was born.'

The reason Gramps cried when he carried Gram into the
house was that there, in the centre of the bedroom, stood
his own parents' bed – the bed that Gramps and each of his
brothers had been born in – the one his parents had always
slept in. This was where his father and brothers had disap-
peared to during the supper. They had been moving the bed
into Gram and Gramps' new house. At the foot of the bed,
wiggling and slurping, was Sadie, Gramps' old beagle dog.

Gramps always ends this story by saying, 'That bed has been
around my whole entire life, and I'm going to die in that bed, and
then that bed will know everything there is to know about me.'

So, each night on our trip out to Idaho, Gramps patted the
bed in the motel and said, 'Well, this ain't our marriage bed,
but it will do,' while I lay in the next bed wondering if I would
ever have a marriage bed like theirs.

JOHN ANDERSON MY JO[1]
Robert Burns

John Anderson my jo, John,
    When we were first Acquent,[2]
Your locks were like the raven,
    Your bony brow was brent;[3]
But now your brow is beld,[4] John,
    Your locks are like the snaw;
But blessings on your frosty pow,[5]
    John Anderson, my jo.

John Anderson my jo, John,
    We clamb the hill thegither,[6]
And mony a canty[7] day, John,
    We've had wi' ane anither;
Now we maun totter down, John,
    And hand in hand we'll go,
And sleep thegither at the foot,
    John Anderson my jo.

[1] jo: dear
[2] Aquent: acquainted
[3] brent: smooth
[4] beld: bald
[5] pow: head
[6] thegither: together
[7] canty: cheerful

READING NOTES

A group leader in Scotland said: 'When reading this passage with a group of young people with English as an additional language, we were first drawn to Sal's assertion: "I watched them and then I repeated everything they had done . . . After the first night, I just followed along behind them, doing everything they did." This led to discussions about the contrast between how we view our elders and the difference between "being in the know" and not. The conversations took two strands: first, the relationship between ourselves and our own grandparents and what we had learnt from them; and second, who the people were that the group members had implicitly followed when they first arrived in the UK or first came to school. We had some great discussions about role models and how useful or otherwise the acquired knowledge had actually been!

'Readers have also been interested in the closeness of Gram and Gramps's relationship with the enduring playfulness between the two of them really shining through. How can they still be so happy after so many years together? How much of the "wildest, most untamed, most ornery and beautiful creature" can we still see? Readers were also surprised at how simple and fast the whole process from first meeting to getting married really was, with the female members of the group shocked at the simplicity of Gram's reasoning before committing to marriage: "I figure if you treat a dog that good, you'll treat me better." Is this the best way to pick a life partner?'

A group in a care home in London enjoyed the tenderness of the poem very much, but attempts at a Scottish accent took them to Wales, India and Birmingham.

I Rest in Peace in You

♥

HANNAH COULTER

(THE ROOM OF LOVE, CHAPTER 14)

Wendell Berry

(approximate reading time 16 minutes)

Hannah Coulter is twice widowed and now, an old woman, she looks back on her life and considers the changes to the community in which she lives. Her first husband was killed in the Second World War. Her second husband, Nathan Coulter, also saw action in Europe but returned to become a farmer. He and Hannah bought an old farmhouse where they worked hard and raised a family. Andy Catlett is a neighbouring farmer.

I was twenty-six years getting from my birth in the old house on the Steadman place at Shagbark to a house and place of my own, and to a long-going, day-to-day marriage. As I said before, the marriage had troubles in it, which is easy to say. It had something else in it too, which is not so easy. As I go about quietly by myself in my days now or lie awake in the night, I hunt for the way to speak of it, for it is the best thing I have known in this world, and it lays its peace on everything else I know.

What the marriage had in it, of course, was Nathan and me. We were in it together because of our plighting of troth, his to me, mine to him, and that was one thing. But we were together in it also because, from time to time, often enough, we were in it by desire, we met entirely in it and were one flesh. What that was and is and means is not altogether going to be found in words.

This was a marriage that did not begin with a honeymoon, and that tells one of the important things about it. We got married and went to work. We had to, we didn't have any time or money to spare. And a honeymoon was something we never greatly missed. Nathan said, 'It would have been nice if we'd had it, but we didn't have it.' We had our living to make, and our place to make while we made our living. We were at work pretty quick after the groom kissed the bride. We had debts to pay and a long effort ahead of us.

The making of the place was the thing that ruled over everything else, for we were living from the place. Little Margaret, and our boys after they came, were living from the place. You can see that it is hard to mark the difference between our life and our place, our place and ourselves.

As the years passed and our life changed, the place changed. It emerged, you might say, from what it had been into what we needed and wanted it to be, never perfect of course, but always a little better. It came under the influence of what we foresaw in it, and our ways of using it and going about in it.

Though we talked of what was possible and what needed to be done, the shaping of the place, the look of it, was mostly Nathan's doing. He had a way of getting it right.

He didn't want to come out and say so, but he was proud of his work.

When Andy Catlett would come back after one of his longish absences from home and would come to see us, Nathan would ask him, 'Well, do you see anything different?'

It would be a new building or an old one renewed or a new fence, or a coat of paint somewhere. Andy would shake his head and grin, knowing he was being tested and was failing the test. Nathan would have to tell him, 'Look at the barn' or 'Look at the lot fence' or 'Look at the corn-crib.'

Andy would say, 'Oh!' and make the proper compliment, for he would be honestly pleased as soon as he saw what he needed to see.

Later Nathan would laugh. 'He's the same damned dreamy kid he's always been.'

But this wasn't exactly Andy's fault. What Nathan had done was what should have been done. The place never looked as if something had been changed. It looked right. It looked the way it ought to have looked. It looked right because the right man was doing the work. If the wrong man had done it, Andy, even you would have noticed.

Nathan always got up before I did. If it was winter he would build the fires. As the children grew big enough to have their own morning chores, he would get them up. I would hear them go out. The nighttime quiet would fill the house again. And then I would get up and dress and go to the kitchen. I would have breakfast ready by the time they came in with the milk.

Except when I was needed in the crew work of the busier farming seasons, I kept the house, worked in the garden, and took care of the chickens, doing the work again that I had done with Grandmam when I was a girl, except that now I usually didn't do the milking. As I went about my work then as a young woman, and still now when I am old, Grandmam has been often close to me in my thoughts. And again I come to the difficulty of finding words. It is hard to say what it means to be at work and thinking of a person you loved and love still who did that same work before you and who taught you to do it. It is a comfort ever and always, like hearing the rhyme come when you are singing a song.

The house, its furnishings and surroundings, took on the appearance given it by my ways of work and my liking, just as Nathan's work and his liking altered the looks of the farm. And as our work shaped our workplace, our work and our workplaces shaped our days. Our work brought us together and drew us apart. Sometimes we would be together only at mealtimes and at night. Sometimes we would be together at the same work most of the day.

We had differences. There were the agreed-on differences of work. There were the accepted, mostly happy differences between a man and a woman. There were the differences of nature and character that were sometimes happy and sometimes not. Some of the things that most endeared Nathan to me – his quietness, his love of his work, his determination – were the things that could sometimes make me maddest at him.

He hated waste, and he was not a waster. It is not surprising that he did not waste words. He said exactly what he had to say, and he meant what he said. He was inclined not to say again what he had said before. You had to listen to him, as the children knew, because he wasn't going to repeat himself. Sometimes he would be finished talking before we had started listening. He didn't rattle. I liked that and was proud of him for it, but I have to say too that it could be a burden. There would be times when he didn't have much to say about anything. If that lasted long enough, I began to feel his quietness as distance. There he would be – so I would think to myself – outside love, outside marriage, way off by himself. Which of course left me by myself. Sometimes it would make me mad, and then I would make him mad. This was not something I did by deliberate intention but was just something I did. When we were both mad, we would have something to say to each other. It wasn't love, but it beat indifference, and sooner or later, mostly sooner, it would come to love.

Sometimes Nathan would do the same thing to me. We would get strayed apart somehow, he would get lonesome, and first thing you know he would do something to make me mad. I think husbands pick fights with their wives sometimes just to get their attention. If you can't get her hot, make her mad. You can't hold it against them. Or anyhow I can't, for as I've just confessed, I did it too.

Sometimes, too, Nathan's eagerness in his work would come across as nothing but impatience. That was his father in him. There were times when he was apt to run over you if you didn't get out of his way. He wasn't stubborn exactly, he was determined. There was a demand in him that you could feel. He didn't have to speak.

When I would be helping him with the cattle and would make a misstep and let one get by me, he would never say anything. He would just give me a look. Sometimes, doing that, he could make me so mad I could have shot him right between the eyes. He knew it too.

Once when I gave him his look back with interest, he laughed. He said, 'Hannah, you'd be a bad hand to carry a pistol.'

I didn't laugh. I stayed mad at him for about a day. And then finally he asked me, 'Are you a pretty good shot with a pistol?'

'I couldn't hit the side of a barn,' I said. 'Lucky for you.'

We both laughed then, and it was all right.

We had often enough the pleasure of making up, because we fell out often enough. But now, looking back, it is hard to say why we fell out, or what we fell out about, or why whatever we fell out about ever mattered. Even then it was something hard to say.

One time we were fussing and Nathan looked at me right in the middle of it and said, 'Hannah, what in the *hell* got us started on this?'

I said, 'I *don't* know.'

'Well, I don't know either,' he said. 'So I think I'm going to quit.'

'Well go ahead and quit,' I said.

He said, 'I already did.' And that was the last word that time.

You have had this life and no other. You have had this life with this man and no other. What would it have been to have had a different life with a different man? You will never know. That makes the world forever a mystery, and you will just have to be content for it to be that way.

We quarrelled because we loved each other, I have no doubt of that. We were trying to become somehow the same person, one flesh, and we often failed. When distance came between us, we would blame it on each other. And here is a wonder. I maybe never loved him so much or yearned towards him so much as when I was mad at him. It's not a simple thing, this love.

It wasn't always anger that came between us. Work could come between us. Thoughts could come between us. Feeling in different ways about the children could come between us. We would go apart, Nathan into whatever loneliness was his, I into mine. We would be like stars or planets in their orbits moving apart. And then we would come into alignment again, the sun and the moon and the earth. And then it would be as if we were coming together for the first time. It was like the time when I had decided I would belong to whatever it was that we would be together, and I looked straight back at him at last. He would look at me with a grin that I knew. He would say, 'Is it all right?' And I would say, 'It's all right.' The knowledge of his desire and of myself as desirable and of my desire would come over me. He would come to me as my guest, and I would be his welcomer.

What I was always reaching toward in him was his gentleness that had been made in him by loss and grief and suffering, a gentleness opposite to the war that he was not going to talk about, and never did, but that I know at least something about, having learned it since he died.

The gentleness I knew in him seemed to be calling out, and it was a gentleness in me that answered. That gentleness, calling and answering, giving and taking, brought us together.

It brought us into the room of love. It made our place clear around us.

Nathan said, 'You've seen those dragonflies flying together joined. How do they know to fly in the same direction?'

'They know,' I said. 'They know the same way we know.'

That was what I wanted to say, and as I said it I realized it was what he wanted me to say.

It would be again like the coming of the rhymes in a song, a different song, this one, a long song, the rhymes sometimes wide apart, but the rhymes would come.

The rhymes came. But you may have a long journey to travel to meet someone in the innermost inwardness and sweetness of that room. You can't get there just by wanting to, or just because the night falls. The meeting is prepared in the long day, in the work of years, in the keeping of faith, in kindness.

The room of love is another world. You go there wearing no watch, watching no clock. It is the world without end, so small that two people can hold it in their arms, and yet it is bigger than worlds on worlds, for it contains all the longing of all things to be together, and to be at rest together. You come together to the day's end, weary and sore, troubled and afraid. You take it all into your arms, it goes away, and there you are where giving and taking are the same, and you live a little while entirely in a gift. The words have all been said, all permissions given, and you are free in the place that is the two of you together. What could be more heavenly than to have desire and satisfaction in the same room?

If you want to know why even in telling of trouble and sorrow I am giving thanks, this is why.

from **THE COUNTRY OF MARRIAGE**
Wendell Berry

1

I dream of you walking at night along the streams
of the country of my birth, warm blooms and the
   nightsongs
of birds opening around you as you walk.
You are holding in your body the dark seed of my sleep.

2

This comes after silence. Was it something I said
that bound me to you, some mere promise
or, worse, the fear of loneliness and death?
A man lost in the woods in the dark, I stood
still and said nothing. And then there rose in me,
like the earth's empowering brew rising
in root and branch, the words of a dream of you
I did not know I had dreamed. I was a wanderer
who feels the solace of his native land
under his feet again and moving in his blood.
I went on, blind and faithful. Where I stepped
my track was there to steady me. It was no abyss
that lay before me, but only the level ground.

3

Sometimes our life reminds me
of a forest in which there is a graceful clearing

and in that opening a house,
an orchard and garden,
comfortable shades, and flowers
red and yellow in the sun, a pattern
made in the light for the light to return to.
The forest is mostly dark, its ways
to be made anew day after day, the dark
richer than the light and more blessed
provided we stay brave
enough to keep on going in.

4

How many times have I come into you out of my head
with joy, if ever a man was,
for to approach you I have given up the light
and all directions. I come to you
lost, wholly trusting, as a man who goes
into the forest unarmed. It is as though I descend
slowly earthward out of the air. I rest in peace
in you, when I arrive at last.

READING NOTES

'I love it when he says in the poem "I went on, blind and faithful" and it turns out that he is actually on steady ground and there isn't a pit waiting for him to fall into,' said a reading group member. 'I don't think I understand all of this poem but it has an atmosphere I want to be part of and so I will keep reading it.' Readers have commented on the idea of marriage being also a sense of place – the country of marriage. They have talked about the idea of dark and light in the third verse and the importance of trust.

People have spoken of the quality of the marriage in the story. While the couple undoubtedly have had their share of quarrels, they were able to come out of them without having inflicted lasting damage. What it takes to make a successful marriage; what is meant by 'differences'; gentleness; the sense of place; the pros and cons of working together, and even the need for honeymoons have all been thought about and discussed. The penultimate paragraph is one that people wish to come back to, as it seems to sum up the idea and the ideal of marriage. 'It sounds like something that might be read at a wedding,' said a reader, 'but Hannah is saying it after a long married life. She is right to give thanks.'

If Ever Wife Was Happy
in a Man

♥

HAPPINESS
Guy de Maupassant

(approximate reading time 14 minutes)

It was tea-time, before the lamps were brought in. The villa looked down on the sea; the sundown had left the sky all rosy and golden, and the Mediterranean, without a wrinkle on its surface, without a tremor, smooth, and still shimmering as the day departed, seemed like a huge sheet of polished metal.

In the distance, away to the right, the jagged peaks of the mountains stood out black against the faint purple of the western sky.

They were talking about love, that old subject, and they were saying things that had already been said very often. The gentle melancholy of the twilight brought a feeling of tenderness into the discussion, and this word 'love', which was constantly being uttered, now in the deep voice of a man, now in the higher tones of a woman, seemed to fill the little room, to flutter round it as a bird, to hover over it as a spirit.

'Can one go on loving for several years in succession?'

'Yes,' said some.

'No,' asserted others.

They recognized distinctions of degree, set down limits, and brought forward examples. And all of them, men and women, filled with recollections, which rose up within them and disturbed their souls, which came to their lips and which they could not quote, spoke of that something, commonplace and all-powerful, the tender and mysterious agreement between two human beings, with profound emotion and devouring interest.

Suddenly, someone who was looking out over the sea, shouted: 'Look down there. What is it?'

Away out to sea could be seen just above the horizon a great grey mass, rising, indistinct, from the water.

The women had risen and were looking, uncomprehendingly, at that strange thing which they had never seen before.

Somebody said: 'It is Corsica. It can be seen like this two or three times a year in certain exceptional atmospherical conditions, when the air is perfectly clear, and it is no longer hidden by those sea-mists which always veil the distance.'

They could just see the mountains and thought they could distinguish the snow on their tops. They all stood surprised, disturbed, almost frightened, by this sudden apparition of an unknown world, this phantom rising from the sea. Perhaps those, who, like Columbus, set forth across unexplored oceans, had the same strange visions.

Then, an old gentleman, who had not yet spoken, said: 'I have known in this island, which is now rising before us, as if itself to answer the question we have been discussing, and to recall to me a curious memory, an admirable example of constant love, of love which was quite marvellously happy. Let me tell you about it.

'Five years ago I took a trip to Corsica. The wilds of that island are less known to us and farther away from us than America, though we sometimes see it from the coast of France, as we can just now.

'Picture to yourselves a world still in a state of chaos, a confused mass of mountains divided by narrow ravines through which torrents rush. There is not a plain – nothing but immense masses of granite and great stretches of rolling country covered with scrub or chestnut and pine forests. It is a virgin, uncultivated, barren country, though from time to time one comes across a village, perched, like a heap of rocks, on the top of a mountain. There is no culture, no industry, no art. One never comes across a single piece of carved wood or sculptured stone or anything to remind one of the feeling, be it primitive or refined, of the ancestors of these people for what is charming and beautiful. What indeed, impresses one most in that magnificent but rough country is the age-long indifference of the people to that seeking for charm in expression which we know as art.

'Italy, where every palace, full of masterpieces, is itself a masterpiece; where marble, wood, bronze, iron, metals and stone, all bear witness to man's genius; where the smallest objects scattered about in old houses reveal the heaven-born instinct for charm; Italy is for us the divine country, which we love because there we see the greatness, the power, the unwearying striving, and the triumph of the creative intelligence of man.

'And opposite it, Corsica has remained as barbaric as it was in the beginning. There man lives in his rude house, indifferent to everything that does not concern himself or his family feuds. And there he has existed through all the years, with all the defects and all the good points of half-civilized races, easily moved to anger, malicious, thoughtlessly cruel, yet hospitable, generous, loyal, simple-minded, opening his door to the passer-by, and giving his faithful friendship in exchange for the smallest mark of sympathy.

'For a month I wandered through this magnificent island, with the feeling that I was at the end of the world. No inns, no taverns, no roads. You reach by mule-paths those little villages, which seem to be hooked on to the side of mountains, and which look down on winding abysses, from which you hear, at night, the everlasting, melancholy, long-drawn-out roar of the mountain torrent. You knock at a door and ask for shelter and food till next morning. You sit down at their poor table, and you sleep under their poor roof, and in the morning you shake the hand of your host as he leaves you at the end of the village.

'Well, one evening after a ten hours' tramp I reached a little lonely house at the bottom of a narrow valley which opened out to the sea a league farther on. The two steep slopes of the mountain, covered with brushwood, loose rocks, and big trees, shut in this inexpressibly melancholy valley, as with two dark walls.

'Round the cottage were to be seen a few vines, a small garden, and, at a little distance, some big chestnut trees, something to live on, anyhow, and a fortune in this poor land.

'The woman who opened the door was old, stern, and exceptionally clean. The man, sitting in a rush chair, rose to greet me, and then sat down again without saying a word. His companion said: "Excuse him, he is deaf now; he is eighty-two."

'She spoke perfect French, to my surprise.

'I asked: "You are not Corsicans?"

'She replied: "No. We come from the mainland, but we have been here for fifty years."

'I had a feeling of sorrow and of fear as I thought of those fifty years spent in this dark hole, so remote from man and his towns. An old shepherd came in, and we began to eat the one dish which was our dinner, a thick soup of potatoes, bacon, and cabbage.

'When the little meal was over, I went and sat outside, my heart full of the melancholy of the desolate countryside, with the feeling of distress which travellers sometimes experience when the evening is gloomy and the place is desolate. On those occasions it seems as if all were nearly at an end – one's own existence and the world itself. One sees, with a flash, the awful misery of life, the loneliness of mankind, the emptiness, and the dark solitude of hearts which lull and deceive themselves with dreams to the very end.

'The old woman came out to me, and worried by the curiosity which ever exists in even the most resigned hearts, she asked: "Are you from France?"

'"Yes, I am having a holiday here."

'"You come from Paris, perhaps?"

'"No; from Nancy."

'It seemed to me that an extraordinary agitation shook her. How I saw, or rather felt it, I do not know.

'She repeated slowly: "You come from Nancy?"

'The man appeared in the doorway, impassive, as the deaf always are.

'She continued, "It doesn't matter. He can't hear."

'Then, after a few seconds: "You know a good many people in Nancy, then?"

'"Certainly, nearly everybody."

'"The Sainte-Allaize family?"

'"Yes, very well. They were friends of my father's."

'"What is your name?"

'I told her. She looked at me steadily. Then in the low voice of one who is calling back the unforgettable past, she went on: "Yes, of course, I remember quite well. And the Brisemares? What has become of them?"

'"They are all dead."

'"Dear, dear! And the Sirmonts? Do you know them?"

'"Yes. The last of them is a general."

'Then, shaking with distress, with some indefinable feeling, at once powerful and sacred, with some desire to lay bare her heart, to tell everything, to speak of those things which, up till then, she had kept securely within her, and of those people whose names so moved her, she said: "Yes: Henri de Sirmont. I know him well. He is my brother!"

'I looked up at her, thunderstruck. Then, all of a sudden, a bygone memory came back to me.

'There had been a great scandal in high circles in Lorraine. Suzanne de Sirmont, a rich and beautiful girl, had been carried off by a non-commissioned officer of a regiment of hussars which her father commanded.

'He was a good-looking boy, of peasant parentage, but handsome in his blue tunic, this soldier who had run away with his colonel's daughter. No doubt she had seen him, noted him, and loved him as she watched the squadrons go by. But how she had been able to speak to him, how they had been able to meet, to understand each other, how she had been bold enough to make him see that she loved him – that was never known.

'What followed was neither guessed nor anticipated. One evening, just when his term of service was finished, he disappeared with her. They were hunted but not found. No news of them was ever to be had, and she was looked upon as dead. And now I found her in this gloomy valley!

'Then I said, in my turn: "I remember quite well. You are Mademoiselle Suzanne."

'She nodded, and tears fell from her eyes. Then, looking towards the old man standing motionless on the threshold of his cottage, she said: "That is he!"

'I knew then that she was still loving him, and that she still saw the enticing light of bygone days in his eyes.

'I asked: "Have you at least been happy?"

'She answered in a voice that came straight from her heart: "Oh, yes! Very happy. He has made me very happy. I have never had a single regret."

'I looked at her, sorrowful, surprised, wonder-struck by the power of love! This rich girl had followed this man, this peasant. Herself had become a peasant. She had fashioned for herself a life, like his, devoid of grace, of luxury, of any kind of daintiness, and she had trained herself to become accustomed to his simple habits. And she still loved him! With her peasant's bonnet and cloth petticoat she had become a peasant herself. Seated on a rush-bottomed chair at a plain wooden table, she ate out of an earthenware dish a stew made of cabbages and potatoes and bacon. She slept on a straw mattress at his side. She had never thought of anything but him. She had never regretted her jewels, her fine clothes, the softness of chairs, the scent of warm rooms with their tapestries, or the delicious comfort of a feather-bed. She had never needed anything but him; as long as he was there, she desired nothing else.

'Quite young, she had given up life, society, and those who had brought her up and loved her. She had come, alone with him, to this wild valley. He had been everything to her, everything that one desires, everything that one dreams of, everything that one is always waiting for, always hoping for. From beginning to end he had filled her life with happiness. She could not have been happier.

'All night, as I listened to the hoarse breathing of the old soldier on his pallet beside her who had followed him so far, I thought of this strange and simple adventure, of this happiness, which was so complete yet made up of so little.

'At daybreak I left the house, after shaking the hands of the old couple.'

The story-teller finished. One of the women said: 'All the same that woman had too simple an ideal, with her too primitive needs and her little wants. She must have been a fool.'

Another said quietly: 'What does it matter? She was happy.'

Away on the horizon Corsica buried itself in the darkness, disappearing slowly in the sea, from which it had risen as if itself to tell the story of the two humble loves whom its shores had sheltered.

TO MY DEAR AND LOVING HUSBAND
Anne Bradstreet

If ever two were one, then surely we.
If ever man were loved by wife, then thee;
If ever wife was happy in a man,
Compare with me, ye women, if you can.
I prize thy love more than whole mines of gold
Or all the riches that the East doth hold.
My love is such that rivers cannot quench,
Nor ought but love from thee give recompense.
Thy love is such I can no way repay;
The heavens reward thee manifold, I pray.
Then while we live, in love let's so persevere
That when we live no more, we may live ever.

READING NOTES

A project worker who has shared the story many times with groups said: 'This story is a little slow to get going but by the end people have usually forgotten that and want to talk about the possibility of happiness in such a situation. We have had conversations about the nature of the old woman's family if she was once prepared simply to abandon them; about the way that young people look at old people without being able to imagine that they could ever have had passionate love affairs; about regret, and even about the desirability or otherwise of Corsica as a holiday destination. The question at the end of the story often prompts talk of what it takes to be happy.'

The poem is seen as an unashamed declaration of abiding love. There have been times when reading-group members have told of taking their copy home to give to their partners. 'It says everything that I would like to say,' said Eileen. Of course not everyone believes in an afterlife, but there have been interesting discussions about what can survive of love.

Read On

♥

The aim of this section is to offer enthusiastic recommendations for further reading.

POEMS

The format of this anthology means that many great love poems are not included. Here then are just few more poems it hurt to leave out.

16th Century

William Shakespeare

A dozen favourite sonnets:

Sonnet 18: 'Shall I compare thee to a summer's day?'

Sonnet 22: 'My glass shall not persuade me I am old'

Sonnet 29: 'When, in disgrace with fortune and men's eyes'

Sonnet 30: 'When to the sessions of sweet silent thought'

Sonnet 33: 'Full many a glorious morning have I seen'

Sonnet 43: 'When I most wink, then do mine eyes best see'

Sonnet 57: 'Being your slave what should I do but tend'

Sonnet 71: 'No longer mourn for me when I am dead'

Sonnet 73: 'That time of year thou mayst in me behold'

Sonnet 104: 'To me, fair friend, you never can be old'

Sonnet 116: 'Let me not to the marriage of true minds'

Sonnet 129: 'The expense of spirit in a waste of shame'
See: *Sonnets*, William Shakespeare (Vintage Classics, 2009)

More Shakespeare
  Twelfth Night: Act II, Sc iv, lines 87 to end
  As You Like It: Act IV, Sc i, lines 38–161

Samuel Daniel
'If this be love, to draw a weary breath'

John Donne
'The Good-Morrow', 'The Sun Rising', 'Air and Angels'

Michael Drayton
'Since there's no help, come let us kiss and part'

Francisco Gomez de Quevedo
'Love Constant Beyond Death'

Edmund Spenser
'My Love is like to ice, and I to fire', 'One Day I Wrote Her Name Upon the Strand'

Sir Philip Sidney
'My true-love hath my heart and I have his', 'If I could think how these my thoughts to leave'

Thomas Wyatt
'They Flee From Me', 'Whoso List to Hunt'. See: *The Penguin Book of English Verse* (Penguin Classics, 2004)

17th Century
John Hoskins
'Absence'

Richard Lovelace
'To Lucasta, Going to the Wars', 'To Althea, from Prison'

Andrew Marvell
'To His Coy Mistress'

John Milton
From *Paradise Lost*, Book IV: 'With thee conversing I forget all time'; from *Paradise Lost*, Book IX, 'Thus Eve with countenance blithe her story told'

John Wilmot, Earl of Rochester
'Life and Love', 'Song of a Young Lady to Her Ancient Lover'
See: *Palgrave's Golden Treasury* (Oxford Paperback, 2002)

18th Century
Robert Burns
'My Love Is Like a Red, Red Rose', 'Ae Fond Kiss'

Lord Byron
'It Is the Hour'; from *Don Juan*, Canto II, CLXXXVI–IX: 'A long, long kiss, a kiss of youth, and love'; 'They Say That Hope Is Happiness'

William Wordsworth

'She Dwelt Among the Untrodden Ways', 'Surprised by Joy'
See: *Six Centuries of English Poetry, Tennyson to Chaucer* (Kindle edition)

19th century

Matthew Arnold

'Dover Beach', 'The Buried Life'

Elizabeth Barrett Browning

Sonnets from the Portuguese. Sonnet 43, 'How Do I Love Thee?', is perhaps the most famous of all love poems, but there are forty-four altogether in the sequence. Try Sonnet 13: 'If thou must love me, let it be for nought/ Except for love's sake only'. Try also Sonnet 44: 'Beloved, thou hast brought me many flowers'.

Robert Browning

'Life in a Love', 'Two in the Campagna'

Emily Dickinson

'My life closed twice before its close', 'He fumbles at your Soul'

John Keats

'Bright Star', 'La Belle Dame Sans Merci'

Caroline Norton

'I Do Not Love Thee'

Coventry Patmore

'A Farewell', 'The Toys'

Christina Rossetti

'Remember', 'I wish I could remember that first day'

Alfred Tennyson

'Now Sleeps the Crimson Petal', 'If I were loved as I desire to be'; from *Maud*: 'Marriage Morning'. See: *English Victorian Poetry: An Anthology* (Dover Thrift Editions, 2000)

20th and 21st centuries

W. H. Auden

'Lullaby'. See: *Tell Me the Truth About Love: Fifteen Poems* (Faber, 1999)

Wendell Berry

'The Dance': VII from *Leavings*: 'I know I am getting old and I say so'. See: *Leavings* (Counterpoint, 2009); *New Collected Poems* (Counterpoint, 2013)

John Betjeman

'Pot Pourri from a Surrey Garden', 'Myfanwy'. See: John Betjeman: *Poems Selected by Hugo Williams* (Faber, 2009)

David Constantine

'As Our Bloods Separate'. See: *Collected Poems* (Bloodaxe, 2004)

Carol Ann Duffy

'Valentine'; *Rapture*: this outstanding collection is a love poem made up of about fifty individual poems. See: *Mean Time* (Picador, 2013); *Rapture* (Picador, 2005)

Douglas Dunn

'Modern Love'. See: *Selected Poems 1964–1983* (Faber, 1986)

Thomas Hardy

Poems 1912–13: poems written after the sudden death of his first wife. See: *Poems of Thomas Hardy* (Penguin Classics, 2007)

Philip Larkin

'Talking in Bed', 'Lines on a Young Lady's Photograph Album'. See: *Philip Larkin Poems* (Faber, 2013)

D. H. Lawrence

'Green', 'On the Balcony'. See: *The Complete Poems* (Penguin, 1994)

William Meredith

'Accidents of Birth'. See: *The Cheer* (Knopf, 1980)

Sharon Olds

'True Love', 'This Hour'. See: *Selected Poems* (Jonathan Cape, 2005)

P. K. Page

'Cross'. See *Staying Alive*: Real Poems for Unreal Times (Bloodaxe, 2002)

Marge Piercy

'To Have Without Holding'. See also: *The Hunger Moon: New and Selected Poems, 1980–2010* (Knopf, 2011)

Judith Viorst
'True Love'

Derek Walcott
'Love After Love'. See: *Collected Poems 1948–84* (Faber, 1992)

W. B. Yeats
'When You Are Old'. See: *A Little, Aloud* (Chatto & Windus, 2010)

STORIES
Here are a few more short stories about love

Elizabeth Bowen
'The Good Girl'. See: Elizabeth Bowen, *Collected Stories* (Vintage, 1999)

Anton Chekhov
'The Darling'. See *The Essential Tales of Chekhov* (Granta Books, 1999)

Margaret Drabble
'Faithful Lovers'. See: *A Day in the Life of a Smiling Woman: The Collected Stories* (Penguin, 2012)

Charlotte Perkins Gilman
'Mr Peebles' Heart'. See: *The Yellow Wallpaper and Other Stories* (Dover Thrift Editions, 2000)

Joanne Harris

'Tea With the Birds'. See *Jigs and Reels* (Black Swan, 2005)

O. Henry

'The Defeat of the City'. See: http://www.literaturecollection. com/a/o_henry/241/

Sarah Orne Jewett

'A Winter Courtship'. See: *Collected Works of Sarah Orne Jewett* (Kindle edition)

Rose Macaulay

'Miss Anstruther's Letters'. See: *The Penguin Book of Modern Women's Short Stories*, ed. Susan Hill (Penguin, 1990)

Guy de Maupassant

'Claire de Lune'. See: *The Best Short Stories; Guy de Maupassant* (Wordsworth Classic, 1997)

George Saunders

'Tenth of December'. This brilliant story will take longer than half an hour to read. See *Tenth of December* (Bloomsbury, 2013)

Elizabeth Strout

Olive Kitteridge is a novel of connected short stories. In the chapter called 'Winter Concert' a husband and wife, on the verge of old age, go out for the evening, meet friends, come home, and realise their need for each other. See: *Olive Kitteridge* (Simon and Schuster, 2011)

Elizabeth Taylor

'In the Sun'. See *Complete Short Stories* (Virago, 2012)

Edith Wharton

'The Other Two' and 'The Muses Tragedy'. See *Short Stories by Edith Wharton* (Dover Thrift Editions, 2000)

Acknowledgements

♥

First of all our heartfelt, grateful thanks must go to the authors, poets and copyright holders who so generously and supportively allowed us to include their work in the anthology.

My thanks to all the great readers at The Reader especially Jane Davis, Philip Davis, Brian Nellist, Clare Ellis, Megg Hewlett, Penny Fosten, Caroline Adams, Lynn Elsdon and Helen Wilson who willingly and enthusiastically shared stories with me.

Thanks to Beth Pochin for her long work on permissions.

Love and thanks to my loyal daughters Fiona and Frances for their record-breaking typing up of texts.

Sincere appreciation and thanks to Chatto & Windus for working with us once again. The Reader owes them a real debt of gratitude for their wholehearted support and belief in the charity. In particular my thanks must go to Becky Hardie and Susannah Otter whose attention to detail and all-round expertise has been much relied on and who have always given it with kindness.

Every effort has been made to trace and contact all copyright holders. If there are any inadvertent omissions or errors we will be pleased to correct these at the earliest opportunity.

Margaret Atwood: 'Habitation' from *Habitation*, published by Toronto: Oxford University Press Canada 1976. Reproduced with permission of Curtis Brown Group Ltd, London on behalf of O.W. Toad Ltd. Copyright © Margaret Atwood 1970

W. H. Auden: 'O Tell Me the Truth About Love' from *Tell Me the Truth About Love: Fifteen Poems*, published by Faber and Faber Ltd. Copyright © 1940 by W. H. Auden, renewed. Reprinted by permission of Curtis Brown, Ltd.

George Barker: 'To My Mother' from *Collected Poems*, published by Faber and Faber Ltd. Reprinted by permission of Faber and Faber Ltd.

Alan Bennett: 'Bed Among The Lentils' from *Talking Heads* by Alan Bennett, published by BBC Books. Reproduced by permission of The Random House Group Ltd.

Wendell Berry: 'The Country of Marriage', copyright © 2012 by Wendell Berry, from *New Collected Poems*. Reprinted by permission of Counterpoint.

Wendell Berry: Extract from 'Hannah Coulter', published by Counterpoint Press. Copyright © 2004 by Tanya Amyx Berry, from *Hannah Coulter*. Reprinted by permission of Counterpoint.

Michael Blumenthal: 'A Marriage' from *Against Romance*, published by Pleasure Boat Studio. Reprinted by permission of Michael Blumenthal.

David Constantine: 'Witness' from *The Shieling*, published by Comma Press. Reprinted by permission of David Constantine and Comma Press.

Wendy Cope: 'My Lover' from *Making Cocoa for Kingsley Amis*, published by Faber and Faber Ltd. Reprinted by permission of Faber and Faber Ltd.

Julia Copus: 'In Defence of Adultery' from *In Defence of Adultery*, published by Bloodaxe Books. Reprinted by permission of Bloodaxe Books.

Sharon Creech: Extract from 'Walk Two Moons' by Sharon Creech, published by Macmillan Children's Books. Reprinted by permission of Sharon Creech.

E.E. Cummings: 'I carry your heart' from *Complete Poems*, published by Liveright Publishing Corporation. Reprinted by permission of W.W. Norton & Company, Inc.

Babette Deutsch: 'Solitude' from *The Collected Poems of Babette Deutsch*, published by Doubleday.

U.A. Fanthorpe: 'Atlas' from *Collected Poems 1978–2003*, published by Peterloo Poets. Reprinted by permission of Dr R. V. Bailey.

Robert Graves: 'Sick Love' from *Complete Poems*, published by Penguin. Reprinted by permission of Carcanet Press Limited.

Philip Larkin: 'Whitsun Weddings' from *Collected Poems*, published by Faber and Faber Ltd. Reprinted by permission of Faber and Faber Ltd.

Laurie Lee: Extract from *Cider with Rosie*, reproduced with permission of Curtis Brown Group Ltd, London on behalf of The Beneficiaries of the Estate of Laurie Lee Copyright © Laurie Lee 1940

Doris Lessing: 'He' by Doris Lessing from *The Habit of Loving*, published by Harper Collins. Reprinted by permission of Faber and Faber Ltd.

Rosina Lippi: Extract from *Homestead* by Rosina Lippi, published by Harper Collins. Reprinted by permission of Harper Collins.

Carson McCullers: 'A Tree, A Rock, A Cloud' from *The Ballad of the Sad Café* by Carson McCullers. Reprinted by permission of Pollinger Limited (www.pollingerltd.com) on behalf of the Estate of Carson McCullers.

John McGahern: Extract from *Amongst Women* by John McGahern, published by Faber and Faber Ltd. Reprinted by permission of Faber and Faber Ltd.

Stanley Middleton: Extract from *Valley of Decision* by Stanley Middleton. Reprinted by permission of Estate of Stanley Middleton and Random House.

Edwin Muir: 'The Confirmation' from *Collected Poems 2003*, published by Faber and Faber Ltd. Reprinted by permission of Faber and Faber Ltd.

Haruki Murakami: 'On Seeing the 100% Perfect Girl One Beautiful April Morning' from *The Elephant Vanishes*. Reproduced with permission of Curtis Brown Group Ltd, London on behalf of Haruki Murakami. Copyright © Haruki Murakami 1993

John Frederick Nims: 'Love Poem' from *The Iron Pastoral*, published by William Sloane Associates.

Jennifer O'Hagan: 'The Car' from *The Reader*. Reprinted by permission of Jennifer O'Hagan.

Micheal O'Siadhall: 'Between' from *Poems 1975–1995*, published by Bloodaxe Books. Reprinted by permission of Bloodaxe Books.

Edith Pearlman: 'Unravished Bride' originally appeared in *Pleiades* in 2001. Collected in *Binocular Vision*, Lookout Books / Pushkin Press, 2012. Reprinted by permission of Kneerim, Williams and Bloom.

Marge Piercy: 'The Book of Ruth and Naomi' from *Mars and Her Children*, published by Knopf. Copyright © 1990, 1999 Marge Piercy. Reprinted by permission of the Wallace Literary Agency, Inc.

Mary Robison: 'Yours' from *Tell Me: 30 Stories*, published by Counterpoint Press. Copyright © 2002 by Mary Robison. Reprinted by permission of The Wylie Agency (UK) Limited.

George Saunders: 'Puppy' from *Tenth of December*, published by Bloomsbury. Reprinted by permission of ICM partners, on behalf of the author.

Jane Smiley: Extract from *The Age of Grief* by Jane Smiley, published by Harper Collins. Reprinted by permission of Harper Collins.

Jan Struther: 'The Weavers' from *The Glass Blower and Other Poems*, reproduced with permission of Curtis Brown Group Ltd, London on behalf of The Beneficiaries of the Estate of Jan Struther. Copyright © Jan Struther 1940.

Joyce Sutphen: 'What the Heart Cannot Forget' from *Coming Back to the Body*, published by Holy Cow! Press. Reprinted by permission of Joyce Sutphen.

A. S. J. Tessimond: *Not Love Perhaps*, published by Faber and Faber Ltd. Reprinted by permission of Bloodaxe Books.

Helen Thomas: 'Two letters' from *Under Storm's Wing* by Helen Thomas, published by Carcanet Press Limited. Reprinted by permission of Carcanet Press Limited.

Miller Williams: 'Love Poem with Toast' from *Some Jazz a While: Collected Poems*. Copyright © 1999 Miller Williams. Reprinted by permission of the University of Illinois Press.

Tobias Wolff: 'Lady's Dream' from *The Night in Question*, published by Bloomsbury Publishing plc. Reprinted by permission of Bloomsbury Publishing plc.

William Woodruff: Extract from *The Road to Nab End*, published by Eland Publishing Ltd in 2011. Reprinted by permission of Helga Woodruff.